...EPORTER, AN INTUITIVE ...BEHAVIOR WHO HAS ...URAL SKILLS IN THAT ...OSSIP, A BEAUTY PARLOR."

—*The Boston Globe*

AND EVERYONE'S HOT FOR HER.

PRAISE FOR *BUBBLES IN TROUBLE* . . .

"Even more over the top than her debut. . . . Bubbles smacks you with humor as broad as a whoopee pie in the kisser."
—*Kirkus Reviews*

"With a zany cast of characters . . . this story is hilarious. . . . Strohmeyer has another winner in this fantastic follow up to *Bubbles Unbound*. . . . I can't wait to see what further adventures await this savvy gal." —*Old Book Barn Gazette*

"High humor and high jinks make *Bubbles in Trouble* a delightful, effervescent read. Strohmeyer imbues her story with warmth and charm, giving us an endearing cast of characters."
—*Romantic Times* (4½ stars)

"Strohmeyer successfully navigates the fine line between humorous stereotype and sympathetic amateur investigator."
—*Publishers Weekly*

. . . AND *BUBBLES UNBOUND*
Winner of the Agatha Award for Best First Mystery

"Bubbles is fun, and so is Strohmeyer's book."
—*The Philadelphia Inquirer*

"Possibly the first novel of its kind to offer beauty tips."
—*The Boston Globe*

"Rollicking good fun. Bubbles rocks!"
—*New York Times* bestselling author Susan Andersen

"This is a wonderfully energizing and skillful page-turner of a book. Strohmeyer will go far."
—Fay Weldon

continued . . .

DUBUQUE COUNTY LIBRARY

"A strong debut . . . a mystery for every taste. There is a riotous world waiting in these pages."

—*Houston Chronicle*

"Meet Bubbles Yablonsky, beautician-reporter-sleuth and blazing star of Strohmeyer's entertaining, establishment-bashing debut. Hop in [her] Camaro and buckle up: Bubbles is behind the wheel, and a wild ride awaits."

—*Publishers Weekly*

"Fizzy as a bicarb, funny as Evanovich. Should bubble right to the top of the mystery bestseller lists."

—*New York Times* bestselling author Carolyn Hart

"A breezy and funny mystery. . . . Bubbles is a wonderful creation. My only gripe? Who is going to believe a character whose first name is Bubbles?"

—Sparkle Hayter, author of the Robin Hudson mysteries

"A sexy, irrepressible heroine, riotous supporting characters . . . and even a makeup tip or two make this a highly recommended series debut." —*Library Journal*

"If Stephanie Plum had a cousin, she would be Bubbles Yablonsky . . . sure to be a rip-roaring series."

—*Romantic Times* (Top Pick)

"Bubbles Yablonsky is Pennsylvania's answer to Erin Brockovich, cracking her gum, murder cases, and the hard heart of a love-'em-and-leave-'em photojournalist without breaking a sweat. You're going to love her!"

—*New York Times* bestselling author Jennifer Crusie

"In an era of pluckier-than-thou females, a nitwit heroine could be a welcome change. Enter Bubbles Yablonsky—a breath of fresh air." —*Kirkus Reviews*

"Blond, beautiful, and dumb? Maybe so, says hairstylist Bubbles Yablonsky, but definitely not boring. This is a fast-paced story with delicious sidetracks . . . and lots of homey 'blue collar' humor." —*The Tampa Tribune*

"Worth checking out, say? Oh yeah. Humor and great characters aren't all Sarah Strohmeyer has to offer."
—*Mystery News*

"You don't have to be from the Lehigh Valley to love reading *Bubbles Unbound.*"
—*The Morning Call* (Allentown, PA)

"A humorous cozy starring a plum of a character whose philosophy on life will keep readers wanting to know more about her. Mystery fans will bubble over [her] amateur investigative skills (or lack of)."
—*The Midwest Book Review*

"Strohmeyer's book is both funny and believable, two qualities often in short supply in the mystery genre."
—*Pittsburgh Post-Gazette*

"The outlandishly intricate plot has more layers than Bubbles' makeup . . . A confection held together by gossip and hairspray." —*Booklist*

THE BUBBLES BOOKS

Bubbles Ablaze

Bubbles in Trouble

Bubbles Unbound

Bubbles IN TROUBLE

Sarah Strohmeyer

A SIGNET BOOK

The treatments in this book are to be followed exactly as written. The publisher and author are not responsible for your specific health or allergy needs that may require medical supervision. The publisher and author are not responsible for any adverse reactions to the treatments contained in this book.

SIGNET
Published by New American Library, a division of
Penguin Group (USA) Inc., 375 Hudson Street,
New York, New York 10014, U.S.A.
Penguin Books Ltd, 80 Strand, London WC2R 0RL, England
Penguin Books Australia Ltd, 250 Camberwell Road,
Camberwell, Victoria 3124, Australia
Penguin Books Canada Ltd, 10 Alcorn Avenue,
Toronto, Ontario, Canada M4V 3B2
Penguin Books (N.Z.) Ltd, Cnr Rosedale and Airborne Roads,
Albany, Auckland 1310, New Zealand

Penguin Books Ltd, Registered Offices: 80 Strand, London WC2R 0RL, England

Published by Signet, an imprint of New American Library, a division of Penguin Group (USA) Inc. Previously published in a Dutton edition.

First Signet Printing, July 2003
10 9 8 7 6 5 4 3 2

Copyright © Sarah Strohmeyer, 2002
Excerpt from *Bubbles Ablaze* copyright © Sarah Strohmeyer, 2003
All rights reserved

REGISTERED TRADEMARK—MARCA REGISTRADA

Printed in the United States of America

Without limiting the rights under copyright reserved above, no part of this publication may be reproduced, stored in or introduced into a retrieval system, or transmitted, in any form, or by any means (electronic, mechanical, photocopying, recording, or otherwise), without the prior written permission of both the copyright owner and the above publisher of this book.

PUBLISHER'S NOTE
This is a work of fiction. Names, characters, places, and incidents either are the products of the author's imagination or are used fictitiously, and any resemblance to actual persons, living or dead, business establishments, events, or locales is entirely coincidental.

BOOKS ARE AVAILABLE AT QUANTITY DISCOUNTS WHEN USED TO PROMOTE PRODUCTS OR SERVICES. FOR INFORMATION PLEASE WRITE TO PREMIUM MARKETING DIVISION, PENGUIN GROUP (USA) INC., 375 HUDSON STREET, NEW YORK, NEW YORK 10014.

The scanning, uploading and distribution of this book via the Internet or via any other means without the permission of the publisher is illegal and punishable by law. Please purchase only authorized electronic editions, and do not participate in or encourage electronic piracy of copyrighted materials. Your support of the author's rights is appreciated.

If you purchased this book without a cover you should be aware that this book is stolen property. It was reported as "unsold and destroyed" to the publisher and neither the author nor the publisher has received any payment for this "stripped book."

For Bubbles's inspiration, Ann Marie Gonsalves—who worked her way from being a South Side hairdresser to publisher of *The Valley Voice* without taking a bit of guff in between

Acknowledgments

While this book is not intended to be an authoritative work on the Amish or their struggles to preserve purity amid rapid commercial development in Pennsylvania, I did research these issues with the help of reputable sources. Most notably, Randy-Michael Testa, at the time a Dartmouth College professor of education, patiently answered my many questions about his experiences with the Lancaster County Amish. Though he may cringe upon reading certain parts of this book, I am deeply grateful for Professor Testa's observations, which he discussed in telephone interviews, E-mails and in his own fascinating book, *After the Fire* (University Press of New England). I am only sorry I could not implement all of his advice.

Further Amish insights came from my mother-in-law, Rosemary Merriman, who shared her amusing anecdotes about living and working with the Ohio Amish, as did my sisters-in-law Jennifer Merriman and Amy Herrick. Alas, they never knew any Amish who wore golden toenail fungus medicine or used a quilting stapler. That I made up.

Thanks to the advice of Jay Mulvaney and his beautifully illustrated *Jackie: The Clothes of Camelot* (St. Martin's), I did not need to make up the wardrobe of Jacqueline Kennedy Onassis.

I also owe a great debt to the multilingual Thomas Vitzhum of Montpelier, Vermont, who translated my rather odd requests for German phrases. Whether it was Fleischwolf or Hackmaschine we'll never know. Tom's hunch to go with Hackmaschine was enough for me.

The vinegar cuticle softener and honey-protein mask

recipes (as well as other tips) were cheerfully contributed by Sharmaine Nunes, although at times I fiddled with the ingredients. Other vinegar tips were offered by Vera Feld, Kay Geibel, Carol Griffin, Vicky Para and Kathy Roland—Bubbles Heads all. Thanks much to Fredericka Naylor for the watermelon pickle recipe which has brightened our Christmas tables for over a decade.

During what proved to be a tough year, my husband, Charles, never got on my case even when reading a first and horrible draft. My agent, Heather Schroder at ICM, continued to perform wonders that have made her legendary in my eyes. The Naughty Girls of Middlesex offered me wine and support when I needed it most. Lisa Sweterlitsch continued her thirty-four-year track record as a best friend and source of Lehigh Valley info. No Bubbles book could be written without her aid.

Finally, I owe every good thing here to my beloved editor, Ellen Edwards, whose uplifting encouragement, professional criticism and unfailing trust brought me out of the dark and into the light. I truly am one of the lucky ones.

Chapter 1

This is how Steve Stiletto, drop-dead gorgeous, globe-trotting photographer, finally got me, Bubbles Yablonsky, Pennsylvania hairstylist and occasional newspaper reporter, to break my chastity vow.

I was relaxing on the back porch one golden, late-summer evening, polishing my nails to a deep and glossy plum. A few of my neighbor Mrs. Hamel's red tomatoes in our shared garden were plump on the vine. The tiny green grapes were coming into their own and the steel mill was closing down for the night with a *pump, pump, pump*.

Suddenly the backyard gate swung open and there stood Stiletto, tall and tanned from India's hot sun. He was wearing tight jeans, the familiar worn leather bomber jacket over his broad shoulders, and those Mel Gibson eyes of his were twinkling their mischievous blue.

"You're back," I whispered, the nail polish bottle tumbling down the porch steps.

"Yablinko," was all he said before leaning down to kiss me, hard and long. He smelled of dusty winds and brutal war. With one movement he swooped me up in his strong arms, and I felt helpless as he kicked open the screen door and carried me upstairs.

"But . . ." I protested weakly.

"Shhh." He placed me gently on the bed and let his lips trace the curve of my neck. "Listen. I nearly went mad in the desert without you, Bubbles. Marry me."

He had done it. Stiletto had uttered those two magic words and I was now released from my chastity vow, free to respond with a lusty abracadabra.

After our first, passionate moment of lovemaking, which was furtive and desperate, I ran my plum nails over his broad chest and down his muscular thighs, drinking in the warmth of him, the tingling satisfaction of our mingling.

"Oh, Steve, you're so—"

"For the one thousandth time it's Chip. Chip. Chip. Chip! When in the hell are you gonna get that straight, Bubbles?"

My eyelids flew open in a flash and I found myself staring into a fleshy, white shoulder.

"Aaaagh," I screamed. My hands squeezed what they had been gripping under the covers. Not muscle. Flab. Mounds and mounds of gut.

"Oww, stop that. You're hurting me."

I bolted upright, pulling the sheets tightly around me. "Oh . . . my . . . God."

Dan the Man, my fat, adulterous, ambulance-chasing lawyer of an ex-husband, lay next to me in bed, arms behind his head, a scowl on his face.

"No one calls me Dan anymore," he said. "Everyone calls me Chip. All except you and those buffoons down at Legal Aid."

"Where's Steve?"

"Steve? You mean that punk photographer? How in the bejeezus am I supposed to know?"

Stiletto's return from overseas must have been a dream. My stomach felt weak and nauseous. I was afraid

I'd throw up, maybe. And a headache. Oh, such a headache, like I'd been crowned by an anvil.

"I think I'm going to be sick," I croaked.

"Wouldn't be surprised considering the condition you came in last night, Bubbles." Dan threw back the covers, revealing his blubbery belly and a pair of ripped, yellow-striped boxer shorts. "Boy, were you sloshed. You passed out here, right on the convertible couch."

"I was not sloshed," I lied. "I was just very, very tired."

"Right. And as a former Lehigh University frat boy I don't know from tanked." Dan snorted as he made his way to the bathroom. "Getting blotto was my major. I graduated summa cum laude in alcohol overload."

Could Dan have been right? Could I, Bubbles Yablonsky, thirty-four-year-old single mother, hairdresser, aspiring investigative journalist and one of the few living Polish-Lithuanian Barbie dolls in Lehigh, Pennsylvania, have allowed myself to get, *gasp,* tipsy?

No. I never touch alcohol. It tastes gross and . . .

I dropped the sheet. I was still wearing my spiffy fire-engine-red sequined dress, now wrinkled and reeking of cigarette smoke. My black hose were bunched at the ankles and a gigantic run exposed my big toe.

Ohhh. I collapsed in a heap of self loathing, painfully recalling how I'd spent the night before—at the bachelorette party for Lehigh Police Department records clerk Janice Kramer, fiancée of Detective Mickey Sinkler and my best source for sealed search warrants.

It was those darn strawberry-kiwi Jell-O shots Janice's coworkers at the police department brought to the party. They must've been spiked.

I winced at the memory of me howling Lynyrd Skynyrd's "Free Bird" into the karaoke machine at Uncle Manny's Bar and Grille, which had opened on a Sunday night just to host our festivities. Janice had covered her mouth first in shock and then in delight when I jumped onto the pool table to play air guitar while the other partygoers whooped and cheered. Only Manny had remained glum, his eyes glaring at my spiked heels digging into the green felt.

To top it off I had evidently teetered home and passed out next to my ex, Dan the Man, who—at the insistence of our daughter, Jane—had been sleeping on our pull-out couch ever since his socialite wife Wendy had given him the heave-ho two weeks ago. Of this I was certain, however: while I had slept with Dan, I had not *slept* with Dan. A bug trap full of Spanish flies couldn't make me do that.

What I needed was sleep, a tall glass of ginger ale, two aspirin and a hot shower with plenty of Ivory soap. But mostly sleep. I closed my eyes and drifted off.

"Hey, aren't you supposed to be getting ready for that wedding?" Dan was suited up for his Legal Aid job and munching on a hoagie. "I thought by the time I returned for lunch you'd be long gone. It's eleven-thirty."

Mickey and Janice's wedding. It was supposed to be at noon. And I was the maid of honor!

"How long did I sleep?"

Dan checked his watch. "About four hours."

"Why didn't you wake me?"

"What do I look like? Your personal valet?"

I leapt out of bed. Here I was, unwashed and hungover, lazing about while Mickey's sweet bride, a kind and shy woman who had *trusted* me to lead her down the aisle, was probably pacing the narthex in frantic worry. Ugh.

I pushed Dan aside and scrambled up the stairs to the bathroom. Usually a Bubbles Deluxe took a good forty-five minutes if my Sunshine Blonde Number Eight locks were to be teased and sprayed into an indestructible beehive. Eyebrow penciling alone could eat up five.

I had, what, ten minutes tops to shower and change into a Bo Peep bridesmaid's outfit complete with hoopskirt, bonnet and satin-covered staff.

There was no way I could get to the church in time. At best, I'd arrive right when Mickey and Janice were exchanging vows.

But I needn't have rushed.

For as I was soon to discover, there would be no blushing bride and beaming groom emerging from St. Lenny's South Side Catholic Church. No dollar dance at Walp's and fancy smorgasbord. No four-night, three-day honeymoon in the Pocono Mountains sipping sparkling wine by a Hotel Paupack heart-shaped bathtub.

There would be no wedding. Only murder.

Looking back, I blame the Skynyrd.

Chapter 2

It took extra effort to squeeze the Bo Peep hoopskirt under the low wheel of my three-toned Camaro. With one final shove I closed the door and stuck the satin-covered staff out the passenger side window. Then I stepped on the gas and headed pell-mell for St. Lenny's on the South Side.

I zipped through the heart of Lehigh, Pennsylvania, a gritty steel town on the New Jersey border and my lifelong home. I sped down Main Street, past Orr's Department Store, the Moravian Book Shop and the Hotel Lehigh, onto the cobblestone streets of the historic district and past the modern library. Then I crossed the Fahy Bridge—where once I had dangled in peril—straight to the South Side, home to Lehigh's massive rust-red steel factory, railroad and shipping yards.

Lehigh's South Side is the side of town where the steel executives with their big stone houses, backyard tennis courts and crystal blue swimming pools *don't* live. The South Side is lined with neat row homes housing workers of Czech, German, Italian, Puerto Rican and Polish descent. The people who actually labor in the suffocating steel plants, pouring molten metal into big sand molds and passing iron bars under supersharp fiery blades that can cut and sear a man's fingers in one quick slice.

I pulled up in front of St. Lenny's, which was run out of the former Big Strike Bowling Alley on Polk Street, next to the Portuguese Club, and held services only at lunchtime, Monday through Thursday. Already the sound of taped organ music was flowing from the open doors, along with the *bing-bong* of pinball, since the priests had had the foresight to retain the bowling alley's old game room for restless children.

As I made my way to the front steps, a short Puerto Rican man in white robes ran to meet me, his face a mask of worry.

"Ju Bubbles Yablonsky?" he asked, wringing his hands.

"I'm so sorry," I apologized. "I slept late and—"

"So glad you made it." He grabbed both my hands in his, shaking furiously. "I'm Fernando, de sex-don. Ju god de ride?"

It took me a minute to comprehend the words Sex Don, until I realized he was saying sexton. "I drove."

Fernando cupped his ear to hear over the music. "In wha car?"

I pointed to the Camaro.

"Aha." He glanced over my shoulder and nodded. "Okay. We ready?"

He ushered me up the steps to the foyer where Myrtle, Mickey's zaftig cousin, was waiting in her pink-and-pale-green shepherdess outfit. The foyer still smelled of spilled beer, cigarette smoke and hot dogs, odors left over from the Big Strike days. An odd contrast to the sickening sweet incense wafting from behind the statue of the Madonna and Child.

Myrtle shoved a bouquet of pink and white carnations into my hand. "Mickey's gonna kill you," she whispered. "You're twenty minutes late. Where's Janice?"

"Where's Janice?" I repeated stupidly. How was I supposed to know where Janice was? She was coming with her uncle Elwood. Janice said he had rented a limo. White with a sunroof and minibar.

"You don't have her?" the Sex Don asked. "I thought you said you got de bride."

"I said I got a *ride*."

"You forgot to pick up Janice?" Myrtle squawked.

The Sex Don and Myrtle exchanged glances and I was struck by a bolt of panic. Elwood *was* supposed to bring Janice, wasn't he? I played back Janice's last words in my brain. This was not easy, as my recovering brain was like a tape recorder on low batteries. It moved very, very slowly.

Suddenly there was a swell of taped organ music and everyone in the church turned to face us.

"Wha are we gonna do?" the Sex Don moaned.

"I don't know about you two," Myrtle said, lifting her skirts, "but I'm faking it." She marched straight ahead toward an expectant Mickey.

What choice did I have but to follow?

I grasped the staff and carnations, my high heels clicking ominously down the varnished wooden bowling lane.

Mickey, his big ears redder than a Ford truck's taillights, smiled beneficently. His eyes fell on me for only a moment, though, before searching for his raison d'être. Modest, gray-eyed Janice. Demure. Soft-spoken. And totally, madly, completely in love with Mickey.

Or so it had seemed.

Like spectators at a tennis match, the congregation craned to look at the door, then Mickey, then the door again. Mickey pasted on a smile and stood straighter. The tape was rewound to "The Wedding March" for another go.

My feeble brain reeled and my dress itched. The

priest clutched his prayer book a bit tighter and raised his eyebrows at Fernando the Sex Don standing at the opposite end of the aisle. Fernando lifted his hands in helplessness and Mickey went paler than Cream of Wheat boiled in milk.

"Where is she?" Mickey mouthed at me.

Before I could answer, Myrtle tattled. "Bubbles didn't bring her. She forgot."

The music stopped and everyone faced forward. "You forgot, Bubbles?" Mickey asked in a hurt tone.

His best man, Detective Frye, shook his head and reached for his cigarettes. Soon members of the congregation were bending their heads and murmuring, "Bubbles forgot the bride."

Mama, who was sitting in the front row, slapped her forehead, the accepted Polish hand gesture for dimwit.

The priest motioned for the wedding party to gather around him. "What's the situation here?" he asked, wiping off a trickle of sweat sneaking down the side of his face.

Mickey pointed to me. "Bubbles forgot to pick up my bride."

"I did not. Her uncle Elwood's bringing her," I countered, relating Janice's specific instructions to the best of my hampered ability. "And besides, where is Elwood anyway?"

Good point. As it turned out, everyone acknowledged that Elwood, too, was a no-show. Mickey leaned over the front pew and asked his mother if she had seen Elwood. No Elwood.

"I knew something like this was going to happen," Myrtle said as Mickey and Detective Frye left to search the church. "Janice was too good to be true. What right-in-the-head woman would take on Mickey and his five kids? You shouldn't have sung 'Free Bird' last night, Bubbles. You gave her ideas."

Figuring they were in for the long haul, guests stood and stretched. Mama and Mrs. Sinkler swung around the front pew.

"Hey, when you're maid of honor, you don't let the bride slip your mind like an RSVP," snapped Mama. "You can't waltz into church a half hour late. It's a Monday. These people have got to get back to work." She adjusted her oversized dark sunglasses.

My wider-than-she-is-tall mother, LuLu Yablonsky, was going through a Jackie O phase. It had been brought on by the stress of opening a pierogi shop with her friend Genevieve and shifted into full gear after she watched a three-part *Biography* special entitled "Jacqueline Bouvier Kennedy Onassis: America's Queen."

A week ago, Mama had showed up at my house with her gray hair dyed jet black, a big pair of tortoiseshell glasses on her nose and a silk scarf around her head. That had been the least of it.

She was also wearing a British equestrian wardrobe including a used navy gabardine coat and Bombay jodhpurs that strained so tightly over her wide thighs they revealed the outline of her girdle underneath. Worse, the elastic tops of her queen-size No Nonsense knee-highs didn't quite fit under the jodhpurs, so a lump of white flesh bulged below her knees.

"What's all this about?" I had asked as Mama flipped open a silver cigarette case and tapped out a Dunhill.

"I'm trying to recapture the lost glamour of yesteryear, from the days of Camelot," she proclaimed, plunking herself on the same living room couch she had once encased in plastic.

After checking with her doctor to make sure Mama hadn't tinkered with her blood pressure medication—she hadn't—I came to accept the petite Polish Jackie Osky as a new member of our family. Pavlova and pierogis. That was the new LuLu.

Now, at St. Lenny's, she was dressed in an off-white Chanel suit with black braid edging donated by the wife of a Lehigh Steel executive to the local Trinity Episcopal Church rummage. It had a small coffee stain on the skirt, which Mama hid with a black plastic purse.

"Here comes Mickey," Mama announced, adjusting the lace mantilla on her head. "And it don't look good."

Indeed it didn't. Mickey's brows were furrowed and his lips were pursed tightly. Detective Frye marched by his side like a bodyguard.

"She's gone," Mickey said. "The wedding's off."

"There must be some misunderstanding," Mrs. Sinkler suggested, batting her eyes. "Maybe Elwood's stuck in traffic."

Mickey shook his head. "Tried calling her home. The phone is off the hook, the operator told me so."

"Police privilege," Frye interjected importantly, "getting the operator to tap into the line."

"Elwood's behind this," Mickey said. "He despises me. Last night at dinner he told me he'd rather see Janice sold away into the white slave trade than have her serve as mother to my kids. Can you imagine?"

Mickey's five unruly, undisciplined savages were busily kicking the video games in the back room. I recalled the times they had keyed cars in the mall parking lot and set fire to a cat's tail. I could imagine.

Mickey rolled up the sleeves of his powder-blue tuxedo. "I'm gonna drive to Elwood and Janice's condo and get to the bottom of this. No woman's gonna stand me up at the altar in front of all my friends and get away with it. No woman's gonna—"

"You'll do *no* such thing, Michael Allen Sinkler," his mother barked.

Mickey immediately hung his head. "Oh?"

"No. It's undignified. You need to send a representative."

The priest, Detective Frye, Mickey, Mama, Mrs. Sinkler, Myrtle and I thought about this for a while. Then Myrtle said, "Bubbles should go 'cause it's her fault Janice no-showed."

"My fault?" Why would it be my fault? I adored Janice and was ecstatic that she and Mickey Sinkler, King of the Romantically Challenged, had found each other. "I'm dying for them to get married."

"Is that so?" Myrtle put down her staff. "Then how come at the bachelorette party last night you sang this." She started playing air guitar and doing a bad Lynyrd Skynyrd imitation.

"You did what?" Congenital mouth-breather Mickey dropped his lower jaw.

Myrtle couldn't wait to fill in the details about how I had jumped on the pool table down at Uncle Manny's Bar and Grille and crooned to the blushing bride-to-be a song about a guy leaving a girl because he has to be free. At least, that's what I think "Free Bird" is about.

"Whatever happened to the days of 'Que Sera, Sera'?" Mama mused nostalgically.

"Mercy!" Mrs. Sinkler waved her wedding program. "Bubbles definitely has to be the one to find Janice, then."

I started to object, but Mama gave my hoopskirt a quick kick. "Don't give me no lip, Bubbles." She turned to Mickey. "Where does Janice live?"

Mickey snatched his mother's wedding program and clicked a pen. He began scribbling down directions. "She and Elwood live in a survivalist compound out by the Lehigh Golf Club."

I took the directions. "A survivalist compound?"

Survivalists were a growing problem in Pennsylvania. Compounds were popping up all over, built by men with a deep distrust of government and a religious devotion to the Second Amendment. They dressed in head-to-toe camouflage, stockpiled Dinty Moore stew by the truck-load, eschewed the IRS and prepared daily for the Armageddon of gun battles with federal agents.

I didn't know about this traveling to a survivalist compound business.

Mickey read my mind. "It's a very nice place, Bubbles. It's called the Final Frontier and it's not what you think."

Mama clapped her white-gloved hands. "The Final Frontier? Count me in. I've been trying to worm my way in there for years."

"Lucky dog," Mrs. Sinkler said under her breath.

Mama eager to visit a survivalist compound? You would have thought she was off to a wake, she was so animated.

Mickey clutched my arm and looked deeply into my eyes. "If you find Janice, Bubbles, make sure you tell her that no matter what, I still love her."

"I will, Mickey," I said, patting him on the shoulder.

"And if you see Elwood, belt him one for me." Mickey punched the air, swinging so hard he lost his balance and nearly sent his string-bean body hurtling over the communion rail.

Thank God his mother was there to catch him.

Mickey was right. The Final Frontier was unlike any survivalist compound I could have imagined. It was surrounded by a freshly painted white rail fence and stately sycamores through which I glimpsed a bright green rolling lawn and heard the hum of motorized golf carts.

"What is this place?" I asked as we approached a tidy, clapboard guard house.

"It's a widow's paradise." Mama sighed, flipping open a compact to apply a thick coat of coral lipstick. "Fifty acres of golf courses, swimming pools and the wealthiest retired bachelors north of Philly."

"You mean it's a retirement community?"

"A golfers' retirement community. For widowers only." Mama snapped the compact shut. "The Final Frontier. Where the women have gone before."

At the sound of my rattling, beat-up Camaro, a uniformed security guard popped out of the gatehouse, his walkie-talkie out of its holster and ready for activation.

"Good morning," he said as he leaned in the window and glanced around my car, his eyes finally resting on my pink, satin-covered staff. "And whom are we visiting today?"

Mama nervously sucked in a breath.

"We're here to visit Elwood Kramer and his niece, Janice," I said. The guard's name tag read RUSSELL. "Say. You look familiar. You go to the Two Guys Department Store Community College, Russell?"

Russell's face brightened. "You know me?"

"Possibly. I attended Two Guys for eight years."

"Eight years at Two Guys, no kidding?" Russell nodded in understanding of my academic difficulties. "I graduated last May with an associate's degree in Security Science. Started right away here at six bucks an hour." He stood up and stuck out his chest. "Promoted to Chief Safety Engineer last month."

"Ooooh," Mama cooed, impressed.

I wasn't so impressed. These days companies were handing out fancy titles like penny candy. "You get a raise with that, Russell?"

"Sure did. To six twenty-five. We got an opening. You should apply."

Mama punched my arm. "Forget journalism, Bubbles. This is where the real money's at. Security."

"Great bennies, too. Gotta take a drug test though."

I groaned. It makes me uncomfortable when strangers ask for my urine.

"Anyway, just sign your name and I'll let you pass."

Russell handed me a clipboard and I scrawled my name, quickly glancing at the others on the list. Most were pompous sounding—Pomeroy, Winchester, Rothschild. I wondered if Russell made them up in his spare time.

"Okay, Bubbles," Russell said, handing me his business card. "If you need a recommendation for that security post, I'm your man. We Two Guys alums gotta stick together."

I thanked him politely and carefully obeyed the 25 mph speed limit as Russell waved us a minimum-wage farewell in the rearview.

"If you're not going to take up Russell on his offer, I am," Mama said. "Be a great way to meet eligible bachelors, being a security guard at a swanky retirement community like this. A little unsure about that uniform, though. I don't look so hot in trousers."

I ignored her, concentrating instead on the numbers of the condos. So far, they had all been double units set back in the woods with slate walkways, pink begonias and redwood porches. Tasteful and private. Elwood Kramer's was number thirty-five. Mickey had told us to look for a wooden planter of purple and yellow petunias by the door.

We found it easily and I was disappointed to see that the curtains were drawn and there was no sign of activity.

"Hmm," Mama said. "Not too promising."

I parked the Camaro. "No. Not too."

Mama and I got out and stretched. For the last week in August it was wonderfully comfortable and dry, not muggy like the end of summer usually is in the Lehigh Valley. Today the sky was a robin's-egg blue and the air was perfumed by newly mowed grass, of which there was a generous, chemically fed amount in the Final Frontier.

Mama walked and I rustled in my hoopskirt up the

newly paved driveway to the front door and rang Elwood's bell. No answer. No sound of movement inside, either. We rang it again. Mama even tried the doorknob. It was locked.

While Mama checked the back, I tried the unit next door. No one answered.

"No one's here," Mama said, rounding the corner. "Let's ask Russell the security guard if he's seen Janice and Elwood. Get me one of them applications, too."

We were about to get in the Camaro when a canary-yellow Porsche zoomed into the driveway. A trim and dapper man with silver-gray hair and mustache, tan leather jacket and matching driver's gloves stepped out and sent my sixty-something mother into quivering teeny-bopper hysteria.

"May I be of assistance, Madam?" he said, extending his hand toward Mama. "Carmine Humphries. I live here." He pointed to the unit next to Elwood's, number thirty-four.

"Oh, my." Mama started patting her chest, our understood sign for *heart attack is imminent, get the nitro*. I put my arm around her shoulders to slow down the adrenaline.

"*The* Carmine Humphries?" she gasped.

He bowed. "In the flesh."

Pretty well-preserved flesh at that. Humphries couldn't have been a day under seventy-five.

"Bubbles, do you know who this is? This is Fast Car Carmine. The most famous race car driver out of Nazareth, Pennsylvania, since Mario Andretti."

"Correction." He twirled the ends of his mustache. "That was before Mario Andretti, as I put him on his first tricycle."

"Oh, of course." Mama stuck out her white-gloved hand. "LuLu Yablonsky. And this is my daughter, Bubbles."

Fast Car didn't give two hoots about me. He bent down low and gracefully kissed Mama's hand, never taking his eyes off her face. Mama blushed deeper than the coral on her lips.

"I used to watch you race forty years ago at the old Schnecksville Speedway," Mama gushed. "Tragedy they closed that 'cause of the neighbors. Noise pollution, schmoise pollution, I say. They didn't have to torch the place."

"Ah, yes. A grand track that was until that dreadful fire." Fast Car's blue eyes became misty. "Those were the glory days. Before NASCAR and Pepsi took over the sport. Some Sunday afternoons I find myself there in Schnecksville, sitting on the remaining wooden stands, reminiscing about—"

"Ahem," I coughed, nodding toward Elwood's door. "Janice?"

"Oh! I nearly forgot." Mama hurriedly explained about the wedding and how Janice hadn't shown and how we had been sent here to ask how come. Since Fast Car lived next door, did he have a key? And, if so, could he let us in for a peek?

"Certainly." Fast Car examined a set of keys on a BMW key chain. "I believe this is the one."

Taking Mama by the elbow, he led the way to the front door. They made an elegant couple, he in his leather driving outfit and she in her Chanel. Trotting behind them in the pink flounces from Miss Petunia's Wedding Emporium, I felt like their slightly off, slightly dim-witted charge out for her daily constitutional at the insane asylum.

Fast Car slipped the key in the lock and turned the knob. He opened the door to a perfectly immaculate living room decorated in shades of sage green, cream and lavender. Everything seemed to be in order. Not a slipcover out of place.

I swished over to a set of French doors that opened to a slate patio with wrought-iron furniture and more begonias. A sliding glass door on the right of the patio opened to the dining room. Another glass door on the left appeared to provide an exit for a bedroom.

"Holy crow," I exclaimed. "This is like a palace."

"It's okay," Fast Car said, running a gloved finger along the mantel. "A tad nouveau riche, if you ask me. Hello? Elwood? Janice?"

We listened. Silence.

Mama began to poke around. "Looks as if no one's home, that's for sure." She moved to the kitchen done with pine floors and granite countertops.

"Elwood's clunker isn't in the driveway," Fast Car observed, "so he and Janice must have left. Come to think of it, Janice's car wasn't there this morning, either, when I went outside for the paper. I simply assumed they were off to the blessed event."

"You hear any noises last night?" I asked. "Car doors slamming? People shouting? Arguing?" I was looking for any evidence that Janice and Elwood had fought over her proposed marriage to Mickey.

Fast Car pointed to his ear. "Sorry. My hearing aid is on the bedside table when I sleep. Without it I'm stone-deaf. Damage after years of racing, you know."

"Aww," Mama clucked sympathetically. "What's this?" She lifted a set of long white papers that had been lying on the kitchen counter.

Fast Car joined her for inspection.

While Mama and Fast Car shamelessly rummaged through Elwood's personal papers, I headed down the short hallway in search of Janice's bedroom. It suddenly struck me as odd that Janice had never invited me here before. There had always been an excuse—my house on West Goepp Street was closer, let's just go to a local restaurant or a movie after work. Since it was always more convenient to get together in town, I'd never second-guessed Janice's motive.

Now I wondered what her true motive was.

I knocked briefly and then opened the first door on my right. I stopped still.

Janice's white satin wedding dress, still encased in its zippered plastic cover, hung from the door to her closet. Her tulle veil awaited, pouffed and ready, on her bureau. The bed was neatly made. Unslept in. A half-packed suitcase was propped open on the floor. I began to seriously question whether Janice had made it home from the party last night.

A blue box with a white bow on Janice's bureau caught my eye. It was next to a smaller white box with a card addressed to Myrtle. Bridesmaids' gifts. I brazenly opened the card for me.

Upon reading the first few sentences my heart sighed. "Dear Bubbles," the note began. "You will never know how much you've meant to me. You were my first friend when I moved here and my best driving instructor."

I pictured my initial face-to-face encounter with Janice, a plain woman with thick brown braids and a pleasant, friendly face. She was near tears in the driver's seat of her Ford Fiesta from which steam was rising after thirty-two attempts to wiggle out of a tight space on Fourth Street. So I introduced her to the infamous steeltown girl's bump-and-clutch method not taught in most driver education programs.

Janice was immediately grateful. But I quickly said it was *I* who should have thanked *her*. A week before, Janice had leaked confidential records to Mickey, who had requested them on my behalf for a story I was working on. With those records, I was able to solve the mystery behind a decade-old murder and write the first blockbuster article of my budding newspaper career. This big break couldn't have happened without Janice's assistance, of that I was certain.

But I was certainly surprised to discover that my request had led to a bit of clandestine bonding between Janice and Mickey, which eventually blossomed into a rich romance and their speedy engagement—as her note pointed out.

"And if it hadn't been for you, I never would have met the sweetest, kindest, gentlest man in the whole wide world," it concluded. "I am proud to have you as my maid of honor on this, the most wonderful day in my life."

Oh, that was too much. The waterworks opened and I started bawling. This was not the letter of a nervous bride, a woman with cold feet. Something awful had happened to Janice. Where was she?

I searched on the bureau for a Kleenex. Finding none, I went on a hunt for toilet paper, turning the handle to what I suspected was a bathroom door. I flicked on the light, stepped over the body lying on the tile floor and reached for the roll. After a good blow, I tossed the crumpled tissue into a wastebasket and did a double take.

Body lying on the tile floor? Yipes!

I scrambled into the tub and assessed the sight in front of me.

He was in striped pajamas and a navy blue robe. His faded eyes were staring at the light fixture on the ceiling and his skin was a pale bluish gray. Altogether, it was a picture of white and various shades of blue.

Elwood.

I put one foot over the edge of the tub and reached for Elwood's wrist to feel for a pulse, although usually I have a hard time finding my own heartbeat when I do aerobics to Richard Simmons on video. In this case, I was pretty positive there was none, as the wrist was clammy cold. There was, however, a pool of dark red blood behind his neck that had seeped into and soaked the back of his robe.

Turning him ever so slightly, I saw a deep gash running the length of his scalp and I concluded—although I have no degree in mortuary science—that Uncle Elwood had not met his Maker by hitting his noggin on the vanity during a midnight trip to the john.

No. Whoever had clocked Elwood had clocked him good.

The question was—what had the murderer done with Janice?

Chapter 3

"So, what's your theory here, Bubbles?" my boss Sandy asked, lighting a Virginia Slims. "You think Janice beaned her grumpy uncle and then skipped town?"

"What're you, nuts?" I bit into a blueberry muffin fresh from the bakery owned by Sandy's husband, Martin, and warmed via the House of Beauty microwave. "Janice couldn't step on a cockroach. More likely Janice has been kidnaped."

"Kidnaped, eh?" Sandy stroked her toy poodle, Oscar, the salon mascot. "That's a bit dramatic. Maybe she came to her senses. Finally realized she didn't want to be a mother to a four-year-old in diapers."

I wiped crumbs off my hands and pondered the lyrics to "Free Bird." "You don't suppose the song I sang to Janice influenced her to run out on Mickey, do you?"

"Nah." Sandy dismissed this with a wave of her hand. "Only men take Skynyrd seriously. Who else would be so egotistic as to assume that a man's leaving would change a woman forever? Don't give it a second thought, Bubbles."

This kind of automatic support is why I love Sandy—if not her taste in clothes. Today she was dressed in a pink polyester nurses' style uniform with a matching kerchief around her brown wavy hair. Oscar sat on her lap crunching on a Milk-Bone.

Having eaten no breakfast or lunch, I found myself famished. I scarfed two of Martin's bursting-with-blueberry muffins and downed a nice cup of hot coffee thick with Cremora and plenty of sugar. For the first time that day I felt almost normal.

Even though it was my day off, The House of Beauty was the only place I wanted to be after the cops arrived at the Final Frontier with a stricken Mickey in the passenger's seat of a Lehigh Police Department cruiser.

I wasn't permitted to say toodle-do to the boy. His cohorts ushered him into the condo and shooed us out as paramedics ran in from an ambulance. After answering a long list of repetitive questions about how I had found Elwood and then filling out two police reports, Mama, Fast Car and I had been free to go.

Fast Car was in total shock. "He was only seventy-two," he kept murmuring. "The prime of life."

Mama, overcome by a thirst for iced tea and the immediate need to put her feet up on Fast Car's comfortable redwood chaise longue, stayed at the Final Frontier. I drove back to Lehigh, stunned and saddened by the day's events. Not to mention deeply worried about Janice's whereabouts.

It was the first day of the first week of school, so Jane wasn't around when I got home. I put on a pair of black Capri pants, a hot-pink knitted tank top and matching high-heeled sandals with Velcro straps. Then I headed over to the House of Beauty, located right next to Uncle Manny's Bar and Grille, to unload on Sandy.

The House of Beauty is your typical 1960s, pink-walled, neighborhood salon, big on the blue hair jobs and weekly comb and sets. Faded photos of models in Dippity-Do flips hang in the front window along with the Liberty High Hurricanes football season schedule and numerous F.O.P. stickers on the screen door to indicate union loyalty.

As soon as I arrived, I decided to straighten out drawers to keep my mind occupied. I wished to hell I still smoked.

Sandy leaned back in the green chair and shooed Oscar off her lap. "I agree with you that Janice is a sweetheart, but, still, she is a bit odd."

I dropped brushes into a sanitizing solution. "How so?"

"For starters, she acted like she had never gotten her hair cut before. Had a part down the middle of her head wider than Route 22. And when I suggested getting rid of those braids, she nearly flipped. Can't imagine her fuss if I had pushed the highlights."

"Janice is a country girl, Sandy. Maybe her mother never took her to the salon." Although that was, admittedly, an alien concept. Saturday morning visits to the salon on the corner were as mandatory as Sunday church, according to my mother. To miss either would have been sacrilege.

"Janice is no girl. She's twenty-four. And that's another thing. What about her family? How come they weren't invited to the wedding?"

I separated bobby pins from hair clips. Janice had been rather vague when I inquired as to why only her uncle had been invited from her family. She had mumbled something about it being difficult for her parents to travel and there being a "religion issue."

"What does it matter? So she wanted an intimate ceremony. Doesn't make her homicidal." My voice reached a high pitch. "Why are you climbing all over Janice?"

"Geez, Bubbles. Take a pill. What's wrong with you? Your skin tone is all blotchy and your hair's limp and lifeless. You stressed?"

I examined myself in the mirror. Indeed, I was not my usual Bubbles best. My black-rimmed eyes were red and even through a layer of foundation and powder my skin was pale and unhealthy.

"I found a dead body today, Sandy," I said, adding under my breath, "and I'm a little hungover."

"I'd say more than a little." Sandy walked over to the cupboard under the cash register and brought up a bottle of V8. She combined a bunch of ingredients from her stash in the minifridge and handed me the glass of thick, red juice.

"For bad girls," she said, dropping in a vitamin. "This'll put the Maybelline back in those cheeks."

I eyed the concoction skeptically. "No way."

"Do as I say. And don't skip the vitamin."

I pinched my nose and did as she instructed. It wasn't too disgusting, although the drink was so spicy my face flushed as my blood revved its circulation. When I was done, I blurted, "I woke up next to Dan this morning."

Sandy put her hands on her hips. "What about that doggone chastity vow? It's only been what, four months?"

I checked my watch. "Ten weeks, six days, five hours and nineteen minutes ago. Anyway, it wasn't like that. I just passed out from too many Jell-O shots."

She shook her head in disappointment. "Let me get this straight, Bubbles. You got drunk at Janice's bachelorette party, danced on top of the pool table—"

"I was playing air guitar."

"Manny told me you were dancing."

Manny, that snitch. Next time I throw a bachelorette party, I'll think twice about hosting it at the bar right next door to my place of employment.

"Then," Sandy continued, "you ended up sleeping with Dan. May I remind you of what happened the last time you got drunk and slept with Dan?"

I opened the third drawer filled with assorted curling irons and scattered clips. I did not need to be reminded of that night nearly eighteen years ago when, as townie teenagers, Sandy and I had sneaked into a Lehigh University fraternity. That was the night I met Dan, attractively adorned with two beer cans strapped to either side of his head. I downed one Dixie cup of frat punch and an hour later I was flat on the fraternity floor, Dan over me, one of his Schlitz cans dripping beer all over my face.

"You got pregnant with Jane."

I emptied that drawer on the vanity. "This time I did not sleep sleep with Dan. I simply *slept* with Dan."

"Oh," Sandy replied. "Well, that's *much* better."

Sandy and I burst out laughing.

The front doorbell tinkled and in walked Tiffany, our on-again, off-again stylist and resident vegetarian hippie.

"What's so funny?" she asked, depositing her macramé purse on the vanity.

"I was teasing Bubbles about how she got sloshed on Jell-O shots at Janice's bachelorette party last night," Sandy said, wisely avoiding any mention of dead Elwood or Janice's no-show at the wedding. Tiffany could not be trusted with gossip.

"Yeah, I heard all about it," Tiffany said, plugging in the hot water pot for tea. "I ran into Manny's bartender in the co-op. Is it true you did a striptease to 'Free Bird'?"

"I did not do a striptease! I played air guitar."

"That's okay, Bubbles," Sandy said soothingly. "We all overindulge once in a while. Look at Martin—"

Uh-oh. I braced myself for another bizarre story about Sandy's mild-mannered husband.

"The other evening Martin and I went contra dancing at the Elks in Allentown. I left at nine to go home to bed, but Martin was so taken with a new mouth harp one of the boys had, he stayed up until midnight learning how to collapse his cheeks to play 'Will the Circle Be Unbroken.' " She slapped her thigh as though this was the most outrageous moment in her life. "He didn't get to bed until one. When the alarm rang at four a.m. he was one tired baker, let me tell you. Whoo. What a crazy night that was."

Tiffany and I stared at Sandy in dull awe.

"Speaking of Allentown," Tiffany said, thankfully changing the subject from Martin's wild antics, "you won't believe who I saw drinking coffee at the Java Man's Café this morning, Bubbles."

"Who?"

"Stiletto."

My right index finger shot to a strand of hair and began twirling. "Stiletto? Are you sure?"

Sandy cleared her throat behind me.

"Yup. I'm sure because I said, 'Hi, Steve, when did you get back?' and he told me a few days ago but he was rushing down to Philly and didn't have time to chat." She took a long sip of tea. "Although he seemed to have plenty of time to talk to some busty brunette. God, she was all over him like a sherpa on Everest."

I figured this was another Tiffany tall tale until I spun around and caught Sandy trying to mime a shut-up signal behind my back. "What? You knew, too?"

Sandy dropped her hand. "I didn't want to say anything until you heard from him yourself. But my Saturday nine a.m., Mrs. Coleman, said her friend Velma got a call from Stiletto asking if she had a few hours to clean his house."

This was such stunning news I collapsed against the vanity, my body like wet spaghetti. "Why didn't he call me?"

"To clean his house?" asked Tiffany.

"Oh, Tiffany," Sandy sighed.

DUBUQUE COUNTY LIBRARY

Stiletto and I had a powerful animal attraction for each other. He was everything I was looking for in a man—tall, broad shouldered, a dead ringer for the lust-of-my-life Mel Gibson, smart, rich, funny and, especially, worldly. He had traveled from Bosnia photographing wars for the Associated Press to Peru shooting village tribes for *National Geographic*. They didn't make men like him in Lehigh.

We first met while I was reporting on a murder for the *News-Times*. Had I not taken the chastity vow weeks before our introduction we would have released all that sexual tension between the sheets long ago.

But for once in my life I had made a conscious decision to be a good girl and to play it proper until I got a commitment, preferably one signed by a judge or consecrated by a priest—or at least notarized by a travel agent. So I had held off Stiletto's soft caresses and tried to ignore the desirous way he gazed into my eyes as he brought my mouth up to kiss me. It had required every ounce of steely resolve not to drag him into bed by his boot strings along with two bottles of conditioner to undo the rat's nest into which I had twisted my hair—a sure sign of sexual frustration.

To my surprise I discovered that my reserve only drove him more crazy. At least, that's what I *thought* I had discovered. Until Tiffany opened her big trap.

"Whoops." Tiffany clapped her hand over her mouth. "You haven't heard from Steve? I assumed he called you as soon as he got in. I am *such* a Sagittarius. Always putting my foot in my mouth."

I folded my arms on the vanity next to the scattered curling irons and hair clips. I was looking forward to a hearty cry when the door opened and in strode a sadder sack than myself.

"What's wrong with her?" asked Mickey, nodding in my direction.

"Hey, what're you doing here?" exclaimed Tiffany. "Shouldn't you be with your new bride heading off to that honeymoon in the Poconos?"

"Yo, Sagittarius, can it," Sandy chided. "I'm gonna have to buy you a muzzle."

"It's okay," said Mickey, sitting down in a wicker chair by the door. He was out of his rented, powder-blue wedding wear and was now in jeans and a polo shirt. "It's gonna be all over town by dinnertime anyway."

"What's gonna be all over town?" Tiffany asked.

Well, the cat was out of the bag now. It could not be helped. We listened patiently as Mickey retold the whole story about how Janice hadn't shown up at the wedding and then the call from me about what we had uncovered in Elwood's condo. He said the cops were waiting for the coroner to determine whether Elwood had simply fallen and hit his head in the bathroom or if he had been the victim of foul play.

"One thing's for sure," Mickey concluded. "Janice did *not* bludgeon her uncle. She loved Elwood like a father."

I wanted to know why Mickey was in the House of Beauty instead of searching high and low for his bride-to-be. "I mean, she could've been kidnaped by Elwood's murderer," I told him.

Mickey shook his head. "When I got to work a few minutes ago there was a message from Janice on my voice mail left around eleven p.m. last night. She said something had come up and she needed to go back home. She'd explain it all to me later." His gaze wandered to the window. "The department's confiscated the tape."

Tiffany announced she was going to brew him a pot of chamomile tea. Sandy did a load of towels in the supply room as I delicately pried information from Mickey about what the cops had learned so far.

"Did they question Russell the security guard? He's the chief safety honcho," I said, wondering what I'd done with Russell's business card. "Seemed on the ball to me."

"That guy's gonna get canned. The condo association is demanding that the whole security team be replaced with a high-profile agency from Philly, according to Frye." Mickey picked invisible lint off his shirt. "The association is extremely nervous about Elwood's death, what impact it's going to have on the resale value at the Final Frontier. They want to sweep it under the rug. You know how these snotty gated communities are. Murders just don't happen there."

I suppose if I were paying a three-hundred-dollar-per-month security charge, I'd expect to live in a homicide-free zone, too. "Yes, but did Russell see anything suspicious?"

"He wasn't on duty. Homicide's trying to track down the night watchman. Apparently the guy's so freaked about what happened that he's gone on some sort of bender."

"You must be freaked, too, Mickey," I pointed out, choosing my words carefully, "what with Elwood being found dead on the same day Janice didn't show up for your wedding."

"You can say that again." Mickey stopped picking the lint and leaned forward. "I've thought about it and thought about it and I keep coming back to her state of mind these past few days."

The tea was ready and Tiffany poured him a cup. "State of mind?" she asked, dipping in a bag of chamomile. "What was her state of mind?"

"Antsy." Mickey took the cup. "Worried. Anxious. Fretful."

"She was about to get married, Mickey," I said, placing my hand comfortingly on his knee. Married to a guy with five undisciplined maniacs, I wanted to add—but didn't.

"It was more than that," he said, blowing on his tea. "She was preoccupied with this case our department's been dealing with. Very controversial."

"I thought all she did was compile records," I said, curious since Janice—who normally divulged every police department detail to me—hadn't said boo about working on a highly controversial case.

"She was called in to be a kind of cultural liaison to help with a couple of kids from Lancaster County caught taking a joyride. They were from her hometown. Whoopee."

"Yahoo!" echoed Sandy, entering the salon with a load of fresh towels.

"No, I mean Whoopee," Mickey corrected. "As in Whoopee, PA."

Sandy, Tiffany and I gave each other glances.

"Where's Whoopee, PA?" Tiffany asked.

"It's in Dutch Country. A tiny town halfway between Intercourse and Paradise." Mickey said this matter-of-factly. "Beautiful place."

Sandy's lips twitched. "You mean, to get from Intercourse to Paradise, you've got to go through Whoopee?"

"That's right," said Mickey. "Actually, you have to make a right at Whoopee from Intercourse on the way to Paradise."

That was too much for Sandy who, I am ashamed to admit, has a pitifully low tolerance for silly humor. She stifled a giggle.

"With my last boyfriend," Tiffany said, "he only wanted Whoopee. He never took me to Paradise after Intercourse."

Tiffany and Sandy bent over in hysterics.

"What's so funny?" Mickey asked. "Whoopee's a famous Amish community. It's where whoopee pies come from."

"Oh, wait until I tell Martin," Sandy howled. "His Chocoholics Anonymous group is going to love this. I can see the T-shirts now."

Mickey rubbed his thighs. "God, I'm restless. The kids are at my mother's for a week. I took off work 'cause of the honeymoon and now I need a chore or something. You got a chore for me to do, Sandy?"

"The front doorknob sticks," Sandy said, composing herself. "How about you fix that? My next client doesn't come in for fifteen minutes. Now's as good a time as any."

Mickey nodded and Sandy fetched a toolbox after calling him a prince. Meanwhile I thought back to what Sandy had said about Janice's wide part and her fear of salons, about how, at age twenty-four, she hadn't been able to parallel park on Fourth Street.

"Janice isn't Amish, is she, Mickey?"

Mickey unscrewed the knob casing. "Born and raised, though never baptized." He pulled off the casing and peered in. "Geesh. You got a lot of rust here, Sandy. You sure this door is watertight?"

Sandy shrugged.

"Is that why she didn't invite anyone from her hometown to the wedding, except for Elwood?" I knelt next to him. " 'Cause she's Amish?"

"Basically." Mickey rummaged through the toolbox. "She didn't want folks in Whoopee to find out about us until the marriage license was filed proper in the Court of Widows and Orphans. She was afraid a few of her relatives might come up here and try to stop her otherwise. Hey, Sandy, you got any WD-40?"

I sat back in the chair, now doubtful about the depth of my friendship with Janice. For some reason she hadn't trusted me enough to confide that she was

Amish. She had let me prance about in my cleavage-baring, butt-hugging Bubbles wear, never letting on that she secretly found my clothes morally offensive.

And all those talks we had about sex! I slapped my cheek. No wonder the poor girl had been as startled as a deer in headlights when I detailed for her my past experiences in the backseat of the Camaro with Ken the RadioShack woofer installer.

"That's why Janice no-showed, Mickey," Tiffany offered. "Maybe one of her relatives found out about the wedding and snatched her."

"Dubious." He spritzed the lock with WD-40. "Her car was gone, the Ford Fiesta. Then there's that answering machine tape where she sounds calm and perfectly in control. Nah. Janice left of her own free will."

"I still can't understand what you're doing at the House of Beauty when you could be out investigating this," I persisted.

"No can do," he said, fastening the strike plate with slow, deliberate twists of the screwdriver. "I'm not allowed to go near the case. I'd get in trouble even if I drove down to Whoopee to break the news to Janice about her uncle."

"How come you can't go near the case?" asked Tiffany. "You're not a suspect."

Mickey sat back on his haunches. "Actually, I am. I'm a suspect because I had dinner with Elwood last night at his home while Janice and the girls were off at the bachelorette party."

"So?" said Tiffany.

"So that makes me one of the last people to see him alive. Like I told Bubbles at the wedding, I was not one of Elwood's favorite people. Homicide's gotta follow all leads."

He turned the greased doorknob easily. "And then there's that will."

Boy. The surprises never ended here at the House of Beauty.

"Will?" Sandy asked.

"The will left on Elwood's kitchen counter," he said. "The will that has a clause stating if Janice gets married before Elwood dies, she gets nothing of his estate. Not one red cent." Mickey sipped the cooled tea. "All his money goes to the Professional Goatherders of America. Elwood showed it to me after dinner."

The Professional Goatherders of America? Shepherds in business suits flashed before my eyes.

"Elwood cornered the goat cheese market years before feta started popping up all over pizzas and salads," Mickey said. "But Janice didn't care about his money. She cared about him—even if he was a feta tycoon."

"He didn't seem *that* rich, Mickey," I noted.

"You didn't see his car. That's missing, too."

"If Janice's car is missing," I said, "then who took Elwood's? The murderer, obviously."

Mickey shrugged. "Any way you slice it, there are more than enough murder motives to go around. You'd better believe that with all this intense pressure from the millionaires at the Final Frontier, homicide's gonna want to tie this up fast."

He shook his head. "I only hope that in their haste the detectives don't screw up and pin the rap on my sweet Janice. Frye leaked it to me that homicide considers her suspect number one since none of Elwood's cash and valuables was stolen, except for the car. Crime of passion, I guess. The condo association is leaning on the chief to arrest her within forty-eight hours after the coroner issues his report."

"They are?" I asked. "But you said they wanted to sweep this under the rug."

"It's like this." He closed the toolbox and fastened it shut. "If it has to be a murder, then the condo association would like it to be a domestic situation. You know, someone in the family. That's much more preferable than the possibility of an outsider sneaking past security and beating some rich resident over the head."

I stood up, incensed, my hands balled into fists. "This is not fair, Mickey. We cannot simply sit here, helpless, waiting for the cops to arrest Janice for a murder she didn't commit. You say Janice was calm and in control when she left a message on the answering machine, but maybe that was before someone, Elwood's murderer perhaps, got to her."

Mickey stood up too and placed a steadying hand on my shoulder. "I hear you, Bubbles, but what can I do? I'm solely responsible for the support of five kids. If I violate the law by tracking down Janice, my job and paycheck are in jeopardy. I'll never work in law enforcement again."

I glanced at Sandy, who lit another cigarette and pointed to the door.

"The *News-Times* awaits, Bubbles. I don't know how you held out this long."

Sandy's "Bad Girls" Hangover Remedy

In the world of my boss and best friend, Sandy, there are two types of women: bad girls and girls like her. I've long forgotten what separates the two, partly because I have the feeling Sandy has always lumped me with the latter. But one point I remember is that good girls don't drink alcohol, and if they do, it's disguised in either a sickeningly sweet drink, such as a Mud Slide, or a fruit-flavored wine cooler.

Of course, I could point out to Sandy that, like a true bad girl, she still smokes (unlike me), but Sandy would just pull out that mental notebook she keeps of all my missteps, including my infamous romp with the RadioShack clerk, and I'd be at an immediate disadvantage. Anyway, here is her recipe for the hangover remedy. Funny. You'd think a girl like Sandy wouldn't have this at her fingertips, say?

8 ounces V8 or plain tomato juice
2 tablespoons white vinegar
Dash of celery salt
A few drops Worcestershire sauce
A grinding of pepper
Dash of hot sauce
Ice

Mix first six ingredients and pour over ice. Sip gradually. Follow with two glasses of water for cleansing and beauty purposes.

Chapter 4

I would like to say that I clicked my heels five blocks to the *News-Times* emboldened by faith in the Fourth Estate and motivated by a noble pursuit of truth and justice.

But I have to confess, I was partly prompted with boy craziness, too. *News-Times* night news editor Mr. Salvo was a longtime pal of Stiletto's. He would know for sure if Steve had rolled into town and, if so, why he hadn't called me.

I entered the three-story brick building across from the Tally Ho! bar and took the stairs to the newsroom. The *News-Times* was like most local newspapers. City council meetings, high school sports, lengthy obituaries and weddings were the big stuff. International conflict and possible nuclear wars were buried on page four.

At the entrance to the newsroom, there was a fresh new receptionist whose nameplate said PAULA PURDY. The old receptionist, my pal Doris Daye, had left the paper and was off to Seattle making gobs of money fooling around in computers. This new Paula was efficiently reorganizing Doris's Rolodex. Her hair was a lacquered auburn shag and her black suit was cut in a way that indicated she didn't plan on being a receptionist for long.

With confidence I pushed against the wooden gate to the newsroom when, much to my amazement, I discovered a lock had been installed.

"May I help you?" Paula chirped.

"I'm here to see Mr. Salvo."

Paula picked up the phone. "Your name?"

I had to be careful how I answered that question. Executive editor Dix Notch had recently suffered a temporary cut in pay and an inconvenient adjustment in work schedules thanks to yours truly. At the sight of me Notch became nervous and agitated; his eyes watered and his muscles started to tic. Something about women wearing tube tops and short shorts in the newsroom. He called it unprofessional attire or some such nonsense.

"Your name?" Paula asked again.

"Bubbawabensk," I mumbled.

Paula's eyes narrowed. She glanced back at her computer where I was surprised to see taped to the monitor a miniature picture of my face with a black Magic Marker X over it. Underneath was a yellow Post-it that said: NO BUBBLES.

Paula's eyes flicked to me and the photo and then at me again. Her crimson-nailed index finger pressed zero. Security.

"I'm sorry," she said, sweetly. "I didn't quite catch that."

Mr. Salvo was making his way to the newsroom copy machine in the hub of the forbidden zone. At the top of my voice I yelled, "Hi, Mr. Salvo!"

"Hey, Bubbles!" He stepped quickly to the gate and pressed a buzzer to let me in. "It's okay, Paula. She's with me."

Paula flashed him an I'm-not-taking-responsibility-for-this glare and returned to the Rolodex.

"She's new," Mr. Salvo said by way of explanation as I entered the newsroom.

Already reporters had their heads together, whispering and staring at my hot-pink Velcro sandals. Geesh. You'd think they'd never been in the presence of a real feminine woman before.

"Maybe we should talk in the conference room," Mr. Salvo suggested, pulling me into a dark, windowless office. He flicked on the light and closed the door. There was one long table, several chairs, a water cooler, a chalkboard and a TV. I sat at one end of the table and Mr. Salvo sat across from me.

He was the same old Mr. Salvo, pasty white skin and tiny eyes like a mole from working nights and sleeping days for more than twenty years.

"Good to see you, Bubbles. Boy, you look great. Such rosy cheeks," he gushed. "What's up?"

"Is Dix Notch here yet?"

Mr. Salvo checked his watch. "He's upstairs in a meeting with the publisher so we can steal a few minutes. You got a news tip?"

I began with the missing Janice and described how I had found Elwood's corpse and how Mickey was pretty certain that Janice was about to be unjustly arrested for murder. I had run this by Mickey and he had granted permission for me to speak to Mr. Salvo. He agreed that having a newspaper probe the case might cause the chief of police to think twice about caving to the condo association.

When I finished my tale, Mr. Salvo merely stroked his chin and played with a pencil on the table. You'd expect that he'd have been thrilled to learn one of his own reporters had an inside scoop on a blockbuster news story.

"Hel-lo?" I waved my hand in front his face. "Did you hear what I just said? I have an exclusive on the Elwood Kramer murder."

"Yes, yes. It's a bit more complicated than that, Bubbles. All day Dix Notch has been fielding calls from—"

At the sound of his dreaded name, the conference room door was flung open and there stood Dix Notch in a bad mood. He was carrying a fancy attaché case and wearing khaki slacks, a navy coat and a blue-and-white-striped shirt with a yellow tie. Per usual, his nearly bald head was sunburned red from all those afternoons playing golf with the steel executives. Paula Purdy cowered behind him.

"Mr. Salvo said it was okay, but I knew, I just knew you'd object, Mr. Notch," she prattled. "It wasn't—"

Dix Notch slammed the door in her face. If I were Paula, I'd grieve.

"What's the Bimbo doing here?" he said, pointing a trembling finger at me.

"Bubbles has a damned good angle on the story Lawless is working on."

Lawless. Ooooh. The mere mention of his name made my blood boil. Lawless was the *News-Times* revered police reporter whose idea of sourcing was knocking back a few brewskies at the Tally Ho! with the detectives. My experience with Lawless was that I did all the work and he got all the credit.

"Alright." Dix Notch crossed his arms. "Let's hear it, Miss Yablonsky."

I laid out what I knew of the Uncle Elwood murder. As I spoke, Notch's right jowl began to quiver.

"So what?" he barked when I was done. "Lawless has been on the case all day. It's bogus."

I opened my eyes. "Pardon?"

"Nothing to it. There was no murder. See, this is what distinguishes a trained veteran like Lawless from a dabbling wannabe like—"

"But, Mr. Notch," I interrupted, adjusting the pink tank top strap that kept slipping down my shoulder, "I *saw* Elwood Kramer's body with my own eyes. That gash didn't come from any bathroom sink, and what about his niece, Janice? She's missing. She was supposed to get married to Mickey Sinkler today. She's such a nice person, so innocent, and Mickey is distraught—"

Notch flapped his hand. "Don't drag me into your middle-class soap opera, Miss Yablonsky. I'm not interested in who was supposed to marry whom. The bottom line is that Elwood Kramer was a seventy-two-year-old man who slipped on the bathroom floor." He threw up his hands. "Happens every day. Get over it."

Get over it? I sat stunned as Dix Notch casually picked up the attaché case. "I had hoped," he continued, "that you were here to offer a beauty feature. Perhaps a piece on those wild haircuts I see skateboarders sporting these days. You know, an article for the women's pages."

Something inside me went snap and I was about to bounce out of my seat and lunge for Dix Notch's buttoned-down collar when Mr. Salvo grabbed my hand and patted it.

"Bubbles understands," Mr. Salvo said, shooting me a knowing glance.

"Good," Notch said, "because I don't want to find that she's been pestering residents of the Final Frontier like some sleazy tabloid reporter and putting the *News-Times* in yet another humiliating situation."

To compose myself, I concentrated on my manicure. My cuticles had been neglected and were threatening to rebel into painful hangnails.

"Don't forget the news meeting in ten minutes, Tony," Notch said, walking to the door. "It's a bimbo-free one today."

I stuck out my tongue as he exited. "How come Notch is so opposed to the idea of Elwood Kramer's death being a murder?" I asked Mr. Salvo. "It's not because Elwood lived in a gated community, is it?"

"Bingo," Mr. Salvo said, aiming his finger at me. "Like

I was about to tell you when Notch came in, he's been on the horn all day handling calls from his golf buddies at the Final Frontier, and what a crowd they are. Retired lawyers, doctors, steel execs. The last thing they want to see are the words *Final Frontier* and *murder* in the same headline. They've even retained their own counsel."

"You're kidding. For what?"

"To sue us if we imply, in any way, that Elwood Kramer's death was made possible by a lapse in security. College campuses, shopping malls, gated communities. They all have the same circle-the-wagons approach when fessing up to crime. Ask any editor. You can't go near the story, Bubbles, not after last time."

I gave him a look to remind him that "last time," had resulted in me landing a page-one humdinger in the *Philadelphia Inquirer*.

"I know what you're thinking, Bubbles. Not to sound like a jerk, but there's an expression in the newspaper business: You're only as good as this morning's story and this morning's story is already birdcage liner."

"I'm sorry, Mr. Salvo, but I cannot stand by and do nothing. I *know* Elwood Kramer was murdered. I *know* Janice Kramer didn't do it. She used to volunteer at the hospital rocking babies, for heaven's sake. And now she's missing and her uncle's dead." I took a deep breath. "If I have to drive down to Whoopee in search of her myself, I will."

At the mention of Whoopee, Mr. Salvo's face brightened. "Whoopee?"

"Whoopee. That's where Janice is from and Mickey said that's probably where she's headed, at least according to the message she left on his answering machine at work."

"Hmmm." Mr. Salvo picked up the pencil and began tapping it. "Turns out we might be able to use you for a story after all."

"Really?" I pulled in my chair.

"And, if along the way you happen to *accidentally* trip upon Janice Kramer or dig up some information on her whereabouts, well, so be it, right?"

I smiled. "Not like I'll be snooping around the Final Frontier."

"Of course not," Mr. Salvo agreed soberly. "Wouldn't want to go against a Dix Notch directive."

"Not us," I said. "What's the story in Whoopee?"

Mr. Salvo grabbed a white tablet and began writing—an involuntary action I've noticed seasoned reporters and editors slip into when talking. "It so happens that last week two teenage brothers with the last name Hochstetter, twins actually, broke down in a stolen car, a Buick Electra 225, on I-78, right by the Lehigh University exit."

Okay. So far not up to par with a murder and a missing bride, but I remained open-minded. I took out a nail file and went to town on a budding hangnail.

"Those boys in the Electra were Amish, which explains why they were driving without a license. But for some reason that neither Lawless nor the *Call* has been able to ferret out, they got the full treatment by the Lehigh police, who confiscated the Electra and placed the kids in a halfway house. The cops are treating them like Mafia hit men. Twenty-four-hour guards, no phone calls." He paused. "Here's the hook. The Hochstetter kids are from Whoopee."

The file slipped across my nail. This must have been the case Janice was working on last week, the one that Mickey said had made her so fretful and worried.

I explained this to Mr. Salvo, who pounded the table in glee.

"A connection. That's great. I'm telling you, Bubbles." Mr. Salvo wagged his finger at me. "Something funny's going on with this case. I'm thinking the kids are part of a gang. That would explain the hot car. Lawless is laying bets on them being Pagans."

"Pagans, Mr. Salvo? I thought you said these kids were Amish."

"Not *that* kind of pagan. I'm talking about the infamous Lancaster County gang. Mostly made up of young outlaws, including a few lapsed Amish. Like to steal cars. Supposedly there's a strength requirement to enter. They have to be able to bench-press five hundred, wrestle an alligator, dive off cliffs. Tend to wear a lot of black leather à la James Dean."

I gulped. Outlaws in black leather? James Dean? Bench-pressing?

Mr. Salvo, who had never bench-pressed more than a hoagie with extra cheese, nonchalantly twirled the pencil on the tablet. "If Janice was working on that Hochstetter case, then maybe the people she's running from—or with—are the Pagans."

"You don't know Janice," I said. "She's very innocent and proper. She wouldn't hook up with a gang."

"I wouldn't be so sure. My neighbor's twenty-year-old daughter ran off with them once. She left home a prissy virgin coed and came back—"

He glanced up at me and blushed. "Well, you know."

I leaned closer. "No," I practically panted. "I don't know. Tell me."

"Oh. I couldn't." He cleared his throat. "Let's just say that when she rode off with the Pagans she was still in loafers and Peter Pan collars. When she returned from her, um, stint, she was in skintight leather jeans and a low-necked top that, well, didn't leave much to the imagination. Guys she knew from college started making trips to her house like it was Mecca. Her dad bought a Rottweiler to keep them away."

"So she wasn't . . . hurt . . . by the Pagans."

"Hurt? Oh, no. Liberated was more like it. Unleashed. Ripened. Matured. Whatever those Pagans did, it transformed her from an awkward girl into a voluptuous woman." He let out a long sigh. "Oh, to have been twenty-two again."

I waited patiently as Mr. Salvo daydreamed about lost youth. After a few minutes he snapped to attention, straightened his tie and returned to those notes. "Anyhow, back to Whoopee. You're not swimming in bucks, and considering Dix Notch's current mood, I wouldn't risk asking him for an expense account. So do you think you could stay with friends down in Whoopee?"

"I believe I can find a place," I answered, suddenly charged by the idea of *me* being "out of town on assignment," looking for Janice and the outlaw, mysterious, sexually gifted Pagans. Wait until Stiletto found out about this! That is, if he could drag himself away from busty brunettes to listen.

"Super. I'll jot down the information for you. The twins' names are Amos and Levi," he said, writing. "We haven't printed that yet because they're juveniles, but we did run a small story on two Amish kids driving a stolen car without a license." He stopped for a moment. "I'm sure you read it."

Uh-oh. As my former professor, Mr. Salvo used to scold us in the Two Guys Community College course if we didn't read the paper every day. He said no reporter was worth his salt if he didn't read his own newspaper. However, I have to confess. I hardly ever read the paper except to clip coupons and match the weddings with the birth announcements to see who had put the cart before the horse.

I slipped the nail file back in its case. "Must have missed it."

Mr. Salvo returned to writing. "Oh, I hope you're not getting out of practice, Bubbles. Being sent out of town on assignment is a whole new ball of wax. You won't be reporting in Lehigh where people recognize you from Schoenen's Grocery."

He ripped off the top page and slid it to me. I couldn't read his scrawl worth beans.

We stood and shook hands. He smiled and escorted me out of the insulated conference room to the gate. Paula Purdy was typing away, all ears.

"I'm sure we'll be in touch," he said. "Call me as soon as you get down there."

I lingered. Deadline was approaching in a few hours and reporters were either shouting at editors or preparing for the night meetings they would cover. The volume on the police scanner was turned to its highest, issuing a constant stream of ten-fours, diabetic shocks and fender benders.

If I had been smart, I would have asked about Stiletto while we were still in the conference room, out of range of questioning ears. However, a Phi Beta Kappa brain surgeon I ain't and desperate I was.

"Is there anything else, Bubbles?" I could tell he was impatient to get to that news meeting.

"Uhmm, I wonder if you've heard from Steve Stiletto. I understand he's in town."

Mr. Salvo shoved his hands in his pockets. "From the very beginning I warned you about him, Yablonsky. Stay away! He's not worth it. He'll break your heart. How do you think he got to be his age and still single?"

I had an answer for that. He hadn't met me yet.

"So is that a yes or a no?" I pressed.

"Yes. We had beers last night at the Tally Ho! But please don't drag me into this mess. Jesus. I'm late for the meeting." He spun on his Florsheims and headed toward Notch's office.

Paula Purdy lifted her fingers off the keyboard. "By Steve Stiletto do you mean that tanned Mel Gibson type who stopped by here yesterday looking for Salvo? The photographer in the bomber jacket?"

"That's the one."

Paula resumed her typing. "What a hunk. You'd better find that guy before I catch him first. Men like that don't stick around for long in Lehigh, honey."

Chapter 5

The next morning, a Tuesday, I was lying in bed, wondering where Janice was and what length of miniskirt would be acceptable in Amish country, when the portable phone rang. I snatched up the receiver.

"You found her!" I yelled.

"Who?" said a strange voice.

"Oh." I lay back in bed. "You're not Mickey."

"No, I'm Mitchell."

"Mitchell?"

"Mitchell from PSAC. The Pennsylvania Student Assistance Corporation. I've been leaving messages on your machine every day for a week."

I sat up. The telephone answering machine and I have what might best be described as a personality conflict. We simply can't work with each other. Plus, I did not trust an entity called the Pennsylvania Student Assistance Corporation. It was suspiciously vague and disturbingly familiar.

"I'm sorry," I said, sliding out of bed. "I didn't get those messages."

Mitchell let out a long-suffering sigh. "Is this Bubbles Yablonsky?"

"It is." I crooked the telephone under my chin as I slid my arm into a robe. "What's this about?"

"It's about the fifteen thousand dollars in student loans you took out. They're due. In fact you're two payments behind. One thousand, two hundred and sixty-three dollars in arrears, actually."

What kind of bill was that? What kind of bill was one thousand, two hundred and sixty-three dollars? I sat back on the bed.

"Student loans? But my husband paid for my community college education."

"Hmmm." There was the clicking sound of fingers on a keyboard. "Is your husband Chip Ritter?"

"His real name is Dan and he's my ex." I heard Mrs. Hamel outside stomping through the garden, picking tomatoes and swearing in German at the awful evil perpetrated by potato bugs.

"Well, according to our records, Chip, I mean Dan, Ritter was the cosigner on your loans, but you are listed as the party responsible. It was you and not your husband who used the money for the Two Guys Community College, is that right?"

"I did, but I don't remember signing any paperwork. Dan was court-ordered to pay for my education. A judge said so."

"I see," said Mitchell, as though court orders of this nature were quite common. "What we have here, it seems, is a domestic relations dispute between you and your former husband. Likely you'll have to go back to court if you can't work it out amicably."

"Back to court!"

"Nevertheless, the loan payments are due and they will impact your credit rating if you don't pay them in a timely fashion. Already one's been reported to the credit bureau, unfortunately."

I bit a nail. How low could my credit rating go was the question. Already I was at the Visa tin-card level—silver, gold, platinum and titanium having been yanked from my reach long ago. Visa didn't issue foil ones, did they?

"How much do I owe again?"

"One thousand, two hundred and sixty-three. Of course, in a few days another payment of six hundred and thirty-one will be due, too."

I hung up the phone, shaking with anger. How could Dan do this to me? Especially since for the past two weeks he had been sleeping on *my* couch, eating *my* food and watching *my* cable. His freeloading had been mildly annoying before. Now it was darn intolerable seeing as I was pretty certain he had forged my signature to a few student loan documents eight years ago.

"Dannnn!" I hollered, stomping down the stairs.

But Dan was nowhere to be found. The fold-out bed was back in place. His suitcase was gone and a handwritten note lay on the counter informing me that he and Wendy had reconciled the night before. He would retrieve the rest of his belongings that afternoon.

It was a heck of a way to start the day.

Later that morning, Mama called to tell me that her old buddy Magdalena Yoder, proprietor of the Penn Dutch Inn in Benton, PA, could offer me a room cheap if I didn't mind staying fifty or so miles away from Whoopee. I told her that was too far, although it was kind of Magdalena to extend herself.

Fortunately, my mother's best friend and pierogi business partner, Genevieve, sent word through the grapevine to an old Amish buddy of hers, Fannie Stoltz, who insisted I stay with her.

"Doesn't matter where I crash," I said. "Just as long as there's coffee, a shower and a makeup mirror."

"There's a bed," Mama said. "Don't get picky."

By that afternoon, Tiffany had agreed to handle my clients at the House of Beauty, Sandy had lent me her phone card to use for long-distance calls on the road, Mickey had given me a photo of Janice, the bank teller had handed me a fresh fifty dollars from my account and the gas station attendant had filled the Camaro. I was ready to roll.

My sixteen-year-old daughter Jane was so keyed-up at the prospect of me going out of town for a few days, she had rushed home from school to help me pack, practically pushing me out the door.

Her half-strawberry, half-blueberry hair was growing out nicely, although she had obtained yet another nose ring. Oh, and she had a new boyfriend who went by a one-letter name: G.

"Like God," was how he introduced himself, holding out his hand for a limp-wristed shake. "Or genius, depending."

G was no trophy. In fact, he was every mother's nightmare.

At age eighteen, he already had a slight potbelly and an annoying stud in the corner of his lip that he licked while he lounged on our couch engrossed in Comedy Central.

To Jane, G was "artistic" and "sensitive." He drew pictures of people watching television in which there were people watching television, etc., until the people and the televisions were tiny dots. Jane pointed to this artwork as proof positive of G's untapped talent.

If Jane was under the delusion that I was leaving her alone with G, she had better wash her hair to its natural brown.

"You're not?" she whined when I broke the news. "Then who's staying with me since Dad's getting back with Wendy?"

"Grandma. She'll sleep in my bedroom."

"Not Grandma! It'll be nonstop *Wheel of Fortune*." Jane pouted. "Why can't I stay by myself? I'm old enough."

I would have been more comfortable leaving Jane alone four years ago than now. Now she had G and high school friends who sniffed out parentless houses with more energy than bloodhounds hunting bunnies. They'd be at my doorstep with a keg of Schlitz and a case of condoms before I had made it to the Allentown border.

"Sorry, honey," I said, removing two miniskirts from their coat hangers. "No can do. If I had it my way, all teenagers would be locked in their rooms until they were old enough to pay taxes."

Jane plunked herself on the bed where I was laying out my essential wardrobe. Two pairs of black Capri pants, four miniskirts—white, lavender, black and denim (because I was headed to the country)—assorted sets of Lycra hot pants, four tank tops, blouses, including a white polyester sleeveless, a hot pink number and a red-checked tie-shirt, plus two V-necked light sweaters that clung to my body like Saran Wrap. Just in case, I threw in a violet cocktail dress and a black one, too. Oh, and I couldn't forget my brand-new Valentine-red Super Wonderbra.

"Uhh, perhaps we ought to discuss this," Jane said, pinching my Valentine-red Super Wonderbra and holding it up for display.

"My mind's made up, Jane. Grandma's on her way as we speak."

"I'm not referring to Grandma. I'm referring to your clothes." Jane waved the bra. "You do realize, Mom, that you're heading to the heart of Amish Country? A place where women don't wear makeup or even buttons because buttons might attract unnecessary attention to themselves and make them vain."

I picked through a collection of dangle earrings. "And your point is?"

"You're not leaving for a vacation getaway with Steve

Stiletto. This is work, undercover stuff. That Amish family's gonna take one look at you and—"

"And what?" I snapped.

Jane gulped. "I don't know. Skip it. Hey, why so sour? Ten minutes ago you were elated about this job."

I gathered up my makeup. Foundation. Concealer. Powder. Blush. Blush brush. Eyeliner in three shades—black, green and navy. Eye shadow in pastel multicolors and my black and blue mascara. I shoved them into the suitcase.

Goddamn Steve Stiletto. Why did Jane have to mention his name? I had been dealing with his absence just fine until Paula Purdy shot me that parting comment. She was right. Stiletto couldn't remain free for long without some witch casting a spell over him. He was too good-looking, too confident, too nice, too . . .

"It's . . . Why . . . hasn't . . . he . . . called?" I wailed.

"Oh, Mom." Jane knelt on the bed and put her arms around me. "It's Stiletto again, isn't it? I have to say, he seems like more trouble than he's worth. Always flitting to foreign countries, never in one place for more than two weeks."

I patted Jane on the back, took a deep breath and picked up the suitcase.

"And besides," Jane added, "maybe he did call. Did you check the answering machine?"

"The answering machine?" I said, my palms starting to sweat. "I tried to play back the messages but I got that *click-click* sound again."

Jane jumped off the bed. "Last I checked there were eleven messages on there. My friends E-mail me so I don't even bother with the phone."

"E-mail?" I followed her down our brown-carpeted hallway, dragging the suitcase behind me. "You have E-mail?"

"Remember the computer Dad bought me last Christmas? I offered to teach you but—"

A shiver ran down my spine. No thanks. If this is what the world was coming to, E-mail instead of phone calls, I was destined for a lonely old age.

We got downstairs and Jane began to work her magic, pressing Play and Rewind and Stop in the sequence I can never remember.

"That's one aspect of Amish living you'll like," she said as the tape rewound. "No machines. Heck, no electricity. Or, at least not much. Of course, you won't be able to plug in your blow-dryer."

"You mean for four or more days I'm going to have to walk around with wet hair?"

"How're you gonna get it wet? Not like they have showers down the hall. Amish women rarely wash their hair. They just brush it and cover it with caps. Okay, we can start playing the messages."

Caps?

The first three messages were from Mitchell of the Pennsylvania Student Assistance Corporation reminding me that I had missed two student loan payments. Jane stopped the machine.

"You had better pay them, Mom. If you don't, it could screw up my financial aid applications for college next year."

"It's a domestic relations dispute between me and your father."

Jane cocked an incredulous eyebrow. "It is?"

"That's what Mitchell told me."

"Whatever." Jane pressed Play again. There were bill collectors from the electric company, the telephone company and, for Dan, American Express. There were a couple of peevish messages from Wendy about marriage counselor appointments. Sandy called to chat and—

"This might be it," said Jane.

"Hey, Bubbles, this is Steve—"

"Turn up the volume," I shouted, dropping the suitcase and bending down to hear better.

"As Dan might have told you, I'm in town—"

Jane and I looked at each other. Dan?

"He said the two of you were back together. I would have found that hard to believe if he hadn't been standing in your living room in his shorts when I showed up to surprise you this morning."

Jane clicked it off. "Did you know about that?"

"Of course not. When was this message left?"

Jane fast-forwarded to the next message to figure that out.

So, this was Dan's cheap and rotten way of getting even. Ever since the big row with Wendy, he had blamed his crumbling marriage on me. Even though Wendy and Dan, in their grasping, greedy ambition, had been the ones who had deep-sixed their own vows.

"Hmm. Looks like Saturday morning," Jane said. "Where were you, at the House of Beauty?"

I nodded.

"Let's hear more." Jane turned it back on.

"If what Dan said is true, I have to say I'm mighty disappointed, Bubbles. You and I were working on something pretty nice, something with a lot of potential when I left."

"Hear that, Mom? He said something with a lot of *potential*."

I felt my cheeks blush. "Oh, stop. Is there any more?"

"So you haven't seen the last of me. Unfortunately, I just learned that a rugby buddy of mine got the crap beaten out of him while on a magazine assignment. I'm headed down to Philly to visit him in the hospital. But I'll be back. And when I do . . . watch out, Dan."

Jane turned it off and I was sure I would faint right on the spot. Watch out, Dan? Stiletto's voice was more ardent than I'd ever heard it. So male. So me Tarzan, you Jane. You could practically smell the testosterone wafting from the tape. It made me all googly inside.

"Wow," Jane said. "You know I've read about this type of male behavior."

Oh, no. Jane was going to rip the romance right off this bud with her academic analysis. "Which male behavior?" I asked cautiously. "Dan's or Stiletto's?"

"Both, actually. We discussed this in the psychology course I'm auditing at the university. You know, the independent study?"

Jane was so far ahead of me intellectually that I had lost her somewhere back in eighth grade. Having exceeded her requirements for graduation, she was now enrolled at the university. G, meanwhile, was still in remedial shop class whittling perches and spending most of his time on the Liberty High School patio smoking clove cigarettes. Ohhh. Where had I gone wrong?

Jane flipped through a psychology book she had pulled out of her knapsack. "Yup. Here it is. Feingold's Two-Factor Theory of Male Emotion. In a nutshell, the male of the species becomes emotionally aroused when it senses another male intruding on a potential mate. Pure Darwinism. Survival of the fittest and all that."

"Male of the species? Potential mate? It sounds so technical."

Jane slapped the book shut. "Seems to me that the key to Stiletto's heart is to make him think that other men are after your attention. It's kind of manipulative—"

"Oh, not me," I said, twirling my hair. "I'm not manipulative."

"No, never," said Jane, rolling her eyes. "And you had better stop that with the hair. If you continue to date Stiletto we'll have to shave you bald."

There was the crunch of a car entering the driveway.

Jane yanked back the curtain. "Hey, it's Genevieve."

"Genevieve? What's Genevieve doing here?"

"Maybe she brought Grandma."

Jane ran out the door while I stiffly carried the suitcase. Mama and Genevieve were unloading the Rambler. Two suitcases, a picnic basket and Genevieve's Civil War–issue musket.

"Going somewhere, Genevieve?" I asked as the suitcase bump, bump, bumped along the walk.

"Oh, boy, am I." She grinned, placing her broad hands on her massive blue polyester hips.

Besides being my mother's best friend, Genevieve also lived with LuLu in the senior high-rise across town and ran the pierogi shop with her on Wyandotte Street. Together the two old ladies were the Mutt and Jeff of the senior circuit, as Genevieve was twice as tall as my mother was short. Genevieve's hulking figure was further emphasized by a pair of shoulders that would cause a Pittsburgh Steeler to seethe with envy and thighs that could crush slab. This was often a dangerous combination, considering Genevieve's penchant for conspiracy theories. She hadn't brushed with fluoride toothpaste since the beginning of the Cold War and drove miles out of her way to avoid high-tension power lines.

I opened the rear of my Camaro and pulled back the flap. "Yeah? Where you going?"

"To Pennsy Dutch country." Genevieve threw in her suitcase. "With you."

I froze in shock.

"Don't forget me." Mama heaved in her suitcase so that there was barely room for mine.

"Not you." I pointed a finger at Mama, who stared back at me behind her Jackie O tortoise-framed sunglasses. "You're staying with Jane."

"Oh, Jane's old enough to stay by herself."

"That's what *I* told her," Jane added.

"Besides," Mama continued, "Genevieve and I got a good deal on a time-share in Paradise. We're switching so they can use our apartment in the high-rise for the Allentown Fair and we can go down for the Pickle Fest in Lancaster this week. We need a break from the pierogi shop."

"Although it does mean we're missing Engelbert Humperdinck." Genevieve sighed. "Front-row tickets, too."

"Ahh. He wears a girdle." Mama waved her hand in disgust.

"I cannot let Jane stay alone," I began, "not when G—"

Beep. Beep. Beep. Speaking of the devil, G drove his rusted, orange, diesel Volkswagen Rabbit up West Goepp Street and double-parked. *Beep. Beep. Beep.*

Jane started skipping toward him when I grabbed her elbow. "Let him get out of the car. Don't run over there when he beeps for you."

"G doesn't like to get out of the car for me. He says it expends too much of his personal energy." She wriggled free and ran to the Rabbit.

I clenched the suitcase handle until my knuckles were white.

"Don't fret over the juvenile," Genevieve said, taking my suitcase and squeezing it into the back. "Your ex will mind her. Meanwhile, your mother and I will keep an eye on you while you're in Whoopee. We've already got a name for the assignment."

"Yeah, Operation Schmutz," Mama said. "Schmutz means kiss in Pennsylvania Dutch. No one will suspect you're tracking a murderer."

I covered my face. I hadn't even left town and already this trip was a disaster.

"Say, what's going on?" a male voice asked.

Dan and Wendy were in front of me, arm in arm. Wendy was dressed in a black pantsuit with some fancy

French scarf wrapped around her neck. She scowled like she always does.

"Jane says you're leaving town. How come?" Dan asked.

I related the recent turn of events and how Dan must stay with Jane. I decided now was not the time to confront him about the student loans and Stiletto, not if I wanted him to serve as baby-sitter.

Dan took me aside. "Lookit. Wendy and I have just reconciled. We're planning a second honeymoon. Don't you think Jane is old enough to stay by herself?"

I nodded to where Jane and G were French-kissing in G's Rabbit. "Yeah. If she were staying by herself."

Dan frowned. "Gotcha."

My thought exactly.

Chapter 6

Driving Mama and Genevieve two hours to Lancaster County was worse than carpooling a couple of ten-year-old girls to the movies. You would have thought it was their first time out of Lehigh.

Besides their constant tittering and yapping, Genevieve would at unexpected moments yell at the top of her voice, "Road trip!" which would send Mama into such a spasm of hysteria I'd have to find a rest stop.

I suppose they were bored with the stop-and-go traffic through small Pennsylvania towns with names like Virgin Run, past billboards, car dealerships and crumbling motels, shoe stores and banks. You'd expect there to be an easier route from Lehigh to Lancaster, but there wasn't. It was Main Street most of the way. And when it wasn't, we were stuck behind a green tractor that wouldn't let us pass.

But what I really came to dread were the Chinese fire drills. We'd be stopped at a red light and the next thing I knew Mama was scrambling over me from the backseat and Genevieve was out the door.

Of course, being two rather out-of-shape women in their sixties, they weren't the world's fastest sprinters and, inevitably, the light would turn green, cars behind us would beep and Mama and Genevieve would be leaning against the Camaro trying to catch their breaths.

"Listen," I barked after the third Chinese fire drill. "You two do that again and I'm turning right around and heading back to Lehigh."

"Can't stop," Genevieve explained, breathlessly. "Gotta keep moving. Otherwise we'll get clots in our legs."

Thankfully we hit a patch of highway and the women settled down to eat. They opened the picnic basket and produced a stack of Tupperware containers filled with deviled eggs, celery with cream cheese, applesauce, pickled herring and dried fruit. All food I hated.

"Okay, here's the plan," Genevieve said, scraping out the orange middle of the deviled egg with a plastic spoon. "Fannie Stoltz and her son are the only family members who have been debriefed about your mission. The rest of the household is under the impression you're in Whoopee seeking a husband."

I nearly slammed into the back of a Wise Potato Chip truck. "A husband? Who?"

"Fannie's son, Jacob, aka Jake, Stoltz. I got his dossier right here." Genevieve opened an oaktag file folder on her lap. Inside was a tea-stained note. "Age twenty-five, Fannie's youngest son. Grew up Old Order Amish and lives at home. Unlike most Amish, though, he went to college. Penn State. Studied animal husbandry."

"They got a course in that?" Mama asked from the backseat. "I figured most husbands were pigs naturally."

Genevieve whipped her head around. "You take your medicine today, LuLu?"

"Musta forgot." Mama unfastened her purse.

"Anyway, as I was saying—" Genevieve straightened the folder on her lap. "Jacob Stoltz is still unmarried and his mother wants to see him hitched. That's where you come in."

"That's why we called it Operation Schmutz," Mama said, swallowing her pill. "With the kissing and all."

"But I'm not Amish."

"Can't pull one over on you, Sally." Genevieve nicknamed all girls Sally and all boys Butch. "You're going to pretend to be an Amish woman from Middlefield, Ohio. Sally Hansen."

I gave her a little smirk. "Sally Hansen? Like the nail products? I've used that name before."

"That's why I chose it. Plus, seeing as how it's a well-known brand in the cosmetics industry, I figured it was one alias you wouldn't forget." Genevieve smirked back. "Anyway, you're going to park your car out of sight, dress in Amish clothes and go barefoot."

"But what about all that work I'll have to do? Milking cows and churning butter, baking bread, sewing by hand, tilling the garden, canning vegetables—"

"Relax, Princess Di. It won't be much. Besides, manual labor is how the Amish say thank you. The Amish don't have much truck with courtesies. No one says please. Instead, without being asked, offer to wash the dishes, scour the floor, slop the pigs—"

"Slop the pigs!"

"Merely in the morning. As part of your cover you'll leave the house early each day, ostensibly to take the bus into town and do filing for a local doctor. That gives you an excuse to work on your newspaper story. Only Fannie and Jake will be the wiser."

"No makeup, Bubbles," Mama said.

No makeup. That I could not abide. Wearing long cotton dresses and caps was bad enough, but no makeup? Forget it. I should check into a hotel and scrap all of Genevieve's arrangements immediately. Of course, it's kind of hard to check into a hotel when there are exactly twenty dollars of credit left on your Visa Tin card.

"Isn't this a bit over the top, Genevieve? I mean, why can't I simply be me?"

Genevieve swallowed a herring. "And risk that exposure? No ma'am."

"What exposure? You think the Pagans are going to be fooled by me dressed Amish?"

I hadn't been able to shake the image of a prissy, virgin coed being transformed into a sensual, worldly woman. Exactly what kind of man could inspire that? And what was it that the Pagans did to women anyway?

"Excuse me. Who's had the militia training here?" Genevieve ripped open a packet of Wash'n Dri with her dentures. "I don't remember seeing you in the field during End Times exercises, Sally."

She had me there. I rolled down the window. With all the deviled eggs and pickled herring, this car was beginning to stink in the heat.

"Roll up that window," Mama barked, clasping her Jackie O "brioche" do. "My hair!"

"But it smells in here," I protested.

"Got just the ticket." Genevieve produced an old Final Net pump bottle and began spritzing away. The odors disappeared and were replaced by a lavender smell.

"That's not Final Net," I said.

"Nope, it's my homemade lavender-and-vinegar air freshener. It sanitizes and"—she sprayed her underarm—"deodorizes, too."

When we hit the Lincoln Highway, the congested and bumpy main drag through Lancaster County, Mama moved into backseat driver mode. Get in the right-hand lane, now the left. Stay in the center.

Lancaster County looked completely different from when I was a child. Gone were the quiet roads and tidy homes. In their places were back-to-back outlet malls—Eddie Bauer, Speedo, Ann Taylor—and tons of chain restaurants—Applebee's, Olive Garden, McDonald's along with the Dutch theme parks featuring giant wooden clogs.

"Where's the farmland?" I asked, as we idled in a hot traffic jam.

"Don't worry. It's behind the malls," Mama said. "They've hidden it. Take Lincoln Highway to the second right. That's where our pickle-season time-share is."

"Or base camp, as I like to call it," Genevieve added. "You can shower there. Change and check your phone messages." She clutched her musket. "And rest assured there will be round-the-clock security."

We parked in front of the first of three attached condominiums. I got out and helped Mama and Genevieve with their luggage.

"How long are you staying?" I asked when we got to the door.

"Until Sunday night. That's when the time-share switches," Mama said, pushing a key into the lock. "On the last day of Pickle Fest."

We entered a beige-carpeted living room done in the neutral tones of most condos. The evening sun was setting in a bay window opposite the door.

"Fast Car's coming down this weekend," Mama said, standing on her toes to check her reflection in the hall mirror. "Hope the weather's nice."

Fast Car? Now my mother was dating Fast Car? Guess he got that nickname from more than just speeding around the track.

"Oh brother," Genevieve sighed. "It's gonna be Fast Car this and Fast Car that all week until he gets here. Nothing worse than going on vacation with a boy-crazy girl."

As I was nearly out of gas, I stopped at M&M Gas and Garage on the corner of Whoopee Highway and

Paradise Road to fill up my car and to grab a package of Tastykake Krimpets (butterscotch, what else?) and a bottle of A-Treat birch beer—my dinner. I also tried to call home from the gas station pay phone but the line was busy, so I dialed Mickey instead.

"Did you find her?" he asked as soon as I said hi.

"No. I just pulled into town." I bit into the Krimpet and ripped off the butterscotch frosting in one strip. "You find any info on that Stetson?"

"You mean Electra? A Stetson is a hat."

"Right. Electra."

After my discussion with Mr. Salvo at the *News-Times* yesterday, I had grilled Mickey about the Hochstetter case back at the House of Beauty, where Sandy had put him to work replacing weather stripping on the front door. Mickey laughed when I mentioned the Pagans and insisted Mr. Salvo had blown the joyride way out of proportion.

The Hochstetter kids were straight-laced Amish who'd merely played a teenage prank, part of their rum springa or running around period, Mickey had informed me. The department considered the case controversial merely because of the cultural differences. Still, he promised to do some digging for me.

"Here's what I learned from a dispatcher who's handling Janice's job while she's out of town." Mickey made Janice's disappearance sound so normal. "The dispatcher said the police reports indicated the boys broke down at mile marker 113 at around six-thirty p.m. a week ago Friday night. The registration on the Electra hadn't been renewed in three years. It was last registered to . . . you got a pen?"

I wiped my fingers on a telephone book and fished out the pen. It was getting dark and a wind was whipping up from the south, bringing with it a faint smell of fertilizer through the car exhaust. "Got it."

"Marian Snyder, 305 Brecksville Road."

I scribbled this down on the back of a PSAC student loan bill, one of the ones I had neglected to pay.

"Okeydokey," I said when I was done taking notes. "Anything else?"

"Yeah. Janice's parents live on Hunkel Road in Whoopee. The people you're rooming with probably know it well. You still got the photo?"

I opened my purse and removed the black-and-white photo of Janice taken in one of those booths at the Westgate Mall. She smiled back at me, wide-eyed and friendly, her hair in braids, looking like she hadn't even hit puberty yet.

"Still got it. I'll show it around to as many people as I can." I gave him the phone number for Mama's pickle time-share, in case of emergencies.

"You know, I assumed tonight Janice would be lying in my arms and we'd be staring at that harvest moon from our bedroom in the Poconos."

I craned my neck to look up at the darkening sky. But there were so many streetlights and mall lights and lights from the gas station that I couldn't see anything. It's a sad day when it's harder to see the moon in the country than in a steel town.

"Sorry, Mickey."

"Yeah, me too."

Next I dialed Jane, who sounded less than enthusiastic when she answered.

"Dad can't do anything," she complained. "He's always asking, where's this, and where did your mother put that. It's like, don't you have two eyes, Dad? Also, he's got a bug up his butt about G. Won't let us— Wait. He wants to talk to you."

Dan got on. "Bubbles. Where's the goddamn ketchup? It's not in the refrigerator."

"Did you check the door?"

Pause while brain fathomed concept of refrigerator door. "Uh, no."

"What wouldn't you let G and Jane do?"

"We'll discuss it later. Okay, here's Jane."

Jane was back. "Mitchell from PSAC called again to talk about those student loans. Did you know he went to Liberty? I think his cousin's in my English class. Also Steve Stiletto called a few minutes ago."

I tried not to choke on the A-Treat. "Oh?"

"Yeah. I told him you were down in Lancaster County in Whoopee and that you were unreachable by phone and that you were on assignment. And do you know what he said?"

"What?"

"He said, 'Maybe I'll catch up with her.' "

I lifted my chin and practiced self-control. "Is that all?"

"Is that all? I figured you'd be thrilled."

"Ho hum."

"Oh, I get it. It's Feingold's Two-Factor Theory of Male Emotion, right? You're applying it in the field."

"Something like that."

"Well, document your results. I might be able to write them up as a lab report."

I reminded Jane to get to bed by eleven and to let Dan wash his own laundry. Then I hung up, mumbled a silent prayer to the Goddess of Virginity to keep watch over my precious, smart and vulnerable daughter, and strolled into the gas station for another package of Tastykakes. This time chocolate cupcakes—creme filled.

The gas station was a junk-food utopia. Racks and racks of candy, four coolers of soda, dangerous-looking sandwiches wrapped in plastic and stacks of chips, pretzels and cookies.

I slid over the Tastykakes, a road map of Lancaster County and the picture of Janice to a young cashier sitting below a dirty white pegboard of keys. He was sporting a mighty spiffy mullet haircut—long in back, short in front—a black Santana T-shirt and a nametag that said in proud gold lettering, NIMROD.

"Your name's Nimrod?" I asked, skeptically.

"Don't josh. It's from the Bible." He started to ring up the Tastykakes. "Doesn't mean I'm stupid. Just means my parents had a sick sense of humor."

I asked if he recognized the woman in the photo.

"Where are you from?" He glanced out the window at my Camaro.

"Lehigh. She's from Whoopee originally."

Nimrod picked up the photo with his gray fingers, pressing smudge marks into the clean white borders. "Oh, wow, man. Those braids. She's like . . . Heidi."

"She's Amish," I said impatiently.

"Looks Swedish or Swiss or something. Whaddaya want her for? Reckless yodeling?"

"She's a friend of mine. Her name is Janice Kramer. Know her?"

He squinted and turned the photo sideways. "Kinda familiar. She work at the mall selling cheese logs?"

"I doubt it. Her area of expertise is law enforcement. My theory is that she may be running from—or with—the Pagans. Either undercover or as a victim."

"The Pagans?" The cash register drawer opened with a *bing!* "Didn't they like open for Megadeth at the Hershey Arena last summer?"

"Unlikely. They're a gang."

"Really? I thought Carpal Tunnel was their lead singer."

"I don't think so," I said, opening my wallet and handing Nimrod a fiver only to have him give me sixteen dollars and forty-two cents in change.

I stared at the money. "Umm, that was a five-dollar bill I gave you."

Nimrod reached under the counter and pulled out a very wrinkled copy of *Spin* magazine. "Yeah?"

"So, you gave me sixteen and some dollars in change."

"Dang." Nimrod hopped off the stool and opened the cash register. "Where'd I put my brain?"

Not in your head, I replied silently as I helped him sort out the change mess.

"Hey," he said when I dropped the last penny into his palm, "you're smart. What did you say your name was?"

I was taken aback. It is very rare—in fact, it is downright unheard of—that anyone uses the adjective "smart" to describe me right off. "Yablonsky. Bubbles Yablonsky. Hairdresser."

"And you were teasing me about *my* name." He laughed. "Anyway, you're not a Bubbles. You're more of a Tastykakes." He made a frame with his thumb and forefingers as I backed up toward the door. "See ya around, Tastykakes."

The Camaro started up with an unusually loud roar when I left M&M and headed down Paradise Highway, away from the malls and into farm country. The eau de manure was stronger now, there were no streetlights and I had to be careful about not running over slow-moving Amish buggies in the darkness.

Boom!

The entire car rattled and I grasped the steering wheel to maintain control. The explosion had come from beneath and now there was a deafening roar.

My mind raced. A bomb had been detonated in my car. Either that or the Pagans had found me and I was in serious, serious trouble. Heaven only knew what those outlaws in black leather would do to me.

Oh, who was I kidding. It was only my muffler.

Genevieve's Miracle Spray

Like many women her age, Genevieve's a stickler when it comes to spending money on so-called frivolous items such as air freshener. That's why her miracle spray is quite a bargain. Not only does it cost mere pennies to make, but it emits no harmful chemicals into the air and, if the bottle is refrigerated, actually cools the skin on hot days. Plus vinegar is a natural skin softener, so spritz some on hands after doing dishes. Mama also tells me this spray is a wonder at removing the lingering odor of frying fish in the kitchen on Fridays.

1 cup water
4 teaspoons baking soda
2 tablespoons white vinegar
A few drops of lavender oil

Mix vinegar and baking soda until foaming stops. Add oil and then water. Refrigerate for best results.

Chapter 7

"*Schteh uff!*"

It sounded like a dog barking or a fat man sneezing. I opened one eye. As it was still dark outside my window, I assumed it must be the middle of the night. So I closed the eye and tried to sleep.

"Get up, Bubbles. *Schteh uff!*"

I rolled over. A tiny old woman dressed all in black who could have been Mama's twin sister was placing a kerosene lamp on a night table by my bed where a china bowl and pitcher stood.

"*Gut marriye,* Bubbles. I'm Fannie."

I hadn't met any of the Stoltzes last night. After my muffler had blown, I had parked the Camaro far away from their farmhouse behind a stand of trees. By the time I arrived, the house was dark and only a lamp awaited me on the kitchen table, along with a welcome note directing me to a small bedroom at the top of the stairs. I was so tired, I had stripped off my clothes and collapsed onto the hay-filled mattress.

Fannie picked up the hot-pink tank top I had thrown on my bed last night. "This yours?"

"It is," I replied with hesitation.

"Nix." She rolled it up and stuffed it under the mattress.

I sat up and watched as she pulled down a cobalt-blue dress, a black apron and an organdy cap from pegs on the wall. "Here," she said, holding them out to me. "Come downstairs for breakfast when you're dressed. And, from now on, I suppose I'll be calling you Sally Hansen." She smiled and left.

I stared at the bulky, formless, sexless clothes. Already my body—which is allergic to cotton, wool or anything drab—was threatening to break out in a rash. Well, I couldn't complain. I was lucky to have a free place to stay and grateful to the Stoltzes for taking me in.

Unlike my room back home, which was cluttered with dirty clothes on the floor and knickknacks on the bureau, not to mention a television, an electric alarm clock and lamps, this one was refreshingly spare and tidy. The walls were painted white. There was no closet, only pegs for clothes, and a nightstand held a pitcher of water in a china bowl. My single bed with its hay-filled mattress was covered by a patchwork quilt and was positioned next to the only window in the room.

I poured some water into the bowl and washed my face, being careful to remove all traces of makeup that appeared in the reflection of my compact mirror. I combed out my permed blond hair, braided it and stuck it under the cap. Then I tackled the clothes.

Hmmm. I turned the dress around and around, trying to figure out which side was front. Finally I decided the open side faced outward since I would never be able to pin it up in the back. I tied the apron around my waist and headed down the narrow stairs and into the large, open kitchen.

It was filled with warm, aromatic smells. Baking bread. Boiled milk and fried scrapple. Fannie Stoltz was standing before a massive, cast-iron, wood-burning stove flipping pancakes when she saw me and nearly dropped the spatula.

"Acht!" she exclaimed, clamping a hand over her mouth.

She rushed over and quickly untied the apron, her thick fingers deftly removing the pins in my dress. "Before Katie sees," she hissed, turning the dress around and pinning me up the back. She giggled as she retied my apron. "City folk."

A large woman in her twenties entered the room humming to a baby burping on her shoulder. She was wearing a blue dress, a black apron and her big bare feet stopped on the wooden plank floor at the sight of me.

"Sally?" she asked, smiling widely. "Are you Sally Hansen from Ohio?"

"This is Katie, my youngest daughter," Fannie said, returning to the flapjacks.

If Amish didn't say please and thank you, did they say hello? Seeing as how I was wearing a dress, I decided a curtsy was in order.

"Huh?" said Katie, pointing to my toes which, to my distress, were still covered in bright gold nail polish. "What happened to your feet?"

"Katie," Fannie chided mildly, although I could tell she was slightly alarmed.

"Oh that," I replied, wiggling my toes. "Medicine. Nail fungus."

"Ahhh." Katie sat on the bench at the kitchen table and bounced the baby in her lap. "Seems everyone's eaten but us, Sally. We're the sleepyheads."

"No wonder. You were up all night with the baby." Fannie clucked sympathetically. "I heard him on our side of the house, too."

Katie shrugged as though staying up with a baby was no big deal. She certainly did not look the worse for wear, what with her pink complexion and full, young face. Fannie gave us each a plate of breakfast—eggs fried in milk, pancakes, scrapple and applesauce—which we ate at a long wooden table.

The baby sat in a bouncy seat facing toward me, banging a spoon against his dimpled knee. I tickled his tiny feet. He laughed and gurgled. Baby flirting.

"Do you have any children of your own, Sally?" Katie asked as the baby blithely gnawed on the spoon.

"One." I bit into the thick pancake slathered with butter and drenched in molasses. My spandex was going to turn into expandex if I kept up this diet while I was here. "A daughter."

"Ohh. What a shame." Katie sighed. "Couldn't you have more babies?"

"More? One was enough. What with the cost of daycare and—"

"Ahem." Fannie cleared her throat as she pumped water into a soapstone sink. "Sally lost her husband, Katie."

Katie gasped. "Poor dear. Was it a farming accident?"

I thought back to how I had come home early from the salon ten years ago to find Dan the Man—who I had worked two jobs to put through college and law school—engaged in a serious game of naked wrestling with the Avon lady, her black bra wrapped around the standing lamp in our living room.

"A pig," I said. "He fell in with a pig."

Katie shook her head. "Have to watch out for those hogs. Sows especially. They've been known to eat men, you know."

"Oh, I know."

There was a rapping at the kitchen door. Fannie bustled over and welcomed a portly, middle-aged man who stood on her doorstep holding a freshly baked pie. His face was doughy soft and a pair of thick, steel-framed glasses gave him the appearance of being almost cross-eyed. The protrusion of his buckteeth was exaggerated by the sad fact that the fellow had been born chinless, and the only supports holding up his rotund belly were wide black suspenders.

"Omer!" Fannie exclaimed as he handed her the pie.

"Mudder baked dis yesterday," he said, taking off his feeder cap. "Shoofly." Omer spoke in a thick regional accent that was fairly difficult to understand.

"How wonderful!" Fannie pulled him in and shut the door. "Sally, this is Omer Best. Our neighbor. Omer, this is Sally Hansen. From Ohio."

"Hey, naw," he said. "Vat part of Ohio are ya from den?"

"Middlefield."

His cross-eyed gaze wandered over my hair. "Boy, dey're blond in Middlefield, Ohio, say?"

"Lots of sunshine there," I said, absently touching a strand.

"Really?"

Fannie slid a plate of breakfast in front of Omer, who helped himself eagerly.

"Dere's anudder environmental conservation commission meeting next week, naw, Fannie," he said, cutting into a scrapple patty. "Has Samuel come ta any decision?"

Fannie sat down and folded her arms. "He's still praying on it. Not my place to ask him."

"Vell," said Omer, after gulping down a tall glass of milk. "Da state is gonna wanna response. Dey's got a mind to slap youse vid anudder hefty fine and I can't stall dem on your behalf much lonker."

Fannie nodded. "I know he appreciates it, Omer. He's out in the field haying if you want to speak with him now."

I picked up my plate and Katie's from the table and carried them over to the sink where Katie was washing dishes. "What's going on with the environmental commission?" I whispered, grabbing a kitchen towel.

DUBUQUE COUNTY LIBRARY

Katie handed me a rinsed platter. "More environmental regulations. The state says we have to redo our system to handle manure runoff and gray water. The tests have found no contamination of local aquifers, but still we're getting fined for not building buffers and retention pools and I don't know what else." She pumped in some more water. "It's become so crazy. Father's thinking of selling the farm altogether. Moving the entire family south to Kentucky where there are fewer people, fewer laws."

I stacked the plates and pondered environmental regulations. Clean air. Unpolluted water. They seemed like good ideas. So why would they be causing headaches for honest, hardworking folk like the Stoltzes?

"Omer's been very helpful, trying to work out a compromise with the commission for us. My father prefers not to attend those meetings. It's not our way to argue."

"Bye naw, Sally," Omer said, plunking on his feeder cap and waddling to the door. His eyes flicked to my golden toes. "Guess dey got da blond toenails in Ohio, too, say?"

I tucked my toes under my dress. "It's medicine for a nail fungus."

"Sure," said Omer agreeably.

When he left, Fannie asked me what time I had to catch the bus to the doctor's to do filing. I lied that I had to be out the door by eight, which, considering how early I had gotten up, still gave me about two hours to pitch in. I offered my services as Genevieve had instructed.

"There are potatoes that need picking," Fannie said. " 'Course, the ground is a bit dry and—"

I shuddered. Digging my hands into hard, dry earth to pick potatoes was equivalent to chomping down on Styrofoam or dragging my nails across a blackboard. No thanks.

"That reminds me," Katie said, "has Ephraim washed Dolly yet?"

Washing Dolly? Hey, wait a minute. That didn't sound too bad.

"No. Samuel and your husband have got Ephraim out there cutting hay, working the thresher. He is ten, after all, Katie."

Katie unplugged the drain. "My oldest," she said. "Almost a man."

Katie seemed barely old enough to have a baby, let alone a ten-year-old who could operate a thresher. "How many children do you have, Katie?"

She held up all five fingers of one hand. "I'd like to have at least two more. They are such gifts from God."

It was as though I had stepped into the Twilight Zone.

"I could wash Dolly," I offered.

"Oh, no, Sally. That's a boy's work," Katie said. "Ephraim can do it when he gets in from the field." She hesitated, though, and I got the impression that she wanted to have this dirty duty done and over with.

"Nonsense." I folded the dishtowel. "In Ohio we wash lots of dollies. Where is she?"

"The barn. And I'm afraid you'll have to use the scraper. Ephraim hasn't cleaned her in weeks. She's caked in manure."

The scraper? Manure? "What, exactly, *is* Dolly?"

"Ephraim's heifer. He's hoping to get a good price at auction on Saturday."

I swallowed hard. Okay. A heifer was a baby cow, I rationalized, heading out to the barn. Baby cows were cute. And certainly, as a hairdresser, I had washed even the toughest cases before.

The sun was coming up over the green fields behind the Stoltzes' barn where the men were tiny black figures on the hillside, cutting hay. A tall, thin windmill blew merrily and chickens scattered as I made my way from the Stoltzes' stone farmhouse, past a shed of unhitched black buggies, to the red barn where Dolly lived.

Five large black-and-white cows were waiting, chewing their cud. The rest were out in the field grazing or lying down in the shade, so I deduced that one of these five must be Ephraim's heifer. They didn't look like babies to me.

A small boy in a straw hat, black pants and blue shirt ran past me and snatched up a pitchfork. I stopped him on his way out.

"Do you know which one of these is Dolly?"

The boy pushed back his hat and pointed to the other side of the barn where a large bovine was slumped on a pile of straw. "That's her. The big girl. You gonna give her a warsh?"

"Thought I might."

The boy reached up and yanked a devious metal claw off the wall. "You'll be needing this, then. She's covered in shite."

Shite? I gripped the claw and made my way over to Dolly. She didn't look so bad from this side, although she was intimidating. About the size of a large bear.

"Get up!" I ordered, pulling her by the cowbell. "C'mon, Dolly. Upsy daisy."

To my surprise, Dolly complied willingly, if slowly. As soon as she stood, I spotted the problem. One side of her, the side on which she routinely lay, I supposed, was completely caked in hard, black tar. Gently, so as not to hurt her, I dragged the scraper along her flank and produced nothing but a few flakes.

I braced my bare feet on the straw and sank the claw in deeper. This time I managed to pry off one chunk, but there were still several layers below that and miles of cow to go. *Oh, I'll never finish this*, I thought, picking at the hardened, smelly cow dung. There had to be an easier way.

Of course there was. Wasn't I a hairdresser? Didn't I deal with stubborn beauty problems all the time?

I dropped the claw and raced into the house and up the narrow stairs. At the bottom of my suitcase I found it. Alberto VO5 Hot Oil Treatment. In my opinion, this stuff could soften cement. I grabbed that, Genevieve's lavender spray and a bottle of moisturizing shampoo with conditioner. Then I headed toward the kitchen.

The wood fire was still burning in the stove on which sat a large pot. I filled the pot with water and heated up the tubes of oil, keeping my eye on Fannie, whom I could see through the window was busy in the garden picking beans. Heating didn't take long and I hurriedly tossed the tubes into my apron.

Dolly was sitting down again when I got to the barn and this time sensing, perhaps, that I was up to mischief, she took her sweet time standing. I ripped open the tubes and quickly massaged the oil into Dolly's side, imagining that my fingers were working the firm flesh of George Clooney's broad shoulders and not a pile of dried cow shit.

Success! After ten minutes the cow dung came off in strips and Dolly mooed in delight.

"Aha!" I said to myself. "Who says I couldn't be a farm girl? Green Acres here I come."

With the cow dung removed, I felt a surge of motivation. Ephraim wouldn't know what had happened. He'd think it was a miracle that his dirty old cow could be so clean and shiny. Why, I'd have that hide of hers gleaming. The auctioneer would be floored. Folks would applaud and slap Ephraim on the back. They'd bid thousands.

"What did you do to your heifer, Ephraim?" they'd ask, astonished. "She looks as though she's been to the salon."

I giggled in glee as I danced over the straw and around the cow, squirting every bit of conditioning shampoo over her massive body. I hummed the tune of

"I'm Gonna Wash That Man Right out of My Hair," while I pumped water into the bucket and carried it back to the barn.

Three buckets later, Dolly was a heap of suds. There were suds everywhere. Dripping off her tail. On the floor. In the straw. And I wasn't giving up. My expert fingers rubbed and rubbed. Dolly's tail wagged in delight.

"Bubbles," said a man's voice.

"You bet there are. Tons of 'em." I looked up from my work. A tall, clean-shaven Amish man stood in front of me studying the bubble-covered Dolly with a quizzical glare. He was handsome in a healthy, farm-boy way. Big hands. Nice shoulders. Black hair under his straw hat. Brown eyes. A sad smile.

"No, I mean, are you Bubbles?" he asked.

"You must be Jake," I said, wiping off my hands.

"Do you know what you're doing?" he said, picking up an empty hot-oil tube.

"I should hope so. I've only been washing and conditioning professionally for my entire adult life. Okay. So where's the hose?"

"Hose?"

"Sure, to hose her down. There's a lot of soap on this gal."

"We don't have a hose. You'll have to use the bucket. And I'd suggest you use it fast before Dolly loses her temper."

"Loses her temper?" I pointed to her flapping tail. "Look. She's ecstatic."

"She's not a dog, Bubbles. When cows flick their tails they're angry. And when Dolly gets angry she tends to—"

"What?" I asked nervously, stepping back.

At that point a clump of suds slipped down Dolly's forehead and over her golf ball of an eye. It was the final straw. She turned toward me and lifted her snout in rage.

Mooooo!

"Charge," Jake said, lunging for her, his hands slipping in the soap. "She tends to charge."

He made another attempt, but it was too late. I was already out of the barn, running across the field, soapy Dolly right on my heels, sending suds everywhere.

Chapter 8

"Bubbles, don't run!" Jake shouted as I headed pell-mell into the pasture. "That will only make her charge faster."

But I wasn't about to stop now. The organdy cap was hanging by its strings around my throat, the pins were coming undone on my dress and I was trying to break the four-minute mile, leaping over manure piles, dodging cows and heading toward the open field ahead.

And still Dolly kept coming. *Clump, clump. Clump, clump.* Every once in a while she snorted and sneezed as the bubbles blew back into her nose. There were shouts all around me from the men who had stopped their haying to try to grab the runaway, soapy cow. There were whistles and a lot of German words that I presumed were not very nice.

Clump, clump. Clump, clump. Dolly, furious that she had been hot-oiled and shampooed, would not be swayed from seeking her revenge.

I was a goner.

I imagined myself being trampled by one of those big hooves. My face squished into the glop below. My spine broken in two places. I predicted my obituary. Bubbles

Yablonsky. Hairdresser, reporter, mother. Squashed by a shampoo-crazed cow.

There had to be some way to stop her, right? I couldn't die in a cow pasture. What would Jane tell her friends? My hands ran over my clothing, looking for a pin to poke Dolly with—and then I found it.

I pulled the bottle out of my apron, uncapped it and sprayed it in the direction of my would-be bovine assassin.

Dolly stopped on a dime, blinking, snorting, sneezing and shaking her head. Jake, almost out of breath, sweat pouring down his neck, caught up and grabbed her collar.

"Don't ever, ever run away from a cow," he said, panting. "When a cow's mad there's no telling what she'll do."

"Oh sure," I replied, clutching my middle. "Now you tell me."

Jake yanked Dolly's collar and led her back to the barn. I grabbed my knees, which were weak and rubbery. My lungs were working overtime, trying to fill up with the breath they had lost. I felt awful. Simply awful. Here I had been trying to help and what had I done? I had disrupted the entire farm and enraged a perfectly docile animal.

"What's that you sprayed in her face anyway?" Jake called over his shoulder. "She smells funny."

I displayed the bottle of my personal cow mace: Genevieve's Miracle Spray. Good for removing odors, softening skin and now, stopping cows.

Jake pushed himself out from under my car. "You couldn't have picked a worse place in your muffler to get a hole, Bubbles. The whole unit will have to be replaced."

I kicked the left rear tire out of spite. "How much do you think that will cost?"

He stood and wiped the black grease off his hands. "About one hundred and fifty without labor. Get me a part and maybe I can fix it if I have some time. I've got the equipment."

Now why would Jake have equipment to fix a car? "How do you know so much about cars anyway if you grew up Amish?"

"I've always been a motorhead. That's one reason why I could never be baptized." He popped open my hood and pulled out the dipstick.

"You can do that? You can live here and drive cars and not be Amish?"

"As long as I keep my cars out of sight, which I do in the garage behind the barn. Not being baptized, I can't be shunned. Boy. You sure are down a quart, Bubbles."

For a second there I thought he was calling me stupid. Dan used to say I was "down a quart" when he ran out of synonyms for dim bulb, ditzy, dumb blonde, etc., etc. But then I realized Jake was just being truthful. Not only had my muffler blown a hole, now the Camaro was burning oil.

"I gave it a quart last week," I said, biting my lip. "That's not good, is it?"

"It's an old car, Bubbles. You've got close to two-hundred-thousand miles. Might want to trade up to a buggy." He smiled and then frowned when he saw I wasn't in the mood for a joke.

I couldn't afford a new car. And how was I going to get a loan with my credit scraping bottom, thanks to the "domestic relations dispute" with Dan over the student loans?

Jake and I stared at the crusty Camaro. "How come you went to college, Jake? Or, more importantly, why'd you come back?"

He slipped the dipstick back in. "It's complicated. Coming back was the easy part. I love my family. I love this farm and the folks I grew up with, their values of community, honesty, hard work and simplicity." He slammed down the hood. "I guess the deeper question is why I could never fully commit by being baptized."

"Why couldn't you?"

"I don't know," he said softly. "I hoped you might be able to help me answer that."

"Me? Why me?"

"You came here to look for your friend Janice Kramer, didn't you?"

"Yes," I said cautiously.

"Long before she ran up to Lehigh, Janice was a nice, regular Amish girl named Elspeth for whom I had—" He paused, unsure of how much to say.

"Fond feelings?" I offered.

"Beyond that. She was the one Amish girl I'd met who could—or, rather, who wanted to—discuss more than who was getting married and having babies. We'd steal moments together during the summer of rum springa and take the buggy to the creek." His cheeks reddened. "My sisters claimed Elspeth and I were bundling—you know, making out—but actually we were talking."

"Talking?" I said, dubiously.

"About what it meant to be Amish, mostly. Elspeth and I both had reservations. Turning our backs on the modern world seemed like a pretty high price to pay for our faith. Elspeth read books she wasn't supposed to and shared them with me. She and I really bonded during that summer. There was no doubt in my mind that she was the woman I wanted to spend the rest of my life with."

"So what happened?"

"I suppose those books she read took hold. She changed, became worldly." He picked up his toolbox and placed his straw hat back on. For a few minutes he stared across the fields, his mind and heart in some long-ago place.

"What am I doing?" he asked suddenly. "The milk truck will be here any minute."

He headed down the road toward the farm, leaving me to mull over the concept of Janice Kramer—who could not parallel park, who flinched at the sound of blow-dryers and was more gullible than a child at a magic show—being a deep thinker and a worldly woman to boot.

Since I was still in my Amish wear, albeit soapy, dirty and manure-stained Amish wear, I decided now was the perfect time to drive over to Janice Kramer's home-stead and knock on the door. Hunkel Road, where her Amish parents and, apparently, extended family lived, was about a mile away, according to my Lancaster County map. Terribly convenient.

Not so convenient was the cruiser, WHOOPEE POLICE cheerfully emblazoned on its doors, stationed at the entrance to the Kramers' driveway. There was also a small band of reporters who were shooting the breeze, drinking coffee and schmoozing with law enforcement in a pathetic attempt to win favor with Whoopee's finest.

This meant that Elwood's death must have been ruled a murder by the Northampton County coroner and that an all-points bulletin had been put out for Janice. In an effort to mute my broken muffler, I drove my Camaro slowly along the road, past the driveway. There was no point in my stopping, anyway.

Because I had a plan.

With the Camaro tucked out of sight behind a grain silo, I grabbed the lunch basket Fannie had thoughtfully packed for me and trundled boldly toward the waiting crowd of police and reporters.

Frankly, I was not surprised to see two television news satellite trucks from Philly. Janice on the run was a story destined for Jerry Springer. Amish girl gone bad. Film at eleven.

As reporters gathered around me, the Whoopee cop put down his coffee and squinted at my face to check whether I was Janice. After determining that I wasn't, the reporters immediately lost interest and resumed their grousing about low pay and high stress, moronic editors and job prospects elsewhere.

"*Gut marriye,*" I said to the officer.

He pulled out a clipboard. "Name?"

I didn't want to get the Stoltzes in trouble so I spit out the first Amish name that popped into my head.

"Magdalena Yoder," I said, stressing the second syllable in each word as some Amish do. I patted the basket. "For the Kramers in this sad time."

A reporter rolled his eyes, as though mourning a loved one was for sissies.

"Sorry for the"—the cop waved his pen around awkwardly—"you know."

I smiled. "It's fine. May I go?"

"Of course."

It was darn hard not to throw those other reporters a triumphant look, but I had new things to worry about. Like how I was going to introduce myself to the Kramers without them thinking I was either insane or untrustworthy.

The Kramers' house was a plastered, rambling structure. Many houses or apartments for family members had been added on over the years. A large woman answered the screen door, and she looked so much like Janice I was almost speechless.

"You must be Janice's sister," I said.

"Emma," the woman said. "And you?"

No sooner had the words *Bubbles Yablonsky* left my lips than a cry went up and Emma grabbed me, calling for her mother and sisters to come. Suddenly I found myself being embraced by five Amish women from various generations—grandmother, mother, sisters, daughters—

all smelling of apple pies and cleaning solution and chattering away in German.

Emma insisted I sit down on a wooden bench in the living room as Janice's mother wiped her eyes and offered me a range of liquids—coffee, tea, milk, water, root beer. The other women hung back, staring at me, shaking their heads and muttering in wonder.

"I'm confused," I said, clutching the basket. "What's going on?"

"You brought back our Elspeth," Emma cried, gripping my knee.

Afraid that I had caused yet another misunderstanding, as I had at St. Lenny's Church, I quickly clarified. "No. I'm a friend of Janice's—I mean, Elspeth's—from Lehigh. We're very worried about her and—"

Emma nodded. "We know. We know. But because of you Elspeth came back to us Sunday night."

"Monday morning," Janice's mother corrected, still dabbing her cheek with a handkerchief. "We hadn't seen her in months. We'd heard she was about to get married without even telling us, but then you sang that song and her heart changed." Mrs. Kramer blew her nose. "That freeing the bird song. Is it a hymn?"

" 'Free Bird'? Janice came home because of 'Free Bird'?" Oh, wait until Mickey heard about this. He was gonna throttle me. "No, it's hardly a hymn."

Emma touched her chin. "Elspeth said it was a line you sang about the Lord reminding us that we cannot change. That's what did it. She knew then who she was and where she belonged—home."

"She wants to be baptized," Mrs. Kramer whispered. "It's a great joy to us."

So much for that wedding to Mickey. To think that Lynyrd Skynyrd, the bad boys of Southern rock 'n' roll, were responsible for an Amish religious rejuvenation. Could Armageddon be far behind?

I leaned against the wooden back and sighed. "But if Janice came home Monday morning, then where is she now?"

Mrs. Kramer rattled off a torrent of guttural dialect to Emma, prompting her to shoo all the other women, except her and her mother, out of the room and close the door. When Emma was sure they weren't listening in, she pulled up a chair and clasped my hands.

"We, too, are very worried about Elspeth. She had no idea about Elwood."

"He's my husband's uncle," Mrs. Kramer cut in. "Or rather more like a cousin several times removed."

"She told us she left the party in Lehigh Sunday night and drove straight here. Didn't even stop to pick up her belongings," Emma said. "What belongings did she need? We were all she wanted."

I recalled Janice's open, half-packed suitcase on the floor in Elwood's condo. There was a ring of truth to what Emma was saying.

"And we were celebrating, happy that our prodigal sister had returned home, when our neighbor came running up the road to tell us that a message had been left on the phone-shack machine. Elspeth's betrothed, Mickey Sinkler, had called with the awful news that Elwood was dead. That he had hit his head and the police were investigating it as a possible murder."

Forget the fact that Mickey had apparently violated his own police department's orders and given Janice a heads up. I was more concerned about there being a dreaded answering machine in an Amish phone shack. These machines were like aliens, invading every house, even Amish farms. Was no place safe from their evil Playback, Rewind, Stop and Record?

"You have a message machine in the phone shack?"

"For business," Mrs. Kramer said. "Cabinetry orders. It's digital."

Emma flashed her mother an annoyed look at our digression. "Anyway, upon getting that message, Elspeth stood up and screamed, 'He meant to kill me. I'm the one he's after. I shouldn't have come home!' "

Mrs. Kramer burst into tears. "And then she was gone. Out the door in a flash."

"We haven't heard from her since," Emma said quietly. "Soon after that the police arrived and they've been parked in our driveway since Monday evening."

The three of us fell silent. My gaze drifted around the dark room to its light blue walls and boxy, propane lamps. No family photos. Just calendar pictures of waterfalls and fields, framed and mounted like priceless Monets.

"Do you have any idea who *he* was?" I asked this more to Emma who, as a sister, stood the best chance of being Janice's confidante.

She shook her head dejectedly. "You are familiar with rum springa, say? The period where we let our young folk act up before they offer themselves to baptism and settle down. The running around time?"

"Vaguely," I said, not eager to relate what Jake had confided to me only minutes before. It was during rum springa that he and Janice had shared their existential thoughts and built their romance. "Isn't that kind of . . . risky . . . to let your teenagers mingle with our world?"

"Not usually. During the running around period, the young folk see the English world for what it is," Janice's mother said. "Busy. Pointless. Unhappy. At least, to us. After that they willingly give themselves over to baptism and raising their families Amish."

"But not our Elspeth," Emma added. "Elspeth ran around so much she kind of . . . ran off. She took a job at the mall selling cheese—"

"Hickory Farms," Mrs. Kramer interjected. "She became a certified specialist of cheddar logs. The tourists loved her."

No kidding, I thought, thinking of Nimrod's statement to me at M&M, which I had blithely passed off as unfair typecasting. Not all women with braids were in the dairy business.

"And she met more English than we knew." Mrs. Kramer smoothed her apron. "She liked the men's cars and the girls' makeup, their so-called freedom. When it came time to commit, she rebelled."

"She left the family and worked mostly at local resorts that offered rooms and free food." Emma's eyes began watering. "That lasted four years. And then, this winter, Elwood contacted her and invited her to live with him. So she moved to Lehigh. And now he's dead."

Gee. There was so much Janice hadn't told me about herself. She had never mentioned that she was Amish or rebelling. Or even that she had been a certified Hickory Farms cheese log expert.

"Was Elwood Amish?"

"That's a long story," said Mrs. Kramer between tight lips. She declined to say more.

It was too bad that the Amish disdained gossip—my lifeblood. Damn. This was going to be a rough road, living among a people who abhorred what to me was as natural as breathing and sleeping.

I left the Kramers with me politely turning down offers of cake and jars of applesauce, plum preserves and whatever else the women could yank from their pantry shelves. Instead, I gave them the phone number to Mama's pickle time-share and urged them to have Janice get in touch with me no matter what.

The hike to the Camaro was hot in my heavy, dark clothes and I was badly in need of a shower. My skin itched like mad. My feet were dirty and there was straw and flakes of manure in my hair.

Once I was in the car, I unpinned the cap and rolled up my sleeves. Then I popped open the glove compartment and pulled out a pack of Virginia Slims I keep for emergencies and occasionally sneak when no one's looking. After turning on Van Halen full blast and rolling down the windows, I began to feel half human.

I revved up the Camaro and roared past the waiting pack of reporters, smoke trailing out my window and David Lee Roth howling from the bottom of his leopard-spotted jeans. The cop dropped his cup at the sight of me and a television reporter gaped.

It was not the proper way for a modest Amish woman to behave, I admit. And, Magdalena, if you hear about this, I deeply apologize for whatever smirch I might have inadvertently placed on your name.

Chapter 9

Mama and Genevieve were almost out the door on their way to register for the Pickle Fest when I pulled up to the curb outside the time-share.

Mama slapped her hands on her hips. "What's that you're driving, a Sherman tank, then? I could hear you a mile away."

"I know, I know. I got a hole in my muffler." I stepped inside.

Genevieve was in the living room, musket in hand. "Can't be too careful. Could've sworn your car was a couple B-1 bombers overhead on reconnaissance. You're a sight, say?"

I undid the apron. "I nearly got killed by Dolly the charging cow."

"Uh-oh," said Mama, lifting her nose in the air. "I smell VO5. Tried to shampoo the poor creature, I bet. As a little girl you were always giving the cat a good sudsing. Prell from head to toe."

I told them about my morning, eliminating the last part about the cigarette, since Mama would have whooped me if she had heard about me smoking. Meanwhile, Mama fixed me a half cup of decaf coffee that tasted pretty much like hot water with coffee grinds at the bottom.

"So, who do you think *he* is?" I asked Mama. "Who's the *he* that Janice said meant to kill her? You think he might be one of those Pagan gang members?"

"Strikes me like the MO of a hit man," replied my mother, who watched an unhealthy number of late-night police dramas. "Maybe Janice is really Sicilian."

"Sicilian Amish?" I asked, dubious.

"Of course, it's obvious who *he* is," piped up Genevieve, who was still waiting on the couch, the musket on her lap. "Then again, no one asked me—even though *I've* had the appropriate training."

"Oh?" said Mama. "Who is it, smarty pants?"

"*He* is The Man."

"The Man?" Mama said. "What Man?"

"The head honcho. The big kahuna. The guy who designs washing machines so they break one day after the warranty. Big Brother."

"Janice's big brother wanted to kill her?" I asked. I wasn't sure Janice even had a big brother.

"Not *a* big brother. *The* Big Brother. He who knows all, sees all. He who makes it so you get charged a late fee on the mortgage payment based on when the bank got around to cashing your check—not when you mailed it."

I removed a piece of straw from behind my ear. "I don't know, Genevieve, it seems—"

"Seems what? Crazy? Think about it. How does Big Brother keep tabs on us? Through the telephone. How does he screw with our minds? Television. Ultimate control? The banking and credit system that keeps us in debt. What don't the Amish have?"

Mama and I stared, partially clueless and partially afraid that Genevieve had really gone off the deep end this time.

"Electric washing machines!" shouted Genevieve. "Do the Amish watch TV? No. Do they use credit cards? Not any I've met. I'm telling you, an Amish woman like Janice mingling amongst modern society is a threat. Big Brother needs to rub her out."

Eager to change the subject, Mama opened a shopping bag by the kitchen door and lifted out the ugliest garden gnome ever. Not only was it painted a disquieting shade of green, but the gnome's face belonged to that of a true sourpuss. He looked as though he were just itching to kick somebody with his stubby plaster legs.

"Whaddya think?" asked Mama, who was dressed in Jackie O casual wear—pink Capri pants and a white acrylic sweater set. Only, unlike Jackie's, the Capris were made out of a thin, stretchy material that did my mother's thighs no favors. "As soon as I saw this adorable little guy I thought of you," she said.

"You did?" What did that say about her perception of me?

"Sure. Gnomes keep watch over the land, to protect it. With all your complaining about the disappearance of Amish farmland yesterday, thought you'd get a kick out of him. Put it in the garden you share with Mrs. Hamel."

"And that's another thing," Genevieve persisted, nodding toward the gnome. "Graven images. The Amish don't keep 'em. Like I told you, LuLu, that statue's a jinx. I'd chuck it."

Mama sighed and examined her watch. "My God. Look at the time. We'll miss the Pickle Fest shuttle if we don't get a move on." She grabbed her purse and rushed to the door.

But Genevieve was still building a head of steam. "You mark my words, Sally," she said, setting the musket in the umbrella stand. "If Big Brother finds out about you searching for Janice, you're a marked woman."

Mama had the door open and was tugging on Genevieve's arm.

"And never trust the ATMs. They're Big Brother's automated henchmen," she shouted. "Charging a buck fifty to withdraw your own money. That Big Brother's evil, I say. Evil!"

Mickey's line back home was busy each time I tried it, indicating he'd left his phone off the hook. Since I didn't have "police privilege," like Detective Frye, to test if that were true, I gave up and dialed the number on the business card of Russell the security guard at the Final Frontier. I got one of those dreaded machines and left only my first name and the pickle time-share number in case any members of the Final Frontier condo association also had access to the machine.

I figured if he were inclined to chat, Russell would put two and two together and give me a ring—unless he whimsically assumed I was calling for a recommendation as a security guard. The chances of that were pretty slim since, according to Mickey, Russell's name was now mud with the condo association. Perhaps Russell was holed up at home, building a deep resentment toward his former employers for canning him. That could only be good for me.

As soon as I hung up the phone rang. I recognized the voice right off. Mitchell from PSAC.

"Hello. I'm looking for a Bubbles Yablonsky."

"*¿Que?*" I responded.

"Her daughter gave me this number as a place to forward her calls."

"*No problema. Yo quiero Taco Bell.*"

"Hmmm. When she gets in, could you ask her to call me? It's important."

"*Sí, sí,*" I said, not bothering to write down the number. The only words I wanted to hear from Mitchell were that I was not responsible for student loans that Dan had taken out. I do not trust bill collectors who insist their concern is "important."

Because I hadn't a clue where to begin looking for Janice or the Pagans or even Big Brother, I decided the only alternative was to shower, bubble up and get to work on the story to which Mr. Salvo had ostensibly assigned me, i.e., the Hochstetter boys in the stolen Stetson. Wait, Electra. A Stetson was a hat.

My hair teased into its rightful fluff, eyelashes properly mascaraed and curled, cheeks rouged, lips painted and eyelids swathed an alluring teal green (as God had intended), I donned a denim miniskirt, red high-heeled sandals and a red-and-white gingham shirt that tied in a bow an inch above my navel. Hey, it was hot. A girl's gotta dress sensibly in those kind of conditions.

Back in the Camaro, I studied the Lancaster County map and plotted my route to Marian Snyder, owner of the Electra. I found her on the patio of her ranch home, immersed in an all-out campaign to terminate weeds between the bricks by spritzing them with a salt-and-vinegar solution.

A pleasant, plump woman, Marian didn't even blink when I mentioned that I was a reporter from Lehigh investigating why the police back home were making such a fuss about two Amish boys who, allegedly, had stolen her car.

"Oh, they didn't steal it," she said, cracking open another bottle of Heinz white vinegar. "They were taking it on a test run."

"A test run?" I flipped open my notebook and clicked my pen. "Where'd you get that information?"

"From Wolf. Wolf Mueller. He's the mechanic who's working on my car and the one who let the boys take the Electra for a spin."

I wrote this down. "But they ran the car all the way up to Lehigh? Don't you think that's extreme?"

"Not when you're talking about Wolf. Wolf is a stickler for details. What you'd call a perfectionist." She mixed the salt and vinegar together in a plastic bowl. "He would never return a repaired car until he was positive it was in smooth working condition."

Something was fishy about this story. "When did you take the car in for repairs?"

"July."

"Last month?"

"Don't I wish. July of three years ago. My baby had a snapped fan belt and, while replacing it, Wolf discovered the engine was burning oil. Engine block could've busted on me. Took some time to fix what with ordering parts from Detroit." Marian smiled innocently. "It is a classic car, after all."

I thought about this as Marian emptied the bowl into a large spray bottle and set to work on the other patio weeds. I wasn't any Ralph Nader, but I had enough consumer savvy to know that it didn't take three years to repair a car—no matter how classic.

"He bill you for those repairs?" I asked.

"Monthly. One hundred bucks. The easy-pay plan."

I multiplied one hundred times twelve times three on my notebook and after fifteen minutes arrived at the total: thirty-six-hundred dollars. That was how much Wolf Mueller had bilked Marian for a broken fan belt. Smelled like another blockbuster story to me. A Big Break in the making—crooked mechanics who bleed naive, trusting women. I'd have to meet this legendary Wolf Mueller.

"You know where I can find Wolf?"

"Sure. He's at M&M Gas and Garage by the Paradise Highway. Can't miss it. He can tell you all about the Hochstetter boys, too. But you have to go there in person 'cause Nimrod the cashier can't be trusted on the phone. Guy can't remember to deliver a telephone message for nothing."

* * *

So there I found myself, roaring in my Camaro up and over the hilly back roads from Marian Snyder's to M&M Gas and Garage, enjoying the breeze through the windows and doing my best to avoid the Lincoln Highway traffic jams and Whoopee Police speed traps. My unmuffled car was so loud, the Amish reigned in their horses and glared at me in alarm when I passed their black buggies.

This was no way to ease into a community incognito.

I decided to travel past the "scenic area" marked on the Lancaster County map and was glad I did. Endless green cornfields, red-winged blackbirds and vegetable gardens lined with marigolds and bursting with tomatoes, cucumbers and melons of all sorts lay on either side of the road. I sucked in a lungful of clean air and questioned why I lived in a gritty, gray steel town.

A white plastered farmhouse by the road was so neat it shined. A group of barefoot Amish women in long dresses and white caps were gathered on the lawn behind it, stirring a large vat of boiling water. Canning vegetables. All that manual labor to do, including raising dozens of kids without the baby-sitter of television, and still the porches were spotless, the flower rows were without weeds and the laundry hung fresh on the line. How did they manage?

I crested the hill and slammed on the brakes, narrowly missing a line of Pennsylvania State Police cars with flashing blue lights parked alongside a cornfield. It was more than a cornfield, it was a construction site. The site of a future retirement village and nursing home called the Whoopee Gardens Estates to be built by Dutch Enterprises, according to the architect's billboard.

Two television news satellite trucks from Philadelphia, Channel Three and Channel Five, were double-parked along with an assortment of radio vans. They were interviewing a group of screaming protesters. Environmentalists. Whatever was happening, it was news to me.

I parked the Camaro behind a cop car, grabbed my purse, along with my reporter's notebook, and crossed the street. A young woman with a sign that read BUILD TODAY, DIE TOMORROW stepped into my path.

"Citizens for A Livable Lancaster," she said, handing me a sheet of information. "C-A-L-L. Join our protest against the latest blight."

"What's going on?" I asked, instead of reading the sheet as I was supposed to.

She pointed to the scene behind her. All construction had stopped. Bulldozers and backhoes were lined up, their engines still running, as they waited for police to remove a string of protesters who had laid themselves on the construction site in protest.

"This is the last unspoiled spot in Lancaster County," she said, throwing her arms wide. "And it's going to be ruined by people who don't give a damn."

She was right. All around this "scenic area" was pristine farmland for as far as the eye could see. No shopping malls. No highways. Not even a streetlight. After less than a day in Lancaster County, I had come to appreciate undeveloped land as a rarity.

"You should write about this devastation," she said, pointing again to my notebook. "This is a national story."

Suddenly a gasp went up and everyone pressed their faces against the fence. I tried to see over their shoulders and signs.

"Now what's going on?" shouted a woman, jumping up to get a peek.

A man with a TV camera on his shoulder pointed to the left. "Over there, can't you see him?"

"Who?"

"How did he get in there?" the cameraman asked.

"Cops won't let the rest of us photographers past the gate, but he manages to get behind police lines—per usual. No wonder he takes home all the prizes."

"Uh-oh," said another TV reporter, "the fuzz are getting into the act."

The crowd fell silent as a squawking bullhorn blurted out unintelligible orders.

"He's not listening."

"Of course not," the TV cameraman explained. "You should've seen his shots of Tiananmen Square. He stood in the path of a Chinese tank to get *the* perfect angle on the student facing certain death, and still he kept clicking away just like he's doing here. He's gonna get his ass tossed in jail for trespassing if he doesn't get out soon."

Risks? Tiananmen Square? Trespassing? Ass in jail?

It couldn't be.

I wormed my way to the fence until I had a clear view. As the last of the protesters was limply being carried away by two police officers, the bulldozers revved forward, oblivious to the photographer perched on a pile of rocks a mere few feet from their blades.

One slip in any direction and he could lose a foot, an arm or his life. One minute more and he was about to be arrested by four state troopers hustling down the hillside.

Who else but Stiletto?

Marian Snyder's Other Uses for Vinegar

Marian Snyder told me she has been using vinegar for years, long before the no-phosphate, don't-harm-the-earth, antichemical movement began. She used it because it was effective, handy and, most of all, cheap. Here are some of her favorite uses.

As a brightener in the wash. Marian adds one-third cup to a load of laundry. Not only does it brighten clothes, but it cuts down on lint and stops colors from running. To remove perspiration stains, soak shirts in a five-gallon bucket filled with water with one cup of vinegar for two hours.

Revive wilted vegetables by soaking them in two cups of water with one tablespoon of vinegar.

A tablespoon of vinegar instantly cures hiccups.

Dab poison ivy patches, bee stings, mosquito bites and sunburn with vinegar to eliminate itching and burning.

Marinating beef and chicken in vinegar—especially in the fancy, flavored vinegars now on the market—tenderizes meat.

Soak a showerhead overnight in heated vinegar—not to boiling—to unclog.

Disinfect wooden cutting boards by wiping with full-strength vinegar.

Warm slightly and use to remove bubble gum from hair.

Chapter 10

"*Stiletto!*" I shouted at the top of my voice. "*Over here!*" I jumped up and down, waving my notebook.

"Gee whiz," commented a hard-hatted worker, who was guarding the door in the chain-link fence. "The guy's even got a fan club. And, oh mama, what a fan." He winked at me lasciviously.

I turned my back to him. Construction sites are the equivalent of modern jungles for women—filled with wolf whistles and catcalls, big apes, low-down dogs and manly beasts. Women have to fend for themselves.

My antics hadn't caught Stiletto's attention, anyway. He was still engrossed in his photography, shooting the last passive protester who was being carried off by the state police. The driver of the bulldozer about to bear down on Stiletto killed the engine and stepped out of the cab for a better look.

Good. Now maybe Stiletto would get the heck out of there.

Then an awful thing happened. Believing that the path was finally clear, the bulldozer operator returned to his cab and started up again. And what was Stiletto doing? He was climbing down the rocks. He was even closer to the bulldozer blade than before! Stiletto crouched down and brought up his camera.

The bulldozer operator plugged his ears and stepped on the gas. He stared straight ahead, oblivious to Stiletto, who was in front of him, out of sight.

That did it. I'd had enough of this macho photographer stunt. I needed to shake some sense into Stiletto before he got himself flattened.

I tapped the cameraman on the shoulder and asked for a boost over the fence.

"What're you, nuts? You'll be trespassing if you do that."

"I'll chance it."

Two seconds later it was alley-oop over the fence.

"No way, sweetheart," objected the hard-hatted bouncer. "You can't—"

But I had no time for lectures. Stiletto was in trouble and he was too full of stubborn machismo to realize it.

"Stiletto!" I screamed, running down the hill. *"Watch out!"*

For a brief moment Stiletto took his eye from his beloved camera and my heart skipped a few beats. Steve Stiletto, prized Associated Press photographer, was never more alluring than when he was intent at work. Underneath his khaki photographer's vest, his gray T-shirt hugged his washboard chest and his faded tight jeans didn't conceal too many secrets, either. I wasn't close enough to be mesmerized by his Mel Gibson blue eyes, but I guessed they were twinkling. He was like a Greek statue, hard, chiseled and timeless.

"Yablinko!" He lifted his arm.

Then it happened. The pile of rocks Stiletto had been standing on gave way, crumbling like an avalanche. Stiletto tried to catch his balance, but could not steady himself. He slid, protectively clutching his Nikon to his chest, as the bulldozer pushed a large pile of debris toward his legs.

A few construction workers standing by with picks immediately spied the danger. They tried shouting and waving at the bulldozer, now no more than two feet from Stiletto, to no avail. The operator, deaf to all sounds but his inner ruminations, continued to face forward and chug, chug, chugged ahead, clueless to the homicide he was about to commit.

"Stop!" I screamed, waving my arms and purse. *"You'll kill him!"*

Nothing. Zip.

I had to catch the driver's attention, but how? I needed to wave something bright that he would spot out of the corner of his eye and stop his bull—

Red. That was it. Red like the capes they use in the bullfights. And I had just the thing on my person, literally. My Valentine-red Super Wonderbra with the front closure.

Quickly I untied and unbuttoned my red-and-white gingham blouse, unhooked the bra and slid it off my shoulders. I retied the blouse and furiously waved the brassiere, its brilliant red cups making a crimson arc in the sky.

I ran until I was so close to the bulldozer I could see the earplug in the driver's ear.

"Stop!" I shouted.

The driver glanced at the waving red bra, then at me, and slammed on the brakes. I only hoped it wasn't too late. He removed his earplugs and stared, mouth open.

"You have to stop," I said, pointing. "There's a man."

"Don't look much like a man to me, sister." He was ogling me, practically drooling, and I felt a slight breeze on a part of my body where most women employed outside the exotic dancing industry don't feel slight breezes very often.

I dropped my eyes. Oh my God! My tied blouse had come undone and here I was, hanging out—at a construction site. This was suicide! A goldfish in a piranha tank was safer.

"Whoops, gotta go," I said, clutching my blouse. I turned and ran up the hill, my sandals slipping on the grass as a chorus of whistles, shouts, jeers and male voices applauded my free peep show.

"Where you going? Don't leave, darlin'."

"Hey, I didn't get to see."

"Show us your ti—"

"Woo, woo, woo."

The word mortification was inadequate. It had been one-hundred-percent public humiliation. How long had my size 38Ds been bouncing al fresco back there? Removing my red Wonderbra? What was I, the dumbest dumb blonde ever?

I made it to the chain-link fence and confronted the bouncer.

"Oh, sure. Now you wanna go." He blocked the gate. "Coming back for a second act this afternoon?"

"Come on," I pleaded, "let me out."

"Hmmm. I'll have to think about that."

The jeers and calls and whoops were louder now. After another minute of this, I kicked him in the nuts (no steel-covered protection there, I learned) and opened the gate while he bent over, contemplating his more sensitive side.

The cameraman stopped me. "That was really brave of you. What's your name?"

I dropped my purse and finished buttoning up. "Why?" I looked around for my bra. It was nowhere in sight.

" 'Cause you're gonna be on the six-o'clock news." He patted his TV camera. "A-slot."

Shoot. I must have left my bra back at the construction site and I wasn't going there again. No siree. While the cameraman pelted me with questions, I searched my purse and backtracked to the gate, looking for the bra.

It was no use. It was gone. I thanked the cameraman and crossed the street to my Camaro. I got in. Locked the door. Put the key in the ignition. Checked my side mirror and pulled out with a screech and roar.

"If you don't mind, my Jeep's a half mile that way. Oh, and what are you going to do about this?"

I turned my head and nearly hit a tree. There riding shotgun was Stiletto, my Valentine-red Super Wonderbra dangling from his fingers.

I drove a half mile down the road, parked behind Stiletto's Jeep and snatched the bra out of his hands.

"It was because of you that this happened."

"Because of me what happened?" Stiletto slid his arm along the back of my seat.

"That I took off my bra and then ended up exposing myself to fifteen construction workers pumped with high-octane testosterone."

"Not quite following you, Bubbles. You did what?"

My reflection in the rearview mirror revealed a haggard mess. Hair everywhere. Makeup smeared. "I was trying to stop the bulldozer from killing you so I took off this red bra and waved it."

Stiletto thought about this, the crow's-feet at the corner of his eyes deepening. I loved the lines and wrinkles on Stiletto's tanned face. They hinted at a full life outdoors in the sun, lots of experience. Most of it sexual.

"I'm afraid I'm not getting the picture. How about a demonstration? A brief reenactment."

I punched him. "So you did see?"

"More like heard. Too bad I was on the other side of the dozer. To think for weeks and weeks I've been trying to get to second base with you and you go out and show it to a bunch of strangers on a whim."

"What were you doing there anyway?"

"Remember Shep, that rugby buddy I told you about?"

"You didn't tell me. You left a message on my answering machine."

Stiletto opened his blue eyes wide. "And you actually picked up the message?"

"Jane played it back for me. So, go on."

"Well, Shep used to be a photographer for the AP. Now he freelances. He was in Lancaster County last week shooting some cornfields for a magazine puff piece on farm country when he got the crap beaten out of him. Three bones in his face broken, two smashed ribs and a concussion."

"Who did it?"

"All Shep can remember is some tall, wild-looking jerk, carrot-colored hair sticking out everywhere." Stiletto brushed clay off his knees. "He was yelling in German and Shep is questioning whether the guy was a crazed neo-Nazi, since Shep is Jewish."

"How would his attacker have known Shep was Jewish?"

Stiletto shrugged. "That's the mystery, I guess. That's what I'm trying to find out while I'm here, finishing Shep's assignment for him."

"That's decent of you."

"Some people think I'm a decent man. So what brings you to the Garden Basket of Pennsylvania?"

I told him about dead Elwood and my search for Janice, how she had announced to her family that a *he* had meant to kill her and not Elwood.

"There's a lesson in Mickey Sinkler," Stiletto said, shaking his head. "This is what happens to nice guys. Offer a woman marriage, financial support, a house and what does she do? Run away."

I ignored that last comment, delivered solely to get my goat. "What do you know about the Pagans?"

"The gang? I hear they got a hankering for statuesque, stacked blondes who give free shows at construction sites." He smiled.

I blushed.

"I do know," he added, "that a few years ago a couple of Amish kids on rum springa got messed up with them and served time for dealing drugs. You aren't thinking of mingling with a few Pagans, are you?"

I blinked innocently. "Who me?"

"Because if you are, Bubbles Yablonsky, I want to be right by your side for protection. It wouldn't be safe for you to meet them alone."

"Safe? Don't forget I was raised on the South Side of Lehigh, Stiletto. South Side girls know how to take care of themselves, probably better than a prep-school—"

A pair of flashing blue lights appeared in my rearview.

"Uh-oh." I pointed to the lights.

"Guess that's my cue to go. You available tomorrow or, um, is Dan here, too?" Stiletto eyed me slyly.

Now was the perfect time to explain about the Dan misunderstanding. However, that Feingold's Two-Factor Theory of Male Emotion so intrigued me, I was kind of curious to test it out. Besides, the results of this experiment might help Jane's grade in psychology. Willing to make any sacrifice for higher education. That's me.

"No. Dan's at home. Lot of work."

"Ahhh." Stiletto checked the rearview. "So I suppose he wouldn't know if I did this—"

With one swift movement Stiletto leaned over and kissed me, his warm lips pressing against mine with a great deal of gentleness and a touch of passion. His chest was broad and warm as he grabbed the back of my head and brought me into him. He smelled of dirt and dust and good ole Stiletto. Spicy. Hot. Ready for action.

"I missed you, kid." He ran a rough finger along my

jawline. "Thought about you all the time when I was away."

"If you missed me so much, then where were the passionate letters you promised to send from India?"

Stiletto quit with the stroking. "What do you mean? I sent one every other day."

"Every other day? How? By camel?"

"If you didn't get them," he said with irritation, "then I'd like to know who did, because I crafted some pretty sensitive prose."

Pretty sensitive prose? That I *had* to read. Would've been nice to have read some sensitive prose instead of the notes Dan used to leave me on the kitchen counter when we were married. "Bubbles: Wash my shirts. I got a big meeting tomorrow. Oh, and buy different toothpaste. No more ShopRite generic. We can afford Crest. Christ. Can't you do anything right?"

I had that classic memorized.

There was a knock on the window. "Hey, lover boy." Two state police peered in. "You got a couple of minutes? We'd like to discuss your trespassing back there."

Stiletto held up his hands. "I'm all yours, officers."

He grabbed his camera bag and opened the door. "Take care of yourself, Bubbles. Maybe I'll see you around."

And he was gone.

Chapter 11

Nimrod was still on the job behind the counter when I arrived at M&M, hot, disheveled, dusty and braless.

"Tastykakes!" he exclaimed, finishing the last bite of a chocolate and cream-filled whoopee pie. "Man, you look awesome."

"I need to use your bathroom," I said. "And I need to speak to Wolf Mueller."

"Wolf's not here." Nimrod handed me a key attached to a Plexiglas *W* the size of New Jersey. "But the boss is in. He'll talk to you. He loves blondes. Especially that Pamela Anderson. Yes, sir."

"The boss?"

"Yeah. And when you get back remind me to tell you about something someone told me about that woman you were looking for."

"Janice?"

"I *think* that's her name. The dudette in braids whose picture you showed last night?"

"That's Janice."

Nimrod returned to his *High Times*. "If you say so."

I shook my head at the pitifulness of Nimrod's brain. As I strolled around the corner to the bathroom, I debated whether he was a victim of chemical infusion or if he had merely been born stupid.

In the too-gross-to-describe green-tiled bathroom, I rehooked my red Super Wonderbra and touched up my makeup in the warped metal mirror over the dripping faucet. The mirror may have been warped, but it was good enough to expose my dark roots. If Stiletto had noticed, he had had the decency to keep his mouth shut.

I decided to find a local hairdresser for an emergency touch-up before my next rendezvous with the International Man of Photography. I didn't want him to suspect that I might not be a natural bright bleached blonde, for heaven's sake.

Outside, I took the long way around the gas station, past M&M's small used car lot lined by multicolored plastic flags. There was a Dodge Colt for five hundred. A Datsun for three hundred, or best offer. Three Chevy Cavaliers for under three grand, each. Marian Snyder's classic roadster must have stood out like a debutante at the Pottstown roller rink during its three years here.

Back inside M&M I handed Nimrod the Plexiglas *W*, purchased a twenty-ounce bottle of Diet Pepsi along with another package of butterscotch Tastykake Krimpets, and reminded him to tell me about something someone had told him about Janice.

"Huh?" he said, ringing up my order. "What're you talking about?"

"Skip it," I said, handing him exact change to be safe. "Is the boss in?"

"Sure." Nimrod slid off his stool and knocked on a grimy glass door next to the shelves of blue coolant, motor oil, boxwood repair cream and STP. "Got a pretty blonde wants to talk to you, boss."

"She a customer?" came a gruff voice from the other side.

Nimrod turned and squinted at me. "Are you a customer?"

"Only of Tastykake."

"Only of Tastykake, boss. She's the one what came in last night."

"Tastykakes?" There was the sound of a chair scraping and then the door was flung open. A short man with Elvis sideburns and a gray worksuit appeared. The name embroidered on his breast pocket was Mac. He was a wiry little guy who chewed gum like a chipmunk and probably met all the risk factors for high blood pressure and popping aneurisms.

"C'mon in. Nimrod, hold my calls."

Nimrod honored him with a tiny salute. "Will do, boss."

I sat in a white plastic chair across from a desk littered with bills, invoices, a *Playboy*, a *Penthouse* and oil company magazines. The walls were painted an institutional green and decorated with fuel oil calendars and plaques that attested to M&M's reputation for quality service or an allegiance to the NRA. Oh, and a Pamela Anderson poster. Mac shut the door, perched himself on the edge of the desk and grinned broadly.

"Nimrod said you came in last night asking about Janice Kramer," he began, helpfully.

"Yes, but Nimrod said he didn't recognize her."

Mac waved that away. "Nimrod. Can't bank on a thing he says. Guy's stoned twenty-four hours a day."

You're making that up, I was tempted to say. "So why don't you fire him?"

"Can't. He's my dimwit sister's numb-nut son. A charity case. Some people give to the United Way. I give Nimrod employment and a room over the garage. Anyway, whaddaya want Janice Kramer for?"

I explained about the wedding and how Janice had run away. The thought had crossed my mind to hold back on the part about me being a reporter, but then I recalled Mr. Salvo's insistence in the Two Guys Community College journalism course about full disclosure. So I whipped out my reporter's notebook, revealed my identity and told Mac about Elwood's murder, too.

"Yeah. Saw it on the news." Mac snapped his gum rapidly. "Funny, 'cause I never heard of Janice Kramer before last week when she started calling here three times a day."

I swallowed hard and tried to look calm. Robert Redford as Bob Woodward. Only in heels. "Janice Kramer called . . . here?"

"Yeah. She works at the Lehigh PD, right?"

"As a records clerk."

"Called wanting to talk with Wolf. About them Hochstetter boys that got in all the trouble and what was up with the car they stole. Wolf handled the whole thing. I don't know nothing about it."

"Nothing?" I wondered if this was Mac's way of distancing himself from the scheme to defraud Marian Snyder.

"Nothing." He held up his two hands. "I swear. I give my mechanics free rein and only the good Lord knows why Wolf had that car for three years. One day it disappears off the lot and the cops show up asking about it. Wolf tells me, 'I'll take care of it, boss,' and he does."

The phone rang.

"Goddamn Nimrod. I told him to hold all calls," Mac said, answering the phone. When he hung up, he continued as though there had been no interruption.

"You should talk to Wolf. He's at his dad's out on King's Road. Geesh, he must've spoken with that Janice Kramer six times. And then the next thing I know, *bing!*" He snapped his fingers. "I turn on the eleven o'clock news last night and see that the police are looking for Janice Kramer in the murder of her uncle up in your neck of the woods. Took me for a loop, it did."

I twirled the pen between my fingers. "Wolf Mueller isn't a Pagan by any chance, is he?"

"Wolf Mueller a Pagan?" Mac stared at his boots. "I don't think so. I think he's Lutheran."

The phone rang again.

"Shit for brains," Mac said, yanking the receiver.

As I wrote down what Mac had said while he chatted with what sounded like a distributor, I heard a disturbing, almost frightening, sound outside the door to his office. It was the clunking of boots and the deep, hearty laughs of male voices. Lots of them.

"Shoot!" I said, capping my pen, envisioning the worst. Perhaps I could slip past them without notice. I was ready to bolt when there was a loud banging on the glass door.

"Hey, boss," called Nimrod. "I got some guys here who want to meet Tastykakes. They're from the construction site down the road."

Mac put his hand over the receiver. "We done here?" he asked me.

I felt like crying. "You have a window? An escape hatch?"

He scrunched up his face, but didn't pry. "Only one window." He pointed to the one behind his desk. It would do. I scurried over to his chair, stood on it, unlocked the window and squirmed out. Mac, still holding the phone with one hand, propped the window open with the other.

I dropped my purse, slipped outside the building, my legs scraping against the concrete wall of M&M Gas and Garage, and fell onto the macadam. Now the challenge was to run to my Camaro without the construction crew noticing.

Whew! I opened the car, slid in, slammed the door and zipped the key into the ignition. Nimrod came flying out of M&M hollering, "Wait!"

But I wasn't waiting. I stepped on the gas and was about to pull out when Nimrod threw himself on my hood. I screeched to a stop.

"I remember what I was supposed to tell you about Janice."

A couple of construction workers stood in the doorway, grinning.

"Make it fast, Nimrod."

He slid off the hood and stuck his head in my driver's side window. "She used to work at Hickory Farms in the mall selling cheese," he said. "I was right."

"I know. Her sister told me." The construction workers were making their way toward me. "Now, I gotta go."

"Also, after work she used to hang out at the Stayin' Alive, a disco next door. I saw her there every night, I swear."

I must have looked incredulous because Nimrod added, "She didn't come to dance. A friend of mine who waitresses at the Stayin' Alive told me Janice hung out with the dude who ran the joint. A total ditwad named Dutch. A real control freak."

For a moment I forgot about the approaching construction workers and considered what Nimrod was telling me. Perhaps this Dutch was the guy from whom Janice was fleeing, the *he* who was supposed to have killed her instead of Elwood. What else did I have to go on?

"If I stop by the disco tonight, do you think you could get me an introduction with this Dutch?" I asked.

Nimrod nodded. "Sure. I'd do anything for you, Tastykakes. Meet me at the bar after nine. It'll be sweet."

According to the phone book, Wolf Mueller Sr. lived at 11 King's Road in Whoopee. The street name sounded familiar and as soon as I took a left off the Paradise Highway onto King's Road I knew why. King's

Road was the road I took to get to the Stoltzes. When Mickey described Whoopee as small, he wasn't kidding. It couldn't be more than five farms wide.

Eleven King's Road was nothing to crow about: a small, blue vinyl-sided cape with a cement stoop, weeds for landscaping and a weathered For Sale sign out front. Like a playground monitor standing between a weakling and the school bully, the house was all that separated a lush cornfield from the sprawling Amish Wunderland Museum next door.

The Amish Wunderland Museum was an "old-fashioned family fun center" with a large stone "authentic" Amish house and a real working waterwheel, according to a billboard at its entrance. There were five-dollar buggy rides, a wooden playground bordered by swaying weeping willows bending over a babbling brook, a small roller coaster next to a few poorly maintained carnival rides, picnic tables and even a place to park one's RV for overnight camping.

In contrast to the bustling Amish family fun center, the field waved silently in the warm, August breeze, row after row of brown-tasseled corn ready for harvest. On a dark green stalk a red-winged blackbird sent out a trill to his feathered friends warning that this undeveloped field, like summer, might be witnessing its last days.

With my trusty reporter's notebook in hand and my faux leather purse jam-packed with cosmetic comforts, I marched up the cracked cement walkway to Mueller's front door. I hoped that Wolf Mueller was home and that he would invite me in graciously. Not merely because I wanted to make some headway on finding Janice, but because I desperately needed a bathroom. One cannot consume a twenty-ounce bottle of Diet Pepsi without consequence.

I rang the doorbell and shifted my feet on the stoop. The front door opened and a short old man in a rumpled plaid flannel shirt appeared. His gray hair was smushed as though he had just risen from the couch after taking a nap.

"Hi! I'm Bubbles Yablonsky from Lehigh," I chirped. "I'm looking for Wolf Mueller. He in?"

"I'm Wolf," he said. "You interested in the house?"

This was Wolf Mueller? The mechanic who had scammed poor Marian Snyder into donating her Electra? Funny. I had pictured him as being much younger.

"Well, uh," I stalled, debating whether to take the bait. It would be such an easy way to gain entrance to that bathroom. "You see—"

"Asking price is four hundred thou," he said. "And that's my minimum."

"Four hundred thousand?" I asked, shocked that a crumbling old cape like this one could be worth more than forty thousand. "Dollars?"

"Of course, dollars. Whaddaya think? Wampum? So what is it? You a taker?"

I'd like to take this guy to the funny farm. "Actually, Mr. Mueller, I think it's your son I want. The one who works at M&M."

"Why?" He put his hand on his hip. "I'm the one who owns the house. Not him. He's just a squatter here. I'm the one you gotta negotiate with."

This was getting ridiculous. So I explained about being a reporter and how I wanted to ask Wolf about the Hochstetter boys, about why Janice Kramer had called Wolf so many times and if he knew why she was so preoccupied with this simple stolen car case. It was right after I mentioned Janice Kramer's name that Wolf Sr.'s demeanor turned from obstreperous to downright obnoxious.

"Wolf ain't available. He's in dispose." Wolf Sr. started to close the door. "No comment."

I shoved my foot in as an obstacle. It was a bold move,

sure, bordering on rude. But, hey, when a girl's gotta go, a girl's gotta go. "I"m sorry to be a pest, but I really need to—"

"I said, no comment," Wolf Sr. grumbled. "If you're not interested in buying the house, then I'm not interested in talking to you. Now git." He kicked my toe.

"Ow!" I yelped, grabbing my foot. "What was that for?"

"Watch it, missy. If you're not off my property in five, you're gonna be looking at the business end of a DeWALT three-eighth."

I stopped rubbing my toe. "A what?"

"Okay. You asked for it." He reached behind the door and retrieved a yellow power drill. He aimed it at me with both hands. "If I was you, I'd get cracking."

I stepped off the stoop. "Wait a minute. It's unplugged and it doesn't even have a drill bit."

Wolf Sr. examined the DeWALT three-eighth. "Yeah. But if it did you'd be one sorry sob sister."

I wasn't afraid of a bitless, unplugged power drill in the hands of an eccentric old man, but I left anyway. Nature called.

I threw my reporter's notebook on the seat next to me in the Camaro, along with my pen and purse, and backed into Mueller's driveway so I could make a K-turn and head to the nearest public bathroom.

That's when I saw him standing in the garage. He was incredibly tall with broad, sloping shoulders and steely gray eyes. An unmistakable shock of bright orange hair stuck out from his head.

Shep's attacker. The one who had pummeled him in the cornfield. It must have been Wolf Mueller. How many giants with red hair could there be in a town the size of Whoopee?

But if this guy was such a brute, if he had attacked an innocent photographer who was merely shooting a glossy spread, then how come he was wearing matching quilted oven mitts and a pink ruffled apron that said, KISS ME I'M DUTCH?

Somehow it didn't seem like a neo-Nazi fashion statement to me.

Chapter 12

"May I help?" I asked perkily, walking into the kitchen of the Stoltzes looking once again like Sally Hansen Plain and Tall.

An hour before, I had stopped by Mama's condo. Mama had talked me into trying a homemade cuticle softener she'd made with vinegar. I was reluctant, but after that cow-cleaning experience my nails were a mess and since I couldn't wear nail polish all the time—or at least when I was Amish—I had to keep them in condition naturally. Mama's lotion did the trick.

When I was done, I removed my makeup and changed into my Amish wear that Mama had thoughtfully washed and ironed. Then I drove back to the Stoltzes, parked the Camaro in its hiding spot and pretended to be tuckered out from a long day of filing in a doctor's office.

"I'd really like to help," I said, picking up the meat cleaver lying on a wooden board. "Here. Let me chop up this pork." I lifted the cleaver high in the air and considered the tenderloin with purpose.

Katie and her mother looked at each other in alarm.

"What'll you be cutting the pork for?" Fannie Stoltz asked as I whacked off several hunks.

"Stir-fry. Mix it with a bit of soy sauce, some ginger, scallions." I lifted the cleaver for another go.

"That was supposed to be the pork roast for tomorrow's dinner," Fannie said, gazing sadly at the mutilated meat. "Special. For Samuel."

"Oh, I'm so sorry," I gushed, genuinely embarrassed, as Katie removed the cleaver from my hand and replaced it with a butter knife. "I just assumed—"

"That's okay, Sally," Katie said softly. "You can help by trimming the beans. There's a pile on the porch." She led me outside to where two children, barefooted girls in bonnets, sat swinging their legs, cutting off the tips of bright green snap beans.

I sat beside them and smiled, picking up a handful and joining in. Although I was glad to be contributing, I couldn't help wondering if the Stoltz women didn't trust me after that Dolly fiasco. It wasn't just because they wouldn't let me wield the cleaver or that they had relegated me to children's duties. It was because the ten-year-old girls had sharp paring knives whereas I was only permitted to use a butter knife.

"Trade ya?" I said, holding up my dull instrument.

"Nuh-uh," replied the little girl with freckles. "My ma warned me about you." She glanced behind me. "You're not carrying any shampoo . . . are you?"

We giggled over the rhyme and the girls repeated more poems they had learned in school. I was about to make a limerick about pierced ears and Britney Spears before I caught myself. After that we debated the virtues of scooters over roller skates and then we were done with the beans. I was disappointed to see that each had trimmed twice as many as I had. I blamed inadequate equipment.

Katie opened the screen door, handed one of the girls a large Tupperware jug of water and rattled off something in German about Jake.

"Where's she going?" I asked the girl with freckles as her sister skipped away with the jug.

"To give Uncle Jake water. He's got a new automobile and has shut himself in the garage working on it," she said, padding across the grass to deposit the bean ends into the compost heap by the garden. "Usually he only stops for supper when he's got a new automobile."

But Jake didn't stop for supper. Moreover, when I asked at the table where he was, everyone became silent. Samuel quickly changed the subject.

"Do you have your own meat grinder then, Sally?" he asked, passing a bowl of chow-chow to an old man next to him.

I nearly spit out my creamed chipped beef on toast. "Excuse me?"

"Yah. We saved up and bought one last year. Fannie loves it. So convenient," said Samuel, stabbing a piece of pie. "How about you?" He repeated the question in German. *"Hast du deine eigene Hackmaschine?"*

Samuel would have preferred to discourse in German, but I had explained that I had no knowledge of the mother tongue because German was passé among the Ohio Amish. Ohio folks had given it up years ago—though I had absolutely no idea if that were true.

"I think I have one," I said, recalling Mama's old hand-operated steel grinder she used for making hamburger out of cheap cuts of beef. "It's my mother's."

Samuel nodded with satisfaction. He was a sturdy man with a long gray beard trimmed to the outline of his face. There was no doubt in anyone's mind that he was the head of the family. I noticed that Fannie acquiesced to him in nearly all matters and let him make the important choices—whether it was to raise the price of eggs or to respond to the conservation commission concerning the water regulations.

In return, Samuel regarded his position seriously and

benevolently. He was a thoughtful man who approached cows and bureaucrats with equal patience. Katie told me that in the evenings her father would either read the German Bible by the propane lamp or recline in his reverse gravity machine, a strange device that suspended him upside down. She said she'd never known him to make a decision without sleeping on it at least one night.

So no one laughed or teased Samuel about discussing the ownership of meat grinders. They listened quietly and ate swiftly from heaping plates of Lebanon bologna, thick, homemade bread, applesauce, green beans, chow-chow and Omer Best's shoofly pie.

Samuel chattered to the man sitting next to him. "I told him in German that you have your own meat grinder. You try saying it, Bubbles. *Ech hab' meine eigenen Hackmaschine*. I have my own meat grinder."

"Ech hab' meine eigenen Hackmaschine," I repeated slowly. My first complete German phrase.

"*Gut, gut,*" said Samuel. "There may be hope for you yet, Sally Hansen from Ohio."

It was around 9:00 P.M. and a summer thunderstorm was rumbling overhead when I tiptoed out of the Stoltzes' house after evening prayers. The family had all turned in for the night, weary from a day of excruciating labor—cutting hay and alfalfa, baling it and performing the many chores required on a dairy farm.

Having risen at five that morning to wash a cow, I, too, was beat. In fact, my sincerest wish was to strip off the hot Amish clothing and collapse on the patchwork quilt in my tiny bedroom. But I had asked Nimrod to stick his neck out for me in requesting an audience with Dutch and I couldn't very well blow him off.

In the bathroom of a nearby McDonald's I slipped into my dazzling rhinestone-studded purple cocktail dress and spruced up my hair with matching combs. My eyelids wore a delightful shade of orchid rose and my lips were the color of cotton candy. To top it off, I applied a quick coat of gold nail polish to match my toes.

My body sighed in satisfaction at being reunited to polyester and spandex.

At a pay phone outside McDonald's, I used Sandy's telephone card to place a call home. Dan answered in a sour mood. I was all prepared to grill him about his treatment of Stiletto and that lingering student loan issue when Dan said, "It's after nine on the first week of school and Jane's not home."

There was a clap of thunder and a burst of rain. Having bagged out when Jane was six, Dan had missed the bumpy transition into the day-to-day, chaotic world of her teen years. "Maybe she's at drama," I offered, opening my umbrella, "or at the library over at Lehigh University. You know how she likes to do research there."

"Get real. She's with G. And G's mad at me."

"No. What did you do?"

"I didn't do anything."

Dishes clattered in the background. Dan doing dishes?

"We were sitting around after dinner and I said to him, 'See my thumb? Gee you're dumb.' And poked him in the eye. In a fun way."

I slapped my cheek. "You poked him in the eye?"

"Yeah, but like I said, in a fun way. That's not what got him mad. What got him mad was the *gee* part. He thought I was calling him stupid—like *G*."

"Well, weren't you?"

"Of course I was. But I figured he wasn't smart enough to pick up on it. Kind of a test. Anyway, he left and Jane went with him and I haven't seen them since."

Twenty-four hours with Dan running the show and my daughter was on the road, probably in the rain, heading God-knows-where on the arm of an MTV addict hailing to a one-letter name. I told Dan to leave a message at Mama's time-share as soon as Jane got in. In my heart of hearts I predicted that would be around midnight, but I didn't tell Dan that. Better to let him sweat it out for a bit. He deserved to squirm and tear out his hair.

I was ready to hang up when Dan said, "Oh, and Bubbles?"

"Yes."

"You know where there are any clean shorts? Wendy always used to keep a fresh supply in the rear of the walk-in closet but I can't find any left in my suitcase."

I introduced Dan to that miraculous invention called the washing machine and hung up. Next I called Mickey.

"Hulloo," he answered laconically.

"Mickey. Where have you been? Your line was busy all day yesterday."

"Took it off the hook." He yawned loudly. "Too tired to get off the couch and answer all those questions."

I briefly considered that Mickey might be drunk and dismissed that notion. Mickey hardly ever drank. More likely he was just depressed.

"I have good news about Janice," I announced cheerfully.

"You found her?"

"Not quite." I told him about my encounter with Janice's family.

"That's old news," Mickey said dejectedly. "I learned that from the Whoopee police long ago."

I wasn't about to mention Lynyrd Skynyrd's role in Janice's epiphany or that her mother and sister had indicated that Janice was home to stay—as a full-fledged, baptized Amish woman. Janice would have to break that heavy news to Mickey herself.

"And did the Whoopee police tell you that Janice had

run out the door after screaming that some *he* had meant to kill her and not Elwood?"

"Yeah. I have no idea who *he* is. She never mentioned another man's name to me, which wasn't surprising." Mickey's voice dropped to a whisper. "She was a virgin, you know."

"More information than I needed, Mr. Mickey Sinkler." Best to change the subject before Mickey spilled out more secrets. "What about Elwood's car? They find it yet?"

"The Rolls? Nope."

I nearly dropped the phone. "It was a Rolls? You didn't tell me that!"

"Not just a Rolls. A Rolls-Royce Corniche. Price tag $360,000. Most expensive car in the world. So long it didn't even fit in the garage."

"Then why'd he buy it? What would a little old man want with a Rolls-Royce Corniche?"

"I dunno. To drive it on Sundays maybe?"

Mickey and I left it that I would call if I found any more information about Janice. I debated about whether to ring Mr. Salvo, but already it was nine-thirty, the night deadline crunch, and Mr. Salvo would have no time to chat. Plus I was getting sleepier every minute. I had to head over to the disco before I was too tired to shake my booty.

The Stayin' Alive Disco was wedged between Hickory Farms and Payless ShoeSource in the Paradise Mall. After mall hours, it was accessed in the rear by an unmarked black door next to the dark blue Dumpsters bursting with rotting remains of pizza and fruit smoothies from the mall's food court. I was certain that if I parked the Camaro back here I'd find a rat in the driver's seat blasting the radio and smoking a cigarette when I returned.

Seeing as how I was so dolled up, a bouncer spared me the cover and directed me to the bar across the disco. Dancers were clustered on either side of a multicolored, pulsating dance floor, talking and drinking. Oddly enough, no one was dancing. I spotted Nimrod, who was sitting at the bar waving for me to come over.

I was click, click, clicking across the pulsating floor when a frightening police siren blared and a blinding spotlight swept the room until it landed—on me.

I shielded my eyes and looked up, trying to signal someone to turn off the darned thing, but all I could see was a mirrored disco ball twirling madly. And then this voice boomed as a bass beat grew louder.

"Ladies and gentlemen, disco guys and disco gals, we have the first contestant."

A roar went up as a man in a white suit and black shirt slid in white cowboy boots across the floor. His hair was jet, swooped in a pompadour and sprayed for that "dry look." He was the spitting image of John Travolta, give or take eighty pounds. Mostly give.

"Maestro!" he yelled to a disc jockey spinning records in a glass booth. "I believe we'd like to check in at the YMCA." Once again the crowd cheered while I winced at the opening strains of the Village People.

Steel-town girls don't dance to the Village People. Bruce Springsteen, yes. A sprightly Bon Jovi or a particularly raucous Van Halen, perhaps, and, when inspired by Jell-O shots, Lynyrd Skynyrd. But men dressed as cops, construction workers and Indians prancing about the stage? Please.

Unfortunately, I was not given an opportunity to object. The emcee tossed the microphone and grabbed me so forcefully my purse nearly fell off my shoulder. After that I don't know what happened except that I was spun, lifted, rear-ended and nearly pushed over. I was turning black and blue.

Eventually we were joined on the floor by the other couples. The emcee took my hand and led me over to the bar before scooping up another victim. My head was spinning.

"This is how you must feel all the time," I said to Nimrod, who was perched on the stool next to me, a huge grin on his face. "Dizzy."

"I hate disco. Disco sucks. But when you hustle, Tastykakes, it's positively bodacious," he exclaimed. "Love the purple, by the way. Or is that eggplant?"

"Are you old enough to be consuming that?" I said, pointing to the Yuengling beer in front of him.

"I'm twenty, aren't I?"

"The legal age in Pennsylvania is twenty-one."

Nimrod smacked his head. "Oh, yeah. I keep forgetting."

Excellent role model that I am, I ordered a Diet A-Treat cola with lime. In a lowered voice, Nimrod said that he had spoken to Dutch, had told him all about my search for Janice and that Dutch had agreed to meet me in private, tonight.

"What's this Dutch guy like anyway?" I asked, grabbing a handful of pretzels from the bar supply.

"Well, he's really big. Like huge." Nimrod spread his arms wide.

"You mean in girth?"

"No, I mean in power. He runs this disco, owns dozens of other businesses and as for land, forget about it. He's on the verge of owning this whole town." Nimrod finished his beer. "He's a feudal lord, man."

I munched on the pretzels and thought about feudal lords. Nimrod shook his beer bottle at the bartender, but I cut him off.

"That'll be a Coke," I said, sternly. "This boy's underage."

"You're like a mom." Nimrod stared glumly at the soda.

"That's because I *am* a mom. I don't get it about Dutch. How did he get so powerful?"

"He's intimidating, you know? He asks for land and farmers give it to him or else—"

"Or else, what?" I stopped munching.

"I don't know. He breaks their legs. Burns their barns. Shoots their cattle."

"That's horrible! Do you know that for a fact?" I knew the question was stupid as soon as it left my lips. There were no facts in Nimrod's hallucinogenic universe, only rippling, technicolor theories.

Nimrod shrugged. "That's what someone told me down at the gas station once."

I was about to pry more information from Nimrod's soggy mind when two men suddenly appeared by our sides. Each was dressed in black flood pants and white, short-sleeve polyester dress shirts. More uncool henchmen I had never seen.

"This her?" one asked Nimrod.

Nimrod gave him the thumbs-up. "Good luck, Bubbles. Tell Dutch I said hello."

"Wait a minute," I protested as I was being lifted off the stool by one of the goons. "Where are you taking me?"

"Ya wanted to see Dutch," replied the goon. "Now you got your chance."

I grabbed my purse and trotted between the two out a side door and up a flight of stairs to Dutch's office.

I don't know what I expected. A big crime boss's office, I guess. Lots of red oriental carpeting and dark wood. Cut-glass decanters and a Colt magnum in the top right-hand drawer.

What I walked into was a simple white room with a worn wooden floor and multicolored braided rugs. A long table covered by a baby-blue vinyl tablecloth awaited at one end under a wall dotted with framed pictures of deer and ducks that I recognized right off as being from Kmart's art department.

"Dutch'll be here in a moment," a thug said before closing the door. "Cool your heels." He shut the door and left me staring at a cheap white china vase holding pink and purple plastic flowers.

An intense aroma seeped under the door and my stomach rumbled. It smelled of molasses and pastry. The door opened and closed behind me and I turned to face Dutch, nearly falling off my seat when I saw him.

A bucktoothed man in an orange feeder cap holding a tray with steaming shoofly pie and a glass of frothy milk eyed me with disturbing suspicion.

Fannie's helpful neighbor—Omer Best.

Mama's Cuticle Softener

This softener is nice because it contains no chemicals and can be assembled from ingredients already found in most kitchens. And, of course, it contains that miracle ingredient—vinegar.

2 tablespoons fresh pineapple juice
1 egg yolk
½ teaspoon vinegar
½ teaspoon glycerine
1 teaspoon rosewater

Mix all ingredients and soak nails for fifteen minutes. Wash off and push back cuticles. Refrigerate any remaining mixture.

Chapter 13

"Don't I know ya naw?" Omer asked, walking to the other side of the table. "Sure and ya look familiar." He placed the tray on the table and studied my hair.

I swallowed hard, trying to absorb the concept that Omer Best, Fannie's goofy, cross-eyed neighbor who lived with his mother up the road from the Stoltzes, was the feared and revered feudal lord of Whoopee, PA, named Dutch.

From my purse I retrieved a Maybelline compact and a tube of Purple Passion lip gloss, which I smeared on seductively. I wanted to look as non-Amish as possible, lest Omer remember where he had seen these bright blond locks before.

Omer snapped his suspenders and sat down, adjusting his steel-frame glasses.

"Na, I guess not," he said, unrolling a steel fork and knife from a paper napkin. "Don't got dat many pretty girls here. Most of dem keep demselves plain."

He began carving into the pie. "Soes, you're looking for Janice Kramer, den?"

"Yes, she's a friend of mine," I replied calmly, putting away the lip gloss. "She was supposed to get married to my friend Mickey and didn't show up for her wedding and then her uncle was murdered—"

Omer nodded and sipped from a glass of milk. "Ya. It was on da noose I saw. It was junk. Janice is a nice girl. She didn't kill nobody."

I watched his face carefully for a flicker of murderer's guilt, remorse or worry. There was none. Only stupidity.

"Did you know Janice?" I asked conversationally.

"Aw, sure. She use ta vork next door at da Hickory Farms. Hung aut dawnstairs sipping ginger beer."

Although Nimrod had implied that Janice and Omer socialized, there was not the least hint of erstwhile romantic longing in his voice. Though, admittedly, imagining Omer Best in a romance was a pretty difficult picture to conjure. When I tried, all I could see was *Hee Haw*.

Omer took a bite of pie and quickly grabbed the milk glass. "I dug in too fast. My tongue I burned."

Boy, whoever nicknamed this guy Dutch knew his stuff. Omer was a veritable stereotype, and after surveying his deluxe office, I decided he was also "tight viss a buck," as they say in this part of the woods.

"Dat's vat you vork for? TV noose? Dat's vat Nimrod says." He chewed with his mouth open.

Disgusted, I averted my eyes. "No. I'm a correspondent for the *News-Times* in Lehigh." How did Nimrod find out I was a reporter? Mac must have told him.

"Ahh. Da noosepaper." He belched silently into his napkin and leaned forward. "You know vat story you should do on? Me."

"You?" I tried to sound interested.

"Ya. I'm gonna hit it big. Amish Vunderland, you seen dat, say?"

"Yup."

"Dat I own and soon the haws next door. Once dat price comes dawn. Four hundred towsand. Oooh boy."

"Mueller's?"

"Ya know it?"

"I stopped by there today for another story I'm working on. Two Amish boys from the area stole a car from a lot at M&M Gas and Garage and broke down outside Lehigh. Apparently Wolf Mueller has the inside scoop on what happened."

"Rum springa. Dat's vat I heard."

Hmmm. I bit my lip. How much should I tell Omer? Probably this guy knew everything anyway. "My editor wonders if it's more than that, if the Hochstetter boys are part of a gang. The Pagans."

"We got da hex signs for dat." Omer held his side as though this were a hoot. "Dat's a joke, naw."

I smiled thinly.

"Forget da Hochstetters." Omer wiped his lips. " I'm gonna put Whoopee on da map viss a development so huge it's gonna befuddle."

"Where?" I asked, thinking that Whoopee was rather small for a befuddling development. "You gonna rip down the Amish Wunderland?"

"Naw." Omer put his hands behind his head. "Dat's a moneymaker. But next to it, sure. It's gonna be da first ever residential community viss an Amish deme park. Come home from vork and ride da coaster."

"Theme park?" I asked, trying to understand Omer's dialect. "You're gonna need acres and acres."

"You said it, girlie. Dat's vat's gonna make me da Donald Trump of Lancaster County, naw."

I played with the plastic flowers on the table until I saw Omer glancing at my golden nails, which I swiftly hid in my lap.

"But it's all working farmland. And Amish farmland at that," I pointed out. "The Amish hardly ever sell their land, just cut it up and distribute it to their kids."

"Dat's vat you tink. The Amish I got da touch vid.

Mennonite, too. Dey trust me 'cause I'm Dutch, say? Fancy New Yorkers. Flashy folks from Philly. Dey don't stand a chance next ta me."

A strange heat began to rise in my chest as I recalled this morning's events. Fannie generously greeting Omer at the door. Omer's dire predictions of doom regarding the water issue with the conservation commission and Katie's fear that Samuel would pick up the whole family and move to Kentucky.

Had Omer insinuated himself in the Stoltzes' dispute with the state just so he could position himself for the moment when Samuel threw in the towel? I envisioned him slapping Samuel on the back, telling him that the state had won and that the regulations were too restrictive. Why not sell the farm and be done with it, Samuel? he would say.

It was all I could do to keep myself from standing up and pointing an accusatory finger at this shoofly-swallowing swindler. Cheat, bully, I wanted to yell. But I didn't because that wouldn't help the Stoltzes. I wasn't sure if I ran to their house right now, woke them up and relayed what Omer had told me, what his true identity was, that they would believe me either.

The Stoltzes were the type to trust their neighbors. Ill will and malicious thoughts did not readily spring to their heads. Samuel, especially, worked hard at keeping his heart pure.

"Vat ya muddling about naw, Bubbles?" Omer asked. "Dat story on me?"

"Yes," I said, rising slowly. "It sounds intriguing. Perhaps I'll look into it."

Omer stood, too. "Gotta wait, dough. Dere's gotta be more sells first."

"More . . . sales?"

"Sure, naw. After Mueller's den just one more. Udderwise da Board of Supervisors won't let me build. I need a lot to handle the surage. Vidout it the permit to build I won't get."

"Surage? What's surage?"

"Sew-er-age," Omer said deliberately. "For da terlets. Septic."

I made a mental note to visit the Board of Supervisors and check out the land records for a glimpse of Whoopee's water tables—as much as I truly loathed and detested doing so. Latitude. Longitude. Bequeath. Quit claim. I shuddered. The prospect of opening those dusty tomes was too horrifying for me to think about now.

For all his boasting and questionable table manners, Omer Best turned out to be a gentleman. He politely led me down the stairs to the back door of the disco. He promised to call if he heard anything about Janice. I gave him Mama's pickle time-share telephone number. In exchange, he handed me his business card. It said DUTCH ENTERPRISES.

"You're the one building the nursing home!" I exclaimed. "I drove by the protest today."

"Did ya naw? Ach. Dem protesters is knuckleheads, say?"

But I didn't say. Instead I shrugged and watched him waddle back up the stairs. Omer Best was not the monster Nimrod had made him out to be. At the very least he was a big fish making waves in a little pond. And Whoopee was a very, very little pond. At the very worst he was a savvy Pennsylvania Dutch developer with an "over-the-fence-some-hay-throw" shtick.

Still, that didn't mean Omer Best was above exploiting his friendship with trusting innocents like the Stoltzes. I would have to proceed very carefully before confronting them about their good friend and neighbor Omer though. I'd have to gather solid information—not Nimrod's rumors—and clear evidence to prove to them concretely that Omer was a shyster, not a savior. It was the best favor I could do in return for their hospitality—besides offering free manicures all around.

I stepped out the back door, opened my purse and pulled out my keys. Rain was coming down in buckets and I did not look forward to crossing the wet parking lot to where I had positioned the Camaro directly under the only light, for safety's sake.

There was a flash inside the car. It might have been a reflection, but it appeared as though the interior light was turned on then off. I tried the rear door to the Stayin' Alive with no success. For some inexplicable reason it was locked.

Slowly I circled to the Camaro, making sure I stayed in the shadows by the putrid Dumpster. I was getting drenched standing out here in the rain. Rain was melting my bangs and soaking my shoes. There was a clap of thunder and I nearly jumped out of my skin, especially when a bolt of lightning lit up a figure within the Camaro.

What could I do? I couldn't go back to the bar. The door was locked. Call the police? I was at the far end of the mall. I'd have to walk the entire length of the parking lot in the rain, at night, to get to the street and a pay phone.

Suddenly there was a screech. A car peeled out from somewhere in the parking lot and spun toward me, seemingly out of control. Damn. Here I was, trapped between the Dumpster and the mall. Where could I run?

The car came closer and I wedged myself against the wall. Good thing, since the car smashed into a corner of the Dumpster, sending it crashing against a chain-link fence, white plastic bags of garbage bursting on the macadam.

It was a nondescript vehicle. A middle-America deal. A Ford Taurus or Chevy Cavalier or Chrysler LeBaron.

Whatever, hitting the Dumpster had had little effect on it. The car zoomed off for another donut on two wheels around the parking lot. Now was my chance. It was either make it to the Camaro or get creamed by this maniac.

I was dashing across the parking lot when the careening car came rocketing toward me again. The driver flipped on the lights and stepped on the gas. Out of the corner of my eye I saw a tall shape step out of the shadows. I was caught like a mouse between two cats. Either the reckless driver or—

There was another smash and I felt myself being lifted by two hands and placed onto the hood of the Camaro.

An object had been thrown through the driver's side window of the suicide car, which began to turn and twist from side to side. Suddenly, it righted itself and screamed out of the parking lot. After it left, all was silent except for my pounding heart and shaking body.

Only then did I acknowledge that standing in front me was my other attacker.

Wouldn't you know it—Stiletto.

Chapter 14

"Oh, I'm from the South Side. I know from tough." Stiletto mimicked me in a girly-girl voice. "I can handle an-y-thing. Why, just give me a bottle of nail varnish and a blow dryer and I'm a one-woman Rambette."

"Yeah, yeah, yeah." I slid off the hood and was surprised that my knees were like jelly and my whole body was quivering. I leaned against the Camaro for support. "How'd you find me here anyway?"

Stiletto linked his arms around my waist, his hips pressing against my thighs. "You talk about mingling with rapists, murderers and gangs and you expect me to leave you alone?"

"Well, you didn't appear too concerned back at the construction site. You said you'd see me around."

"And I did. I saw you around M&M, then the Amish Wunderland and at that farmhouse where you're staying—"

But I had stopped listening. My concentration had dissolved, much like Stiletto's white oxford shirt was doing in the rain. It was soaked and now practically see-through under the carbon light. I loved those broad shoulders of his, not to mention those arms. Perfectly muscular, not in a Mr. Atlas way, but in a rock-hard, I-can-take-care-of-business way. Water trickled down his neck in rivulets, around his collarbone and over his chest. If I ran the world, I'd always keep Stiletto soaked to the bare skin.

"You're not answering my question, Bubbles," he said softly, pushing back my hair with his hand. "What were you doing in the disco?"

I hadn't really heard the question the first time. I started to answer when Stiletto leaned down and kissed the spot where he had brushed away my hair. I closed my eyes and he held me tighter. The shaking stopped. I was safe and okay. Yes, I was fine. And Stiletto? He was warm and smelled of clean soap and damp cotton.

Instinctively I brought my left leg up and leaned back against the hood of the car, Stiletto laying me down gracefully. Raindrops splashed on my face and my lips parted, catching them before the rain was replaced with another of Stiletto's soft kisses.

"What was that you threw in the maniac's window?" I murmured, although, to be honest, I couldn't have cared less at the moment. I merely asked to keep myself from going nuts with desire.

"Garden gnome." His fingers caressed first the tops of my breasts and then my cleavage. He was purposeful, intrigued. "It was in the backseat of your Camaro crying to be tossed."

Ahh. Mama's hideous garden gnome, I thought dreamily. Good call. I could feel Stiletto between my legs as his hand stroked my thigh and continued daringly upward. I didn't give two hoots about that stupid old chastity vow now. That chastity vow could go jump off a cliff.

"Let's go someplace out of the rain," I suggested. "Maybe we should—"

I never got a chance to finish. Stiletto bent over and

kissed me with such passion I had to push him away. He didn't take it personally. Instead, he slipped the raincoat and straps of the cocktail dress off my shoulders and smiled mischievously.

"Maybe we should what?" he whispered before kissing my shoulders. I shuddered slightly and this time not because I was scared. Stiletto's lips had moved south, following the edge of my purple cocktail dress, which was threatening to slide down more and expose me in public for the second time that day.

Suddenly, I didn't care that we were in a parking lot and making out like teenagers, or that while getting dressed earlier in the McDonald's I had opted to go braless and now was practically naked, splayed on a Camaro hood with a hunk of Mel Gibson in *Braveheart* proportions having his way with me. Stiletto could have me. He could take it all.

If I didn't get *him* first.

Spaghetti straps be damned, I wiggled free of them. Stiletto studied me with a look of admiration.

"My, my. What's come over my reserved Bubbles?"

I was not in the mood for chitchat. I ran my hands along his thighs and up his back, pulling him toward me. Stiletto started to kiss my lips but I arched my back and pushed him downward instead. While his lips delightedly explored, his hand ventured further under my dress with confidence as my chastity vow waved the white flag of defeat.

"Not here," he said, pausing in his pursuit. I could feel his heart pounding in his chest. "I'm staying in Shep's hotel room. C'mon, let's—"

"Shep. That reminds me. I think I know who Shep's attacker is," I said absently.

Screech! Crash. Halt. Stiletto stood up. "Did you say something about Shep's attacker?"

Uh-oh. Make-out misstep. "Forget about Shep," I

said, grabbing Stiletto's hand. "Let's go back to doing what we were doing. I'll bring you up to speed later."

"No, wait a minute. What did you say about Shep?"

I modestly pulled up my dress. "Shep's attacker. I think I met him today. Well, not *met* him. Ran into him. More like backed into him, if you want to be technical."

Stiletto put his hands on the hood. "And?"

"His name's Wolf Mueller. He's about seven feet tall with orange-red hair out to there. He was wearing a pink—"

"That's the guy," said Stiletto, giving the hood a hard pound. "I gotta meet him in person and even the score for Shep." He yanked open the passenger's side door and got in.

"Now?" I asked, readjusting the straps, grabbing my raincoat and sliding off the hood. "You want to meet him, now?"

"Now," Stiletto said resolutely.

"But it's almost eleven."

"Never too late to put those neo-Nazi punks in their place," he said, his fist making contact with the palm of his other hand. "Violence is the only lesson they understand."

I opened the driver's side door. "Hold on, Stiletto. Mueller might be important in my search for Janice and this stolen car story I'm working on."

"Don't worry. You don't have to be by my side. You just have to get me to his doorstep since I left my Jeep way at the opposite end of the mall. Also, I'd enjoy your company when I'm done pummeling the bastard."

Geesh. What if I had been wrong about Mueller? What if he was really a nice guy and his evil twin had beaten up Shep?

"You have no idea if Mueller's a neo-Nazi, if indeed it was Mueller who beat up Shep," I said, tossing in my purse and getting behind the wheel. "For all you know, maybe Mueller was ticked that Shep was tromping through his cornfield."

"The cornfield isn't owned by anyone named Mueller," Stiletto said as I started up the Camaro. "It's owned by a corporation. Dutch Enterprises. And Shep got permission from the secretary to shoot its perimeter."

The Camaro stalled. "Dutch Enterprises?" I squeaked.

"You've heard of it before?"

"Once or twice," I said, starting up the Camaro again. "I'll tell you on the drive over to Mueller's house. But promise you won't laugh when I explain that it all has to do with shoofly pie."

Since I didn't want Mueller to see the Camaro when Stiletto arrived to throw his first punch, instead of roaring up to Wolf Mueller's doorstep, I decided to park it in the Amish Wunderland RV area. We sat in the car and talked for a bit. Stiletto was floored by what Omer Best had said about acquiring land by putting the touch on the Amish.

"You're onto something, Bubbles," Stiletto said, flipping open the glove compartment to get my Lancaster County map. "Did you get Omer on tape?"

Darn. I'd left my large yellow tape player back at Mama's condo. Too bad, since with its large Play, Rewind, Record and Stop buttons in the colors of red, green, blue and purple, it was the one recording device I could operate all by myself.

"What you need is one of those minicassette recorders," he said, unfolding the map. "They've got microphones built in them now that would pick up a conversation a half a room away, even if they were hidden in your purse."

"I think it's illegal to tape a conversation without the other person's knowledge, Stiletto."

He clicked on the flashlight from my glove compartment and shined it on the map. "It's not too illegal. Swindling honest farmers, that's illegal. Okay, here. This is where Shep was beaten," he said, pointing to a white space on the map a few inches down from Amish Wunderland.

"And this is where Mueller's house is," I said, "which means Shep's beating probably took place in the field behind his house."

Stiletto shook his head. "That SOB," he said, folding up the map. "Accosted Shep in the middle of the field, left him there, bruised and battered, too."

"I thought you said the secretary at Dutch Enterprises gave Shep permission to shoot the *perimeter* of the field. What was Shep doing in the middle of the field, then?"

Stiletto cleared his throat. "Well, you know, Shep's used to war zones. Bosnia. Chechnya. Boundaries and perimeters, they're kind of fuzzy concepts to him. Shep's not one to be told where he can't go. So, are you gonna drive off or come with me and see what happens?"

What kind of question was that?

Next I knew, Stiletto and I were sloshing through the dripping cornfield to arrive at the back door of Mueller's small house. Thankfully the rain had stopped. I had decided to stay in the field, shivering, wet and out of sight, to watch the first few rounds.

Stiletto walked up to the back door and rapped a few times. There was no answer. He rang the doorbell. Nothing. Then pound, pound, pound. Still no response.

He stepped off the stoop and jogged around to the front of the house. When he returned, he called, "There's no car in the driveway. No one's home."

I felt a great sense of relief. Whew! No fight. That meant I could return to the Stoltzes, get out of these wet clothes and climb into bed. Bed. What a wonderful word.

"Aww, gee, that's too bad," I said, trying to mask the eagerness in my voice. "Guess we better go."

"Go?" Stiletto removed his wallet from the back pocket of his jeans. "I'm not going."

At the sight of Stiletto removing a credit card, my stomach flipped. "Oh, no." I ran out of the cornfield to stop him.

"Oh, yes." Stiletto slid the card between the weather stripping and the casing. "When do you figure this house was built? I'm estimating postwar circa 1952. You think Mueller's changed the lock since then? This will take two seconds, tops."

I heard a click and grabbed Stiletto's wrist. "Hold on, James Bond. This is completely, utterly unethical and illegal to boot."

"Please, Bubbles. No more of this Two Guys Community College journalism propaganda," Stiletto said a tad cockily. "That's the second time tonight with this ethical nonsense. Can't you see I'm on a moral quest here?"

"What moral quest?" He made himself sound like Sir Lancelot.

"To stop neo-Nazis before they inflict more pain. You've read the headlines. You know what a problem they are in this part of Pennsylvania. It's more than kooky, radical talk. That I could deal with. It's murder. These guys kill people. People like my bud Shep."

I waited, breathing hard, hoping that I could restrain myself from following him inside—which I knew, deep down, I couldn't.

"What would Mr. Salvo say if he saw you doing this?" I asked, hoping to play on Stiletto's long-standing friendship with my boss.

"If you knew some of the stuff Tony Salvo and I did as teenagers, you wouldn't be holding him as the moral high bar, Bubbles." Stiletto pushed open the door. "Voilà. Can't go back now. I've broken." He put one foot into a back hallway. "And I've entered. Cuff me."

The next thing I knew Stiletto was inside and the door was shut. I stood outside in the dark by my lonesome for a few minutes, listening to the chirping crickets and the drip, drip, drip of rainwater off the leaves. One breaking branch in the distance was all it took for me to reconsider.

"Thirty seconds, not bad," he said when I let myself in.

"I want separate trials," I mumbled.

"Hello!" Stiletto shouted. He began inspecting the rooms with the flashlight. When he came back he said, "Free and clear. Okay, I'm gonna check the basement. Neo-Nazis love basements." He opened a door off the kitchen and scrambled down the stairs.

"What's that smell?" I asked, lifting my nose. It reminded me of dirty socks and underwear, only more pungent. And yet strangely reminiscent of Liberty High football games on crisp autumn Friday nights, cocoa in Styrofoam cups and woolen plaid blankets.

I moved into the kitchen where a pile of baking pans stood stacked in the sink. There was chocolate goo all around. In bowls. On pans.

"Someone's been baking up a storm," I said to no one in particular.

Stiletto emerged from the basement. "Nothing but piles of laundry and empty bottles. I'm going upstairs. Wanna come?"

No, I was inclined to respond as I climbed the stairs after Stiletto. No, I wanted to leave. Leave now. Leave forever.

There were only two small bedrooms and a bath on the second floor. One was the old man's. It was sparsely appointed and needed a good cleaning. There were dirty clothes thrown over the bed. Empty pizza cartons on the floor lay next to scattered beer cans and rancid socks.

Wolf's room, however, was as tidy as a pin.

Stiletto and I stood in shocked silence as the beam from the flashlight fell on polka-dotted Swiss curtains, a small upright piano with sheet music in the corner, a chintz-covered bed with flowered sheets and cookbook after cookbook specializing in desserts neatly stacked next to a life-sized cardboard cutout of Julia Child holding a tray of puff pastry.

"Some neo-Nazi," I said, letting out a whistle. "Oooh. I'm quaking in my heels. Wouldn't want him to sauté me."

Even in this darkened room, Stiletto looked sheepish. "May have made a mistake here," he said, clicking off the light. "Sorry, Bubbles. I guess I expected to find papers disputing the Holocaust. Rants against the Jewish race and posters of Hitler—not . . . her. Whoever she is."

"Julia Child." I sighed. "It's okay, Stiletto. No harm done. Not as long as we get—"

Slam! From the driveway outside Wolf's window came the sound of slow steps and an elderly groan. Both of us froze.

"Roll out the barrel, roll out the barrel of fun—" Hiccup. Hiccup!

Old Man Mueller was home, crooning to the moon and three sheets to the wind.

We could only pray that he hadn't plugged in his drill.

Chapter 15

"Can't say our relationship lacks spark," Stiletto said. "We're not exactly a *boring* couple."

I pretended to explain the situation to the powers that be at the *News-Times.* "See, it's like this, Mr. Notch. My friend Steve Stiletto thought this guy he'd never met was a neo—"

"Alright, alright. I've learned my lesson." Stiletto pulled me behind the bedroom door, closing it to a crack. "Let's hope he heads straight to bed so we can sneak out later."

"What if his son comes home? Then what?"

"Then we'll hide behind Julia over there. She's . . . shhh!"

The back door downstairs opened and closed. There was a crash of pans in the kitchen sink and then running water. A voice. Old Man Mueller was talking to himself in loud tones, most of which consisted of vigorous expletives.

Footsteps stumbled across the living room. They were odd. Uneven.

We heard a hand thump against a wall and the creaking of springs. Mueller Sr. must have taken one look at those stairs and surrendered to the living room couch.

Stiletto opened the door slightly. "He left the lights on."

After a while there came the deep rattle of a loud snore. Stiletto gripped my hand and I followed him down the stairs, tiptoeing softly. In order to get to the back door we would have to pass right by the old man.

It wasn't pretty. Mueller Sr., mouth open, gray-haired chest bare, lay spread-eagle on the couch. Even from the bottom of the stairs I could smell the wafting waves of whiskey, partially because of the half-empty liquor bottle on the floor beside him.

We had barely passed him and made it to safety when my conscience called. He looked so . . . pitiful there. So neglected and unloved. Once upon a time he had been some mother's baby boy and now—what a mess.

Mueller yawned and smacked his lips. "Where's the ducky?" he mumbled.

I walked softly over to him.

"What in the Sam hill are you doing?" Stiletto wanted to know as I pulled a multicolored crocheted afghan off the couch and covered his naked chest.

Then I picked up the whiskey bottle with two fingers and carried it daintily to the kitchen sink. Stiletto followed me and stared in confusion as I poured its remnants down the drain. I considered writing a brief note touting the virtues of Alcoholics Anonymous and loving oneself, but thought better of it. A drunk needs to hit rock bottom on his own before he wants help.

"You're a regular Carry A. Nation," Stiletto said after we stepped outside and closed the back door. "What gives?"

"Just being a human being, Stiletto," I said, heading toward the cornfield.

By the time we made it back to the mall parking lot, I was so tired I wouldn't have cared if Stiletto had made love to me or dumped me. All I wanted was sleep.

"So what're you doing tomorrow?" he asked.

DUBUQUE COUNTY LIBRARY

I yawned. "Continuing my pursuit of Janice. She's gotta turn up sometime. This town isn't that big. What are you doing?"

"Shooting a train wreck in Baltimore," he said with a shrug.

Damn. Why did this always happen? As soon as Stiletto and I spent five minutes together he was off.

"A train wreck?" I whined.

"Yeah. The Associated Press bureau chief called me this evening. They wanted me to hightail it down there tonight, but I told them the train would have to wait. I had to look after my Bubbles first."

He chucked me under the chin to cheer me up, but my chin wasn't giving in. This was my pout and I was sticking to it.

"I'm sorry, Bubbles, but you're a journalist, too, now. You know what this business is like. Nothing's sacred. Not holidays, Sundays. Not gorgeous, adventurous women whom you—"

I turned to him. "Whom you what?"

Stiletto cleared his throat and said, "Whom you wish would bag their cheating ex-husbands once and for all."

"What?" I said, confused. "Ex-husbands? What are you talking about?"

An aha! expression came over Stiletto and I winced. Oops. That's right. I was supposed to be engaging in Feingold's Two-Factor Theory of Male Emotion.

"Dan and I are simply, uh, friends," I said, covering. "He's been living with me as an experiment." Not a lie, per se. A bit of understatement of facts, as Jane would term it, but not an all-out, bold-faced fib.

"I see," said Stiletto. "Well, then, let me do you one last favor, Bubbles."

"Yes," I said, closing my eyes and pursing my lips.

"Let me advise you to stay away from the Pagans. Do not go near them under any circumstances."

I opened my eyes and unpursed my lips. "Why? What do they do?"

"You don't want to know."

"How come no one will tell me what they do? How come everyone's stingy on the details?"

He leaned over and kissed me. Embarrassingly, I yawned.

"Bubbles! Am I that old hat?"

"My apologies, Stiletto," I said, stifling another yawn. "I'm dead on my feet."

Because of my obvious exhaustion, Stiletto insisted on trailing me back to the Stoltzes', lest I fall asleep at the wheel and drift off the road. When we got there, he walked me from where I had hidden my Camaro behind a stand of trees, across the wet, mowed field to the Stoltzes' front door before kissing me on the forehead and running off.

It wasn't Paris. He hadn't bought me diamonds or a gourmet dinner or tickets to a Broadway play. But his simple acts had warmed me to the tips of my golden-painted toes and inspired me to lay awake for a few minutes more, smiling at the moonlit clouds outside my window.

And wish on a star that for once in our relationship he wouldn't have to leave to photograph a train wreck in Baltimore.

I awoke the next morning, a sunny Thursday, to a damp lump of cocktail dress at the foot of my bed, to worries about Jane and to the pounding disbelief that I had committed a felony.

If any neighbors reported that a high-haired blonde in a purple cocktail dress and a hunk in tight jeans had been seen snooping around Mueller's house, we were dead meat. Old Man Mueller would recognize me in a second as the pesky reporter who had tried to enter his abode earlier in the day. I'd be burglary suspect numera una.

After I dressed in my Amish clothes, I washed my face and braided my hair. My hair was not up to its usual par and the braiding only exposed more of my dark roots. The result was a two-toned look I hadn't sported since Northeast Junior High. And though it was expensive to do and not conducive to finding Janice, I resolved to visit a hairdresser's that morning. As a beautician I've observed that once a woman decides to take action with her hair, whether to cut it or color it, it's virtually impossible for her to wait until it's done.

After breakfast and "redding up the house," as Katie called it, Fannie put me to work in the cool pump room scrubbing bottles with a wire brush. There wasn't much damage I could do there, besides breaking a few bottles (two), and it was a true help to Fannie and Katie, who admitted detesting the work.

I could see why. Scrubbing bottles was tedious and frustrating. There always seemed to be bits of hardened gunk or, gulp, bugs at the bottom. It would have been a breeze with an automatic dishwasher, but I couldn't suggest that, of course. In this instance *I* was the automatic dishwasher.

The cleaned bottles were the first step in preparing Fannie Stoltz's famous root beer, which was a tradition at the Lancaster County Fair, Katie said. The secret of its appeal was Fannie's insistence on old-fashioned ingredients. No purchased extract for her. No siree. Her root beer was made from fresh ginger root, burdock and sassafras, steeped for twelve hours, left to sit for a day and then skimmed, bottled and stored for a month.

It seemed like a heck of a lot of work for a bottle of A-Treat.

Still, the repetitive rinsing and swishing let my mind focus on what steps to take next in searching for Janice.

I had stalled on that front. Her parents hadn't seen her. Mickey hadn't heard from her. The police were clueless and Wolf was, apparently, inaccessible.

I was stumped.

I had finished the last bottle and was drying my hands when I heard the back door close and the familiar, now alarming, regional dialect of Omer Best fill the kitchen. He had another pie baked by Mother. Shoofly again. And he was hankering to know where I was.

"Vere's dat Sally?" Omer asked loudly. "Mudder says dis pie's for her."

I paled and gripped the pump.

"Oh, now don't tell me you're sweet on our Sally." Katie laughed innocently. "And here I thought it would be Jake fixing up the courting buggy."

"You're making me all ferhoodled, Katie."

Katie giggled. "I'll go get her. She's just around the—"

Smash! There was a gasp and then Fannie apologizing profusely. "Slipped right out of my hands. Must've had butter on them."

"Nudding vorse den pickle spills," grumbled Omer. "My shoes, dey got vet."

"I'll get a broom," declared Katie.

"You better change those pants right away," Fannie said, "and come back later this afternoon because Sally's off to do filing at the doc's."

"I need ta spritz me down, naw."

Omer left to change his vinegary clothes and Katie answered the cries of her adorable baby, who had awakened from a nap in her family's side of the house. When the coast was clear, I rushed into the kitchen and confronted Fannie.

She stared at me, a slight smile at the corners of her lips.

"But how did you know—" I started to ask.

"I may be old, but I still remember what it is like to

be a younger woman," she said quietly. "When Samuel and I courted, my stomach was in knots he was so handsome and strong. But Omer"—she shook her head—"no butterflies for you there, say, Sally?"

"No," I said, "no butterflies, Fannie."

"So I did you a favor, then, by sending him off?"

"More than you'll ever know."

Chapter 16

There was no message about Jane when I got to the time-share. And I couldn't ask anyone if she had phoned since Mama and Genevieve had awakened bright and early to go to Hershey Park. I could only assume that Jane's arrival home had been so late Dan didn't want to wake Mama and Genevieve by calling. Either that or Mama had forgotten to write down his message.

The other possibility—that Jane hadn't returned at all—was too frightening for a worried mother, a good eighty miles away from her daughter, to even consider.

I took a long hot shower and stepped into a gathered blue peasant top, a black miniskirt with a slit up the side and knee-high boots. I topped off the outfit with gold hoop earrings and did up my lids in powder blue—to match the peasant top. I twisted my hair and held it fast with a big white plastic French clip.

Then I sat down at the yellow-and-white kitchenette table, opened the phonebook and searched for a decent hairdresser to touch up my roots. I decided to go with Regina's in the Paradise Mall. How bad could the mall salon be? Plus, there was a picture of Regina. She appeared capable and pleasant.

Regina couldn't take me for an hour and a half. That gave me time to place another call to Russell the security guard. I wasn't put off by the fact that he hadn't returned my last phone call. As they taught us in journalism class, the difference between a good newspaper story and a great one is the phone call the writer of the former didn't make.

Still, it was a tad early for rousing canned security guards. So, I poured myself a cup of lukewarm decaffeinated coffee left in Genevieve's Mr. Coffee pot, toasted an English muffin and spread it with the airy yellow paste from a white plastic tub that Mama and Genevieve called margarine. It wasn't margarine. It was worse. It was "I Can't Believe I'm Eating This!" margarine substitute. No fat. No cholesterol. No taste.

I chewed the damp English muffin and sipped the tepid coffee. Mama and Genevieve were always buying fake food. Cholesterol-free egg substitute that came in milk cartons. Fat-free cheese with the texture of vinyl. Potato chips fried in the imitation oil that in federal tests inflicted lab rats with diarrhea. Cookies made with unreal sugar.

Yet, without a second thought, they were off to the Hershey factory to ride through the chocolate-scented museum and to overdose on free candy. Afterward they'd hit the Hershey gift store for discount Kisses and bags of Krackel bars, not to mention thick, rich, fat-filled cocoa and creamy Hershey's ice cream.

Mama claims the fake food offsets the fattening food so that, in essence, she ends up eating a well-balanced diet. I think she's merely a sucker for marketing.

I was done with my second breakfast at eight-thirty and concluded that it wasn't too early now to call Russell the security guard. He answered on the first ring, more wired than a Chihuahua on amphetamines. I introduced myself, pricked his memory by reminding him of my eight years at the Two Guys Community College and asked if he could help.

"For a recommendation? Sorry, Bubbles, I've had a bit of a setback at work. I've been let go."

"I know. Elwood Kramer. I found his body."

Russell coughed nervously. "That was you? My apologies. I had no idea. How insensitive of me."

"Don't give it a second thought." I twirled the tub of margarine substitute. "I don't know if I mentioned this when we met, Russell, but I'm moonlighting as a reporter for the *News-Times* these days. My Two Guys professor is the newspaper's night editor."

Russell was impressed. "No kidding. Gosh that's a great community college. Though it's too bad they didn't teach me what to do if a dead body shows up when you're in command. I still can't believe Kramer's sweet niece Janice is the culprit."

"Me neither, which is why I'm calling." I took a deep breath. "Between you, me and the telephone, Russell, I think Janice is innocent. I think the condo association wants her arrested merely to get the murder off the front page."

Russell was silent for a while. When he spoke again, his voice was so low it was almost a whisper. "That puts me in kind of a tough position, Bubbles. See, as Chief Safety Engineer, or rather, former Chief Safety Engineer, I'm obligated to keep details of the crime scene confidential until they are made public in a court of law."

"But?" I said, egging him on.

"*But* . . . can we go off the record?"

Cripes. I hate that question. I'm too much of a softy to say no. "Sure, what the hay."

"Well, Bubbles, I've been deeply disturbed by the condo association's preoccupation with one minor aspect of that night."

"Which is?"

Russell paused again. I crossed my fingers and hoped his thirst for revenge against the association, which apparently had sacked Russell first and asked questions later, was strong enough for him to break the Chief Safety Engineer's unwritten code of silence.

"Whoever drove that Rolls out of our gate that night knew Kramer's four-digit access code. According to our computer records, it was inputted shortly after two a.m."

An access code? Geesh, the residents of the Final Frontier must think they're living at the Pentagon. "What's an access code, Russell?"

"Each association member possesses an individual code which he is required to input at the gate if he comes or goes between the hours of ten p.m. and five a.m. It's an extra security measure."

"And you have to punch in that code when you're leaving?"

"It's to prevent incidents like this—a stolen car."

"And a murder, Russell."

"How could I forget?" He sighed. "Whoever killed Elwood Kramer killed my career, too."

There was a crisis in progress when I arrived at Regina's and I knew that if I didn't act quickly I'd still be two-toned tomorrow.

A glum, middle-aged woman with frizzy brown hair sat in the third chair on the left. Her shoulders were stooped, her skin was sallow and her eyelashes were scrawny. A hairdresser, whom I assumed was Regina, was opening pages from various stylist magazines and pointing cheerfully to pictures of celebrities. The woman shook her head. She didn't want the gap-toothed sexy look of Madonna or the perky perm of Meg Ryan.

"I want me," she moaned. "I want me twenty years ago when I knocked Harold's socks off."

The two other hairdressers bent their heads and tried to appear insignificant as they tended to their own clients. No one wanted to get roped into this mess.

Cautiously, I stepped to the cash register. Regina placed the styling magazine on the counter and approached me efficiently. She was a pretty woman, about my age. Tall with hennaed hair wrapped in a French twist. She had a full plate back home, I could tell. Probably kids in daycare and a husband who groused about how she should be spending more time in the kitchen and less in the shop.

"You're my nine-thirty, aren't you?" she said, running a chewed pencil down the columns of her book. "I'm sorry, but we may have to reschedule. There's been a backup."

"I understand perfectly." I opened my wallet and flashed my beautician's license. "Bubbles Yablonsky. House of Beauty, Lehigh, Pennsylvania. What seems to be the problem?"

Regina closed the appointment book. "I'm beside myself. I've suggested everything from a perm to a color change. She won't settle on anything."

I sized up Regina's client, who leaned against her right hand, studying her reflection with total loathing. "Sexual disorder?"

"Husband told her this morning she was a fat frump," Regina whispered. "Said the cleaning woman in his office was more of a turn-on."

"Maybe she is."

"The cleaning woman moonlights as the bearded lady during summer carnival."

I winced. "Kids?"

"Three."

"Married for how long?"

"Fifteen years. Husband sells insurance."

I had handled tough cases like this before. And in my experience, there was only one solution.

"Foil," I announced. "Heavier around the face, lighter in the back."

Regina tapped her chin thoughtfully. "Not the cap?"

"Too painful. In her delicate condition it might be traumatic."

Regina glanced at her watch. "I'm afraid I don't have time for foil. I've blown forty-five minutes as it is."

"I'll do it," I offered, "on the condition that you handle my roots after I'm done. I can whip up the mix blindfolded. Sunshine Blonde Number Eight with a touch of drabber."

"It's a deal," Regina stuck out her hand, "and welcome to Regina's, Bubbles . . . what was it?"

"Yablonsky," I said. "Only too glad to help."

An hour and a half later, I was blowing dry the lightened hair of Regina's depressed client Lois Dizelhaus—or rather, Mrs. Harold Dizelhaus, as Mama would say.

Lois Dizelhaus was much improved from her earlier sorry sight. I had cut her hair in a shag with extra layers in front to make the most of her brilliant green eyes. I had applied auburn highlights around her face to lift the color of her skin.

I had even whipped up a honey protein mask from ingredients in Regina's minirefrigerator. It turned her skin smooth and tight. Afterward, while waiting for the color on my own roots to take hold, I plucked Lois's eyebrows, lined her eyes in forest green powder using a tiny angled brush, and laid a rich coat of Max Factor brown onto her lashes.

When I finished, Lois Dizelhaus was dazzling. All focus went from her nondescript body to her mesmerizing emerald eyes and beautiful complexion. She vowed to go on a high-protein diet with lots of fruit and vegetables combined with a walking regimen of two miles a day for starters. In the meantime, I advised staying clear of unflattering jeans and switching to black skirts, taking advantage of Lycra's modern wonders found in tummy-control panty hose and push-up bras.

As for sex, I explained there was nothing wrong with wearing silky, dark lingerie that emphasized her two God-given assets. However, I suggested she force Harold to wait a few days—or at least until he brought home flowers and dinner.

"Thank you, Bubbles," Lois gushed, clasping my hands, "can I make an appointment to have you do the trim next month?"

"No can do, Mrs. Dizelhaus." I told her how I was actually a Lehigh hairdresser-slash-reporter in town on assignment searching for Janice Kramer and, on the side, investigating what happened with the Hochstetter boys.

"The Hochstetter boys!" Lois exclaimed as Regina washed out my color. "Their mother, Anna, used to clean my house. I ran into her last week and asked her to do an emergency floor scrub, but she begged off. Said there was real trouble at home. The boys' arrest in Lehigh must have been what she was referring to."

Regina sat me up and wrapped my head in a towel. "Doesn't Anna Hochstetter sell baked goods down at Hecht's Market?" Regina asked.

Lois snapped her fingers. "That's right. I bet she's there today. She opens her stall Thursday and Friday for a few hours. On Saturday she sells quilts and Amish knickknacks on the lawn outside her home."

Regina walked me over to her chair and began the comb out. Lois followed. My roots had blonded perfectly. People would suspect nothing.

"Is there a Mr. Hochstetter?" I asked.

"Dead," Lois said. "Threshing accident years ago. But

if you get over to Hecht's Market around lunchtime you'll find Anna. She might even stay open until two, considering the Pickle Fest is in town. Any help you can give her, I'm sure she'll appreciate. Last time I saw her she was near tears."

Regina's Face Mask

Spread thinly, this face mask moisturizes by providing natural oils and skin softeners. The recipe below makes enough for one application.

1 tablespoon honey
½ tablespoon cider vinegar
½ tablespoon bee pollen
½ teaspoon wheat germ oil or glycerine
1 egg white at room temperature

Combine the honey, pollen and vinegar. Mix well until the honey softens. Add the remaining ingredients and smooth over the face. Leave on until dry, then rinse thoroughly.

Chapter 17

On my way over to Hecht's Market, I hooked a right into M&M Gas and Garage. I couldn't eat another Tastykake if I were force-fed, but it bugged me that I hadn't been able to interview Wolf Mueller. He had to show up for work sometime, right?

"What? You again?" Nimrod exclaimed. "If you like it here so much, you should move upstairs. Mac's got another room. Still haven't got that muffler fixed, I hear."

"Don't have the time," I said, grabbing an A-Treat from the cooler. "Haven't met any mechanics in this town." I plunked the A-Treat on the counter along with a packet of Dentyne. "Hint, hint."

Nimrod didn't get the hint.

"Speaking of which," I said, leading Nimrod on like a donkey, "is Wolf in?"

"Nope." He shook his head and scanned the Dentyne repeatedly. *Beep. Beep. Beep.* Would've been faster to type in the bar code. Would've been faster to write the price down by hand in a ledger. "He's off. Family tragedy."

I did not like the sound of that. "What kind of family tragedy?"

"His pop. Old man kicked the bucket."

I examined my manicure, the nervous habit I slip into during times of high stress. I could do with a cuticle soak and a buff.

"His dad died?" I said, hoping Nimrod didn't notice the slight quiver in my voice. "When?"

"Last night." Nimrod stopped his incessant dragging of the Dentyne over the scanner and lowered his voice. "Freakiest thing. Wolf came home from a party, you know? Around two a.m. and found his dad on the couch with all this junk stuffed down his throat."

I thought of Wolf Mueller Sr. under his crocheted blanket passed out. Had I been the last person to see him alive? "What do you mean by junk stuffed down his throat?"

"Promise not to tell, 'cause Wolf told me not to say."

I crossed my chest. "Swear."

"Shoofly pie." Nimrod threw up his hands like he was at a tent revival. "I swear to God."

I tapped my nail on the Dentyne packet. "Shoofly pie, huh?"

"Isn't that the *wildest*?" Nimrod handed me the finally scanned Dentyne. "I mean, what a way to enter eternity. Choking on shoofly pie. Man, that's not how I wanna go. When I'm sliding off this human plane, I want me a doobie—"

The office door burst open. Mac appeared looking not at all friendly and helpful, as he had the day before. "What's all the racket? I'm trying to do business here."

"Sorry about Wolf's dad," I said quickly.

Mac shoved his hands in his pockets. "Yeah. It was sudden. I'm gonna be down a mechanic one week." He nodded in my direction. "You back for more Tastykakes?"

I smiled weakly. "Actually, I kinda wanted to talk to Wolf."

"Out of the question," Mac said. "Should never have

suggested you go over there to begin with. His dad called me up yesterday and read me the riot act about you. Cursed me for sending a pushy reporter his way. My fault."

His eyes shifted.

"That's two forty-five," Nimrod said.

"Oh, right." I turned and counted out exact change, for safety's sake.

Mac returned to his office and closed the door. "Wow. What's up with the boss?" I asked.

Nimrod plunked the change into the drawer. "Who knows? He's uptight. Course it might have something to do with you spreading rumors around town that M&M's ripping people off."

I brought my hand to my chest. "Me?"

"Absolutely. That Snyder chick. She called the Better Business Bureau on us. She claimed you told her she was a victim of a scam because Wolf worked on the Electra for three years. Now she wants all her money back. Car, too."

"Well, she did come in for a broken fan belt and—"

"Broken fan belt! Are you for real? That car couldn't run. It was a rusted heap." Nimrod shook his head as though I were a total moron. "Wolf worked on that Electra in his spare time, bought parts with his own money and fixed it up until it shined simply because of his deep appreciation for classic cars. He probably put twelve thousand dollars of labor in it alone."

And Marian had paid $3,600.

"Gosh, I didn't know," I said. "I'm so—"

"Nah, I'm kidding you." Nimrod leaned toward me and winked. "Wolf was ripping her off royally. Other old ladies, too. Man, he should get busted."

Where was Stiletto when I needed him? Who else could I call to share the news, anxiety, fear, whatever, about the death of Wolf Mueller Sr.? No one. Our fingerprints were all over that house. And what if the Whoopee police investigated Old Man Mueller's untimely passing as a murder by molasses?

And it was a murder, oh yes, I thought as I gripped the wheel and roared toward Hecht's Market. Mueller was down for the count when I tucked him in. Shoofly pie was not on his agenda.

No, that agenda belonged to none other than Omer Best, aka Dutch. I had pooh-poohed Nimrod's dramatic assertions that Dutch was the all-knowing, all-powerful landlord who'd stop at nothing in his quest for acreage. Just because Omer talked, dressed and ate like a bumpkin didn't mean he was one. Omer was the type to squash anyone in his way.

Omer had said last night he was waiting for the price on Mueller's property to go down. With Old Man Mueller out of the way, there was a better chance of Omer getting his wish, I'd bet. And what about all that shoofly pie Omer's mother baked? Three times in twenty-four hours I had seen or heard him with shoofly pie.

And now this. Old Man Mueller's asphyxiation by . . . oh, it was too awful to imagine.

I shuddered at the idea of some goon stuffing heaps of baked molasses and Karo syrup down *my* throat. I'd heard of Colombian neckties, the signature throat slitting performed by hit men of various South American drug cartels. This, I'd decided, was the local equivalent. A Dutch gag.

More than ever I had to find Janice and convince her to talk to the police. If she were running away from Omer Best or a tough gang like the Pagans, then she needed the kind of protection and shelter only professional law enforcement could provide. She needed Whoopee's finest.

Anna Hochstetter was my last and now, only, hope. I parked the Camaro in Hecht's lot and applied a new coat of Ruby Rhumba to my lips using the rearview. There. In the mirror I was calm and composed, even if I didn't feel it inside. That's half the battle right there.

Hecht's Market was a low brick building off the Lincoln Highway with live animals out back—including crates of chickens, rabbits and goats—and buses of tourists out front.

I grabbed a brochure near the door and located Hochstetter's Baked Goods in Area 10, Stall 3 near the back of the store. I needed a helmet and pads to rush my way through the slew of old ladies waddling down the aisles with all the urgency of dazed pigeons.

Inside, Hecht's was a glorious feast of warm, spicy aromas. For a while I forgot all my troubles as I drifted over to Bruggels Flowers to inhale the late-summer bouquets of yellow daisies, orange marigolds and purple mums.

My stomach rumbled as I passed delicatessens offering gigantic pastrami sandwiches on thick kaiser rolls. Sausage. Kielbasa. Liverwurst. Lebanon bologna was displayed in fresh white paper under the glass counter next to my least favorite foods—scrapple and head cheese.

Since it was the end of August, the vegetable stands were full to bursting with spinach; Swiss chard; new white potatoes; zucchini; yellow squash; tomatoes; lettuce; giant garlic; red onions; huge, crisp orange carrots and an endless array of sweet, fragrant melons.

Amish gift items were everywhere. Women's sensible calico bonnets, men's straw hats, aprons, patchwork quilts and even furniture painted in that classic Pennsylvania dark turquoise-green.

It took all the willpower I could muster to resist the bakery stands lined with fresh white bread and rolls, chocolate cake, blueberry and apple pies and fat sticky buns oozing with cinnamon syrup and nuts and . . .

Shoofly pie. Aaaaggh! I left quickly, turning my attention to finding Anna Hochstetter.

Anna was packing up when I spied her tiny stall at the rear of the market. She was a large woman in her late thirties wearing a black dress with a black apron. Her thick brown hair was wrapped into a loose bun under her white cap. A pair of wire-rimmed glasses was perched on her nose and her entire body gave the impression of being dimpled. There were dimples in the folds of flesh gathered at her elbows, dimples in her fluffy pink cheeks and dimples over each knuckle.

I was making my way toward her when I stopped still. There, a few feet in front of me, was a tall woman with a horribly dyed blond beehive (not enough drabber in the color—too red). She was wearing a ridiculous yellow tube top that was stretched over her navel and almost up to her chin. (That is not how we wear tube tops. They're supposed to bunch around the bosom.) On top of that she was wearing teeny weeny white hot pants and black high-heeled sandals.

It was me! Or, at least, someone trying to look like me.

I gawked as she teetered over to Anna, falling slightly against a tourist and then a pushcart of dolls. She righted herself and finally reached Anna's stall, collapsing onto a stool in exhaustion.

They spoke animatedly and Anna threw her arms around my twin. Then Anna began crying and suddenly I knew exactly who was impersonating me. That stretched tube top. That shaky walk. This woman wasn't used to heels. She was too inexperienced for the midriff challenge.

"Janice!" I screamed, waving my hand. "Oh, my God. I found you."

She whipped her head around and I saw that the lipstick was all wrong. Don't go inventing lips under your nose, girl. And that mascara. Navy blue eyeliner with yellow? I don't think so.

Oddly enough, Janice didn't stick around for my fashion analysis. She turned and headed into the crowd, click, click, stumble, tripping along the way.

I caught up with her in no time. It takes years and years to learn how to run in heels. Amateurs shouldn't attempt it.

With one firm hand on her bare shoulder, I grabbed her. Janice turned, her body shaking. I pushed her behind a stack of pickle barrels.

"Oh, Bubbles," she sighed. "You shouldn't have found me. Now you'll be in danger, too."

"Janice," I said, stifling a yelp of glee upon finding my long-lost friend, "what is this all about?"

She glanced warily over my shoulder. "It's such a long story and I'm nervous about being out in public." Tears formed at the corners of her eyes. Washable mascara. Poor choice given the circumstances. A more versed makeup artist would know such things.

"Give it to me fast. Why are you on the lam?"

"Two weeks ago I was called to work on the Hochstetter case. You know that, right?"

I nodded.

"The boys were scared to death at being returned to Whoopee, which the Lehigh Police Department was ready to do the night they picked them up on Seventy-eight. But the boys wouldn't tell me why. They refused to talk. They said only that their mother would be in hot water if they screwed up and their lives would be ruined if they went home.

"I'm telling you, Bubbles, they wouldn't eat. They wouldn't sleep. That's why the department called me in. The detectives thought it might be some *Amish* thing. I told them, it's no Amish thing. These boys are petrified. They're being bullied."

Janice was clutching a white handkerchief, wringing it in her hands.

"So I started making phone calls demanding to know what was going on. I must've talked to most of the people here in Whoopee. Finally, that mechanic Wolf, whom I know you've been tracking—"

"How'd you—"

She put a finger to her lips. "I don't have much time, Bubbles. I'm only telling you this so you'll get out and go back to Lehigh—for your own good. Anyway, Wolf told me in no uncertain terms to cut it out with the questions, that there was a . . . a higher authority . . . who wanted me to drop it. And if I didn't . . ."

Her two hands clutched her throat and made a choking sound.

"Who?" I asked. "A Pagan?" Maybe now I could meet this rough and tough motorcycle gang who did unspeakable acts with prissy girls.

"A Pagan?" Janice cocked her head. "The Hochstetter twins aren't into Satanic stuff, Bubbles. They're decent boys."

I waved her on. "So who do you think is the so-called higher authority?"

"I'm not sure. That's why, when I learned about Uncle Elwood's death, I ran away from my family. I wanted this creep, whoever it is, to know that my family was innocent. To stay away from them."

"And, of all places, I find you at Hecht's Market. Why'd you risk coming here?"

"Anna Hochstetter doesn't have a phone and she was the one person I hadn't spoken with. A few minutes ago I told her the boys were alright and asked if she had any idea who the kingpin was. And moreover, what he was the kingpin of. That still isn't clear."

"And," I said, "what did Anna say?"

"I never heard. You showed up and I ran."

"Janice," I was almost breathless, "you've got to go to the police. They're getting ready to bust you for murder."

Her eyes closed and her lips whispered a prayer. "I know that, Bubbles. But I don't want to go to jail for something I didn't do. And I was driving down to Whoopee when Uncle Elwood was killed. Where's my alibi?"

My mind was racing. What had Russell said? That whoever left with Elwood's Rolls had punched in the code at two A.M.?

"Where were you at two a.m. that next morning?"

Janice started to tear up again. I wished she wouldn't do that. Mascara was streaming everywhere. "In the kitchen with my mother and sisters, crying and laughing for joy."

I quickly told Janice about what Russell had said.

"The police must've taken a statement from him, Janice." I smoothed back her brittle, over-bleached locks. "Trust me and go to them."

She let out a sob and blew her nose.

"And then you'll have to call Mickey," I added softly.

"Oh, Mickey," she wailed. "What have I done to Mickey?"

"You want me to drive you to the police station myself?"

She sniffled a bit and nodded.

"There you are! Yoo-hoo, Bub-bles. I saw your Camaro from the bus!"

Mama poked me with her umbrella. Oh, no. She was back from Hershey park and wearing a pink seersucker muumuu. Sure, on Jackie Kennedy a muumuu on the beach of Hyannisport had been fecund and feminine. On Mama it looked like she was off to a junk-food free-for-all at the trailer park.

"And who's this? Why, she's dressed just like you, Bubbles."

Could Mama's voice have been any louder?

"Is this little Janice Kramer? Mickey's Janice? My, you're so—"

It was too much for Janice. She got that deer in the headlights gaze she used to get when I prattled on about sex with Ken the RadioShack clerk, pushed me aside, slipped off those dratted high heels and disappeared into the crowd.

Mama and I stared mutely as she became one with the white-hairs. Anna Hochstetter must have packed up and left while Janice and I were talking. Her stall was empty now.

"Thanks, Mama," I grumbled. "I almost had Janice at the police station."

"Came just in time then." Mama put down her silver-and-brown Hershey's shopping bag. "They'd have arrested her in that getup. They've got decency laws here, you know. Where'd she get those clothes, anyway?"

That was a good question. Where *did* Janice get those clothes? I thought they were pretty darn spiffy, myself.

Chapter 18

Later that evening, after supper, Katie unfolded a large wooden rack over which was stretched a white-and-blue patchwork quilt.

"That's lovely," I said, examining the various blue-patterned triangles. "Why don't you put it on a bed?"

"Oh, Sally." Katie laughed. "What a sense of humor you have. Of course it's not done. C'mon. Help us work on it."

Me, sew? I, who taped hems and Krazy-Glued rips in coats?

Thrilled with the project, Katie, her sisters and cousins carried the frame out to the lawn and brought out chairs. Soon their fingers were busy with threaded needles that they carefully, lovingly slid in and out with teeny tiny stitches as they chattered like the robins twittering their evening songs on the branches nearby.

"What're you waiting for, Sally?" Katie called. "Not like you haven't quilted before." She patted the seat next to her.

"We don't do much quilting in Ohio," I explained, as Katie handed me a needle. "At least, not with thread."

"No thread?" asked Katie, bent over and sewing. "How do you do it then?"

My fingers awkwardly stuck and pulled the needle in and out of the cloth. I made one big stitch. "With staples. We find it goes much faster."

"Ahh." Katie nodded. "We'll have to try that. But staples . . . isn't that . . . uncomfortable? What if a staple comes loose in the middle of the night?"

My stitches weren't too bad. This was actually fun! I crossed my legs and proceeded to embellish the lie. "Doesn't happen with a quilting stapler. Don't you have those here? You can buy them at Jo-Ann Fabrics in Ohio."

"Rebecca," Katie called to her cousin sitting across the quilt, "have you ever seen a quilting stapler at Jo-Ann Fabrics?"

"No," Rebecca said. "We don't have that shimmery gold nail-fungus medicine either. And is it hard quilting with your nails so long like that, Sally?"

I stopped sewing and examined my nails. I had forgotten to remove the polish after my evening at the disco. "If only I could trim them. But the doctor won't let me."

"Poor Sally," clucked Katie. "Funny, those doctors in Ohio."

Throughout this conversation, I had been keeping my eye on Jake, who had missed supper again. Twice he had crossed the field near us. Once carrying a doggy bag of dinner Katie had made for him and then a bucket of water.

"What's Jake up to?" I asked.

"Who knows?" Katie said. "This is what he's like every time he gets a new car. As soon as the day is done and all his chores are finished, he locks himself up in the garage, banging and hammering away."

"How many cars does he have?"

"Besides the one he's working on, none. For Jake the fun is fixing them up and repairing them. Then he sells them at auction and makes a buck. With the auction starting tomorrow, he's working extra hard. We aren't to disturb him."

Hmmm.

"I forgot," I said, putting down the needle. "I haven't checked for messages at the phone shack."

"Who're you expecting a call from, Sally?" Rebecca asked.

"My doctor. Maybe he'll give me the green light to cut these nails, finally."

"Wouldn't *that* be a relief," exclaimed Katie.

The telephone shack was a mile down the road and shared by five Amish families. Like the seventy amps of electricity that coursed through the Stoltzes' electric fence and into their welding equipment, the phone shack was, as far as I could see, a loophole in the Amish prohibition against using electricity. The belief behind that ban was that Amish were not supposed to "yoke" themselves to nonbelievers by tapping into a central power source.

However, this being the twenty-first century and Amish cabinetry being more valuable than gold, many Amish families found that having a phone nearby was handy for business and emergencies. It was fine to accept incoming calls. Making outgoing calls was discouraged, but tolerated if someone needed to dial 911.

Which might explain why I found a woman waiting in the phone shack when I arrived.

"May I use the phone?" I asked politely.

"I'm expecting a call," she said, darning a sock. "They usually call around suppertime."

"Who?"

"Those people who ask for me, Hedda Hossel."

Hedda Hossel? The name rang a bell. "What do they want?"

"Mostly they want to know if I'm satisfied with my long

distance carrier." Hedda tore off a thread with her teeth. "Sometimes it's if I'm interested in reducing my annual Mastercard fees."

I choked back a scoff. "Those are telemarketers. They call everyone around dinnertime. My mother pretends to be from Turkey and gabs gibberish into the phone when they do."

"Hmm. I don't think so. They usually ask for me alone. They say, 'Is this Hedda Hossel?' "

Ding! Now I knew why her name rang a bell. "I think they're asking for the head of the household."

Hedda thought about this. "Okay. You can use the phone," she said, pulling herself up. "But if they ask for Hedda, tell 'em to call back tomorrow."

First on my list of calls to make was Jane. I rang home and prayed that her spry and lively voice would answer right away.

Dan picked up on the first ring. "You got her?"

"Jane?" There was a flutter in my chest. "No, I don't have her. Where is she?"

"Hell if I know. There was a message on the answering machine when I got home from work saying she was heading down to Lancaster County to meet up with you."

"With G?"

"Can't think of how else she'd make it there. I assume G's driving since he has the Rabbit."

I kicked the grass with my heel. This situation did not sound good. It meant that Jane was skipping the first week of school. It meant that she wasn't filling out her college applications or boning up for the next Advanced Placement Exams. It meant that Jane was running away and that she was sleeping overnight with G—which meant that she was *having sex*.

The ultimate parental crisis had arrived.

"You have to contact G's parents," I said. "They should be brought in on this."

"Done it. G's dad is one of my clients."

"At Legal Aid?" My voice was now at an hysterical pitch.

"Sure. A little breaking and entering. Nothing big. Bottom line, he has no idea where his son is. He's not exactly Mr. Cleaver, you know, Bubbles. I'd be stunned if he remembered the kid's birthday. And the mother? Strung out in California."

That did it. "I'm coming home."

"Don't do that. Jane's on her way to you. What would happen if she drove down there and found out you had left?"

Dan had a point. I made him swear up and down to call Mama as soon as he heard anything. He swore.

"When you find her, I'm going back to my house, to Wendy," he said. "That is, if Jane's not coming back here."

"Fine, Dan. And when you get back to your house, would you mind looking up a word for me in your law books? You know, the ones I bought you a decade ago using my waitressing money? I need a legal definition."

He snorted. "*You?* What words do you need defined? Bad haircut?"

"Forgery. As in, I forged my wife's signature to a few student loan applications. I believe, although I'm not sure, that the penalty for that is serious jail time and, oh, could you check to see how a forgery conviction affects a law license?"

There was a pause. A delicious, nervous pause.

"Sure. I'll look that up for you," he said efficiently.

"Remember. It's forgery. Begins with an F as in I am fu—"

But he had hung up.

Quickly I dialed Sandy's home phone. It rang and rang. Shoot. Thursday night was Sandy and Martin's Spanish macramé class. When the machine clicked on I left a message about Jane driving off with G and Dan being no help. I asked Sandy to call me at Mama's pickle time-share number.

Next I dialed Mama. Genevieve answered with a gruff, "Eight, four, six, one."

"Eight, four, six, one?" I asked, puzzled. "What's that?"

"Is that you, Sally? See, we were taught in militia training camp never to answer the phone with either the complete phone number or a name. Just the last four digits, in case it's a stalker. Your mother's out buying supplies for watermelon pickles. She's making Aunt Fritz's recipe. What's up?"

I shook my head. Genevieve was an acquired taste. I told her about Jane's message.

"Yeah, yeah. The juvenile contacted us shortly after seventeen-hundred this evening. ETA in two hours. Why don't we plan on reconnoitering at oh-eight-hundred tomorrow?"

I hung up, surprised to find myself calmed by Genevieve's militaristic style.

Mr. Salvo's answering machine picked up right away, which meant he was on the other line. So I made the phone call I'd been dreading—to Mickey. The last time I spoke with Mickey, he'd been so depressed he could barely hold up his end of the conversation. I was curious to learn if Janice had finally contacted him and if he could go on living.

"Sinkler, here!" There was a grunt, grunt on the other end.

"Mickey? Is that you?"

"Hey, babe. Nice of you to ring. Let me finish this last rep." There was more grunting and then the *clang!* of a barbell hitting the floor. Wait—had he just called me babe?

"Are you lifting weights, Mickey?"

There was a loud slurp. "Ahh. These protein shakes

aren't bad. Yep. I'm up to fifty pounds each arm, twenty reps apiece. My muscles are torn flesh. But no pain, no gain, that's what they say, babe."

"What *who* says?"

"The authors of this book I'm reading called, *Get up off the Couch You Lazy Sack and Find Your Inner Spear.*"

I smacked my head with the receiver. In the wake of public humiliation and loss, Mickey Sinkler had gone macho. "Are you on drugs? Steroids, Mickey?"

"Don't need 'em. Got more testosterone in my loins than a charging bull at Pamplona."

I supposed that line was from the book, too. I had to change the subject before my stomach turned. "I guess you haven't heard from Janice yet, say?"

"Who?"

"Janice Kramer? The woman who—"

"Oh, her. The Amish dame." More slurping. "Yeah, she buzzed this afternoon from the Whoopee police station. Thanks for that, by the way. Good to know she's on the right side of the law again."

"Really? Janice went to the police?" This was *great* news. "They're not going to arrest her for murder?"

"Unlikely. She's been advised not to leave the area, but Frye told me on the Q.T. that her alibi's solid and she lacks motive and opportunity. She's clear. But as far as us becoming bride and groom, that's a no go."

"I'm sorry, Mickey."

"Ahh, would've been a big mistake." He yawned as though this were all water under the bridge. "You know, I've been thinking about what you and I were talking about yesterday, about Janice claiming there was some *he* out to get her. I told you she never had a boyfriend before me. But after you hung up I remembered this one jerk, a friend of the family—so she claimed—who showed up one Saturday to look at Elwood's new Rolls.

Guy was a classic-car freak. Couldn't be bothered to say hello to me, just kept studying the car."

I brushed a cobweb from the corner of the shack. "What was his name?"

"Been racking my brains. Can't recall. But he wasn't Amish, 'cause he drove. Looked Amish, though. Tall guy."

"Hey. Maybe he's the real murderer. We should investigate him, say Mickey?"

"Not me, babe. I'm going to the beach. I got women to see, sex to enjoy. I'm busting out."

"What about your kids?"

"Still with my mother. Payback for all the times I mowed her lawn, did her taxes and cleaned her gutters. She owes me."

She sure did. I thought about the years of Mickey's dutiful obedience to his mother, how she made him take her grocery shopping and wait while she tried on pair after pair of orthopedic shoes at Orr's Department Store. Yes, Mrs. Sinkler definitely owed her son a few favors—a few favors the old wimpy Mickey never would have dared to cash in.

"And this weekend my ex is coming in. I called Sue in Duluth and told her to pack her bags, catch the Greyhound to Lehigh and be maternal for once in her life."

I gulped. Like his mother, Sue had walked all over Mickey during their marriage. He had been her personal doormat, a quivering mass of jelly in her domineering presence. Not now, though.

"How'd she take it?"

"I spoke; she obeyed." Mickey started grunting again. "What's to take?"

After Mickey, Genevieve and Dan, the macho triplets, talking with Mr. Salvo was a breath of fresh air. He was obviously eager to hear from me, and when I told him about finding Janice and what Mickey had said about her being absolved, he was positively giddy.

"That's a scoop, Bubbles!" There was a pound on the desk.

"I thought Dix Notch didn't want to do an article about Elwood's death being a murder."

"Have no choice. The *Call* broke the story in their Tuesday morning edition and Notch got summoned upstairs. Publisher let him have it. Now, two days later, he's been scrambling to find some new angle the *Call* doesn't have. You've got an exclusive, Bubbles."

I told him everything Janice had said. Mr. Salvo promised me a double-byline on the story with Lawless, who would write up my information and add an update from the Lehigh police.

Afterward, Mr. Salvo and I decided to keep the Hochstetter case out of the newspaper—for now. "So, there is a deeper story there after all," Mr. Salvo said. "You gonna stay in Whoopee and try to find who the kingpin is and what's going on?"

"Thought I might. Also, I have to help out my hosts." I filled him in about Dutch, his plans for an Amish theme park and how I suspected him of trying to manipulate the Stoltzes into selling their farm so he could include their land in his development.

"A residential community with a theme park. It's a miracle it hasn't been built before," Mr. Salvo said. "You might just have a super write-up there, Bubbles. Especially if you can prove that this Dutch fellow sought favor with the Amish merely to bilk them of their land. Don't forget to check the land records."

"I won't, Mr. Salvo," I said, smiling. Mr. Salvo worshiped land records.

"And remember, Bubbles. Whatever happens, if someone tries to run you over again, or you get beaten up in an alley or threatened with murder and shot at, keep in mind one thing."

"What's that, Mr. Salvo?"

"Take notes."

Ah, newspaper editors, I thought, as I left the phone shack. Were they animals or humans? Tough to tell the difference sometimes.

The sun had all but set over the green cornfield. Streaks of red and purple shot up from the horizon against which Jake's garage stood out like a black fortress. It was an intimidating structure. Huge. Impenetrable.

Large enough to hold a $360,000 Rolls-Royce Corniche?

I was about to find out.

Chapter 19

It was pitch-black by the time I reached Jacob Stoltz's hangar of a garage, a barnlike aluminum structure that would've given me a fit in a lightning storm. There were no windows, but there was a glimmer of light under the door and evidence that Jake was inside, working.

I put my ear to one wall and listened to the movements within. Along with the *bang, bang, bang* of a hammer, a transistor radio broadcasted the pop-fly-foul hum of a Phillies game. Jake paused his hammer at the bulletin of a possible home run or a double play that the announcer described as bee-u-ti-ful.

But it was the other sound that had me puzzled. Water splashing. And it wasn't coming from inside, either.

I reached into my pocket to search for a weapon and found only a rag, an apple and the butter knife. Clutching the butter knife, I tiptoed around the garage, the grass wet with dew under my bare feet. I was about to turn the corner when I felt a hand slap over my mouth and an arm swing around my waist. It held me so firmly I couldn't kick or twist. The butter knife fell from my hand and a lump of panic filled my throat as I tried in vain to scream.

"You're making a mistake," a deep voice warned.

"Hey, what's going on?" A woman, her hair and body wrapped in towels, stepped into the light. "It's only Bubbles, Jake. Let her go."

The hand dropped and I clutched my waist, now throbbing in pain from the tight grip. "Janice?" I said, squinting at the figure.

"Bubbles?" Jake said.

"Actually, around this town, I'm known as Elspeth. She's okay, Jake. You can relax."

Jake walked over and put a protective arm around Janice's naked shoulders. She smiled up at him and I remembered what he had confided yesterday while checking out my muffler—that Janice had once been the freethinking Amish woman he had intended to marry. But I'd had the impression from that conversation that their relationship was now cold and dead.

"What're you doing with him—*here?*" I asked Janice.

"I was taking a bath and now I'm freezing. Let me put my clothes back on and we can talk in Jake's garage."

Five minutes later, I was sitting on the hood of a '57 Chevy Jake had been repairing, sipping coffee from a Thermos Katie had fixed for him. Janice was wearing a plain blue Amish dress, lying on an old couch with her wet hair turning a more and more garish blond as it dried. Perhaps it was the security of being tucked away in this garage or that she had spoken with the police, but Janice was now markedly calmer and happier than when I had run into her only hours before at Hecht's Market.

Jake, however, still seemed nervous at my discovery of their hideaway, no matter how Janice assured him that I wouldn't blab.

There was no Rolls-Royce Corniche, only Janice's old Ford Fiesta parked on the other side of the garage.

"To tell you the truth, I'm surprised you didn't figure

it out earlier," Janice said, biting into one of Katie's delicious Lebanon bologna and tomato sandwiches. "When Jake told me that he had revealed to you our prior relationship, I nearly went wild. I thought that would have tipped you off right away."

"I'm a hairdresser," I said. "Not a secret agent."

"But what about the tube top and shorts I was wearing? Didn't you recognize those?"

"Those are mine?" I said, alarmed. "Where did you get them?"

"From the bottom of your suitcase. Who else owns that kind of clothing? It provided the perfect disguise, although I apologize for rifling through your stuff."

"It's okay. But you would've looked better in pink. With that hair and all."

"What's wrong with my hair?" Janice pulled down a brittle, bleached strand and examined it.

"We'll talk later. First, I want to know how you and Jake hooked up."

Janice frowned at the strand of frizzed hair and pushed it away. "After I got word about Uncle Elwood, I panicked. I didn't want to stay home and put my family in jeopardy, but I didn't know where to go. Then I thought of the one person who was strong enough, in character and muscle, to protect me."

Jake sat on the edge of the couch and grasped Janice's hand with a steady firmness.

"Jake took me back in a blink," she said, shooting him a coy glance, for which he lifted her hand and kissed it gently.

That's when it struck me. Jake and Janice were still in love. Oh, it was so romantic. All those long years of Jake waiting patiently for the one true love of his life and Janice searching for herself and finding—I felt a sob clutch my throat—that everything she needed in the world was back home in little old Whoopee, PA.

"Elspeth was a damsel in distress," Jake said, blushing slightly. "What choice did I have but to take her back?"

Watching couples so in love made it hard to keep my mind on work and not on Stiletto. Jake and Janice's quiet intimacy, their unspoken words and meaningful looks, reminded me of the many summer evenings Stiletto and I once shared in his Jeep under the Hill to Hill Bridge in Lehigh.

Back then we'd make out until it was dark, Stiletto persistently pushing further and me fighting to keep on strategic items of clothing until we were sweaty with exasperation and lust. Afterward we'd watch the orange flames of the Lehigh Steel blast furnaces lick the night sky while Stiletto described a harrowing trek he took across the Andes Mountains to shoot the remains of a downed airplane. His stories were always so engrossing I didn't notice his fingers snaking up my thighs until it was too late and that darned chastity vow was once again in danger of being violated. Sigh.

For other folks in Lehigh the smell of burning coal and iron ore might be a drawback to living in a steel town. But for me those metallic odors will always bring back romantic memories of me and Stiletto, sex and summer nights under the Hill to Hill Bridge.

Janice's words roused me out of the daydream. "Could've turned me in to the police, Jake," she said, teasingly. "In the back of my mind I feared you would, Mr. Moral."

Jake bunched up a dirty rag and tossed it at her.

"I'm glad you went to the police, Janice," I said. "Mickey says you're free and clear."

"I won't be free and *safe* until they arrest Uncle Elwood's murderer. Ach. Poor Uncle Elwood," she said sadly. "He was the one family member who understood me. I'm going to miss him terribly."

"I'm sorry, Janice."

"I also feel guilty for leaving him. If I had come home Sunday night, maybe he'd still be alive."

"Or you'd be dead," I reminded her.

"That's why I'm still sleeping in Jake's garage. As much as I like the Whoopee police, I don't think they're any match for the kingpin the Hochstetter boys are scared of. And now with what happened to Uncle Elwood, I have to agree with them. This guy's frightening."

I put down my coffee on the hood. Jake promptly walked over and repositioned it on the floor. "Please, Bubbles. I spent three hours waxing this baby." He picked up a steering wheel and began to re-cover it with vinyl tape.

"Sorry, Jake. What else didn't you tell me about the Hochstetters, Janice? For instance, what background did the Lehigh detectives provide you on the case?"

Janice massaged her toes as she considered my question. "Not much. The boys were picked up around nine on their way back from New Jersey. They told the detectives that the joyride wasn't their fault, that a mysterious 'someone' in Whoopee had ordered them to take the car to New Brunswick, New Jersey, where they were to empty some cardboard boxes into a particular Dumpster."

"That's quite a distance for a trash run," Jake said.

"That's what the detectives thought, too, especially when the dogs picked up a trace scent of marijuana in the trunk."

"Marijuana!" I said. "They were transporting drugs across state lines? That's big time."

"Well, if they were transporting drugs, the boys didn't know it. I'm convinced of that. And they weren't charged with any drug-related crimes. You can't be arrested for possessing the smell of marijuana and the New Jersey police never found any of the boxes in that Dumpster."

"If they got the car from M&M, anyone could've put marijuana in it," I said, thinking of my pal Nimrod.

"The police interviewed Wolf Mueller, the mechanic at M&M. His take on it was that the boys snatched the keys to the Electra from the pegboard behind the cash register and took off. Unfortunately, the cops think that's the most reasonable explanation, too. Joyride, pure and simple."

"Okay. So let's say the Hochstetter boys are telling the truth. Why would they have agreed to drive up to New Jersey and dump the boxes in the Dumpster? Did they get paid?"

"No. And this is the part of the story where the Lehigh detectives and I butt heads." Janice sipped from a can of caffeine-free Coke. "The boys told me that the mystery man who ordered them to drive the car threatened to reveal their mother's so-called secret if they didn't do it. The cops think that's all hogwash."

"Secret?" I said, sliding off the hood. "What kind of secret could sweet and motherly Anna Hochstetter have?"

"That's what I'd hoped to find out at Hecht's today before a certain someone burst upon us, screaming my name." Janice cleared her throat and raised her eyebrow at me. "Anyway, whatever secret Anna Hochstetter's harboring, I'm sure it's not half as horrible as she and her sons believe. These people are pure innocents. Perfect prey for someone looking to take advantage of the Amish."

"Dutch," I said. "It has to be. Omer Best."

Janice nearly spit out her Coke. "Omer Best? That flat-footed mama's boy?"

"He might live with his mother, Janice, but he's no patsy."

Jake stopped wrapping the steering wheel and stared at me in puzzlement. I continued. "I met him in his office last night. Omer told me about his plans for building a theme park in the area and how he has a so-called way with the local Amish so that they don't mind selling him their land. You said Anna and her sons were perfect prey for someone looking to take advantage of the Amish. Well, Omer Best sure matches that description."

"You don't know Omer," Jake said thoughtfully. "He's practically a simpleton."

"A simpleton? Do you know how much land he owns? Plus, he runs the disco!" I held back from shouting what I was bursting to reveal, that Omer was poised to snooker Jake's own father. Clearly Jake wasn't ready to believe me.

"You don't have to be a genius to run a dance hall, Bubbles," Jake said. "And most of that land he inherited from his mother's side of the family. He's a good neighbor to us and an ally in my father's tussle with the conservation commission regarding the groundwater issue. But he's not a criminal. You've met him. Did he seem like a criminal to you?"

Darn. Human intuition. It always gets in the way. "No. Omer seemed more like a caricature from a Pennsylvania Dutch gift shop," I said, sighing, "although Nimrod down at M&M called Omer a feudal landlord."

"What does Nimrod Oggledorp know about feudalism?" Janice said. "If anyone put the pot in the Electra, he did. That is if he could bear to part with it."

I started to giggle. "His last name's Oggledorp? Nimrod Oggledorp? That's just cruel."

"You can say that again. His father walked off when he was three and his mother has all but abandoned him. Thank God for Mac, who gave him that room over the garage. I doubt the strapping Hochstetter boys would be afraid of Nimrod, though. One pow from their big farmhand fists and the only secret Nimrod would be hiding is his own cowardice."

So we were back to square one. Janice's hair had dried completely now. It was streaked various shades of blond and parts weren't colored at all.

"We have to do something about that hair, Janice," I said. "If you're gonna stay blond, you've got to learn that all of your hair has to be dyed, not just some of it."

"It'll have to do until Uncle Elwood's funeral tomorrow. He's going to be buried in the Whoopee Cemetery. You should come, Bubbles, since you found his body. Might provide you with closure."

Maybe I would. I'd stayed up for enough late-night movies to know that it's a rule all murderers must watch their victims descend into their graves. It would be very interesting if Omer Best showed up, hiding behind a headstone.

"I'll go Amish, as Sally Hansen," I said. "No one will recognize me. And I'll make an appointment for you at Regina's Saturday to have that hair taken care of by a professional, okay?"

"Great. Oh, and do you have a dress I can borrow?" Janice sat up. "Something simple, yet—"

"I've got the perfect thing," I said, excitedly. "Black with a bit of white around the—"

"Oh, brother," Jake said, opening the door to step outside. "Like I said, I knew Bubbles's coming here was a mistake."

But we barely heard him. We were too busy debating footwear and the art of strolling on stiletto heels.

The next morning was the first day of September, a Friday. It was also the first day of the auction and Pickle Fest, which would last through Labor Day. The Stoltzes were so excited about these two events that we all rushed through the morning's chores as quick as a wink. The entire family would be gone for most of the day since Ephraim was planning to display his hot-oiled cow that morning and Fannie was judging the sour pickles that evening.

I amazed myself by making breakfast for twenty—eggs fried in milk (an Amish specialty), oatmeal mush with honey and applesauce—as Fannie packed a huge picnic basket. Only after everyone left the table did I have a chance to taste my own cooking. Blech! The eggs were like rubber and the oatmeal was undercooked and lacked salt.

"This oatmeal was awful," I said to Katie, who was sweeping the floor.

"Was it?" said Katie. "Not to me. I just assumed that's the way you eat it in Ohio—raw. For healthy fiber."

I groaned. The Stoltzes must think I was the most useless Amish woman the good Lord had had the pity to put on Earth. I couldn't wash a cow, I couldn't quilt or trim beans half as fast as a child. I couldn't even make breakfast. What could I do?

The answer came to me when I visited the pickle time-share that morning. Thankfully, G's Rabbit was parked out front.

"Jane's here!" I exclaimed throwing open the front door.

"Well, well, well," Mama singsonged from the kitchen, where she was standing on a stool stirring a pot that smelled of sugar, cinnamon and cloves bubbling on the stove. "If it isn't Busty LaRue."

Genevieve snickered and whacked at a watermelon. From the looks of it, the two were brewing up another batch of Aunt Fritz's watermelon pickles for the festival—and some private joke about me.

"Who?" I asked, throwing my keys on the kitchen table. "Who's Busty LaRue?"

"And you here dressed so modest." Mama clucked her tongue. "When a mere few days ago there you were skipping over fields, waving a red bra, naked as a jaybird."

I covered my face with my hands. "How'd you find out about that?"

"How'd I find out about that?" Mama waved her wooden spoon so that sticky goo dripped onto the stove top. "The question is, why'd it take me so long. It was all over the TV news last night, says Genny."

"Ya. They've been playing and replaying the shot over and over again," Genevieve said, spooning out the watermelon's pink flesh. "They pasted one of them black rectangles over the juicy parts and the newscaster called you Lady Godiva. If it wasn't taxes, what were you protesting?"

"I wasn't protesting. I was saving Stiletto."

"Saving in what way, exactly?" Mama asked.

"Oh, let's skip it. It's over and done with now." I grabbed a cup and poured some coffee. "Where's Jane?"

"Sleeping. In my bedroom," said Mama. "And don't worry, Bubbles, G's in the car."

"Whew!" I took a big sip and felt much relieved.

"What's your concern?" asked Genevieve. "The juvenile's practically an adult."

"Sex, Genevieve. Since running away from home Tuesday she's spent at least two nights with G alone and I don't like it."

"Hey, I got news for you, Busty," piped up Mama. "What Jane and G can do at night, they can do in the day, too. You forget about twenty-four-hour sex because you've got a job and a kid to look after."

"Twenty-four-hour sex?" That was worse than sex between eleven and seven. "It had never occurred to me that Jane might be having *twenty-four-hour sex*."

"Who's having twenty-four-hour sex?" asked Jane sleepily, as she entered the kitchen.

Her cropped hair was now all lime and her eyes were black-rimmed from going to sleep without removing her makeup first. Tsk. Tsk. She was in her oversized Mensa T-shirt and pink slippers. I ran to her and wrapped her in a crushing hug, kissing her all over until she pushed me away.

"Now," I said, picking up Genevieve's knife, "I'm gonna kill you. What made you think you could run off on your father like that? And with G, too—"

"Bubbles!" Mama snapped. "Jane just woke up. Let her have a cup of coffee before you slit her throat."

"Fair enough," I said, putting down the knife. "Okay. Where'd you go with G? Hershey? The shore? The Poconos?"

"Gettysburg," Jane said, sliding into a plastic seat. "I've lived in Pennsylvania all my life and I'd never been to Gettysburg. It was awesome, looking out over that battlefield thinking of all those young men, cousins some of them, bleeding to death for a cause that had more to do with a burgeoning industrialized economy than the free will of the black man."

I handed her a cup of coffee. "Sometimes I can't figure you out."

"Ditto." She sipped the coffee and looked me up and down. "Hey, nice outfit. Grandma told me you'd taken to this *Little House on the Prairie* shtick, but I didn't believe it. How's it going at the Stoltzes?"

"Yeah," Genevieve said, "you helping out like I told you to? Nothing says thank you like the gift of elbow grease."

I sighed. "I've been trying to, but I keep screwing up. My best contribution so far has been scrubbing bottles for root beer."

"They're making root beer?" Jane asked excitedly. "Cool. We did that in science class once."

I popped a piece of watermelon in my mouth. "Fannie's recipe takes days. She steeps all these roots and lets it ferment. It's painstaking."

"Not the way we did it," said Jane, taking some watermelon, too. "The way we did it took thirty minutes. It was radical."

"You remember the recipe?" I asked, getting ideas. When the Stoltzes were at the Pickle Fest tonight, I could whip up a batch while they were gone. When they came home they'd find the root beer all bottled and ready to go.

"You need dry ice," said Jane.

"That's trouble," said Mama. "Dry ice and Bubbles. I'd hate to think."

"Never fear," Jane said. "I've got time to kill. G and I will pick up the ingredients and I'll write down the recipe and leave it for you here, Mom. The Stoltzes are gonna love it."

When she went upstairs to take a shower, I said to the old ladies, "I don't think she's having twenty-four-hour sex, do you?"

"Nah," said Genevieve. "Twenty-four-hour sex is one of those things that sounds like fun, but when you think about it, what could be worse?"

Mama and I gave each other looks.

I didn't want to fret any more about Jane having sex, so I filled them in about finding Janice and how Mickey had been transformed into Macho Man. Then I made the biggest mistake I had made so far during my stay in Whoopee.

"Pretty soon I'll be off to Elwood's funeral," I said casually, not thinking.

The world stopped spinning.

"Elwood's funeral?" Mama turned down the stove and stepped off the stool. "Why didn't you say so?"

Genevieve clasped her hands in prayer. "Alleluia."

Mama and Genevieve at Elwood's funeral! "No way."

"I'll wear the black veil," Mama said, puffing up her brunette Jackie O flip. "It'll lend an aura of sophistication."

"You brought funeral clothes to Amish country?" I asked, incredulous.

"Of course. You know a fisherman not to pack a rod and reel? You never can predict when they'll be biting."

"Who?"

"Widowers."

"Especially those of Elwood's social set." Genevieve rubbed her forefinger and thumb together. "I might take a cue from Sally here and go Amish. Could widen the field for me."

Mama slapped her cheek, rosy with anticipation of the upcoming soiree. "What if you get lucky, Genevieve? Then I'd have Fast Car and you could have—"

I stood up and stuck my fingers between my teeth, emitting a whistle so piercing that Mama's hearing aid buzzed. The two women quit yapping on the spot.

"No one but me is going to Elwood's funeral," I announced. "It is a solemn occasion and not a pick-up joint for elderly, sex-crazed ladies. And that's the final word."

Mama folded her arms. "Are you finished? 'Cause Genevieve and I have some strategy to map out."

"Right-oh. Strategy." Genevieve pushed aside the watermelon and grabbed a paper and pencil. "Okay, LuLu, you take the flank and I'll scope out the rear. I'll bring the binocs to spot the wedding rings."

An hour later I was headed toward Elwood's funeral in the Camaro with the roaring muffler, accompanied by the Widow Warriors, hand-drawn maps of the Whoopee Cemetery on their laps, binoculars around their necks.

And me here thinking I'd arrive inconspicuous.

Chapter 20

A long string of black buggies and hitched horses tied to posts lined the road next to the Whoopee Cemetery. In addition there were some spiffy Mercedeses and a few gold Lexuses that obviously belonged to Elwood's non-Amish friends from Lehigh. At the sight of them, Mama and Genevieve's spirits brightened considerably. They started spraying up a storm of Estée perfume and whipping out the coral lipstick.

I parked the Camaro behind a black buggy and laid down the ground rules. Mama and Genevieve were not to wave at me from across the grave or shout, "Hey, Bubbles, whatcha doing?" I had a professional assignment to complete and if they wanted a ride home, they had to meet me back at the Camaro at an appointed time.

"Thank God I brought these." Genevieve handed Mama and me tiny yellow walkie-talkies. "I got two sets at Costco. Cheap!"

"Handheld radios. I love them," Mama said. "Mary Alice brings 'em to bingo. What frequency?"

Frequency? What was Mama talking about? I stared at mine. Small. Brightly colored. So innocent—yet, by their very electronic nature—so devious.

"I don't know," I hemmed, my palms beginning to

sweat. "Can't we just arrange to meet the old-fashioned way?"

"Oh, get with the twenty-first century, Sally." Genevieve grabbed mine and fiddled with a dial on the side. "If it were up to you we'd still be using strings and Dixie cups for a telephone."

So? There was a problem with strings and Dixie cups, maybe?

"There. You're all set." Genevieve pointed to a black button on the front. "Press this and talk. All you need to do now is turn it on."

I turned it on and an eardrum piercing screech filled the car.

"Not now!" Genevieve snatched it. "You'll get feedback. Turn it on when we're at the cemetery."

There was a crowd of Amish in black at the far end of the cemetery which was bordered by a white-painted plank fence. Simple, uniform stone markers stuck out of the ground. They merely stated the names of the deceased—John, David, Sarah D., Reuben—and their dates of birth and death. There were no praying angels or Madonnas with outspread arms. No fading plastic flower arrangements or ornately carved granite headstones, our culture's last attempt to keep up with the Joneses.

Genevieve and Mama headed off to the right while I went left. I saw Janice standing under an oak tree wearing the black dress I'd left for her, a veil hiding her face and that blond mess on top of her head. She teetered a bit on the heels and caught her balance on a tree branch. Other than that she appeared in control.

I scanned the crowd for a sign of Omer, with no luck—yet. It was only a matter of time before he showed up and I could be as patient as a spider.

At least I thought I could—until the Amish crowd began a never-ending, monotonous German hymn.

A cool breeze blew through the cemetery, ruffling the white organdy caps of the women and sending a shower of leaves from trees nearby as the hymn went on and on. This day had a touch of fall. The sky was darkening with gray clouds. There was a hint of chill to come, of dying leaves and change.

A tall and trim man crossed the cemetery toward me in long, silent strides. As he got closer I recognized him as Fast Car Carmine, Elwood's neighbor at the Final Frontier and Mama's latest puppy-love crush. He was wearing a dark suit with a stylish gray-and-black silk tie.

I waved at him and he stared until he realized who I was.

"Bubbles? I would've passed right by you if you hadn't flagged me down."

"Part of my cover as a reporter. If anyone asks, my name is Sally Hansen."

"Gotcha. Too bad I'm late," he said in a low voice. "Would've liked to have been there for the funeral back at the house. At least I made it to the burial."

"With your racing career, I wouldn't think you'd be late for anything."

"Speed trap." Fast Car straightened his tie. "Going ninety in a forty miles per hour zone. Police did not approve."

Whoops.

"Is your mother here?" he asked, searching the crowd.

I pointed to across the cemetery where Genevieve's bonnet with purple mums stuck out amidst the black hats of the Amish. "Somewhere on the other side."

"How's the big murder investigation?" he asked as the Amish began another German hymn.

I shrugged. "Seems to have stalled. Have you learned anything?"

"The police haven't been back to Elwood's place for

two days. That unsightly yellow tape is still across the door, though. A dreadful reminder." Fast Car shaded his eyes. "Well, I'll be. Is that the way they do it?"

I followed Fast Car's gaze to where they were lowering the pine casket into the ground. "Do what?"

"They're burying Elwood under the fence. Can't you see?"

Indeed. The crowd was pressed against the fence where Amish men were shoveling dirt over Elwood's remains. Over the shoulder of one, I spied the trademark feeder cap and buckteeth of Omer Best. For a minute there I thought he saw me, too.

"Does that mean anything?" I asked, stepping behind Fast Car to hide myself.

"It means that somewhere along the line, Elwood violated God's law. It never occurred to me that Elwood must have left the Amish faith." He clicked his tongue. "He must have been shunned, the old fellow."

"Shunned?"

Omer stepped back from the crowd. His head craned from side to side, as though he were looking for someone.

"Where the Amish community turns its back on a member who has strayed from the faith. They're not allowed to accept dinner invitations from the shunned, rides in the buggy from the shunned. Can't do business with the shunned. It's quite disheartening. And in the end, the Amish bury the shunned under the fence to let God decide what to do with their souls."

I pondered Elwood's shunned soul. Of course, Elwood had driven a car, owned a television and had a telephone in his house after making a fortune in goat cheese. Made sense that he had been shunned, if he had been Amish.

"That shunning had a strange effect on Elwood. He never could appreciate the bounty of the material world," Fast Car said. "It was as though he felt too guilty. All that expensive artwork, the condo, the car were wasted on him. A shame, really."

The crowd was breaking up and Fast Car strode across the cemetery. I turned on Genevieve's walkie-talkie and announced that Fast Car was looking for Mama. Mama "oooohed" delightedly into the speaker. I dropped it in the pocket of my apron and searched for Omer. He was still missing.

Janice came over to me and whispered that she'd seen Omer by the grave. "Not that I'm saying he's the kingpin," she said softly. "Just thought you'd be interested. He's over there now, in heavy conversation with Anna Hochstetter's cousin. Curious."

I'll say it was curious. So what was Omer Best doing at Elwood's funeral and why was he in heavy conversation with Anna Hochstetter's cousin?

After Janice walked off to be with her family, I slinked along the fence until I was about four feet away from Omer. I dabbed my eyes with a handkerchief and pretended to be immersed in grief.

"Vat's dat I'm hearing about Anna's boys, naw?" Omer was saying to a squat Amish man who, like Anna, was dimpled all over. "I hears dey run into some wonnerful trouble."

The squat man nodded somberly. "Rum springa."

"Ya, ya," said Omer, picking his teeth. "Dat's da noose. Joyriding, vas dey?"

But before Anna's cousin could answer, an awful cry rose up from my dress.

"*Hey, Bubbles. Where'd you say Fast Car was?*" My pocket started squawking with Mama's voice. "*We can't find him!*"

My walkie-talkie was on full volume. I turned my back to Omer and fumbled with the dials.

"*Oops. Forget that, Genny says she's found him.*"

I turned a knob down and sighed in relief. Maybe Omer hadn't noticed.

"*He's giving us a ride so don't wait,*" the radio blared, louder than ever.

I pried open the back with my nail and shook out the batteries. There was a tap on my shoulder. Omer stared at me, his chinless face a mask of childlike confusion.

What to do? Omer had met me only briefly as modest Amish woman Sally Hansen from Ohio, but he had spent a half hour with me as Bubbles Yablonsky, dolled up disco gal from Lehigh. I decided to chance it.

"Dutch!" I said, sticking out my hand. "It's me, Bubbles Yablonsky, the reporter who interviewed you at the Stayin' Alive Wednesday night."

Omer limply shook my hand. "Bubbles? Vas is das?" He nodded to my dress.

"This?" I held out my skirt. "It's an awful, simply low-down act. I admit it. I'm undercover. Undercover at a burial."

"Ahhh." Omer smirked and spread his legs. "So dis is some reporting ting, say? Like dem *Sixty Minutes* folks."

"Sort of," I said, screwing up my courage. "I was wondering if maybe Elwood Kramer's murderer might show up at the cemetery. By the way," I added craftily, "what are you doing here? Don't tell me Elwood boogied on down at the Stayin' Alive?"

"It vas Elwood Kramer dat taught me about selling and all," Omer said flatly. "He vas my first boss und I vas his apprentice. Tirty years naw it's been."

I gulped and immediately regretted my not-so-subtle accusation. "I'm so sorry."

"At first I taught ya vas annudder girl I am knowing. She's got da golden nails just like ya." He started walking away at a flat-footed, galumping gait. Then he stopped and, over his shoulder, yelled, "Her name's Sally Hansen and my mudder baked her a shoofly pie."

Shoofly pie! The words made my heart flutter and sweat trickle down my neck. Omer knew. He knew who I was and maybe what I was up to. Worse, he had threatened me with shoofly pie! I was a marked woman. Just like Genevieve had predicted.

Or was my imagination getting carried away, I wondered, hurrying down the road and around the corner to my hidden Camaro. Omer had a perfectly good reason for being at that burial. And perhaps his comment about shoofly pie was an innocent one. It was true. His mother had made shoofly pie for me.

Maybe Janice and Jake were right. Maybe Omer was a borderline simpleton who padded through life delivering pies baked by Mother.

Or maybe not.

I opened the driver's side door of the Camaro and gasped. There on my dashboard, a bit scratched and broken in places, was the ugly, menacing garden gnome Mama had bought for me. The same one Stiletto had thrown through the window of the car that had tried to run me down outside the Stayin' Alive.

But instead of being afraid as my stalker intended, I was angry. I was pumped and I was on a mission to expose Omer Best for what he truly was. Nothing could stop me now. There was only one ammunition I needed and it was publicly available.

Land Records. A reporter's best friend.

The Whoopee Town Hall was a low brick building set in what once had been the center of Whoopee, PA. With all the shopping malls on Route 30, though, Old Whoopee, as folks around here called it, was nothing more than a post office, general store and rusted gas station.

The secretary of the Board of Supervisors directed me to the basement where the land records were kept.

It resembled every other land records department I had ever had the joy to visit. It was windowless. There were rows upon rows of metal-backed books with numbers on the front that were supposed to be significant. Metal cabinets held index cards galore for cross-referencing names and corresponding numbers that clerks then matched to numbers on other metal-bound books that contained, yet again, more numbers.

The Whoopee land records department wasn't what one might call a happening place on the Friday before Labor Day. Aside from a gaunt bespectacled man at the counter, I was the only customer. Even so, the rather slothlike clerk whom I guessed to be a lifetime member of the *Star Trek* fan club took his sweet time getting to me. Oh, what I would have given for a spaghetti-strap halter top at a time like this.

When he finally deigned to help me, I identified myself as Bubbles Yablonsky, newspaper reporter, and requested to see the plat drawing for the south side of Whoopee.

"We have only one side," he said, pointing to a town map that hung on the wall. I studied it, fairly clueless as to what to do next. I had wanted to show Samuel Stoltz exactly where Omer was purchasing property and what was up with the conservation commission's water requests. Finally, I gave up and asked the clerk.

"Actually," I said, "I'm trying to help the people I'm staying with. The Stoltzes. They've had some dealings with the conservation commission over water regulations—"

"Water regulations?" asked the clerk, eagerly. "Not my department. That's the person you'll be wanting to speak with. He's with the department of environmental protection, the local field office. Lucky you caught him." He indicated the single other customer standing right next to me.

The bespectacled man whipped off his glasses and held out his hand. "Bob Jackson, and I am very well aware of the Stoltz case."

As I shook his hand I explained my situation. The clerk, who earlier couldn't have cared less who I was or what I wanted, was now unable to pull himself away from eavesdropping on our conversation.

"Perhaps there's an office we can use," Jackson said, smiling graciously at the clerk, "so we can be out of your way."

Disappointed, the clerk pointed to what I would have considered a stock room. On the way there, Jackson stopped by a cabinet, pulled out some files; he then led me in, closing the door partway.

"I realize this may seem awkward, what with me not being an official member of the Stoltz family," I said, sitting on a metal chair, "but after staying with the people this week I get the impression that they aren't sticking up for themselves on this issue. I'd like to help them understand what's required."

Jackson nodded. "I've run into this kind of situation before in dealing with the Amish. Often they don't show up to meetings or respond to letters and what started out as a molehill turns into a mountain." He opened the file and spread out the drawings.

"It's not too complicated," he said, pointing to a diagram of Samuel Stoltz's farm. "Here are two major runoff ditches on Samuel's farm and here's Whoopee Creek, a major water source for this area. As you can see, the creek runs through the northern tip of his farm."

I studied the map and traced the winding Whoopee Creek with my finger while Bob Jackson continued to explain. "State regulations mandate that runoff of manure and fertilizers be redirected into retaining ponds, instead of being allowed to leach into the soil, as in

Samuel's current system. This is to prevent a variety of contaminants from entering the aquifer and water sources such as Whoopee Creek. Do you understand?"

I nodded. "I think so. Though it's technical. What will Samuel have to do to comply?"

"Construct new ditches here and there. Build a retaining pond over here," he said, pointing to places on the map. "A buffer there. There are other land management plans that he can design whereby naturally occurring bacteria can break down the wastes. There are a variety of creative options, really."

"It's a lot of work."

"And the state knows this can be a hardship for farmers, so there is grant money available with funds from the federal Department of Agriculture to help finance compliance. Although, being Amish, Samuel probably wouldn't accept the money."

"No," I said, "he probably wouldn't. Maybe if he heard all this directly from you he might be more willing to comply, though?"

"I've written him three letters and visited the farm once," Jackson continued. "So far Samuel Stoltz has only listened to me, never truly responded."

"I think he feels so overwhelmed by these regulations that he's contemplating pulling up his family and moving to Kentucky."

"Kentucky? My, my," said Jackson, putting the pages back into the folder. "Change is hard and for the Amish any dealing with the government is dreaded. They pay their taxes, but otherwise wish to stay by themselves. Can't say I blame them."

"The way Omer Best put it, it seemed like the state was about to levy some heavy fines on the Stoltzes if they didn't comply."

"Ah, yes. Omer Best." Jackson replaced his glasses and smiled. "You've met him?"

"Many times. Between you and me, Bob, I have a feeling he's trying to shoo the Stoltzes off their land."

"I wouldn't put it past him."

"Omer told me he wants to build a huge residential community and a theme park."

Jackson stood up and closed the door completely. "Don't you mean deme park?"

I smiled. The Stoltzes had an undeclared ally in this Jackson. "What can I do?"

"Lay out the facts to Samuel again, although I'm sure Omer's ingratiated himself with them already. That's how he obtained the Beilor property up the road," Jackson said. "If Omer's interested in the Stoltz property it's because the farm sits over that large aquifer."

"How come you know about this?"

"Oh, I've been tracking Omer's theme-park proposal since he first unveiled it, largely because of my concerns about the water resources on that side of Whoopee. But, I can tell you this, without buying Samuel Stoltz's water rights, Omer will not be able to pull off this development. So Stoltz is key. I can give you a map of the water tables, if you like, to show to Samuel."

"That would be wonderful. Though I'm a bit confused. Why would Omer need the Mueller property then?"

"Road access," said Jackson, pulling a sheet out of the folder, "and zoning. It would be pretty hard to expand a theme park with a single-family home right there." He put the sheet on the copier. "Theme park. It's brilliant."

The copier hummed.

"Why is it brilliant?"

"Because local officials would never approve a residential development the size of which Best is contemplating. Sure, it would bring in more taxes, but the drain on services—road maintenance, schools, police—would be monstrous for a town of this size."

He handed me the photocopies. "But with a theme park? Ahh. Then we are talking about serious tax revenues. Once the town got wind of that they started salivating. I think they're ready to push Stoltz out themselves."

"You're telling me that—"

Jackson smiled thinly. "Yes. Omer Best is not Samuel Stoltz's only enemy. His real enemies are the city people who've moved here seeking a cleaner country life for their children. They're the ones who can't stand the smell of manure and the high taxes to pay for struggling schools. They want all the benefits of the suburbs without the downside of rural life. Unfortunately, they're also the ones who are sitting on the various local commissions and boards levying the fines."

"I'm sorry," I said, shaking my head. "I don't get the point."

"The point is that these regulations sat on the books for years without anyone making a fuss. But Samuel Stoltz's neighbors have changed in recent years and it's his new neighbors who are making life hard for him."

From a file Jackson produced a series of letters signed by a Philadelphia lawyer. He photocopied them and then handed the set to me.

"Make sure Samuel reads these," he said. "You should take a look at them, too."

I did as Bob suggested. And when I had read them twice I knew I had all the ammunition I needed to bury Omer Best.

Chapter 21

I decided on the drive over to Mama's pickle time-share to deposit the photocopies Bob Jackson had made for me there, in case someone got to snooping at the Stoltzes' or in my car. Anyway, it would have been awkward to walk through the front door of my Amish home as Sally Hansen with a bunch of maps and water tables under my arm without coming up with another wacky Ohio explanation.

It was shortly after three in the afternoon when I rang the doorbell to the pickle time-share and met Mama in her pink chenille bathrobe.

"You just get out of the shower?" I asked, placing the file by the telephone.

Mama pushed back her dyed black hair. Her complexion was surprisingly rosy for a woman in her sixties whose only exercise was flipping between *Wheel of Fortune* and *The Price Is Right* on the remote. "I'm getting ready for the Pickle Fest. You stopping by or passing through?"

"What a choice. You trying to get rid of me?" I peered in the refrigerator in search of leftovers, and found a promising Tupperware container holding tuna. I was starved. "When was this tuna fish made?"

"You don't want that," Mama said, shutting the door. "Go out and get yourself some McDonald's. You deserve a break."

"That's not a bad idea. Where's Jane? Maybe she'll go with me."

"They're at the Shoot 'N Loot with Genevieve doing some gift shopping and predinner target practice with the musket. Hey, why don't you drive over there? You can catch them before they start the final round, if you hurry."

"No thanks. I've got to head over to the Stoltzes' and make that root beer—"

"Oh, I nearly forgot." Mama bustled over to the foyer and pointed to a gigantic plastic bucket with a green lid. "Jane left this for you. She said all the ingredients and instructions are inside. Gee. I guess you better get brewing. Ta ta." She reached for the doorknob.

"No. I'm going to wait until Jane gets back," I said, throwing myself on the couch. "We have a lot to discuss, not the least of which is her running away and then there are those applications if she wants to apply early admission to Har—"

Mama dropped her hand from the doorknob. "Didn't she tell you? Jane's not going to college. G's got other plans."

I smiled the forced smile of the budding insane. Jane had a 4.0 grade-point average. Her SATs were the highest in the school. She was taking courses in molecular physics and psychology at Lehigh University and her guidance counselor was confident of getting her a full scholarship to an Ivy League school.

"G has other plans?" I asked through gritted teeth.

"Grape picking." Mama folded her chenille arms. "Grape picking in France. That's what G wants to do with her after graduation."

"Grape picking!" I couldn't control my anger any longer. "G doesn't even pick up his socks."

"Jane was afraid you were going to be ballistic."

I put my head in my hands. Mama sat down and put her hand on my arm.

"The next time I see G, I'm going to—"

"You'll do nothing of the sort." Mama's voice was firm. "You'll listen to me."

I lifted my head. "Huh?"

"You rip into G and you can kiss that precious daughter of yours goodbye. Jane's got some valid reasons for not going to those fancy universities you're so enamored of and I think you ought to hear her out."

"You're on *her* side?"

Mama shrugged. "In your mind Jane's the next Alberta Einstein, but basically she's a steel-town kid whose home life, being jerked between you and Dan, has never, shall we say, been stable."

I resented that. I'd done my best, including staying in the same house on West Goepp Street, to reassure Jane that her world had not fallen apart when Dan left me for another woman. Make that, women.

Mama stood. "Here's another piece of gristle to chew on. So Jane isn't doing what you want her to do. Can you stop her? It was a snap for her to skip school this week, defy her father and head down here. Your days of maternal control are over, Bubbles. The only option left is for you to stand back and cross your fingers that all those lessons you taught her as a kid sank in."

I opened my mouth and closed it. Mama studied me, not as the omnipresent authority figure in my life, but as a fellow mother. She didn't have to say what she was thinking. At age seventeen, I'd announced that I was pregnant by some guy named Dan I'd met during a one-night stand while violating her strict prohibition against visiting Lehigh fraternities. As a credit to her, she never once scolded, argued or criticized me. She merely asked me what I wanted to do about it.

"What's all the ruckus, pickle puss?" boomed a voice from the top of the stairs. Fast Car emerged wearing a gray silk smoking jacket—and nothing else. "Woke me from a deep nap I settled into after—"

He saw me and froze. Mama blushed deeper than cranberry relish on a Christmas-red tablecloth.

"Mother!" I exclaimed. "So that's why you were trying to get rid of me."

Mama yanked me up by the hand and led me to the foyer, hooking the bucket of root beer fixings over my arm. "And who said you couldn't take a hint." With that she opened the door.

I grabbed her by the collar. "Pickle puss?" I whispered. "Did he call you *pickle puss*?"

"Kids," Mama said, pushing me out. "No matter how old you get, you're never free of them."

I took Mama's advice and headed to the drive-through of McDonald's, earning a dirty look from the burger boy as he handed me a Diet Coke, large fries and Big Mac. I couldn't understand why he was gaping at me like that, so I said, "You got a problem?"

He ran his gaze along the Camaro. "You Amish?"

Whoops. I kept forgetting how I was dressed. "From time to time."

"Boy, have things changed from when I was a kid," he said before I zoomed off, my broken muffler bouncing on the blacktop.

When I was done with the ultimate grease and sodium splurge, I dialed Mr. Salvo from a drive-up pay phone. Mr. Salvo had just arrived at work, so he was particularly jovial. I relayed what Bob Jackson from the Department of Environmental Protection had said about Best ingratiating himself with the Beilors, another Amish family up the road—evidence that Omer was not above putting the squeeze on the Stoltzes.

"And you'll be very proud of me, Mr. Salvo. I took plenty of notes and have copies of water tables and various other records."

Mr. Salvo let out a breath. "That's great work, Yablonsky. And it seems like a helluva story, especially if you can get interviews with some of the Amish and the developer. But it's out of our circulation area. Can't use it."

Damn. Once again that stupid circulation area reared its ugly head. If I had stumbled upon the Watergate burglars, would *that* story have been out of the *News-Times* circulation area, too?

"How about the Hochstetter kids? You make any headway there?" he asked.

I told him about Janice's conversation from the night before, how the boys claimed they had been strong-armed into delivering boxes that supposedly contained marijuana by a mystery man they refused to name.

"Dope? They were running weed?"

God. Did everyone watch *Miami Vice*? Where had Mr. Salvo come up with this running weed business? "Janice doesn't think the boys knew what it was. She thinks they dropped off the boxes because, otherwise, this mystery kingpin was gonna reveal their mother's secret."

"What secret?" Mr. Salvo asked. "Is she a drug dealer, too?"

A picture of plump and dimpled Anna Hochstetter came to mind. "Hardly. She's a stereotypical Amish housewife. Janice said Mrs. Hochstetter's secret, whatever it is, is probably innocuous in our society. It's just that the Amish are so innocent and rigid in their rules."

"Now *that's* interesting," Mr. Salvo said. "That's a story the *Call* would never get. You got it because you took the time to visit Whoopee and immerse yourself in the culture. You find out what that secret is and that's a

Sunday page one feature on how drug dealers are manipulating the Amish."

"The Lehigh police don't believe the boys even have a secret. They think the mother's secret is merely a ruse, to escape prosecution."

"Better yet," said Mr. Salvo. "Nothing sweeter than publishing a story that points out what cynics cops are, especially when their cynicism obstructs justice. I'm counting on you to finish up there this weekend, Bubbles, and be in the office bright and early Monday."

"Monday?" I shook the last of the Diet Coke ice into my mouth. "Why Monday?"

"Dix Notch wants to meet with you. In the publisher's office."

"But Monday's Labor Day."

"Shame on you, Bubbles. Certainly you know by now that news doesn't take a holiday. And this is news. Big news for you."

I brought my hand to my throat. My dream had come true. "They're gonna offer me a staff position?"

"Er, not quite. To put it bluntly, you're one step from being fired, Bubbles. Permanently. Notch was furious when you called in that report about finding Janice."

"I thought you said that story would save his ass after the *Call* scooped us."

"And it did, it did. Only Notch viewed your traveling to Whoopee as circumventing his orders. He told you to stay away from the Elwood Kramer murder and you didn't."

"But—"

"There's more. The publisher's up in arms. He had no idea you were the one who had found Elwood Kramer's body until his buddies at the Final Frontier called to complain about your double byline with Lawless. They claimed it was an obvious conflict of interest for you to have had any involvement in the story, especially since you were to be Janice's maid of honor. Called their goddamn lawyer, the one on retainer."

The wind had been knocked out of me. "You're kidding?"

"I'm not kidding. That's why nailing down that Hochstetter story is important, Bubbles," Mr. Salvo said. "Would lend credibility to my argument that you were sent down to Whoopee to investigate the stolen car case, not to find Janice Kramer. I tried to explain to Notch and the publisher that you stumbled upon Janice Kramer by accident, but they're not buying it. So I'm in hot water, too. Keep that in mind."

After he hung up I sat back and thought of the Stoltzes. Life was so much less complicated in their world. Animals needed to be fed and watered. Grain had to be harvested. The kitchen had to be cleaned for another day of cooking, after which there was the haven of bed.

None of this mother-may-I world of office politics. No backstabbing and cynicism. Only lots of love, for parents, for children, even for strangers like me. I'd been welcomed, no questions asked—except about the golden toenails.

The truth was, I had come to enjoy being Sally Hansen. I'd even gotten used to the drab clothes and living without light switches, television and dishwashers. And I wasn't sure I'd show up Monday in the publisher's office.

I just might stay in Whoopee forever.

Chapter 22

Jake and Janice were pulling out of the driveway in Jake's '57 Chevy when I arrived at the farm that Friday evening, padding barefoot along the dirt road with my heavy root beer bucket. Jake had stopped by the barn to do the evening chores, slopping the pigs and milking the cows. Freedom is not another word for farming.

Janice appeared to have attacked my suitcase again. She was sitting in the passenger's seat dressed in my favorite black miniskirt and pink sweater set. Her scraggly hair was wrapped under a fuchsia kerchief and her eyes were hidden behind a big pair of white sunglasses that were not mine.

"Say goodbye to her, Bubbles," Jake said. "She's on her way to auction."

"Who, Janice?"

"No, you silly girl. The Chevy." Jake patted the side door. "I've already got four interested buyers."

"How are you gonna explain Janice?" I said. "You gonna drive up with her?"

"Meet one of my interested buyers," he said, pointing to his passenger. "Bubbles Yablonsky from Lehigh, Pennsylvania."

"Don't you dare," I said, shaking the root beer bucket at him.

"I know what you're thinking, Bubbles," Janice piped up. "You're thinking, is this chick ever going to stop raiding my clothes. I promise, after tomorrow I'm through hiding."

"No way! But we haven't found out who killed Elwood and threatened the Hochstetter boys."

"Jake and I discussed it and we decided that whoever that person is, he's not interested in me anymore, now that I'm not working for the Lehigh Police Department."

"You quit?"

"Called the chief today," Janice announced. "It's such a relief."

Jake gripped her hand. "I've asked Elspeth to marry me."

"First we've got to be baptized though," Janice reminded him.

"No more driving for me," Jake said.

"And no more makeup for me," said Janice. "It's not going to be easy. We may have to go down on our knees and ask for forgiveness from the whole community, but it'll be worth it. It's right for us to be married and live with our families."

I sighed and nodded. Poor Mickey. No matter how steely hard his muscles were now, he still had a soft heart. He would be devastated by the news and I'd be sad to lose a friend to this old-fashioned cloistered world.

"One last favor," I said. "Can you come with me tomorrow to Anna Hochstetter's lawn sale? I need you to take one last stab at asking her about her so-called secret. Looks like my career depends on it."

"That's a deal," Janice said. "It'd be good to have that case resolved once and for all. Of course, it might have been wrapped up if you-know-who hadn't interrupted my conversation with Anna at Hecht's Market."

I winced. Janice was never going to let me forget that, was she?

I waved goodbye as they backed down the long lane. When they were gone, I was struck by how lonesome I felt. The golden September sun was setting into a cool evening. At the auction, couples would be putting on sweaters and strolling arm in arm on a cozy Friday night. Jake had Janice. Jane had G, and even Mama had Fast Car.

Who did I have?

I trudged up the front steps of the Stoltzes' farmhouse. *Let's face it, Bubbles,* I said to myself, *you have no one. Oh, sure. You tell yourself you have Steve Stiletto. But where is Steve Stiletto? One moment he's in Lehigh, the next he's in the Indian Desert. Then he's in Whoopee encouraging you to break into houses and,* bing, *he's off to Baltimore for a train wreck.*

The bottom line was that there was no room for me in Steve Stiletto's action-packed life. Mr. Salvo was right, darn it. How many times had he warned me not to get involved with him? Stiletto was single at his age for a reason, Mr. Salvo had said repeatedly. And here I claimed it was because Stiletto hadn't met me yet.

Nope.

I turned on the propane lamps in the kitchen. They illuminated with a *whoosh!* From the pump room I carried the cleaned and scrubbed bottles, lining them up along the counter. Samuel had a transistor radio on which he listened to ball games. I marked where he kept the dial and then found a station that played oldies.

The big house, usually so full of the running feet of children and nonstop German chatter, was now big and empty. The wooden plank floors creaked as I walked to the pump room for water to fill the bucket. My voice, as I read the directions out loud, seemed small and helpless.

Jane hadn't missed a detail, bless her, although I couldn't understand why she had made root beer in science class. A drawback of eliminating home economics from the high school curriculum, probably. Now they were teaching kids to cook over Bunsen burners.

I emptied the root beer extract into the bucket, along with almost a bag of sugar and a bag of dry ice. Then, according to directions, I sealed the bucket with a lid and prepared to wait thirty minutes. Jane's directions said not a minute later.

"Or else," she added.

There was one problem with the Amish. They had a quirk about clocks. There were none in this house. I ran upstairs and found the travel alarm in my room. It was six-thirty. At seven I'd have to remember to open the bucket.

And that's when I heard the noise.

It was a shuffling that started and stopped. At first I assumed it was the radio—until it snapped off. Silence. Then I heard the deliberate steps up the stairs. *Thwap. Thwap. Thwap.* The unmistakable flat-footed gait of Omer Best.

"Hullo!" he called out. "Anybody home!"

I moved across the bedroom to close my door, but Omer was faster. His orange feeder cap popped around the corner as I slunk back into the shadows. At the sight of me he grinned and removed his glasses, apparently to make himself more attractive. He stuck them in his shirt pocket while I murmured a silent prayer of gratitude for his vanity.

"Hey, Sally," he said, licking his buckteeth. "By yourself alone, naw? Vere's da family?"

"Pickle Fest," I whispered, trying to wedge myself past the door and toward the stairs. "Or the auction."

"Ve call dat da vendue. Don't ya call da auction da vendue in Ohio?" He stepped to the right so that I couldn't pass him.

"No."

Omer was holding something behind his back. "Seeing as dey von't be back for hours and you is by yourself alone, Mudder vonted me to bring ya dis."

With a sweep of his arm, he whipped out a freshly baked shoofly pie and pushed it toward my nose. A huge plate of sticky, sweet, molasses death, hidden beneath pastry and sprinkled with sugar. A gagging sensation gripped my throat.

"Nossing fancy, just a shoofly pie. Smells somesing wonnerful, don't it naw?"

I nodded. This was how Old Man Mueller bit the dust, murdered by Omer Best's shoofly pie. Strangled and then suffocated with filling. And I was to be his next victim.

"It sure eats wonnerful good. Mudder'll be upset if it don't get et. Try some."

I managed one breath and composed myself. "I'm sorry, Omer," I said. "It looks delicious, but it's too fattening."

"Aww, a plump wife and a big barn never did any man harm. C'mon."

Omer started to reach into the pie to grab a slice when I saw my opportunity and fled down the stairs. He came after me, the pie plate in one hand, the piece of pie in the other.

"C'mon, Sally," he was saying as I scurried across the kitchen. "Da way ta a man's heart is dru his stomach, Mudder says. Vimmen too, say?"

I turned the corner into the living room and bumped smack into him. He dropped the pie plate on the floor with a crash and clutched my neck.

"Make like a big girl, naw, and open up." He forced the pie toward my mouth.

A figure was in my peripheral vision. A tall, dark Amish man who seemed oddly familiar, yet out of place. He walked briskly up the steps to the kitchen door and rapped on the screen. It wasn't Jake. Jake wouldn't knock on the door. But who?

Omer let go of my neck and went to the door. "Come back later," he said through the screen. "Da Stoltzes is aut."

"I'm not here for the Stoltzes," the man said, pushing the door and Omer Best aside. "I'm here for her."

In walked Steve Stiletto dressed every inch an Amish man. White shirt, suspenders, straw hat and black pants. Even bare feet. I was so happy to see him, so surprised and full of questions, I was practically speechless.

"I'm here to go settin' up with Sally," he said, removing his straw hat and bowing. He gave me a slight wink and I suppressed a smile.

Omer, still holding the pie piece with one hand, put up his other in protest. "Naw, naw. I'm da one she's settin' up vid."

"Steve," I managed to croak. "This is Omer Best."

There was a flash of recognition and anger in Stiletto's deep blue eyes. I thought for sure he would grill Best about the field in which Shep had been beaten and press him to reveal the identity of the attacker, but Stiletto merely put a firm hand on Omer Best's shoulder and grinned.

"Friend," he said, "I don't want this to get ugly." He gripped Best's shoulder so tightly that the shoofly pie in Omer's hand quivered.

When Stiletto let go, Best threw me a sour, cross-eyed look, tossed the pie piece back into the plate, picked it up and left. At the door he said, "Mudder von't be pleased," replaced his eyeglasses and walked out.

"What was *that* about?" Stiletto asked as I collapsed on a bench, shaking. "That was Omer Best, the big land baron of Whoopee, Pennsylvania? Hah! Separated at birth from Elmer Fudd, I'd say."

Stiletto finally noticed that tears were streaming down my face and that I was trembling in a postadrenaline surge.

"Bubbles!" he said, rushing over to the bench and clasping my shoulders. "What's wrong?"

"The shoofly pie," I moaned. "Oh, Steve, you saved me from the shoofly pie."

Stiletto cocked an eyebrow. "I'm missing something here. I saved you from love handles? Fat thighs? A sugar high?"

"Death. Omer Best was about to kill me with shoofly pie." I let out a deep and hearty sob. "That's the way he suffocated Wolf Mueller's father on the night we broke into his house."

Stiletto pulled me to his chest and let me cry it out. When I was done, purged and relieved, he said, "Look at it like this. Perhaps Old Man Mueller wasn't murdered. Maybe he got up in the middle of the night with a hankering for shoofly pie and choked. Or had a heart attack. I think you've been working too hard, Bubbles, if you're frantic about being killed by shoofly pie."

"I don't care," I said, resting my head on his shoulder. "You arrived just in time. Omer was going to suffocate me, I know it. What brought you back anyway?"

"A sixth sense that I shouldn't be apart from you, not after that parking lot incident. Left in the middle of the assignment."

I lifted my face. "You . . . left an assignment . . . for me?"

His lips brushed against mine and then pressed deeper, more passionately. "It was only a train wreck," he whispered into my ear.

We kissed again and there arose in me a bubble of joy I hadn't felt in a long, long time. I was valuable to him. More important than a national story.

"Stiletto, what about your editor? What's he gonna say when he finds out you left a train wreck for me?"

"Editor? Excuse me? When did I ever give a damn about an editor? Hey, I haven't seen you as Amish before. Stand up and let me get a good look."

I groaned. No makeup. My hair dull and braided and these clothes! I might as well have been a nun in this long blue dress and black apron.

I stood up, twirled briefly and sat back down.

Stiletto nodded. "Nice, very nice. And very sexy, may I add."

"This?" I asked, holding out my skirt. "You think *this* is sexy?"

He traced the outline of my face. "No. I think this is sexy. Bubbles Yablonsky. The woman who dodges cars one moment and tucks in cranky old drunks the next, who throws herself into a newspaper story like no other reporter I've ever met. Who cares so much about the people she meets, like the Stoltzes, that she goes out of her way to protect them."

Now I was blushing. And close to tears again, too.

"It was strange," he continued. "At any other time in my life I would have been fired up to cover a train wreck like this one in Baltimore. I got to climb to the top of a bridge—you know how I like to do that—and hang out of a helicopter shooting the mile of twisted metal. And the entire time, do you know what I was thinking?"

"What?" I said, twirling a tendril of hair.

"I was thinking: What's Bubbles doing? Is Bubbles okay? And what's up between her and Dan?"

I quit twirling. Oops. I'd totally spaced on that Feingold's Two-Factor Theory of Male Emotion experiment. Stiletto must still think that my ex and I were back together.

"Uh, about Dan," I began, straightening my posture. "That's not happening."

"No?"

"No. It was kind of a misunderstanding. Long story that I'll tell you someday when I'm not worried about the Stoltzes returning."

Stiletto snapped his suspender. "What's to fear? I look Amish, don't I?"

"Yes, but unmarried Amish women and unmarried Amish men aren't supposed to hang out alone. It's verboten."

"Ahh, well then." He went back to tracing my face again. "How about we sneak off tomorrow afternoon? I know of a quiet place, babbling brook, weeping willows, where we can have a romantic picnic. Very private. Now that Dan's out of the picture, I have an important question to ask you, Bubbles." He leaned down and kissed me softly. "Very important."

I gripped the bench, the tips of my nails digging into its underside. What? What did Stiletto have to ask me?

"I," he started, playing with the ribbon strings of my organdy cap, "I—"

He never got a chance to finish. For from the kitchen floor came a monstrous rumble. It was a gurgling sound that grew louder and louder, followed by a whistle.

I jumped up. "The root beer!"

"The root beer?" Stiletto asked.

"Yes, the root beer. It's about to explode." Indeed. The green lid was bulging like a dome. "This is what Jane must have meant by thirty minutes—or else. I've got to relieve the pressure."

"Don't, Bubbles," Stiletto said, walking swiftly toward it. "It'll blow up in your—"

Kaboom!

Too late. With one terrific explosion the green lid popped off and the entire bucket of root beer sprayed like a geyser, showering every inch of the kitchen with sugar water and root beer extract. There was root beer on the cabinets, the stove, the propane-run refrigerator and even the pretty green plaid curtains Fannie had sewed for the window over the kitchen sink.

Stiletto was soaked. His straw hat on the kitchen counter was now a soggy mess. His white shirt was brown. Root beer dripped down his forehead and onto his collar.

"Yuck," he said, wiping the root beer from his neck. "Now what?"

The timing couldn't have been worse. From behind me I heard the clop, clop, clopping of horses' hooves coming up the driveway.

"Now you leave," I said, handing Stiletto his sticky hat and steering him toward the door. "The Stoltzes have returned. Hurry!"

"What about tomorrow?" he asked.

I kissed a drop of root beer off his nose. "Pick me up at Mama's around three. And go through the cornfield. I don't want the Stoltzes to see you."

Poor Stiletto, I thought as I watched him tromp through the cornfield. What we do for love.

I caught myself. Had I said love? But it was love, wasn't it? That's what had brought him back from Baltimore. That's what had sent him, stickier than flypaper, through the cornfield so that I wouldn't get in trouble. Isn't that what Stiletto was about to say—that he loved me?

"*Ach ta lieben!*" cried Katie, a baby asleep on her shoulder. "What happened?"

"I tried to make root beer, but it exploded."

"Exploding root beer? So soon? Usually that only happens if you leave the bottles to ferment too long."

"This is a new recipe," I said. "From—"

"Ohio, I bet." Katie dipped a finger into a pool of root beer. "Not bad. Not bad at all. Pop, taste this root beer."

At the sight of the ruined kitchen, Samuel Stoltz's

eyes were so bugged out, I feared they were ready to leap out of his head. "*Vas is das?*" he exclaimed.

"Taste." Katie stuck a root beer laden finger in his mouth. "Sally made it quick, just tonight."

Samuel smiled and nodded. "*Gut, gut.*" He glanced behind his shoulder. "Better than your mother's, I think."

Katie laughed and I let out a sigh of relief.

"Let me put the baby to bed and then I'll help you clean up the kitchen," she said. "And then leave me the recipe. Root beer this delicious, this fast, could bring in a bundle at the county fair."

Chapter 23

Because we had stayed up so late scrubbing every inch of the kitchen the night before, Katie and I were excused from breakfast duty. We went to work in the barn instead, hooking up cows to the propane-run milking machines. My job was to disinfect and then wipe dry the udders with old newspapers before Katie attached the nozzles.

Katie was teaching me how to approach a cow so I didn't get kicked—a trick I never learned because the farm where I came from in Middlefield, Ohio, ahem, didn't have cows, you see. Twice I narrowly missed a flying hoof, much to Katie's childlike amusement. Once I jumped back so fast I fell into a bucket of water.

Meanwhile, Ephraim, who was in charge of distributing feed that morning, chatted away, tossing hay so absentmindedly that it fell on the cows' heads and over their backs. He was excited because he had noted several prospective buyers checking out Dolly, his salon-styled heifer, while she was on display the day before. I am proud to report that one farmer asked Ephraim what he had fed her to make her coat so shiny. Thankfully he did not respond by saying "hot oil," as he had proudly informed his shocked cousin the day before.

The bidding would take place today and Ephraim was sure his sleek and smooth cow was going to make a killing. I had my manicured fingers crossed.

"Aren't you coming with us to the auction?" Katie asked as she lifted a child into her husband's black buggy. "Surely you don't have to go to work at the doctor's office on a Saturday."

Yipes! I hadn't thought about that.

"I was thinking of taking the bus to Anna Hochstetter's lawn sale," I said, adding quickly, "to get Fannie a thank-you gift."

"Thank you," Katie said. "For what?"

"For letting me stay here. I'm leaving tomorrow."

"Ach." She dismissed me with a wave. "You can't snooker me, Sally Hansen. You'll be family, soon."

"I will?"

"Sure. Jake is fixing to announce his engagement over Sunday night supper. Won't be any surprise who he'll be marrying." She wagged her finger playfully and stepped into the buggy.

Oh it won't, will it?

After all the Stoltzes had left, I carried the last of my clean clothes—a lavender, faux-leather miniskirt and a black, scoop-necked spandex T-shirt—to the garage where Janice was hiding out. She put them on and I sat on the old couch, staring at her with envy.

"I tell myself I've gotten used to the blue dress, black apron and organdy cap," I said, "but I lie. I can't wait until I'm back home and I can wear what I want."

"Me, too," she said, buckling the jet, strap sandals. "How do you go through the day like this? I couldn't get anything done if I had to trip around in heels this high and bend over in skirts this short."

"I'm not milking cows, Janice, I'm cutting hair."

"Touché."

On the way over to Mama's, to see Jane and get my

messages, Janice and I planned strategy. She would try to steal Anna Hochstetter away from her customers and talk to her privately, preferably out of view, to grill her about the secret. Meanwhile I would stay out front in my nondescript Amish clothes and play lookout.

"Who's gonna drive?" she asked.

"I am," I said, gripping the wheel of my Camaro possessively. "It's my car."

"Yeah, but you're dressed Amish. It's gonna raise suspicions if you pull up to Anna's lawn sale behind the wheel looking like you do."

I didn't know how to break this to Janice, but she was the worst driver I'd ever had occasion to come across. After all, the way we had officially met was when I found her crying in the Ford Fiesta that was wedged between two cars on Fourth Street. After that I noticed Janice stopped on green, drove on red. She sped at sixty miles an hour through school zones and crept at forty on the highway.

It wasn't her fault, I now realized. She had been raised Amish. Not only did she not know how to drive, but no one in her family knew how to drive, either.

"We'll see," I said, as we arrived at Mama's pickle time-share.

" 'Cause I'm not going to have many opportunities to get behind the wheel after tomorrow, Bubbles," she said, stepping out. "This would be my swan song. The big finale."

Coming from Janice, that was downright ominous.

This is what we were discussing on the steps of Mama's pickle time-share when the door flew open and my boss and best friend Sandy greeted us. There were shouts of delight and hugs all around and then Sandy gave Janice in her Bubbles outfit the once-over.

"Trick or treat," Janice said, holding out her arms to show off her new outfit.

"And what are you, little girl?" Sandy asked Janice as she stepped inside.

"I'm a wayward Amish maiden having one last fling," Janice said, swishing her lavender, imitation-leather hips. "Any sailors at home?"

Sandy and Janice giggled while I fumed. "How come everyone makes those cracks about my clothes?"

"Oh, don't be so sensitive, Bubbles," Sandy said. "Aren't you glad to see me?"

"Surprised is more like it. How come you're here?"

"Are you kidding?" Sandy playfully punched my shoulder. "After that message you left on my answering machine Thursday night, about Jane running away, I figured you were in need of some friendly support. So here I am. What's up with your newspaper story?"

Janice and I sat down at the kitchen table and filled in Sandy about the week's events, including the Hochstetter boys and their mother's secret, the mysterious kingpin and how Janice had been hiding out in Jake's garage. I told Sandy about Omer Best and how I had nearly been run down outside the Stayin' Alive. I omitted the breaking and entering at Wolf Mueller's as neither Janice, a former employee of the Lehigh Police Department, or Sandy, a closet prude, would approve.

"You bring Martin?" I pushed an English muffin into the toaster.

It was the wrong question to ask. Before we could stop her, Sandy embarked on a long drawn-out explanation of how her baker husband, Martin, was able to turn the Whoopee trip into a business expense by attending the Pickle Fest as research for his original Bread and Butter Pickle Butter Bread.

Janice's eyes glazed.

"Hey, Bubbles," Janice said. "Do you think your mother would mind if I use the shower? I haven't had a real shower in days."

I directed her to the second floor. Janice nearly sprinted up the stairs.

"Martin's such a genius," Sandy continued, dreamily. "The Bread and Butter Pickle Butter Bread is for hamburgers, you see. He hopes to entice some investors at the Pickle Fest. LuLu and Genevieve are introducing him around right now."

"You need investors for bread?" I asked, pulling the muffins out of the toaster.

"Ringa-dinga-ding. Wake up, Bubbles Yablonsky. This is the twenty-first century. Like, duh!"

"Seen Jane this morning?" I asked, changing the subject as fast as I could.

"Still sleeping. What a teenager."

"You have any idea who she's sleeping with?"

Sandy spooned artificial sweetener into her coffee and gave it a quick stir. "I have no idea. When I pulled up, LuLu and Genevieve were rushing out the door. The place was empty. I assume Jane and G are together since no one's sleeping on the pull-out couch, right?"

I bit into my English muffin and mulled over this crisis, the most challenging I had encountered as a parent so far.

"Do you think Jane and G are having twenty-four-hour sex?" I asked finally.

Sandy spilled her coffee. "Twenty-four-hour sex! There is such a thing?"

"You've been married for eons. You tell me."

She grabbed a paper napkin from the holder on the table and mopped up the mess. "Not to get into personal detail, but after trying out many methods, Martin and I prefer staggering sex."

"Everybody prefers staggering sex, Sandy."

"No. I'm talking about a schedule."

I debated whether to pursue this line of conversation. If it involved Sandy and Martin and sex it could get weird.

"Every other day?"

"Lord no. With Martin's demanding life as a baker, are you kidding? That'd kill him."

"It would?" There was a lot more intrigue to this baking business than I was aware of. Investors. Deadly sex.

"I'm talking every other month."

I plunked the coffee down. "Get out! How do you keep from going mad?"

"I have no idea what you're talking about. Martin is a man's man. He ravishes me. It takes me nearly sixty days to recover. You ever wonder why I close up the shop the first Sunday of every other month?"

"You're always closed on Sundays."

"Well, now you know the truth." Sandy lit a cigarette and struck a worldly pose.

I studied her, in her tidy red cotton sweater and narrow, dark denim jean skirt, and wondered what planet she was from.

"Ohmigod!" Sandy shouted, pointing over my shoulder. "What's that?"

Pressed against the kitchen window was an obscenely bloated face, its lips flattened into an O of horror, its hair a mat of red. Goodness gracious, it was G.

"Speaking of ravishing," I said, getting up to open the kitchen door.

G stumbled in wearing a pair of gray sweatpants cut off at the knees and a black T-shirt that said: TOO OLD TO WORK. TOO YOUNG TO DIE.

"Thanks, man." He collapsed at the kitchen table. "God, am I beat. You got coffee?"

I poured him a cup and slid it over. There was a big mark across G's neck and his hair was crumpled on one side of his head.

"Where were you?"

"In the Rabbit. Spent the night in the backseat." He gulped his coffee, reached behind him and removed a

DUBUQUE COUNTY LIBRARY

Santana cassette from his shirt. "Should've moved those tapes before I crashed, I guess."

"*I?*" Sandy kicked me under the table. "Don't you mean, *we*?"

"Huh?" G's lower jaw dropped. "Oh, you mean Jane. No, she bunked with Genevieve."

I willed a straight face. "You could've slept on the fold-out couch in the condo, G."

"No way. Not after . . . Oh, yeah, did that guy get ahold of you, Mrs. Y?"

G called me Mrs. Y for no practical reason since, when I was married to Dan, I was Mrs. R. "What guy?"

"I don't know. Some guy who was at the back door looking for you when Jane and I got in last night. Said he was a friend of yours."

"A friend of mine?" I moved my chair closer. Probably Stiletto. "What did he look like?"

G screwed up his face and pondered the question as though I'd asked him to explain the Theory of Relativity in Latin. "About my height, but a lot taller. My hair. More brownish. Hmm, maybe redder. Kind of a tool."

Let's hope a murder verdict didn't hinge on G being a key witness.

"Might have been my friend Steve Stiletto."

"At one in the morning? I didn't think any of your friends stayed up that late, Mrs. Y."

"You got in at one in the morning?" asked Sandy, who had no children of her own and therefore no concept of the odd hours teenagers kept. "What were you doing at one in the morning?"

G sneered at her and then said, "Who's she, the playground nanny?"

I ignored his comments. "Did this mystery visitor say what he wanted?"

"Yeah, he wanted to know where you were staying. Jane wouldn't tell the guy. Later she said it might be one of the goons you've been investigating, Mrs. Y, and since you kind of hang with a tough crowd, I decided to sleep in the Rabbit. I got three hundred dollars' worth of tapes there, not including the Alpine I installed this summer."

G stood, stretched and carried his coffee into the living room where he automatically turned on Comedy Central and flopped onto the couch.

Sandy and I stared at each other.

"Strange men coming to your mother's door at one a.m.? Doesn't sound good, Bubbles." Sandy ground out the cigarette. "I'd say it's time for you to get back to Lehigh."

Sandy was right. If it hadn't been Stiletto, then it might have been Wolf Mueller who was looking for me at one a.m. And if so, that was bad. I didn't want to end up like Shep, in the hospital, broken bones all over the place.

"First Janice and I have go to Anna Hochstetter's," I said.

"Ooh. Can I come?" Sandy squealed. "It would be so exciting to watch you two working undercover."

I thought of Janice's request.

"Sure you can go. You can drive the getaway car."

"Cool."

But in my morning daze, I forgot to remind Sandy about a certain trait she inherited from her bargain-hunting mother. A trait that, in the wrong circumstances, can destroy families, clutter an attic and be lethal when trying to flee violent men.

An incurable addiction to yard sales.

"Aww, geesh, there's a tour bus. That's not good," Janice said from the backseat of the Camaro. "Anna's gonna be too busy to talk."

As we approached Anna Hochstetter's large, albeit

slightly run-down, brick farmhouse, Sandy slowed the Camaro and pulled to the side of the road. She killed the engine and we waited as a group of tourists—women with teased hair and coordinated pink pantsuits, men in white bucks and green pants—debarked from the bus and descended on Anna's lawn sale.

Gaily colored quilts hung on clotheslines next to shelves of canned preserves, baked goods and wooden knickknacks. By the barn were antique farming equipment, newly sanded and stained Amish benches and stands of cut flowers.

"Look at that beautiful hand-painted pottery," Sandy exclaimed. "Those pieces would be perfect for my sideboard in the dining room, don't you think so, Bubbles?"

But I wasn't focused on pottery. I was watching Anna smile and clasp her hands in a motherly fashion and wondering how she managed. If my twin sons had been arrested and held eighty miles away through no fault of their own, I would have ripped out my hair—yes, my precious hair—in worry. I would have run to the police, demanding they be set free.

I suppose Anna remained here, selling cookies and quilts, because that was the only way for her to survive. Being an Amish widow, how many ways could she earn money?

"How does an Amish widow like Anna Hochstetter make a living?" I asked Janice. "She can't have any skills. Can't go on welfare."

"No need to go on welfare," Janice said. "That's one of the benefits of our community. A woman who loses her husband is supported by everyone. Same for the elderly. Don't see any Amish nursing homes, do you?"

That was true. If I were Amish, Mama would have an apartment off my house. Fannie and Samuel Stoltz had given over the biggest part of their house to Katie's family and moved into a smaller section, where I had stayed, too. No one was abandoned for being old.

When the tour bus left, Janice and I decided to make our move.

"Leave the keys in the ignition, Sandy, so we're ready to go."

"Aye, aye, farm girl."

I stuck my tongue out at her and marched across the lawn. Janice was ahead of me, making a beeline for Anna while I pretended to examine a display of polished copper watering cans.

Fortunately, Anna seemed very receptive when Janice approached, greeting her in German. Together they made an odd pair—Anna in her Old Order black dress and spectacles, Janice in her heels and super bleached blond hair. Anna must have been willing to divulge the big secret because she and Janice slipped into the shadows of the barn, out of sight.

Following the line of quilts, I made it to the barn wall. I could hear the women talking, but couldn't understand what they were saying because they were conversing in German.

"Excuuuuse me." A woman with blue hair and a sweatshirt tapped me on the shoulder. "Do you know how much this quilt is?"

She had to tap me twice more before I realized that she had mistaken me for a vendor at the lawn sale.

"Oh, I'm not—"

"Not selling?" the woman asked. Her sweatshirt said NEW JERSEY OR BUST. If I had had her chest, I'd have chosen Jersey. "This quilt obviously is for sale. It has a tag."

Well then why don't you read it for yourself, I wanted to suggest. Instead, I ran my hand over the red, white and blue wedding ring quilt and found the price.

"Two hundred and twenty dollars," I said. "Anna

should be right back. Seems like she handles all the money."

Miss New Jersey pressed on. "Yes, but how much is it . . . really?"

"Really?" I scratched under my organdy cap. "Two hundred and twenty dollars. Look. It says so right here."

The woman opened her purse and removed her checkbook. "I'll give you one hundred and fifty."

"One hundred and fifty? What for?"

"My. You're a tough one." She bit her mochaccino-glazed lips. "Okay. One seventy-five and that's my final—"

"You don't understand," I said, "I'm not—"

"If you think I'm hitting one eighty, you got another thing coming."

I was about to explain when a black Dodge Ram pickup pulled up with a screech and double parked. A tall man got out, slammed the door and left the engine running. He was wearing a navy windbreaker and jeans. His hair was red and wild.

Dammit. Just our luck. Wolf Mueller.

"Shit!"

"What was that?" asked Miss New Jersey. "Did you just swear? Did you just say shit?"

"No, I, uhh—"

She adjusted her glasses and brought her face close to mine. "Am I mistaken or is that Sunshine Blonde Number Eight on your hair? I know because that's my daughter's color. You're not Ay-mish. You dye your hair."

"You see, I'm from Ohio—"

But she wasn't buying it. She was from Jersey and she wasn't afraid to nail a fraud when she saw one. I was screwed.

"Arthur. Come over here," she called to her husband, a sallow-faced man who had been comparing corncob pipes. "This woman's not Ay-mish. She dyes her hair."

Arthur slowly put down the pipe. "What's that, Marguerite?"

I turned my attention back to the barn. I could hear a man shouting and then a tiny yelp. A Janice yelp.

"Ay-mish." Marguerite pointed at me. "She's not Ay-mish. She swore. I swear she swore. She's a phony."

"Now, Marguerite," Arthur said patiently, "don't get so upset, it's probably—"

"Don't tell me not to get upset. This Ay-mish imposter was trying to rip us off."

Suddenly a scream filled the barn.

"Aaahhh!" Janice came tripping and stumbling out in my high heels. "He's after me!"

Who? Who was after her?

"Janice!" I yelled over Marguerite and Arthur's squabbling. "What's wrong?"

Janice stopped, teetered a bit on the heels and pointed to the barn. "Wolf. C'mon, Bubbles, we've got to get out of here."

"Bubbles?" Marguerite the Jersey tourist exclaimed. "Your name is Bubbles?" She punched Arthur on the shoulder. "Didn't I tell you she was a phony?"

Janice headed for the Camaro, but I couldn't. Where was Wolf? And what about Anna? I was more worried about what supposed danger we had put her in than what Wolf might do to us.

While Marguerite and Arthur gnashed teeth over what a suspicious witch she was and what a worthless son-of-a-gun he was, I tiptoed to the back of the barn and found Wolf interrogating a startled Anna Hochstetter.

"Don't tell me you didn't," Wolf was saying. "I *saw* you talking to Bubbles Ya-ya . . . whatever her name is. That reporter. Her heap's parked right out front."

My Camaro a heap? I took exception to that.

"But that wasn't Bubbles," Anna tried to explain.

"I've never spoken with a Bubbles. I don't even know a Bubbles. That was another woman."

I moved behind a minisatellite dish to get closer.

"Okay. Forget Bubbles. That blonde who was just here. What did she want?"

"She wanted to know about some secret. She said my boys wouldn't talk to the police because they were afraid one of you people would reveal a secret I had. Is that true?"

"Scared, are you?" Wolf put both his hands on her plump shoulders. "Frightened that people will find out about you and you'll be shunned, is that it?"

"I don't care about that now," Anna said, crying. "The bishops will understand. I'll buy a ticket for the bus to Lehigh and explain to the police myself—"

"Do that and your boys will be in more trouble." Wolf's voice had turned menacing. "And do you know who they'll be in trouble with, Anna?"

She shook her head frantically.

"The Pagans. Ever hear of them?"

Aha! So, Mr. Salvo was right. The Hochstetter twins were members of Pennsylvania's most notorious gang that did unspeakable things to prissy virgin girls.

Anna gasped. "Not them? Not the druggies."

"You got it. So don't go mucking things up by talking to the police. Keep your mouth shut and your sons will come home safe and—"

"There she is!" the shrill voice of Marguerite cried behind me. "There's the phony Ay-mish woman who tried to rip us off. There's Bubbles!"

I spun around. A crowd of Jersey tourists with clenched fists was heading around the corner, Marguerite in the lead.

"That's not why we come to Ay-mish country," another woman shouted, "to be cheated. We can get that at home."

"Bubbles?" It was Wolf and he was moving in my direction, a sneer on his face. "This is Bubbles Yablowski?"

"Yablonsky," I corrected, before diving headfirst into the crowd. I emerged on the other side of them and searched for the Camaro. It was nowhere in sight.

Already Wolf's red head was bobbing over the top of the Jerseyites. Where were Sandy and the Camaro? She was supposed to stay right there. I had instructed her to.

Boom! Screech! Clunk! Suddenly the Camaro came up the road, accelerating, then halting, almost stalling. Its muffler was louder than ever.

I zigzagged through the lawn sale and out into the road. I couldn't wait to escape this crowd and that bizarre Wolf Mueller. I opened the door and got in. And just in time, too, for Wolf Mueller had reached the road and was there, hands on hips, giving me the evil eye.

"Let's not sit here, Sandy," I screamed. "Let's go, go, go!"

"Oh, don't rush me. I've hardly ever driven stick before."

I whipped my head around. Holy mackerel! It wasn't Sandy behind the wheel, it was Janice, her head under the dashboard studying the pedals on the floor.

"The one in the middle's the brake, right, Bubbles?" She stepped on it and we stalled. "Oh, darn. It happened again." She brushed back a strand of hair and turned the ignition. "Patience makes practice."

The backseat was empty. "Where's Sandy?"

Janice pointed to the lawn sale. "Over there. By the pottery."

Sure enough, there was Sandy holding up first a white pitcher with red designs and then a blue pitcher with white designs.

Meanwhile, Wolf was wearing the smile of a smug victor. He strolled casually to his Dodge Ram, jingling his keys. I didn't trust him. He was up to something.

"We've got to get out of here," I said. "I don't know

what to do about Sandy. I should have ordered her not to get out of the car. I forgot how she is with yard sales. We'll never get away."

"I'm sure she won't be long," Janice said. "There, I put it in neutral."

Wolf hopped into the Ram and drove off.

"You don't understand Sandy. Yard sales, lawn sales, moving sales, garage sales. She's addicted to them. And once she's there, she's hooked. They suck her in. You can't distract her."

I leaned over and beeped the horn. Sandy turned. She smiled and held up her index finger.

"Shoot. She gave us the finger," I said. "That's bad."

"Sandy gave us the finger?" Janice asked, wide-eyed.

"Not that finger. What the—?" I pointed to a black dot in the rearview. It was Wolf's truck. He must have driven around the block and was now headed down the road toward us.

"Sandy!" I screamed, opening the car door and pointing to Wolf. "Look!"

Sandy saw the zooming Dodge Ram, quickly plunked down some cash, grabbed a pink-and-cream-colored bowl, ran to the Camaro and climbed over me, into the backseat.

"Step on it, Janice!" I barked.

"Wait. I think I've got it. Clutch. Brake. Shift."

"Oh for heaven's sake." I grabbed the wheel and threw my left leg over Janice's.

Bump! We all pitched forward.

"What was that?" Sandy asked. "It almost broke my bowl."

"It was Wolf," I said, stepping on the gas. "His Dodge rammed us."

"What are you doing, Bubbles?" Janice yelled as I placed my foot on hers, alternating clutch and gas, all the while shifting.

"Very talented, Bubbles," Sandy said with admiration. "You learn that from Jay Roach senior year?"

"Who else?" I said as we hooked a right at the red light.

"I don't think there's right on red in this part of the state," Janice said nervously as the Camaro peeled around the corner.

"It's Pennsylvania law, Janice, the same for the whole state."

"Really?" But Janice couldn't have cared less. She was too busy gripping the door in terror, her skin white with fear as I pulled a U-y.

"That's illegal," she gasped.

"Aack. A buggy!" Sandy covered her eyes with one hand.

"Shoot." I swung the wheel.

"Watch out for that fence!" Janice screamed. "What are you doing?"

With one swift move I pulled the wheel to the right, downshifted between my legs and took us onto a set of wagon tracks running through an alfalfa field. Janice eagerly stepped on the brakes and killed the engine. We held our breaths and stared at the rearview until we saw Wolf's black Dodge Ram pass, oblivious to our hiding place in the alfalfa.

I removed my leg and leaned back in the seat.

"That was," Sandy panted, *"the* most terrifying experience of my life. What got into you?"

"I will never, ever drive a car again," promised Janice, who failed to recognize that I had driven the car, not she. "You cured me, Bubbles. Thank you, I guess."

I rubbed my temples. It had been quite a morning. "Did Anna tell you what her secret was, at least?"

Janice removed a tissue from her purse and dabbed her forehead. "No. She started explaining how her secret came about, but she never actually said what it was.

Then Wolf showed up and hollered that I was a dead woman."

"He thought you were me, Janice. Now it's me he's after," I said. "Or rather, the Pagans will be after me."

Janice dropped the tissue. "The Pagans? That heavy-metal group?"

"No. They're a gang. Anna called them druggies."

"Sounds vaguely familiar," Janice said, "although I thought they had disbanded years ago. Either that or moved to Seattle. Where'd you come up with the Pagans?"

"That's what Wolf told Anna, that if she spoke to the Lehigh police she'd be in trouble with the Pagans. It's exactly what Mr. Salvo, my editor, said. He speculated the Hochstetter boys had joined the Pagans, too, though I've been asking everyone around Whoopee about the Pagans and no one's heard of them."

Janice narrowed her eyes. "You know what I think? I think Wolf Mueller alone is the mystery man who threatened and blackmailed those kids into driving the marijuana to New Jersey. This Pagan stuff came out of the blue, probably because you've been spreading rumors around town by asking your questions, Bubbles."

I straightened in my seat. "I didn't mean to spread rumors. Anyway, where is Wolf, a two-bit mechanic, getting marijuana? I don't think South American drug cartels are dropping off bales of marijuana in Whoopee, Pennsylvania, so that Wolf can blackmail Amish kids into delivering the drug to New Jersey. Something doesn't add up, Janice."

Janice and I thought about this and I remembered a crucial detail I had noticed during my first visit to M&M. I would have to stop by there today and check it out.

"So, where to now, Evel Knievel?" Sandy asked from the back.

"To the place where women go when all else fails," I said, opening the door so Janice and I could switch seats. "The hair salon."

Chapter 24

"What beauty parlor?" Sandy asked as I looked both ways like a proper motorist before backing out of the alfalfa field.

"Regina's. In the Whoopee Mall." Wolf Mueller was nowhere in sight. I took a chance and hung a left at the next stop sign.

"It'll be great to get my old color back," Janice said. "But do you think they'll be able to take me without notice, Bubbles? I mean, it is a Saturday."

"Don't worry, Janice. Regina loves me. If worst comes to worst, I'll color your hair myself."

Sandy went "hmpf," and began efficiently wrapping up the china bowl. "How did you meet this Regina anyway?"

"I helped her out with a temperamental client on Thursday when I stopped by to get my roots done." I slowed down and let a black pickup pass me on the double yellow line. Whew. Not Wolf Mueller.

"You worked there? At another salon?" Sandy asked this as though I had divulged nuclear secrets to the Russians. "Without telling me?"

"Regina was in a pinch. It didn't mean anything, Sandy."

Sandy went "hmpf," again.

We turned onto the Lincoln Highway. The mall was two lights away and in a normal world it would have taken us three minutes to get there. But this was Saturday in Lancaster County and traffic was bumper to bumper. There were charter tour buses, cars packed with shoppers and a few black Amish buggies, the horses in blinders and their drivers praying that a semi wasn't about to slam into them.

When we arrived at the mall, I showed Sandy where the Stayin' Alive was and where I had been nearly killed in the parking lot. I parked the Camaro and Sandy refused to get out.

"That's okay. I'll stay here until you get back."

I removed the keys from the ignition. "Don't be silly. C'mon. I want you to meet Regina. You'll like her."

Sandy reluctantly climbed out of the rear seat. "She probably has a lot of those fancy Nexxus products for sale, say?"

"I didn't notice. What's your problem?"

Janice was like a little kid, clicking on her heels ahead of us to reach the mall first.

"What's my problem?" Sandy twirled through the mall's revolving glass door. "You leave the House of Beauty for days at a time, forcing me to put up with Tiffany and her botched coloring jobs and butcher bobs and lo and behold, I find out that all along you've been working at another salon."

I had forgotten that I still had bare feet, part of the Amish ruse. A security guard standing by the Kay Jewelers glanced at my grass-stained toes and frowned.

"I did not *work* at another salon, Sandy. I required an emergency root job and coincidentally helped out a fellow hairdresser. What's so wrong with that?"

"Nothing." She pouted as we came to Regina's. Sandy inspected a sign by the cash register. "Oh, great, she offers bikini wax. Figures. Probably a tanning bed in the back, too."

"Yes?" Regina put down a pair of scissors and approached the counter. She appeared much more relaxed and cheerful today. Her auburn hair was neatly coiffed and her white blouse was loose and carefree.

"Hi," I said with a wave, "it's me."

"Pardon?" Regina said. "Have we met?"

"That's a mall salon, for you," Sandy muttered under her breath. "No personal touch."

"I'm Bubbles."

Regina cocked her head questioningly.

"The hairdresser? From Lehigh who assisted that client with the sexual issue?"

"Sexual issue?" said Sandy.

"Oh yes," said Regina, nodding now. "You look so . . . different. I didn't recognize you. You were great!"

"I wonder if I could get a color correction for my friend here?" I pointed to Janice, who was staring in awe at the whirl of cutting, coloring, curling and conversation inside the salon. "She's announcing her engagement tomorrow."

I put my hand up to Regina's ear and whispered that Janice was returning to Amish life and needed an application of Monastery Mahogany Number Two with extra drabber.

"I see," Regina said.

Sandy cleared her throat.

"We weren't talking about *you,*" I hissed.

Regina ran her finger down the appointment book. "If you can get her started, Bubbles, I can finish her myself. And, please, let me handle the bill. Your kindness the other day resulted in superb word of mouth about my salon. It's I who owe you."

I stuck my tongue out at Sandy, who stuck out her tongue back while Regina led Janice to a chair. I sat Janice down, combed out her brittle hair and went to the supply closet to retrieve the ingredients for Monastery Mahogany Number Two. Sandy followed me like a puppy.

"What's that?" she asked, pointing to a purple glow beneath a closed white door.

"Looks like a tanning bed to me," I said, taking the supplies into a back room for mixing.

"I told you." Sandy picked up the bottle I'd snagged from the supply closet. "Oh, she uses *that* kind of developer. Yuck. I used to use that brand until I read a report about its carcinogenic chemical content."

I ignored her while I mixed the dye.

"How's it going here?" Regina asked twenty minutes later. Sandy was in the waiting area, petulantly flipping through magazines.

I told Regina everything was positively ducky and complimented her on what a well-organized salon she ran.

"Would be an even better salon if I could convince you to work here, Bubbles."

I sat Janice under the dryer and set the timer. Janice's eyes grew wide when I flicked the On switch. "Is it supposed to be this hot?"

"It wouldn't set your color otherwise, Janice. Relax," I said. "You have eight more minutes. Actually, Regina, I'm really trying to make it as a newspaper reporter, although it hasn't exactly been easy lately. This Amish dress is part of it. I'm undercover."

"So that explains the outfit. You ever find Mrs. Hochstetter?"

"Found her, yes. Spoke with her, no."

"Odd woman, from what Lois Dizelhaus told me."

"Oh?"

"Lois ever tell you why she ended up firing Anna Hochstetter?"

"I don't believe she did."

Sandy was scrutinizing a can of French mousse. She checked to see if anyone was looking and then slyly wrote down the brand name on the back of her checkbook.

"Because the only thing she ever cleaned was the remote."

I stopped the dryer and checked Janice's hair. Janice gazed up at me anxiously, like I was about to commit brain surgery. "Two more minutes, Janice." I stuck her head back under. "What do you mean she only cleaned the remote?"

"She was a TV junkie. Soap operas specifically. Any time Lois's back was turned or she left on an errand, Anna Hochstetter would rush to the TV and click on *One Life to Live*. It was so bad, Lois was forced to can her."

I thought about that satellite dish attached to Anna Hochstetter's barn and turned off the dryer. "Hey, Janice, would a soap opera addiction be a big enough secret to blackmail Anna Hochstetter?"

Janice gingerly touched her hair. "Sure. It's television and sex and electricity wrapped into one. If the church elders had spoken to her about it before, she might even be shunned if she continued watching the soaps. See, I told you her secret was minor in comparison. How's my hair?"

"Because I saw a satellite dish outside her barn," I said.

"How would she get electricity, though?" asked Regina.

"Probably she rents her house from an English family," Janice said. "That's very common. Is my hair back to normal?"

"Fascinating," Regina said, folding her arms. "Every woman I know watches soap operas. No big deal."

"But with Anna Hochstetter being a widow and so dependent upon the Amish community for survival," I said, "a secret that could get her shunned would be serious enough for someone to use against her as blackmail."

"Speaking of black," Janice said, "aren't you worried that that's the color my hair's gonna turn if we don't rinse out the dye?"

Regina escorted Janice over to the sink. "I can take it from here, Bubbles."

"Yeah, don't wait," Janice said as Regina spritzed her scalp with warm water. "I'll hop a bus home."

"You sure you don't want me to give you a ride, Janice? It's no problem for me to stick around."

"No, no. That's okay. After this morning, I'm not sure I'll ever get in a car again."

"Let me get this straight," Sandy said, as I parked in an inconspicuous spot behind M&M. "You want me to walk into the gas station and talk the clerk's ear off until you beep."

"That's right." I slipped my bare feet into a pair of flats I kept in the car for driving.

"And you don't want me to buy any gas?"

"Gosh no. They'd see the car."

"Alright," Sandy said, opening the door. "Try to hurry, though. I don't know how long I can hold a conversation with an individual who calls himself Nimrod."

I watched as Sandy trotted around the corner. As soon as she entered the station, I softly closed the Camaro door and skipped over to the small used-car lot. Not much had changed since I'd surveyed it on Wednesday.

There was the Dodge Colt for five hundred. The Datsun for three hundred or Best Offer. The rusted blue Subaru was a new addition, as was an old brown Volkswagen Dasher. I didn't care about those.

It was the three Chevy Cavaliers for under three grand each that I was interested in. Specifically, the two white ones.

The first white Cavalier was in fairly good condition, at least on the outside. $2,900 was written in soap on the windshield. Every penny worth it, I'd say.

The price was missing from the second Cavalier. I strolled around the car, running my nail along the fender. All four windows were in place and the car appeared as though it had been recently cleaned and, geez, waxed even.

I cupped my hands to the driver's side window and read the mileage. Eighty-six thousand and twenty, although I doubted it was that high before Wednesday night.

"Help you?" A mechanic in a navy jumpsuit was exiting the garage, wiping his hands on a blue cloth. He was too tall to be Mac and I couldn't detect any red hair under his feeder cap.

"Oh, no," I said demurely, casting my eyes downward in exaggerated embarrassment. "I'm just looking. I thought Wolf would be here. He's the one I usually deal with."

The mechanic shoved the rag in his pocket. "Wolf's had a death in the family so he's off this week. I'm filling in and, uh, don't be embarrassed." His name tag said HANK. "We get lots of Amish in here 'just looking.' "

"And this car is how much?" I touched the side mirror lovingly.

"Isn't there a price on this baby?" He leaned over to check the windshield. "Must've come off during the window repair."

"The windshield was broken?" I asked with alarm.

"Only the driver's side. Vandals smashed it Wednesday night." Hank shook his head in disgust. "Mac wouldn't have these problems if he kept a Doberman in the lot nights. Anyhow, we just got the car finished this morning so that's why there's no price. I think it's somewhere around sixteen hundred."

"Ahh," I said.

He pulled out a set of keys. "Wanna give it a test drive? That is, if you know how to drive?"

"Oh, I don't. My husband does."

Hank smiled knowingly. "Well, then how about you sit yourself down behind the wheel. Get a feel for it."

And ruin all those valuable fingerprints? Nothing doing, Bub, I felt like saying. Instead I bowed my head and said, "I should be going."

"Next time why don't you bring your husband, sister?" Hank said, a ring of annoyance in his voice. "Then maybe we can talk turkey."

He hustled back to the garage just as Sandy was rounding the corner with a huge brown bag of groceries. Why was she returning so soon? Both of us got inside the car.

"It was that boss you told me about, Mac," she said, as I backed up the Camaro. "I think he had a security camera because he bolted out of his office and asked Nimrod who was in the lot."

As we rolled out of the gas station, I checked the rearview. Mac and Hank the mechanic were in deep discussion by the Chevy Cavalier.

"What did Nimrod say to that?"

"Nimrod said, 'What lot?' "

"You're not serious."

"I am." Sandy reached in the bag of groceries. "Bubbles, he had to be the stupidest excuse for a human being I've ever met. Do you know I had to count the change out for him?"

"Been there, done that. So why did you buy all that stuff?"

"I didn't know what else to do. First I asked directions to the mall and this Nimrod obviously couldn't give them to me. Then I told him the whoopee pie he was eating looked good and we discussed that for a while. I explained that my husband was a baker in town for the Pickle Fest and Nimrod suggested he try one of these homemade whoopee pies. So I bought a few, along with two cans of soda, a quart of motor oil and some chips. And then Mac came out and that was it."

Sandy put the bag on the floor. "This undercover work is exhausting. Was that car the one that tried to run you down?"

"I'm almost ninety-nine percent positive," I said.

"What're you going to do about the remaining one percent?"

"I don't know," I said, parking in front of the pickle time-share. "First I'm going to take a shower, go on my date with Stiletto and then I'm going to sleep on it."

Sandy picked up the groceries. "What about that chastity vow?"

"I'm going to sleep on this Chevy Cavalier dilemma, Sandy. Not on Stiletto."

"Just checking. Thought maybe you got your pronouns mixed up."

Chapter 25

I must have been exhausted, too, because on the way to the shower I fell asleep on Genevieve's bed. When I awoke an hour or so later, the condo was dead quiet. Mama left a note saying that she had packed me a picnic dinner for my date with Stiletto and that she and Genevieve had taken third prize in the unripened watermelon pickle category at Pickle Fest. They and Fast Car were off to Miller's Smorgasbord to celebrate at the early bird special.

Jane and G had driven into Lancaster to catch an alternative one-man play written, produced and acted by an Amish dissident. The title of the play—*Pounding My Plowshares into Uzis*—gave me the chills, but it wasn't half as frightening as what Sandy was doing this evening—attending a three-hour motivational seminar with Martin called "Turning Bread into *Bread*."

It was nice to be alone, getting ready for a date on a clear, dry Saturday evening in September. And not just any date. A date where Stiletto was going to ask me an "important question."

Mama had been kind enough to wash and iron a few of my clothes. I chose the red-checked gingham tie top—the same one that came unbuttoned at the construction site—and my white miniskirt. After a long, hot shower, I toweled up, unscrewed the eyeliner (Jet Noir) and prepared to draw a thick black line under my lashes.

I paused, holding the eyeliner wand in midair.

When Stiletto had complimented me on my Amish outfit, I hadn't been wearing any makeup. Could it be that some men didn't like makeup? Not to say that I put on eyeliner, mascara and eye shadow for men. Of course not. Those always have been indulgences I've reserved for myself. However . . .

Ten minutes later I was a toned-down version of the old Bubbles. My hair was French braided and tied with a white ribbon. My eyes were done in Smoke Mist with a touch of Light Charcoal eyeliner—to bring out the blue in my irises. I applied a touch of Natural Rose to my cheekbones and Cherry Crisp to my lips.

The new country-casual me was ready to slip into a smashing pair of high-heeled pumps when I had a crisis. My feet, which had been padding around either bare or in flats for days, would not fit. As hard as I tried to squeeze my toes, I could not stuff them into the points of my shoes.

"Horrors!" I cried, falling onto the bed. "No heels! What'll I do?"

The doorbell rang. I bravely slipped on the flats, skipped down the stairs, opened the door and faced Stiletto.

"Yablinko!" he exclaimed, stepping back to get a better view of me. "You look . . . terrific! What's changed?"

I stuck out my foot. "No heels."

"No, it's not that. It's . . . you're—" He suddenly got a funny expression and produced a bouquet of freshly picked purple, yellow and orange wildflowers. "You're an inspiration, Bubbles," he said as I buried my nose in their fragrant petals.

Stiletto lifted my chin and kissed me gently. He was wearing a white T-shirt, black blazer and jeans—the favorite way I like Stiletto. Besides wet.

"You don't look too bad yourself," I said, picking up the basket Mama had left for me. There was a paper bag on top. I opened it and pulled out a tube of Bentley's Boxwood Repair Cream. I couldn't imagine what it was for, but dropped it inside the basket anyway.

"What's that?" Stiletto said, pointing to what I was holding.

"Dinner."

"Oh, no. *I* packed a picnic."

"You?" I led the way to the Jeep. Believe it or not, Stiletto opened the door for me and held my arm as I got in. "How?"

"Well, not me, actually. Harrods."

"That a store in Lancaster?"

"Not exactly," he said, starting up the Jeep. "London."

"London . . . Pennsylvania?"

Stiletto sped forward. "London, England."

I turned around. In the backseat next to a green blanket and an ice bucket with wine was an adorable red picnic basket trimmed with gold. "But how—"

"Overnight international post. Very convenient."

Convenient? Damned expensive was more like it. I have a mind block when it comes to Stiletto's wealth. He's too hardworking, too real to be rich. If I had his money, I sure as hell wouldn't be rolling in front of bulldozers and hanging out of helicopters shooting train wrecks.

"I forgot to ask. You do like lobster, don't you?" he said as we passed Mueller's house and Dutch Enterprises' cornfield.

"Sure do!"

That was a total lie. Lobsters reminded me of my most detested bugs—the indigenous Pennsylvania centipede. It was all I could do to keep from reaching for the Raid when I saw the crustacean in a restaurant.

Still, this night was so magical and sparkling, I thought I just might eat a bit of lobster. I was in the mood to be daring, to try something I'd never tried before.

Unfortunately, I got my wish.

Stiletto led me to a private green glen that lived up to his description. Weeping willows, a crystal brook gurgling over polished rocks and a setting sun to boot.

"Wow," I said, pulling Mama's basket from his Jeep. "This is . . . dazzling."

"Glad you like it," he said, putting his arm around my shoulder. "I like it, too. Reminds me . . . wait. First I want to show you something."

He reached in his pocket and pulled out a photo. It was of another landscape, even greener than this, with stone walls, hedgerows and grassy hills. Similar to the countryside around here.

"I shot it," he said. "What do you think?"

"Lovely. This part of the magazine assignment you finished for Shep?"

Stiletto smiled and put the photo away. "No. Took it last year in—"

"Hey, there's a duck," I said, pointing to a long-legged bird standing by the water's edge.

"That's not a duck. That's a heron. A blue heron."

I tiptoed into the water to get closer to it, but it flew away, its giant wings waft, waft, wafting into the air.

Stiletto opened the bottle of wine, poured me a glass and walked into the brook to hand it to me. Lifting his own glass he said, "To adventure."

"To adventure," I said, taking a sip. Hmm. It wasn't my preferred flavor, Peach Fuzz, but it was pretty tasty.

"So, Bubbles," Stiletto said, placing his glass on the rock, "about that question I wanted to ask you."

I put down my glass, too. If this was the question I expected, I didn't want anything breakable on my person.

"It's true we haven't known each other very long," he said, the setting sun turning his face positively bronze. "But in a short time, I'd say we've been through a hell of a lot together, wouldn't you?"

I stirred the water with my toe. "Dangled off a bridge."

"And don't forget that cabin in the Poconos. That was touch and go."

"Nope. Couldn't forget that. Then there was that felony we committed this week. The breaking and entering."

"Yeah, sorry about that." He reached out and stroked my bare shoulders. "But I've been gone a lot, too. Right when we're getting to know each other it seems I get called off."

He was so close to me now that I could see the crow's-feet at the corners of his eyes, those sexy laugh lines around his mouth. "Bubbles, I have bad news. Good news for my career, but bad news for us."

My heart was pounding. A soft breeze kicked up, sending the willow trees' branches waving over the brook. "You're going away again," I said.

"England. For six months. To oversee a bureau reorganization." His jaw muscles flexed tautly. "That's what the picture and the Harrods picnic are about."

I gave him a good hard push. So hard that he tripped over a rock and fell backward into the brook with a splash.

"What're you trying to do, torture me, Stiletto?"

"What the—?" He sat up in the water and rested his soaking forearms on his knees.

"Was this entire evening a way of saying toodle-do, Yablinko? I'm off to a far cooler place than you'll ever go and, guess what, I'm going without you. It's been fun, toots."

I turned to go, but he grabbed me by the knees, pulling me into the water with him. I twisted away. He caught me, lifted me out of the brook and wrapped his arms around my drenched body, kissing me firmly, passionately. It wasn't fair. I felt like the Wicked Witch, accidentally doused in her final hour. I was melting.

"I want you," he said softly, "to go with me. I want you to go with me to London. There's a town house in Soho I've got a lease on. Jane will be crazy for it and I can get her into an excellent University of London program. From there we can take trips to Scotland, Ireland, Paris, even Italy. Think about it, Bubbles. We'd have the time of our lives."

At first I wasn't sure what he was asking me to do. Did Steve Stiletto want me to travel over the ocean to live with him as a kept woman? Because that wasn't going to happen. Not at my age and after my experience.

I had made a promise to myself when I took that chastity vow. I was going for the whole enchilada. Just as I was aspiring to become a first-rate investigative journalist at a top newspaper, I was not going to settle for less than a loving, nurturing and sexually charged marriage.

It had taken me a long, long time to realize that this is what I wanted. But there comes a moment in a woman's life, after she has compromised herself for her parents and her boyfriend, husband, boss and children, when she takes stock and says, No! From now on, I am going for the golden glories in this world. I want it all. I am worthy.

I broke from Stiletto's clasp. "That's a big question, Steve," I said, standing up and shaking off water that was dripping down my arms. "It's a big step."

"I know," he said somberly. "I wouldn't have asked, except that after missing you in Baltimore like I did, it hit me that I might . . . that I—"

Yessss? I thought. Say it! Say it! Say it, boy!

"I might need some more wine," he said, scrambling out of the stream and onto the bank. "Hey, how about this food? It's getting cold."

Could this guy be any more of a Peter Pan? You're thirty-seven, Stiletto. Take the plunge!

I sighed and, stepping from rock to rock, joined him on the creek bank where the Harrods basket lay open. Inside was a tiny jar of caviar, a tin of pâté, a container of white-and-pink lobster meat, sliced cucumbers and a loaf of French bread. There was cold fried chicken, figs and fresh red grapes. Gruyère cheese and hulled strawberries.

I examined Mama's picnic basket. Smoked tongue sandwiches with bright yellow mustard. Pickles wrapped in foil. Genevieve's deviled eggs, a plastic Baggie with celery sticks, ShopRite brand root beer and ginger ale in cans and ten Fig Newtons. Nothing edible there except the two whoopee pies Sandy had purchased at M&M.

Stiletto dabbed some caviar on cucumber and popped it in my mouth. It tasted salty when the eggs burst. It wasn't *too* disgusting.

"I'll think about it, Steve," I said, biting into a strawberry. "London. Give me a few days."

He grinned and kissed me on the cheek. "That's my girl. And don't worry. Take your time. I know how hard commitments are to make."

Pal, you don't know from commitment, I thought. You wouldn't recognize commitment if it passed you on the street and socked you in the nose.

There was no point in ruining the evening by fuming about Stiletto. I decided to call a truce for now and be pleasant company. So we lay on the blanket, talked, sipped wine and plowed through the Harrods basket. I ate cold chicken and grapes and drank bottled water while Stiletto finished off the lobster and wine.

The whoopee pies Sandy bought at M&M reminded me of Wolf Mueller.

"I think I know who tried to kill me outside the Stayin' Alive," I said, biting into the deep dark chocolate and cream. Odd tasting, but not bad. A bit . . . crunchy. "Or at least, who tried to run me over."

"Omer Best?" Stiletto suggested, lying back and looking at the stars, which were beginning to emerge in the darkening sky.

"Don't think so. I think it was Wolf." I finished the whoopee pie and wiped my fingers on a napkin. "That's my preliminary theory."

"Your preliminary theory, huh. Based on what?"

"Empirical and inferential evidence, mainly. Can't prove the final thesis until all the elements of the paradigm have been either eliminated or verified."

"Eliminated? Paradigm? Was there a dictionary in your picnic basket, Bubbles?"

"Oh, you and your witty quips. Say, look at the moon. The reflection it's casting on the water is perfectly parabolic. And I mean that in a purely aphoristic sense." That struck me as side-splittingly funny and I tittered with laughter. "That's a double entendre, you see. Parabolic being a synonym for allegorical."

Stiletto sat up and stared at me in shock. "Are you okay, Bubbles?"

"I don't know. Depends on how one defines 'okay,' I suppose. A commonly used phrase, part of the American lexicon, although ninety-eight percent of the public hasn't a clue to the derivation of the word."

Stiletto rested his chin in his hands. "Do tell. I'm rather enjoying this. What is its derivation?"

"As any schooled etymologist could tell you, Stiletto, the history of *okay* hails to the 1840 campaign of Democratic candidate Martin Van Buren, dates 1782 to 1862, eighth president of the United States."

"I know," Stiletto said, smiling.

"You know? *Nihil sub sole novum* to you, eh, Stiletto? Or should that be *nihil sub luna novum*? Anyway, Van Buren's nickname was Old Kinderhook, a droll reference to his locus of parturition."

"Pardon?"

"Birthplace."

I was beginning to feel dizzy. Knowledge and words were streaming into my brain so fast my lips couldn't keep up. "Campaign representatives manipulated this fortuitous abbreviation of Old Kinderhook to match a popular, crude phrase of the day, oll korrect. That's with an *O* and a *K*."

Suddenly my body went limp and Stiletto grabbed me.

"You're not Old Kinderhook," he said, lifting me up and carrying me to the Jeep. "You're stoned. I think there was something funny in that whoopee pie you ate."

"Stoned? Why whatever do you mean, my good man?" I said, holding up a finger in furious protest. "Are you insinuating that I, a woman of virtue and temperance, have succumbed to that vile cannabis, the hallucinogenic palliative embraced by the masses?"

"Don't take this the wrong way, professor," he said, placing me in the seat and tucking the blanket around my shoulders, "but while most people get stupid on pot, I believe you get . . . intelligent."

"Do you mean intelligent as in the ability to acquire knowledge and analyze information via reason? Or in a theological sense? As an incorporeal—"

But I never finished. Somewhere between intelligence as thought and intelligence as an angel I drifted off. The only memories I had after that were of being carried into Mama's condo and being laid on the couch.

Stiletto stayed with me through the night, murmuring

calming words and holding me securely as my mind bounced from the origin of man to the periodic table of elements and then the ultimate question:

How come Nimrod was selling marijuana-laced whoopee pies?

Chapter 26

Jane was leaning over, inspecting me with concern, when I slowly opened my eyes Sunday morning. Sun streamed into the condo, across the beige carpet, and I could smell Mama's decaffeinated Maxwell House and G's dirty socks lying near me on the floor.

"Take those away before I get sick," I whispered, pointing to the dirty, crumpled socks.

Jane nodded to G, who jumped out of the wing chair and picked them up.

"How are you feeling, Mom?" she asked, handing me a cup of water.

I emptied the glass. "Thirsty."

"What's pi r squared?" she asked, frowning.

I squinted. "Pies aren't square. They're round."

"I am more powerful than nothing. Nothing is more powerful than God. Therefore I am more powerful than God." Jane sat back. "In philosophical terms, what's that called?"

"Dumb," I said, sitting up. "Where's Stiletto?"

"She's back to normal," Jane announced. "Hey, Steve. We've got our Bubbles back."

Next thing I knew the living room was filled with clucking and chattering. Mama pronounced me a hippie pothead. Genevieve blamed a secret conspiracy perpetuated in processed baked goods. Jane wondered at my innate intelligence. G claimed that this was a good reason why kids should get stoned to do their homework and Fast Car wanted to know what I had done with his tube of Bentley's Boxwood Repair Cream.

I pointed to Mama's picnic basket.

"I'm glad you're better," Stiletto said, kissing me on the forehead. "Although you were pretty great last night," he whispered.

I clasped my hand over my mouth. "I was so stoned. We didn't—"

"No. Of course not." He handed me a cup of coffee. "What kind of guy do you think I am? I was talking about how beautiful and interesting you were." He kissed me again.

"Ahem." Mama appeared, clutching her pocketbook and Sunday coat. "Fast Car, Genny and I are off to church. Sandy called to say she's on her way over and you should know, Bubbles, that we have to be out of this condo by four. Fast Car's driving me home in the Porsche."

Genevieve, wearing her black-and-white-striped church dress, stood behind them, hulking and obviously glum. "With all the luggage, they've got no room for me in that fancy Austrian sports car of his," she said, nodding toward Fast Car. "So I guess I'll walk."

"To church?" Jane asked.

"No, to Lehigh. It's only ninety miles. I did twice that while training in Montana. In the snow, too."

I assured Genevieve that either G or I would take her home. But she didn't seem much happier at the prospect.

"By the way, Bubbles, I got word to Fannie Stoltz," she said as Mama and Fast Car walked out the door. "Lied to her that you ran into a relative from Ohio who insisted you stay for supper and the night."

The Stoltzes. They must have been frantic wondering where I was. And this was the big day, the day when Jake and Janice met with the bishops and church elders and announced their engagement. I could not miss that.

After a quick shower and packing up what items I'd left at Mama's, I arrived downstairs to find Sandy and G smoking cigarettes at the kitchen table where Stiletto and Jane were intently studying a Lancaster County map.

"Oh, Bubbles!" Sandy exclaimed when she saw me. "I'm so, so sorry. I had no idea about those whoopee pies. For some reason, that clerk Nimrod must've thought I was looking to buy drugs."

"What *did* you say to Nimrod?" I asked, pulling out a chair for myself.

"Nothing." Sandy nervously blew a plume of smoke. "I told him that the whoopee pie looked good and said my husband might be interested because this is what he likes to do with his spare time—experiment with different products."

G raised an eyebrow.

"Doesn't sound so bad to me," I said.

"I think what gave him the wrong impression was when I commented on the texture of the cake itself. I said it was nice and high."

G coughed and ground out his butt. "You used the word high? You might as well have come out and said, 'Excuse me, but do you have any marijuana-laced whoopee pies to sell?' "

Sandy scowled. "Nimrod did say the oddest thing. When I asked him if the cocoa he used was from South America, he said no, it was locally grown."

"Aha!" Jane yelled. "See, G, I told you the pot came from around here."

"No way." G shook his head. "Not the right conditions in Pennsylvania. Growing season's not long enough."

"How do *you* know?" Sandy asked suspiciously.

"Gardening magazines," he replied with a straight face.

"I'm betting it's grown in the cornfield out Wolf Mueller's back door," Stiletto said, pointing to the map. "Right here. That's where Shep was taking photos and that's probably why Mueller attacked him and took his film. Didn't want any photos of his plants to be developed."

"He planted marijuana in the open?" I asked. "In the middle of a cornfield?"

"And that's where we've got to go, to see for ourselves," Jane said, eagerly. "Straight to the middle of that cornfield."

"Hey, that's awesome," G said. "I'm telling ya, if the Boy Scouts took hikes like this, I'd still be a member. Always be prepared. That's me."

An hour later, Stiletto and I entered the Amish Wunderland parking lot in his Jeep with Jane and G following in the Rabbit. Sandy, concerned that Martin might try the last of the M&M whoopee pies, rushed back to where they were staying at the Red Roof Inn before he got hold of some pressurized whipped cream and became a danger to himself and others.

Meanwhile, I was darned uncomfortable. I had borrowed a pair of Jane's jeans to avoid scrapes and cuts from the corn leaves. But the jeans were cut so low in the waist that I kept hitching them up as we trudged through the field.

"Gee, Mom. It's not like you never flashed your navel before," Jane said, giving them a yank downward.

It was slow going through the cornfield. The plants were higher than even Stiletto, and once we were a few feet into the field, I didn't have a clue as to what was north, east, south or west.

"How do we know a marijuana plant when we find one?" I asked Stiletto, who was forging ahead like a jungle bushwhacker.

"That's easy—" G began before Jane gave him a nudge.

"Fortunately, it's September, the peak of marijuana harvesting season," Stiletto said. "Marijuana plants now are emerald green and distinctive. When I was starting out at the Associated Press, I used to fly on overheads with the National Guard and the DEA—that's the federal Drug Enforcement Agency, G."

G nodded as though he knew them well.

"Anyway," Stiletto continued, "they could easily spot the marijuana plants in a cornfield this time of year. You'll know one when you see one, Bubbles."

As we marched deeper and deeper into the field, G sang a song he had invented to the tune of *The Beverly Hillbillies*. It went like this:

Oh, let me tell you a story about a dude named G
Took his girlfriend to stay in Dutch Country
Then one day he was hiking through a field
When he accidentally found a marijuana yield.
Grass, that is. Acapulco Gold. Kingston tea.

Well, the next thing you know, old G's a happy guy
He's smoking a spliff and getting pretty—

"That will do, G," I cut in.

"Oh, Mom," Jane said, "he was only having fun. G doesn't smoke pot, do you?"

G trudged on silently.

"Well, at least he hasn't around me," Jane said, drifting off to the right. "I despise the stuff. Unlike you, Mom, it makes me goofy and spacey and—"

I stopped. "When have you smoked pot?"

DUBUQUE COUNTY LIBRARY

"Oh, right. Like you, never."

"I never," I said, breaking through a spiderweb.

"Back in your day, kids used to get high on Pine Street between classes. It was like, legendary, at Liberty."

That was true. After lunch every day, the assistant principal used to shoo them off the street. I could still picture the group of red-eyed losers, marching like zombies back to class. These days all smoking of any leafy material was forbidden. Even on Pine Street.

"So can you honestly—and be truthful now, Mom—honestly tell me you never took even a tiny toke*?*" Jane put her hands on her slim hips.

"I honestly never did. I got pregnant with you at seventeen. There was no chance for me to experiment with illegal drugs. And you shouldn't either. If I find—"

I quit it. Mama had lectured me about letting Jane go, about praying that the values I had instilled in her years before had taken root. What was the point of disciplining her at this late age? Besides, it appeared as though Jane had no use for marijuana. Some parents would argue I had gotten off lucky.

"Skip it," I said, ducking under an umbrella of corn leaves. "What I was about to say, it was stupid."

Jane smiled. "You're not stupid, Mom. I'd like to give you an IQ test someday. After that marijuana experience you had, I think you might be a natural genius."

"I'm a genius," G yelled. "I found one!"

He was holding in his hand a bright green bush.

"The mother lode," he beamed.

"And there's another one over there," said Stiletto, whipping out his camera and taking a few shots. "They're everywhere. All a half mile from Mueller's kitchen window. Shep's gonna love this."

I thought about the baking pans in Mueller's sink, the tray he had been holding in his garage the day I nearly backed into him. I mentioned this to Stiletto who agreed that Mueller was probably harvesting the marijuana, baking it in his whoopee pies and then using M&M Gas and Garage as a distribution center.

"Great," I said, after Stiletto had shot a roll. "Let's go. I don't want Mueller to suddenly attack us, especially with Jane and G here."

"Go where?" Jane asked.

"I've got to confront Nimrod," I said. "My guess is instead of money, Mueller's compensating his salesman Nimrod in whoopee pies, which I've seen him consume sitting behind the cash register. But Nimrod's as much a victim as anybody else here, I think. I'd like him to voluntarily go to the police and turn in Mueller before the state police bust Nimrod for dealing dope."

We started walking back to the cars.

"You can't just walk into the gas station and tell Nimrod to confess, Mom," Jane said. "He knows you're a reporter. He'll clam up."

"Jane's got a point," Stiletto said. "It won't work with you and Nimrod."

"Okay. Why don't you go, Steve?" I said. "He doesn't know you."

"Are you for real?" scoffed G. "Stiletto's like old. Nimrod's gonna peg him as a cop undercover."

Stiletto stopped walking. "I am not old. I could whip your ass with both fists tied behind my back."

G snorted and kept on moving. "Don't bust a hemorrhoid, old man."

I shrugged and told Stiletto to ignore him. "He's just a kid, Steve."

"I'm in much better shape than he is," Stiletto grunted, pushing aside a stalk of corn. "Look at all that flab on the boy. I've got more muscles in my right arm than he has brain cells in his head."

"That I'd believe."

"How about I go?" Jane piped up. "Send in G and me. We'll get Nimrod to show us his stash and then you guys can corner him."

"Nuh-uh," I said, "absolutely not."

"Why?" whined Jane.

We argued about this until we got back to the cars. I refused to put her at risk and Jane was convinced that she could pull off the assignment. Eventually, Stiletto stepped in and promised to provide backup. That was better than nothing.

"Anyway," said Jane, "I'm not an idiot. If I get in serious trouble, I'll talk my way out of it. Not like I haven't done *that* before."

Don't think about it, Bubbles, I told myself. Don't even go there.

Chapter 27

I was wrong if I believed the nature of Jane's relationship with G was the hardest moment I'd had to encounter as a parent. That was zip in comparison to watching my smart and yet slightly naive daughter skip into a dirty gas station to sting a suspected drug dealer. Nor did I gain any comfort in knowing that she was being escorted by a slacker who, in other circumstances, could easily have been Nimrod's best buddy.

"There she goes," Stiletto said as we sat in the Jeep, hidden behind pump number three. "She's some kid, that Jane. The way she helped me analyze that map and figure out that Mueller was growing pot out his back door was impressive. She'll make a great journalist someday."

"She's not going to be a journalist," I moped. "G wants her to go to France and pick grapes instead of going to college."

Stiletto leaned back and laughed. "Ahh. That old line. They're still using that?"

"Who?"

"Teenage boys. I must've suggested grape picking in Europe five times to girls when I was eighteen. Kept fluctuating between France and Italy, whichever got me the quickest action. It's a classic."

I shifted in my seat. "A classic, huh? How about fly with me to London and live in Soho, is that a classic, too? For the older set?"

"Good. I'm glad you're still mulling that over." He put on his Ray-Bans. "See, the difference between lines you spout when you're seventeen and those you say when you're thirty-seven is you can back them up when you're thirty-seven, Bubbles. Hey, there they are."

G had emerged first, holding the glass door open for Jane and . . . Nimrod! Nimrod was wearing an orange knit cap and a black George Thorogood T-shirt. He glanced around and then opened a small door to an internal stairway leading to the apartment over the garage. Jane went in first, then Nimrod, then G, who leaned down to tie his shoe. When he was finished, he flashed us a peace sign and the door closed behind him.

"How are you going to get in if you don't have the key?" I asked, trying not to sound too panicked.

Stiletto hopped out of the Jeep. "Don't worry. I'm sure G thought of something."

I got out, too. "I'm coming with you. She's my daughter, Steve."

He nodded and grabbed his camera. The two of us ran to the door and found, much to my delight, that G had left a packet of cigarettes wedged between the door and the wall. Well, at least those evil cancer sticks had some value.

We gently closed the door behind us, replacing the pack of cigarettes, and softly climbed the creaky stairs. Nimrod's room was to the right off a cruddy hall lined with dust bunnies, empty oil cans and odd bits of trash. His door was closed, though we could faintly make out voices and other noises.

There was the scraping of chairs and Nimrod put in a

CD. It was a group I'd never heard of, although Jane and G began chatting about it eagerly. Smoke wafted out—cigarette, not marijuana—and bottles clinked. *Please let it not be beer*, I thought, stupidly. We were dealing with marijuana whoopee pies and I was worried about beer?

This lasted for fifteen minutes when Jane began talking animatedly, pelting Nimrod with questions. He responded with monosyllables and Jane's voice grew louder.

"Let's go!" I hissed to Stiletto. "It's been too long."

Stiletto did the calm-down motion with his hands. "Jane's up to something. Give her a few more minutes."

That was easy for him to say. He'd never rocked her to sleep as a baby or splashed her in the bath when she was a laughing little girl. What had I been thinking, letting Jane get trapped in a snare like this?

Suddenly there was a thump, a click and the sound of cutting. The cutting of cardboard.

"Springsteen rules!" Jane yelled.

"Are you crazy?" Nimrod yelled back.

"I'm telling you, *Springsteen rules*."

Those were the code words.

I took a deep breath and Stiletto gave me an encouraging look.

"It'll be alright, Bubbles," he said before rushing down the hall and kicking open the door. It flew back instantly.

"It was open, man, you didn't have to kick it in," protested Nimrod. "Hey, what gives?"

I dashed into the room and grabbed Jane, who was standing calmly with her hands in her pockets. "You can chill, Mom. Nimrod's cool."

"Tastykakes?" Nimrod exclaimed, glancing back and forth between me and Jane. "She's your mother? Why didn't you say so? I *love* Tastykakes."

"Tastykakes, eh, Mrs. Y?" G said, tapping his

magenta-dyed temple. "I got that one filed for future reference."

Stiletto began taking photos.

"Hope you get my good side," Nimrod said, removing his cap and fluffing up his stringy hair. "Oh, no. Hat head."

I let go of Jane. "I don't get it. How come he's so cooperative? What did you say to him?"

"After we hung out for a while and started talking, I sensed Nimrod had qualms about selling whoopee pies," Jane said in a lowered voice. "I concluded this so-called sting might go more smoothly if I explained the economic consequences to him."

"The economic consequences?"

"Sure. Most illegal enterprises such as this rely on a dramatic imbalance of power. When I diagrammed the unfair system to Nimrod and explained that he was getting short shrift and that Wolf, who had been reaping the profits, would be the first to snitch on him, Nimrod saw the light. Simply a microcosmic model of the proletariat rising against the bourgeoisie, Mom."

"You know about this?" I asked Nimrod, who had been listening intently to Jane.

"About the pot whoopee pies? Sure I know. I've been selling them for a year," Nimrod said. "Eating 'em, too." He and G high-fived.

"No, I mean about you going to the police and turning in Wolf. There's more at stake here than marijuana whoopee pies. Wolf tried to run me over at the Stayin' Alive, Nimrod. This is very serious."

Nimrod squinted. "Wolf didn't try to run you over. Mac did. And he was only scaring you off. He wouldn't have hit you or nothing."

My mouth fell open like a broken trap. "Mac? What does Mac have to do with selling whoopee pies?"

"Like . . . everything. You think this kind of operation could run under his nose for a year and he'd be, uh—"

"Oblivious?" offered Jane.

"Yeah. That. Thanks." Nimrod nodded at Jane.

"But Mac was so helpful and friendly when I asked him about the Hochstetter kids," I said. "He didn't seem like a drug dealer."

"Ahh, he thought that by acting nice, you'd be satisfied and go away. But you didn't. You kept coming back again and again. And, let me add, the last time in that Amish outfit pretending to be interested in buying a car. Not up to your usual snuff, Tastykakes."

"So where does Wolf figure in this?"

"Wolf's only the baker. That's his hobby. The guy's like Betty Crocker in repair overalls. Cookies. Cakes. I don't see the appeal, but that's the way he is."

"Found more!" Stiletto said, uncovering four boxes.

"So," Nimrod continued, "one day I asked Wolf if he could bake me a marijuana brownie. He said it'd been done. There was no challenge. Where was the creativity? Finally, he showed up at work with a marijuana whoopee pie and it was bitchin'."

Stiletto started dialing Nimrod's phone. "I'm calling the state police and taking you down, Nimrod. I've got a source there who'll give you a break if you make a complete statement. Do it today and the worst you'll get is probation."

Nimrod jabbed his thumb in Stiletto's direction. "Who's grandpa?" he asked G.

"Her boyfriend," G said, pointing at me. "They think they're Bonnie and Clyde or something."

I'd remember that the next time G was looking for free handouts from my refrigerator. "Go on, Nimrod. Wolf cooked a marijuana whoopee pie and then what?"

"Mac found out. At first I thought, there goes my job and room over the garage, but no. He was excited. Kept saying it had financial potential. Bought the seed, even planted it and arranged for whoopee pies to be shipped up to Jersey."

"Until one night the driver couldn't make it," Jane said. "Right, Nimrod?"

"Yeah and that's when the karma changed." Nimrod gulped the rest of his Coke. "Mac got wild and forced these two simple Amish kids who used to watch Wolf fix cars into driving to Jersey. Mac thought they'd be inconspicuous and police proof."

"Because Wolf knew how to blackmail them," I added, "with their mother's secret."

But Nimrod didn't seem to know anything about that.

"What about the Pagans?" I asked.

Nimrod stared absently and then broke out in a big grin. "Oh yeah. That was one of the first questions you asked me. If I knew any Pagans."

"Well?" I was sick and tired of this Pagan business. "What about them?"

"There aren't no Pagans. Though Wolf really appreciated you mentioning them. He said the next time anybody asked about the Hochstetter kids, he'd tell 'em they were Pagans. Hah!"

"*I* didn't come up with the Pagans," I said to Jane and G. "Mr. Salvo did."

"Right, Mom," Jane said, following G out the door. "I've heard about you tabloid reporters. Sensationalize everything."

Once outside, Nimrod turned. "I gotta lock up. No one's here to run the place. Mac doesn't come in on Sundays."

Stiletto and I went in with him, to make sure he didn't try anything. He pulled out a key and locked the cash register then turned off the lights. On the way out, I passed the stand of STP and car wax by Mac's office and picked up a tube of Bentley's Boxwood Repair Cream on display.

"What *is* this stuff for?" I asked.

"That?" Nimrod snickered. "That's for show. No one hardly ever buys it."

"How come?"

Nimrod rolled his eyes. "Because hardly no one owns a Rolls. Only Rolls-Royces have boxwood in the steering wheel. It's a big status thing."

Stiletto and I glanced at each other.

"That's gotta be it, Bubbles," he said. "You want help?"

"No thanks. You get Nimrod to the barracks," I said, rushing to the pay phone outside.

It was the same pay phone I'd first used in Whoopee, back when I was halfheartedly convinced that Janice was not Elwood Kramer's murderer. Now I knew who Elwood Kramer's murderer was.

Unfortunately, I had the sinking feeling I was too late to stop him.

As it turned out, I *was* too late. The phone at Mama's pickle time-share rang and rang. Where was Genevieve? I had to get to the condo—pronto.

G drove the Rabbit as fast as a fifteen-year-old German diesel with clogged fuel injection could sputter. When we arrived at the pickle time-share, I jumped out of the car and threw open the front door. Jane was right behind me.

We found Genevieve, her packed bags by her feet, sitting on the couch with her award-winning jar of unripened watermelon pickles and the musket on her lap, along with a huge pile of used tissues.

"Where's Mama?" I panted.

Genevieve blew her nose with a loud *honk!* "Gone," she said, dabbing her eyes, "with Fast Car. They've eloped."

"Eloped?" I ran to the telephone. "To where?" I dialed Mickey Sinkler's home number. It was busy.

"Niagara Falls." Genevieve sniffed. "She's left me forever, Sally. My best friend is gone."

Jane sat herself next to Genevieve and patted her hand. "Don't think of it that way, Genevieve. Think of it as gaining a friend in Fast Car."

"Fast Car hates my fat ass," Genevieve said. "And I don't like him one bit. He wants LuLu all for himself. He's selfish."

I pressed Redial. "And greedy." Damn. Still busy.

"That, too." Genevieve said. "Do you know he wouldn't even let me come along to be LuLu's maid of honor? Said it wouldn't make sense. Because after Niagara Falls they were going to Canada for an indeterminate stay, he said. I ask you, who stays indeterminately in Canada except no-good draft dodgers?"

"Criminals," I muttered, dialing the Lehigh Police Department on the off chance that Mickey was there. He answered on the third ring.

"Sinkler."

"Hi, Mickey. It's me, Bubbles. Good to see that you've come to your senses and returned to work."

"Well, with Janice in the clear and me eliminated as a suspect, I was welcomed into the department with open arms. Anyway, I got tired of sitting around, lifting weights and drinking those chalky protein shakes. Needed to work. Are you back in Lehigh?"

"I'm still in Whoopee with an emergency and a deal."

"Do I get to choose which?"

"Here's the deal. I will tell you who killed Elwood Kramer and where he hid the Rolls if you promise to give the *News-Times* the exclusive."

"The *News-Times*?" Mickey scoffed. "Took 'em three days to print that Kramer had been murdered."

"Is it a deal or not?"

"I'd like to remind you that I have the bargaining advantage here, Bubbles. I could cite you for withholding evidence from police and all that."

"Look at all the pavement pounding I did for you, Mickey. Coming down to Whoopee and—"

"Awww. What the hay. Deal."

I took a deep breath. "The murderer is Carmine 'Fast Car' Humphries, Elwood's—"

"Next-door neighbor. I know. He's suspect number one. We just haven't been able to find the Rolls or any evidence besides fingerprints on a couple of doorhandles. If we can tie him to the Rolls then he'll . . . roll, we're thinking." Mickey let out a nervous laugh.

"You try the speedway?"

"The Nazareth Speedway? Homicide obtained a search warrant four hours after Elwood's body was found. Scoured the entire premises, even old garages and nearby gas stations. No evidence found around The World's Fastest Mile."

"Not that speedway. The old one in Schnecksville."

There was a pause as Mickey scratched his brain. "Didn't that burn to the ground?"

"If it did there must be something left because Fast Car told Mama when we first met that he liked to go down there and get nostalgic."

There was a scratching on paper. "Not bad, Bubbles. When was the last time you heard from Fast Car?"

"About six hours ago. He and Mama left Whoopee this morning in his yellow Porsche and are headed to Niagara Falls and then to Canada, Mickey. He wants to elope with my mother."

"Romantic. They're on Interstate 81 then, probably. Your mother gonna stop bullets for him?"

"Bullets?"

"Just kidding. Thought it'd add to the romance. I'll take this info to homicide and see what they can do. You'll be hearing from me." And he hung up.

I turned to find Genevieve on her two feet, her beefy

face a brilliant crimson and her fists rolled as tightly as cannonballs.

"Fast Car is Elwood Kramer's murderer?" she boomed. *"And you let him take your mother?"*

"I didn't know," I said, my body beginning to shake. "I just figured it out."

"Step aside, Sally," she said, pushing me against the wall and yanking up the receiver. "This is a job for the Monocacy Militia."

"The Monocacy Militia?" asked G, who had just walked in after finishing his cigarette. "Cool."

"Hello? Give me El Jefe, this is Musket Mo." Genevieve tapped a pencil while she waited for El Jefe to get on the line. "El Jefe? We got a nine twenty-four in progress headed northbound on 81. License plate atta-boy-xray-25C. Call out the entire eastern squad and the mountain motorcycles, too. Don't forget the buckshot."

Genevieve nodded a few times, said, "Yup, mm-hmm and back atcha." Then she hung up.

"How fast can that pathetic example of Nazi-financed engineering of yours go?" she asked G.

He shrugged. "I dunno. Eighty maybe? If I stand on the gas pedal."

"Give me your keys, Butch," she ordered, holding out her large hand. "I'm the only one who's gonna be doing the standing here."

G, as frightened of her as I was, dutifully obliged.

"You juveniles with me or against me?" she said, picking up her bags, musket and pickle jar.

"With you," G said, "since it is my car."

"Wait a minute," I said, pointing to Jane, "she's not going. Oh, no."

"Not this again, Mom."

"Sally," Genevieve said, dropping her bags, "do you actually think I would put your daughter at risk, that I would speed, unload a firearm or try to apprehend a murderer on my own with her present?"

"Yes," I said.

"Well, that's true. I would. But I'd use common sense about it."

I wasn't satisfied.

"Okay, Mom." Jane folded her arms. "Tell me. What are you going to do? Head straight home to Lehigh?"

"Not quite. I've got to visit the Stoltzes one last time to show them the file I obtained from the clerk's office about Omer Best. Then I'm leaving."

"What about Mac?" she said. "He's gonna be very ticked off when he discovers that you and I encouraged Nimrod to rat on him. Wouldn't it be better to have me far away, out of danger?"

Genevieve patted the musket. "Safety first, Sally."

I threw up my hands. What could I do? I was surrounded by illogic.

There was a round of hugs and goodbyes as I watched my daughter, for the third time today, enter another death-defying situation. First she had combed the fields for marijuana, then she had entrapped the dealer and now she was on a military-style mission to find my mother, who was being whisked away by a suspected murderer.

Is that good parenting or what?

Chapter 28

In the hubbub of the elopement and marijuana whoopee pies, no one, not even a disheartened Genevieve, had cleaned the pickle time-share as required by contract. Mama usually relished such tasks—scrubbing toilets, sweeping the kitchen and wiping down every inch of the refrigerator. So I was surprised that she had left the place in such a mess—an omission I chalked up to Fast Car's eagerness to split. But, seeing as I had one hour until four o'clock and I was the only one around, I began cleaning to save the security deposit.

Besides, it kept my mind off Jane.

I had just finished that last detail, scouring the coffeepot and placing it in the dishwasher, when the phone rang. It was Stiletto calling from the barracks.

"Glad you're still there. How're you holding up?"

"Not too bad," I said, examining my hands. During my week of cleaning, milking and scrubbing at the Stoltzes, my hands had turned from well-conditioned hair-trimming machines to rough-skinned workhorses with short nails. "There've been some developments."

I told him about Fast Car's escape with Mama, my conversation with Mickey and Genevieve's roundup of the Monocacy Militia.

Stiletto remained eerily speechless throughout. When I was done he said, "You've got to get out of town, Bubbles. This instant."

"Nothing would give me greater pleasure, Stiletto," I said, "but I have to show this file to Samuel Stoltz and explain how important it is for him to contact the state on these environmental regulations. If he doesn't, he could lose his farm and that's exactly what Omer Best wants."

"Mail it to him. Write a letter. Visit next month. Only get out now. Do I have to drive you myself?"

"Plus, I didn't say goodbye, Steve. It would be very, very rude of me to simply drive away after all the effort that family has put out for me. What's the rush anyway? You can't find Wolf?"

"No. The cops found Wolf. Arrested him at home with all the evidence on the premises. Apparently he dried the marijuana in the oven, of all places, on cookie sheets."

I smiled. Too bad we hadn't peeked in the oven when we broke into his house. I'd be home by now.

"It's what Wolf said that's got me concerned. He said someone else beside Mac is pulling all the strings, though he doesn't know who, and the detectives here believe him."

I walked the phone into the kitchen where I began stuffing the contents of the refrigerator into brown paper bags. "What does Mac say? Maybe he'll talk."

"Can't find him. Car's at home. All the cars at M&M are accounted for, but Mac's disappeared. The detectives have put out an APB on him. Nimrod's terrified. He doesn't want to leave the barracks. He doesn't want me to leave him either."

"That's sweet . . . Grandpa," I teased.

"Grandpa. Hmpf. You really think I look that old?"

"Let me get this straight. A few seconds ago you were

urging me to drop everything and head for the hills and now we're having a conversation about your looks?"

"I don't think I look old. I'm only thirty-seven, for Christ's sake."

"Time waits for no man, not even for studs like you, Stiletto."

"Guess I should stop acting like a reckless youth wandering all over the globe," he said. "Maybe it's time to grow up. Settle down."

Don't hold your breath, Tinkerbell, I told myself, keeping mum on my end of the line. I filled the bag with half-empty jars of fat-free mayonnaise, mustard and no-sugar fruit jam.

"Alright," he said, "if you insist on heading to the Stoltzes, please leave by sunset. And give me a call when you do so I can stop worrying."

"Will do," I said, emptying a container of spoiled skim milk down the drain.

"Oh, and another thing, Yablinko."

"Yes?"

"In case anything should happen, I want you to know that I . . . that I—"

I dumped the empty carton in the dark green plastic garbage bag and crossed my arms. Why couldn't he just say it?

"I had a really great time with you Saturday night. That's not it. What I mean is . . . you know what I'm trying to say, don't you?"

"I do," I said. "Me, too."

For the last time I removed all my makeup, braided my hair and slipped my freshly washed cobalt-blue dress and black apron over the tube top and black shorts I was wearing. That way I could discreetly undress in the barn and leave my Amish clothes there when I left the Stoltzes for the last time.

I pinned on my organdy cap and carried all the stuff that had been left in the pickle time-share into the car. Then I picked up the file for Samuel Stoltz and shut the door.

It had been a productive week, I decided on the drive over to the Stoltzes. What had started out as a jaunt to find Janice had resulted in so much more. We had uncovered a marijuana production and distribution ring, ferreted out a blackmail scheme and paved the way for two innocent teenagers to be set free.

There was a good chance that I had figured out who had murdered Elwood. Should have known something was off with Fast Car when he emerged from that nap, claiming he had been awakened by our conversation. At the Final Frontier, he said he took out his hearing aid when he slept. Yet he had been awakened by the voices of Mama and me at the condo.

So I was dying to hear if Mickey had discovered the Rolls-Royce in Schnecksville and if the cops now had enough evidence to pin Fast Car. I prayed he wouldn't do something ridiculous, like hold Mama hostage when the cops caught up with him—that is if Genevieve's gang didn't catch him first.

But, without a doubt, the most satisfying moments during the trip had been in the day-to-day activities at the Stoltzes' farm. Even making root beer, as disastrous as that had been, was a moment I'd never forget.

I'd especially miss Katie's friendly lack of guile, the way she unquestioningly accepted that all my quirks were due to my Ohio upbringing. I didn't consider her a fool; I considered her a friend—a warm, gracious woman who was raising joyful children in a loving household.

I parked the Camaro in its old hiding spot and then trudged down the driveway, swinging the file in a plastic ShopRite bag. It was almost five o'clock and the

Stoltzes would be sitting down to supper soon. Jake and Janice would be making their announcement. Another happy family in the making.

I took a right into the barn and looked for Dolly. She was gone, I noticed, sadly. Sold at the auction. Her stall was empty, a broken tube of VO5 Hot Oil conditioner, caked with manure, lying in the straw.

"Que sera, sera," I said.

The barn door slammed shut and locked.

"Where is she?" a voice said from the corner.

"Jake?" I ran to the door. "What's wrong?"

He was ashen. That was the only way to describe his complexion. Ashen and drawn, large black circles under his eyes.

"She didn't come back to my garage last night, Bubbles," he said. "I assumed she spent the night with her family as she had planned. But when I went over there this morning they said they hadn't seen her."

I slumped against a wooden post. "Janice?"

He nodded. "Tell me she was with you. That's the only possibility that's kept me from going nuts."

"The last I saw Janice was at the beauty parlor yesterday. Regina's in the mall. She said she was taking the bus home."

Jake shook his head. "Do you think she's run away from me?"

"Like she did from her wedding? I don't know. But I think you should go to the police." I told him everything that had happened over the last twenty-four hours.

"Wolf Mueller saw her at Anna Hochstetter's," I said. "And even though she was disguised to look more like me, the original Bubbles, I'm afraid he did threaten to kill her. The police have to know about her disappearance."

Jake had been pacing the barn, mumbling about "responsibility" and "the outside world" and "corruption," along with several Biblical passages that were over my head. When he was done ruminating, he said, "I'll go. Could you cover for me at supper? My parents are expecting me."

"Do they know about Janice?"

He shook his head. "Because she went off, we were never able to meet with the church elders. I didn't want to say anything until Elspeth and I had received their approval."

I told him I would do what I could and he flew out the door to hitch up the buggy. To me this was an indication of his renewed conviction to turn away from the modern world and toward the faith he had almost abandoned forever. Jake had given up cars.

Now very concerned and filled with purpose, I left the barn and approached the farmhouse. The sun was obscured by clouds which were beginning to drizzle the rain of early fall. Chickens clucked in complaint while a house cat rushed onto the porch to escape the rain.

I wrapped the file tightly in the plastic, dashing toward the screen door. All I had to do was take Samuel aside for ten minutes, pitch my argument and I was free to go.

But no such luck. For the Stoltzes had just sat down to supper. Their smiling faces greeted me with hospitality. Chicken pot pie, red beet eggs, tomatoes, three-bean salad, Lebanon bologna, bread and butter waited on the table—along with a steaming plate of shoofly pie.

I gasped as I spied Omer Best sitting next to Samuel.

"Hurry up, Sally Hansen," Omer said, holding up his fork and knife, "before it's all et."

Chapter 29

"*Komme esse,*" said Fannie. "Ephraim. Move over and make room for Sally."

"No, no," intervened Omer, pointing his fork toward the gap beside him on the bench. "Next ta me sit yourself dawn."

"Ya, sit next to Omer, Sally," Katie said, squirming to the side to make room for me. "I'll rutch over."

"Have you seen Jacob, Sally? We're waiting for him," Fannie asked, as I sat down.

"Yes, I did. He passed me when I got off the bus," I answered calmly, although inside I was a tangle of raw nerves. "Said he wouldn't be making it to supper."

With that said, Samuel began the prayers and the family dug in. It took Omer no time to start in on the environmental regulations and the upcoming conservation commission meeting. I clenched my teeth, barely able to take a bite as he lied blatantly to an unwitting Samuel. The family ate swiftly as he spoke.

"Ya oughta go dawn naw, ta da meetin'," Omer said, helping himself to Samuel's Lebanon bologna.

"With all this alfalfa to bale? No. It's the wrong time in the season," Samuel said, sagely. "The state will have to wait until November when the harvest is over."

"In da tousands da fines will be by den," Omer said. " 'Course I can do da talking fer ya, if ya don't mind, naw, when I go dere Tuesday ta do my own business."

That's because your own business is pushing the state to cite your neighbor, Omer Best, I wanted to scream. You want him to leave his farm quickly and desperately. So desperate that he will sell you his land below market value.

But I couldn't scream that because there was an unspoken rule in this household that when the menfolk were talking, women and children were not to interrupt. We were not even to hold our own conversations. We could only eat, listen and get up to do the dishes.

When Omer changed the subject and began waxing nostalgically about the beautiful, fertile farms he'd seen for sale in Kentucky, I had to take action. My knee banged the table and Omer's glass of water promptly toppled. Water spilled onto the floor and onto Omer's lap.

"*Geb acht*, Sally!" Omer said as he leaned over to help me dab up the water with his napkin.

For one brief second his gaze met mine and there was a spark of awareness.

"Do ya know not vat's da meaning of *geb acht*, Sally?" he asked.

"Sally is from Ohio, Omer," Samuel said. "They've given up the old German there."

"Have dey naw?" Omer said. "I never met an Amish dat didn't speak German. I vonder, Sally, vy ya don't."

"I can speak some," I said. "All Ohio Amish speak some German."

"Ya. If dat's so, den *was hast du denn?* Hey, even I know dat von."

Fannie, the only one at the table who had been clued in to my true identity, sucked in a breath. I was positive Omer had discovered I was a fraud and, moreover, that I was critical of his plan to scam land from Samuel.

"I said," Omer pushed back his plate and regarded me with his crossed eyes, *"was hast du denn?"*

Samuel put down his fork. "Now, Omer—"

"*Ech hab' meine eigene Hackmaschine.*" It was the only Pennsylvania Dutch phrase I had been taught, although, thanks to my sieve-like brain, I had long ago forgotten what it meant.

"*Ech hab' meine eigenen Hackmaschine*?" Omer exclaimed.

Yipes! What had I said?

A nervous silence descended over the table.

"Ya know vat?" Omer said loudly, glancing around the table, "I don't tink dis Sally here is Am—"

"*Was hast du denn?*" Katie cut in, giggling. "And Sally said, *Ech hab' meine eigenen Hackmaschine*. It's funny. What have you? I have my own meat grinder. Good pun, Sally."

Fannie was the first to join in and then Samuel. Both laughed, more at the release of tension than at the silliness of my Pennsylvania Dutch play on words. Omer stroked his double chin sullenly.

I took this opportunity to wiggle out and gather plates, taking them over to the sink. Katie brought a few more over and, whispering, asked me where I had been the night before, that the whole family had been worried. I made up some story about running into a long-lost relative at Anna Hochstetter's but this time Katie didn't believe me.

I avoided eye contact and vigorously pumped water into the sink.

"Omer's right. You're not Amish, are you?" she said after an uncomfortable silence.

My hand fell off the pump. "I'm sorry, Katie. Perhaps you should ask your mother later." I nodded toward Omer whose big ears were positioned to eavesdrop. "Now is not the time."

A look of hurt washed over Katie and I felt like kicking myself. She opened her mouth to ask me another question and then snapped her lips shut.

"Are you . . . in trouble?" she whispered.

I thought about this. "Actually, I may be."

She wiped her hands purposefully. "Well then, I'm glad you're here. There is no trouble in this house." And she walked away.

I wanted to cry. Oh, if that stupid doofus Omer Best would only leave. Then I could explain everything.

Finally, miracle of miracles, he did leave.

It was almost nine and even Samuel was nodding as Omer sat in the rocker, discussing the market price of corn and the cost of a new tractor. Katie was back in her side of the house, putting her family to bed, and Fannie had given up her knitting to go upstairs.

Meanwhile, I sat at the kitchen table, thumbing through vegetable seed catalogs by the kerosene lamp. I tried not to fixate on what was going on with Mama and Jane or that, because there was no telephone, no one could reach me if something horrendous had happened to them. I refused to imagine Mac lying in wait, seeking his revenge against me. I could not wonder about Janice, if she had gotten cold feet for the second time in one week.

Instead I designed gardens of Bugsby's Super Orange Flesh Melon and Big Boy Tomatoes. Southern Delicious Cucumber and Northern Hearty Broccoli with Slow Bolt Buttercrunch.

Then I heard Samuel say the magic words. "I apologize, Omer, but the night is getting the better of me."

"Ach. I don't know ver da time vent," Omer muttered, as he got up and waddled to the door. "Good night, Sally Hansen of Ohio."

"Good night," I mumbled.

"Sweet dreams," he said, opening the door.

Yeah, yeah, I thought to myself, yawning.

"Well, good night, then, Sally," Samuel said, picking up a lamp to go upstairs.

"Samuel," I said softly, "I need to talk to you."

"It is late, Sally. Whatever it is can wait until tomorrow."

I lifted my head from the seed catalog and pulled out the file that had been hidden on my lap. "This can't wait," I said, plunking it on the table. "The future of your family depends on it."

He put the lamp down and glared at me over his glasses. "What have you been up to, Sally? First you do not come home last night, worrying us something sick. Then you show up late for supper. You are rude to Omer, spilling things, and now this." He pointed to the file.

Samuel Stoltz was as mad as I had ever seen him. And I did not think he angered very often.

"My name is not Sally Hansen and I was not raised Amish in Ohio."

"That I gathered," he said, taking a seat on the bench opposite me. "Who are you, then?"

"My name is Bubbles Yablonsky and I'm a hairdresser-slash-newspaper-reporter on assignment undercover." I stood up and took off my Amish dress to reveal my top and shorts, the real me.

"And now I have to help you. In repayment of your kindness."

Samuel put a hand over his heart as his wide gaze traveled down to my tube top, stared in horror and then rose to my eyes in shock.

"What do you intend to do? I've been married for thirty-five years. I'm a very devout man . . . Bubbles."

"Oh, no, not like that, Samuel," I exclaimed, clutching my dress and sitting down. "Help in this way."

I removed papers from the file, first handing him the

state statute on regulating the runoff of manure and fertilizer from farmlands. Then I showed him the diagram Bob Jackson had made, of where Samuel needed to dig drainage ditches and retention ponds.

"This I know," he said. "This is why I'm getting fined. Why are you showing it to me now?"

"Bob Jackson said it would not cost much money to comply with the regulations. There are even grants—"

Samuel held up his hand. "No. Not for us there aren't. We do not take money from the government. Give, yes. Take, no."

I breathed in deeply. "Okay, but this is why I'm so insistent you look at this file now. Here."

I slid him the series of letters from Philadelphia lawyer Crandall Hurd to the Department of Environmental Protection. In the letters, Hurd noted he represented a Whoopee landowner who preferred to remain anonymous at this point for obvious reasons and who had "grave concerns" that Samuel Stoltz was not following "revised groundwater protection standards."

Hurd said that if the state did not take action by citing and fining Stoltz for noncompliance with federal and state law, then the landowner would be forced to sue both Stoltz and the state and federal governments for not protecting his water supply.

"These regulations have been on the books for years, Samuel," I explained, "and even though they are important, they usually are not enforced by fines until a neighbor insists the state cite the farmer. Most often the state works with the farmer to achieve voluntary compliance."

I watched as Samuel compared the threatening, legally written memos.

"In your case, Samuel, your most ardent enemy, the one who has repeatedly insisted that you be fined until you comply is—"

"Omer Best," Samuel said.

I leaned over and looked at the letter. "It says that there?" I hadn't yet pointed out to Samuel that Randall Hurd was also a lawyer representing Dutch Enterprises, Omer's business.

"No. I knew. I've known for a long, long time, Bubbles." He threw the letters down on the wooden table. "Is that what you've kept me up to tell me?"

Okay, I was stunned. No, stunned is too weak a word. Shocked was more like it. Shocked beyond belief or comprehension.

"If you knew, then why do you let him—"

Samuel shook his head. "Omer has his faults. But greed, covetousness, gossip, surely those are temptations to which many of us as humans fall, right, Bubbles?"

I hung my head. I was such a fool. "Right, Samuel."

"That does not mean I do not welcome him into my home or accept his friendship. Deep down Omer is a good man, I believe. However, I do not take what Omer says as gospel." His eyes twinkled with mischief. "And who's to say I wasn't having some fun leading him on."

We smiled at each other warmly. Had Samuel Stoltz not been a proper, married Amish man and I not been dressed in a tube top, I would have reached across the table and kissed his cheek then and there.

"I'm sorry for butting in, Samuel. It was wrong of me to assume that I knew more about local politics and neighbors and farming than you did."

"No, no, Bubbles. I'm touched that you made the effort to go to the town hall and research this." He tapped the file. "And you're right. I will contact this Bob Jackson and meet with him. I should've done it last spring when I received the first citation."

"So you're not going to Kentucky?"

"I didn't say that. It depends on what Dutch Enterprises does with that land it owns all around us. I do not want to be the only farmer in the midst of houses and an amusement park. Omer knows how I feel about that, too."

"Dutch Enterprises needs *you*, Samuel. Without your land to supply water, Omer Best can't build."

"There is always a way to build when money is involved. If Dutch Enterprises can't get my land one way, they'll get it another. Sometimes I think it'd take a miracle to stop them."

A clap of thunder shook the house and rain streamed down the windows. It was cozy and comforting in this tidy red, white and green kitchen with its large iron stove and pump sink. Part of me did not want to leave.

The other part of me was dying to go.

"I'm afraid that this file was to be my going-away present to you," I said. "Some present, huh?"

"It was a fine, fine gesture." Samuel stood. "Will you be here in the morning?"

I shook my head. "Thank Fannie for me and Katie, too, will you please. They were more than hospitable. They were friends."

He nodded.

"Oh, and I wonder if you've discovered any of this in your cornfield." I reached in my pocket and showed him a wilted marijuana leaf.

"Hemp," Samuel said, examining it. "It popped up everywhere in the fields this summer. We've been gathering and burning it. Have to be careful, though. Makes us ferhoodled if we stand too close."

He handed me the leaf, took the lamp and crossed the creaky wooden floor to the stairs.

"Goodbye, Bubbles Yablonsky from Lehigh," he said, pausing on the third step.

"Goodbye," I croaked, tears dotting my cheeks.

I folded my Amish clothes and laid them neatly on the table, along with the file. Then I gathered my keys and jogged up the driveway in the pouring rain to the Camaro, tucked in its hiding place for the very last time.

The rain was so heavy that a river was running down my windshield. I was soaked to the bone and once inside the car I rummaged around in my suitcase for a new bra, blouse and denim skirt. After changing in the front seat I felt somewhat better, although my skin was still clammy. With another dirty skirt I alternately toweled dry my hair and wiped the inside of the windows free of condensation as I blasted the defrost. When I had one tiny hole of vision, I stepped on the gas.

Immediately I sensed that the car was driving oddly. It was dragging as though the tires were low. But I couldn't stop and check the air now. I needed to get to a phone and call Stiletto at the state police barracks. He would know if Jane was okay. Besides, I needed one of those metallic space-age thingamajigs to check the air and I had lost mine from the Shell car-care course I took a few years back.

To calm myself down, I played a bit of Van Halen and toyed with the naughty idea of visiting that secret Virginia Slims pack I keep in the glove compartment. The rain was mercilessly hard with thunder, lightning and pelting rain against which my wipers were virtually powerless.

How much more could a girl take? It was bad enough that my daughter was off who-knows-where with a band of renegade, prune-gumming, senior-citizen militia members after a speeding murderer. Now I had to deal with flooding roads and nil night vision. Didn't I *deserve* a cigarette *just this once?*

Well, of course I did. But as though the Surgeon General were a sniper waiting to shoot a cigarette out of my hand, right when I leaned over to snap open the glove compartment there came a loud *crack!*

I bolted upright. What was that? But there it was

again. *Crack!* And then the most awful, dreadful thing happened that can happen to a thirty-something single woman on the road alone at night. I got a flat tire. *Flump. Flump. Flump*, the wheel went as I rolled to a stop.

Hey, I might be blond and busty, I might base most of my fateful life decisions on what Luke and Laura would do in the fictional soap opera city of Port Charles, but I was not without awareness. Someone—and I didn't think it was the Surgeon General—had shot out my tires. I was doomed.

The choices were slim to none. Sit here with the Van Halen tape blaring David Lee Roth and wait for my would-be murderer to arrive, or get out, pretend for a moment that I'd merely hit a pointy stone, dig around for the jack, fix the car and head off. I chose the latter.

At least the storm had handed me a break. The rain was only constant, not relentless, now. I grabbed my raincoat and got out, trotting around to the rear. I wasn't sure I'd know what to do with a jack once I found it, but I understood the basic premise. Lift up car. Unscrew old tire. Screw on new one.

Never got the chance to try it, though. Because when I opened the rear and threw back the flap, there was no jack. There was, however, Mac. A cold, dead, shot-through-the-head Mac. Great. Just when I could really, really use a mechanic, I discover one in my trunk and he's been murdered.

Funny how my teeth had started chattering. And what was with this shaking of the knees? Or the whole body for that matter. Was I about to . . . I think I was. I was about to throw up!

Holy mackerel, I must be scared. No, correction, I must be frightened witless. Because here I was on this deserted dirt road in the middle of nowhere Whoopee, PA, with a shot-out tire and a dead guy in my trunk. A dead guy that I had assumed was the threatening, blackmailing brain behind the M&M drug business.

So if Mac was dead, then who had killed him? Not Nimrod or Wolf. They were in custody.

I feared the answer was studying me from the shadows and waiting for me to make my next move.

Chapter 30

My next move was obvious. Run.

I pulled my raincoat over my head and, still in my Amish-style bare feet, headed into the cornfield. I zigged and zagged as I had seen victims do on television. I zigged and zagged so much that I ran into a small shed. Literally. Oww.

When I realized what I had found, the local telephone shack, I was nearly giddy. I *knew* this place. I had been here.

I might very well survive.

I pulled open the door and reached for the phone. Even with limited light, my fingers could dial 9-1-1. It rang once and then a dispatcher got on.

"Lancaster County 911."

"I'm—"

Click.

We'd been cut off. Someone—or something—had depressed the receiver. Reaching up, I made it out to be long, cold and wet. A rifle butt.

"It's over, Bubbles," he said.

I turned. The door was open behind him, but in the darkness I couldn't see much. A white shirt. A straw hat. Suspenders.

It couldn't be.

The rifle slid off the receiver and I hung up the phone. There was silence as the gun's steely hollow end pressed into my breastbone.

"Let's go, Bubbles," he said. "Janice is waiting."

I thought about kicking him or fumbling for Genevieve's cow mace, but what would that have accomplished? A hole in my chest, that's what it would have accomplished.

"Who are you?" I asked, the words barely able to exit my throat.

"Who do you *think* I am?"

"Jacob Stoltz?" I said. "Is that you? Don't do this, Jake, because—"

Pleading was no use. He had started laughing a cold, mean, cruel laugh. And with the laugh came images of the damage I had caused. Here I had an entire militia and possibly a police department chasing after Fast Car when Fast Car hadn't stolen the Rolls at all. Jake had.

Hadn't Mickey mentioned that an Amish friend of Janice's had shown up at the Final Frontier to look at Elwood's new car? He had been preoccupied with it, Mickey said, obsessed to the point where he could not pull himself away even to say hello.

"But what do you have to do with Mac?" I asked.

"Forget it, Bubbles," he said, nudging me with the firearm. "We don't have time."

"Where can you take me?" I asked. "Whoopee's not that big, Jake. People will hear things."

There was that annoying laugh again, and then Jake said, "We're going back to the Whoopee Garden Estates, Bubbles. Got to get back to the garden—"

The phone rang. *Brrrring. Brrrring.* Jake and I stood there, dumbstruck. *Brrrring.*

"Aren't you going to answer it?" I said. "Maybe it's

911 and they've traced the call. Got cops on the way right now."

I needn't have said more. In a flash, Jake leaned over and popped off the receiver. It dangled there, swinging back and forth. The rifle butt was still pressed against me, so I was not inclined to yell. Jake and I held our breaths.

"Hello? Bubbles?" came the whiny voice. "This is Mitchell from PSAC. I'm trying to find a Bubbles Yablonsky. Hello?"

With one quick grab I yanked up the receiver. "Help, Mitchell! Call the police. He's taking me to the Whoopee Garden Estates. It's a con—"

Boom!

Jake had fired right into the pay phone, sending pieces flying. A sharp shard of metal hit me on the side of the head, barely missing my eye. It was the last sensation I experienced before sinking onto the dirt floor of the phone shack and wondering about that warm sticky stuff that was oozing down the side of my face and where Jake had learned to shoot a gun anyway.

My first thought when I achieved consciousness was, am I dead or alive? When I opened my eyes and saw that I was sitting behind the wheel of an early model Ford Fiesta, I figured I was indeed dead and that the afterlife was pretty much like the current life. Old Fords. Wal-Mart and McDonald's. Some pie in the sky.

Although it was pitch-black outside the car, I had the distinct impression that I was no longer anywhere near the phone shack by Samuel's farm. My best guess was that Jake had taken me, as he had promised, to the Whoopee Garden Estates—that huge construction site where I had waved my bra to save Stiletto.

"Oh, my head," I moaned, carefully dabbing my temples. "Got such a headache, like I've been crowned with an anvil."

Wait! Where had I had that thought before? Oh, yes. On that sickening morning when I awoke next to Dan the Man after doing Jell-O shots and lip-synching Skynyrd at Uncle Manny's Bar and Grille. If I had only kept my mouth shut, sung some Judy Collins instead, I wouldn't have ended up this way. Janice wouldn't have flipped and run back to Amish life and she'd be married to Mickey by now. Probably changing a diaper on the four-year-old.

"Ohh. Ohhh." The pounding was terrific. Worse than the aftereffects of those Jell-O shots. And what was that noise? Whatever it was, it was not helping.

Bzzz. Bzzzz. It was loud and obnoxious. A chain saw.

"Hey, cut that out!" I shouted, closing my eyes and wishing for a cold drink of water.

The buzzing stopped. "Excuse me?" Jake was outside the car so his voice was muffled. "Did you say something?"

"That sawing. Cut it out."

"Not tonight." *Bzzz! Ping.* "There. That's the last doorhandle."

I tried the handle on the inside of the car. It moved, but otherwise was useless. The door didn't budge. "What did you saw off the doorhandles for?"

"Guess."

"I give up."

"I don't want you two to escape, not when you're rolling down the hill to your death."

Hold on. Back up. "We? Who's we?" I asked through a crack in the window.

"Check out your backseat. You can turn on the overhead."

I turned on the overhead. There was Janice flat out, still in my clothes and heels. I was relieved to see her chest rising and falling slightly.

"What'd you do to her?"

"I went easy on her. She got a nice drink to knock her out. Now turn off the overhead."

I turned off the overhead. "Let Janice go," I said, pulling on that doorhandle. "She didn't do anything wrong, Jake. She was trying to help out a couple of kids. I was the one who found the drugs and convinced Nimrod to turn in Wolf. She was completely innocent."

Ugh. What was the point? There was that hideous laugh again. A high-pitched nasal excuse for a guffaw.

I took a deep breath. Logic. I needed logic. I was sitting behind the wheel of a Ford Fiesta. No doubt the brake lines had been cut. The locks had been rendered inoperable and we were about to die. Plus my brain really, really hurt.

"So, what are you going to do here, Jake?" I asked, rotating with the window mechanism. It, too, had been disabled. "You gonna push us into a river or something? A quarry?"

"Not quite. I'm sending you straight into the middle of the construction site where you'll blow up upon impact with the aid of some blasting caps."

"Why there?"

He walked around to the other side. "You're a kamikaze protester, Bubbles. You and your best friend Janice. Ever see *Thelma and Louise*?"

"No. And I've never protested a thing in my life."

"Not true. You were seen all over the Philadelphia news last week waving your red bra, trying to stop a bulldozer."

I kicked myself. Good move, Bubbles. He was right. My death would be written off as a suicide when people realized that I, the woman who had streaked across the construction site, was now dead in the very same spot. The ultimate protest.

"You also were seen going up to Omer Best's office

on Wednesday night, trying to state your case," Jake continued. "And on Friday a clerk in town hall overheard you asking how you could stop Omer Best from completing his development."

Talk about plugged in. Jake had been aware of my every movement during my stay in Whoopee. He must've stuck a homing device in my Camaro when he inspected my muffler, that's all I could think.

"That should be it," he said, walking to the rear of the Ford. "All I need now is to give you a slight push and down the hill you go. It's perched to rocket. Goodbye, Bubbles. It'll be good to have you out of my—"

"*Hold on, Omer!*" a voice called out in the darkness.

Omer? Where was Omer?

"Jesus Christ, Samuel. What're you doing out here so late?" Jake responded.

Or was that Omer? No. If it were Omer Best, that would have been, *Vat're ya doingk here aut sa late, naw*?

Then again, the man I'd been talking to here, the man who had kidnaped me from the phone shack, had never completely confirmed that he was Jake. Nor had he shown his face. While stuck in the car, all I'd seen were glimpses of his body. Shirt and pants.

And Samuel certainly knew an Omer from a Jake, I thought sadly. Brave, wise Samuel. Oh, why hadn't he merely called the police? Why had he come here, probably unarmed and too innocent to deal with the pure evil of Omer Best?

"*Put down the gun, Omer.*"

There was a long pause. As though Omer might actually obey.

"*It's the right thing to do, Omer. C'mon, give me the gun.*"

"You're not armed, Samuel," Omer said. "You're a dead man."

"*I'm an old man, too. I don't care if you shoot me. Give me the gun. You're no murderer, Omer.*"

Wanna bet? I thought of Mac, bullet in the head, back in my Camaro. My heart was beating so furiously it filled my ears.

I heard the safety catch click and then Omer yell, "Like in the movies, better say your prayers—Ugh!"

Say your prayers—Ugh? What was going on? I hated being trapped in this all-American shell of a compact car. I wanted out. I banged on the window, but no one responded. There was the sound of scuffling and then a shot went off.

"Bubbles?" It was Jake. The real Jake. His face was pressed against the window and he was trying the doorhandle. "You're gonna be all right. Where's Janice?"

I turned on the overhead again and his eyes flicked to the backseat. "Oh!"

"She's okay," I yelled through the glass. "Omer drugged her. Where are the cops?"

Jake was on the other side now, trying that doorhandle. "They're coming. What did Omer do to this car?"

The car began to rock as he yanked on the door.

"Jake. Watch out!" I yelled. "He's got this thing rigged to—"

It was too late. Before I knew it, the Ford Fiesta teetered back and forth and then zoomed forward, almost as if falling off a cliff. We bounced along the ground over rocks and what sounded like various pieces of debris. Old oil drums. Trash cans. Lots of clanging. Quickly, I put on my safety belt—a life-saving detail Omer had forgotten to disable.

The brakes were gone, of course, but there seemed to be a bit of life in the steering. Good old manual steering. Couldn't twirl this baby with my manicured index finger, oh no, I had to yank it to the left. Then yank it to the right. Anything to slow us down. It was working. The rate of acceleration was decreasing. Now if I could only find out where we were and to what we were heading.

For one brief second I took my hand off the wheel to fumble for the light switch. That was my crucial mistake. The car went up and over, rolling twice as I lost control. Finally we landed on our side and I sucked in the unmistakable sweet odor of a budding electrical fire.

Smoke rose from the dashboard and began filling the car. I unfastened my seat belt and felt for Janice, who was now moaning slightly as she lay against the windows. We had to get out of here. I had to break a window, escape and pull out Janice before we blew up.

It was too much. As the smoke filled my throat I began to cough. So did Janice, who gasped pitifully from the back. My eyes were stinging and my lungs ached. I wanted the pain to be over. I wanted this to stop.

Crash! I became vaguely aware of lights around the car. The windshield had been broken and Janice's body went by me. I remember being happy at seeing her legs kick, knowing she had made it. That she would live.

"*Get her out of there!*" someone shouted. "*We need to get her out of there now!*"

I didn't care. My body convulsed in a fit of coughing and I fought the temptation to simply close my eyes and pass out.

Then I heard that damn chain saw again and realized that the door was being removed. There was a rush of cool air and I felt two strong arms wrap around my chest, lifting me out. I was being carried away and up a hill.

"Bubbles! Bubbles! Are you okay?"

The pain in my lungs was too intense. I kept coughing. I couldn't answer.

"Bubbles, it's me, Steve. Say something. Say anything."

I blinked my eyes. Stiletto was leaning over me, stroking my forehead. He was smoky and sweating.

"You," cough, "say it first," I managed to eke out.

He gave me a startled look, but then he smiled. A big, wide, grin.

"I—"

Kaboom!

A flash of bright orange heat exploded below us. Janice's Fiesta burst into pieces, scattering glass and door parts and burning rubber in slow-mo around us. Stiletto had gotten out of saying it one more time, the bum.

I shut my eyes and drifted off, wondering about Stiletto's fantastic bachelor luck, when he bent down low and amidst the police sirens and the static of firemen's walkie-talkies, he whispered in his softest, sexiest voice, "From the moment I saw you hanging from the Philip J. Fahy Bridge back in Lehigh, I knew you were the one. So don't die, Bubbles. You have to live because I love you, Bubbles.

"God, do I love you."

Epilogue

I didn't die. What I did was spend two days in the Hershey Medical Center recovering from smoke inhalation, a concussion and various assorted minor injuries. And if that was death, then it was absolute heaven. Free cable. Maid service. In-house cook. Plus Stiletto refused to leave my bedside. He kept offering to administer sponge baths. Totally unnecessary, as I was able to limp to the shower. Still, it was thoughtful of him to expend the effort.

Samuel Stoltz escaped unharmed. The shot that went off from Omer Best's rifle landed in the architectural drawing for the Whoopee Garden Estates. Meanwhile, Janice spent a day in the hospital, too, mostly to recover from the Mickey Finn that Omer had slipped her. When she stopped by my room to say farewell, she said that while the Amish cannot take oaths, she was making a vow never to step into another car again. They'd been nothing but trouble as far as she was concerned.

I observed that she and I would not have met had it not been for car problems. Janice said that proved her point exactly.

In the end I owed my life to Katie and Mitchell of PSAC. It was Katie who persuaded her father that night to follow me in the pouring rain. After our talk in the kitchen, she had lain awake, unable to sleep because she was convinced I was in terrible danger. When she heard me leave she ran to Samuel and roused him, urging him to take the buggy and search for me. Samuel was headed down the road past his farm when he spied Omer carrying my unconscious self to the Ford Fiesta. Janice's Fiesta never could go much over forty miles per hour, a Godsend in this situation since its pokiness allowed Samuel to follow in the buggy.

Mitchell, who could easily have assumed that my plea for help was yet another way of avoiding the student loan bill, hung up and called the state police like a good boy. Stiletto and Jake were exiting the barracks when the dispatcher received Mitchell's report and radioed the details to troopers in their cruisers. Wasting no time, Stiletto and Jake drove to the construction site. It was Stiletto who had jumped on Omer right when he was about to fire at Samuel.

Later that night, Omer Best was apprehended by the state police and charged with a variety of crimes. He was eventually indicted with murder (in the death of Mac), attempted murder, assault, kidnaping and destruction of private property (the Amish pay phone). Police did not have enough evidence to pin him with the death of Wolf Mueller Sr., however. And Omer may very well slip the murder charge, as Mac's body was blown to smithereens in the Fiesta where Omer had craftily transferred it.

However, according to police sources, Omer is also under investigation for his role in the marijuana whoopee pie distribution ring. It was no accident that the marijuana we found was growing on Dutch Enterprises real estate. When Omer had discovered the plants on his property the year before, he had traced them to Mac and demanded a lion's share of the profits—which he promptly received.

When I showed up asking questions about Janice and the Hochstetter boys, Mac took my visit as an opportunity to renegotiate the contract. He apparently visited Omer that Sunday morning and threatened to reveal the marijuana operation to me if Omer didn't give him a bigger cut. Omer responded by shooting Mac in the forehead.

That done, Omer panicked. He had been many shady things—a greedy developer among them—but before Wolf Sr., Omer had never killed a man. He was worried that Mac had already spoken to Janice and me or that we knew more about his relationship with Mac than we did. So he went after us. With Nimrod and Wolf in custody, we were the only targets he could grab.

To me the brilliance of Omer Best was the phony accent he had learned from a Pennsylvania Dutch book of phrases he purchased during his first week in Lancaster County. Omer, also known as Billy Ray Best, was from Odessa, Texas, originally. Thirty years ago his mother had inherited the farm in Whoopee and decided to retire there. Dutiful son that he was, Omer tagged right along.

The phrase book had been Mudder's idea. She proposed it as a way for her socially inept son to mingle with the natives. Omer saw it as his key to opening the doors of area Amish homes—and bank accounts.

Much of this information I gleaned from interviews with police sources and Whoopee residents who had long been concerned about Omer Best's plans for the community. I found the shopkeeper who sold Omer his first book of ferhoodled phrases, and Omer's mother, a kind old lady who seemed greatly relieved to have Omer out of her house and behind bars with three squares a day, discussed his quirks with alarming frankness.

I relied on these interviews, along with records from

the town hall and the state, to compile an in-depth profile of Omer Best. It was a fascinating tale of fraud, drugs, development and Omer's sneaky manipulation of local Amish families. However, with Whoopee being ninety miles out of the *News-Times* circulation area, my hometown newspaper wasn't interested.

Fortunately, the editors at the *Philadelphia Inquirer*'s Sunday Magazine were. And they showed their gratitude with a hefty check.

So I wasn't too worried when, weeks after I was released from the hospital, Dix Notch arranged for me to meet the publisher for a real, old-fashioned chewing out. Notch gleefully explained how I had violated various ethical obligations, from reporting on the murder of Elwood Kramer to prancing around Whoopee in Amish wear. But by this time the *Inquirer* had already contracted me to write the magazine piece and the only person who got chewed out was Notch, for not recognizing a potential Pulitzer when he saw one.

Speaking of Elwood Kramer's death, Fast Car owned up to his crime shortly after he was accosted at an Interstate 81 rest stop by Genevieve, Jane and G along with thirty or so senior citizens dressed in black leather and driving Harleys. Fast Car admitted that he and Elwood had engaged in a virulent argument on Elwood's patio the night before Janice's wedding. The issue, as always, was Elwood's Rolls. Fast Car had come home that night to find that it took up too much space in their shared garage for his Porsche to fit. It was the final straw.

Unfortunately, words about whose car deserved garage space turned into shoves and soon the old men were in fisticuffs. Elwood fell back at one point and smacked his head on the corner of a wrought-iron table. He died instantly. Fast Car, horrified, dragged his body into the bathroom, cleaned up the blood as best he could and then thought, what the hell? Why not take the Rolls? Which he did. Mickey's search warrant revealed it hidden under an old tarp in a burned-out garage in Schnecksville. Fast Car was charged with manslaughter and grand theft auto. He is free on bail.

For Mama, this was more drama than she ever hoped to enjoy in her twilight years and she has milked it for all it is worth down at the senior center. She has abandoned the Jackie O shtick for the more romantic role as an outlaw's girlfriend. Passing on pudding and shuffleboard, she now shoots billiards and casts wistful looks at women who haven't known the heartbreak and adventure of loving a man at odds with the law. The other day I found her in Kmart shopping for faux leather jeans. Size petite queen.

Jake and Janice, or rather, Elspeth, finally spoke to the church elders and are slated to be married in November. After enjoying a traditional Amish honeymoon of visiting extended family and friends, they plan to build a farm on some land that Omer Best is selling to pay for legal expenses. In fact, Omer has had to sell most of his land back to the Amish at very reduced prices. Needless to say, the massive development and "deme park" will not be built.

Once his farm is completed, Jake has indicated that he would like Nimrod to apprentice with him, working as a laborer and learning more about cars. The judge on Nimrod's case (and, really, who of us isn't on Nimrod's case?) has tentatively signed off on this arrangement. If that agreement goes through, Nimrod will be spared jail time and receive probation instead. Someday he might be able to expunge his record of marijuana charges, if he keeps his nose clean.

There is a good bet Wolf Mueller will endure a light sentence for his role in manufacturing and distributing marijuana-laced whoopee pies and for beating up poor

Shep. However, he has already applied to various cooking schools where he has a good chance of learning gourmet cuisine after he has served his debt to society.

The Hochstetter boys were released into their mother's custody. Anna, who made a clean breast of her soap opera addiction to the Amish community, has left her electrified house for one without cable.

With all this behind me, it was a delight to return to work at the House of Beauty where Sandy is all atitter over Martin's Bread and Butter Pickle Butter Bread. She is convinced that this latest invention of his will be picked up by a fast food chain and that their retirement will be secured.

Meanwhile, Mickey is a changed man. With his ex-wife, Sue, back to mothering, Mickey has moved into a chic apartment in Fountain Hill where he has set up a weight room. Overnight his string bean body has turned to a muscled mass that would rival Arnold Schwarzenegger's and his self-image has improved as well.

"What're you doing all this weight lifting for?" I asked, when he stopped by the House of Beauty for a haircut the other day.

"Why else does a man take charge of himself, turn his muscles to steel, Bubbles?" he said. "For a woman."

I blushed and was about to plant a platonic kiss on his cheek when, much to my shock, I noticed that he was glancing at Tiffany who, in turn, batted her eyes and stirred her raspberry tea dreamily. Why I never!

"It's Feingold's Two-Factor Theory of Male Emotion in reverse," Jane teased me later. "He got you, Mom. He got you good."

Jane was sitting on my bed, cracking her gum and watching me pack for a trip I'd been anticipating for a long time. A weekend getaway with Stiletto. We'd decided that before we ran away to Europe together, we ought to spend, like, a weekend with each other first—

especially now that the heat in our relationship had been turned up a notch, thanks to those three little words.

"I'll fly you any place you want, Bubbles," Stiletto had said while we were sitting in his Jeep at our spot below the Hill to Hill Bridge. "Bermuda. The Caribbean. Greece. Rome. Paris. You name it."

"Scranton," I announced. "Scranton, Pennsylvania."

"Scranton? Why, of all places, Scranton?"

"I've heard it's very nice."

Stiletto slapped his forehead. "I offer you Europe and you choose coal country?"

"I've always wanted to go," I said. "My ancestors are from up there."

So, Scranton it was.

Mama offered to stay with Jane since Dan was back in the McMansion, now that Wendy's wealthy father had agreed to chip in with the mortgage payments until Dan could find a "real" job, which Legal Aid, apparently, wasn't.

And Dan cleared up that nagging matter with the Pennsylvania Student Assistance Corporation. He hadn't a clue as to how my signature had appeared on those loan documents, he claimed. So I reminded him about my forgery theory, which is why Dan quickly promised to pay the bills in full.

"Well," Jane said as I folded up my Valentine-red Super Wonderbra. "Are you?"

"Am I what?"

She rolled her eyes. "Come on, Mom. Look at what you're packing. Lingerie. Perfume. Thongs. Get real."

"First answer this. Have *you* done it?"

Jane's cheeks went crimson. "You mean with G? What do you think?"

"Grandma says you're having twenty-four-hour sex."

"Twenty-four-hour sex! Ewww. For your information,

even though this is none of your business, G and I have not done it. And do you know why?"

I dropped a white lace bustier into the suitcase. "Why?"

"Because of you. I've thought about how premature sex pretty much ruined your life by forcing you into adulthood at an early age, how it degraded your self-esteem, burdened you with unwanted responsibilities and put you at risk for a variety of diseases.

"And I was so impressed by the way you've dealt with Steve Stiletto, how he respects you and admires you for having enough presence to demand a commitment before leaping into bed. If you want to know the truth, Mom, you're my role model."

I removed the white lace bustier.

"All set?" Stiletto said as he took my suitcase and walked me down the steps. "This is going to be some getaway, even if it is in coal country. I love you, Bubbles. I can't wait for us to be alone."

Stiletto opened the door for me and I climbed in the Jeep next to him. On the front porch, Jane and G waved at us merrily.

"Just remember, Mom," Jane called out, "don't do anything I wouldn't."

"Suppose that gives us some leeway, eh, Bubbles?" Stiletto said, starting up the Jeep.

Oh, if he only knew.

Turn the page for a preview of the further adventures of

Bubbles Yablonsky in

Bubbles Ablaze

by Sarah Strohmeyer

Now available from Dutton Books

Looking back, I guess my first mistake was to naively hope that a woman of average means could pursue both a career in journalism and a hot sex life. I mean, what was I thinking? One glance at a crusty old city editor and the truth is obvious: the only time sex coexists with newspapers is on the front page. And even then, it's always followed by the word "crime."

My case, unfortunately, was no exception.

The evening began with me between red satin sheets in the Passion Peak Resort—one of those fancy and romantic Pocono Mountain lovers' hotels that I'd dreamed of staying in since I was a little girl.

Hunky Associated Press photographer Steve Stiletto was late, per usual. As an international photojournalist more accustomed to dodging bullets than punching clocks, he considered punctuality an option. Even when the option was making love to a thirty-something living Lithuanian Barbie named Bubbles who hadn't had sex in five months, twenty days and four hours. Yes, I was counting.

This time he had an acceptable excuse. The President was hitting the hustings for Pennsylvania Republicans and Stiletto was to shoot him at every stop. As soon as Air Force One left for Washington, Stiletto vowed to develop his film, send it off to the AP office in New York and meet me at the Passion Peak for our first night of sexual intimacy.

In the meantime, I made sure everything was perfect. I had arranged and rearranged the cinnamon scented candles around the champagne-glass style Jacuzzi and practiced seductively unrolling my stockings from their black lace garters . . . until one got a run when it snagged on my acrylic nail. Finally, after lying on the circular bed and staring at my reflection in the overhead mirror for so long that I started seriously considering liposuction, I dialed the front desk.

"Has a Steve Stiletto left a message for me by any chance?"

"No Stiletto," said the clerk. "Salvo."

"Mr. Salvo?" Uh-oh. Mr. Salvo was my boss at the *Lehigh News-Times*. "And you didn't put him through to my room?"

"In case you're unawares, this is a honeymoon hotel. We got an automatic do not disturb policy. I told him to fax over the message and I'd get it to you ASAP."

"Bet he took that well."

"Let's just say I never knew ASAP referred to unmentionable body parts." There was the rustling of paper. "I got it right here. On company letterhead, no less."

A fax on *News-Times* stationery meant trouble and I was right. The one-page letter contained an urgent message along with detailed directions to an abandoned coal mine called simply Number Nine in the nearby town of Slagville, where a Lehigh businessman had reportedly been found fatally shot in the chest earlier in the evening. It promised to be a media circus.

Because I was in the area, Mr. Salvo concluded I could beat the pack of other Lehigh Valley reporters and get an exclusive for tomorrow's paper—that is if I hustled. A police press conference was tentatively scheduled for eleven-thirty p.m.—one half hour before the final edition deadline.

The stamp on the fax said nine fifteen.

The time on the heart-shaped bedside clock said eleven p.m.

Mr. Salvo was going to have my bleached blond head on a plate.

I shoved my gartered gams into a pair of black spandex pants, wiggled into an apricot-colored turtleneck and scribbled a note for Stiletto that I intended to sound sexy, but which came off instead as a desperate plea for him to stay awake until I returned. I dropped it off with the front desk clerk and hopped in the Camaro.

The murder scene would be crawling with reporters by now, I thought, as I goosed it down Route 15. Like most Pennsylvania highways it was as smooth as a brick patio. Bumpity bump, bump, bump. I veered off an exit to a deserted, winding road. Occasionally, my headlights illuminated large coal breakers that loomed on the hillsides, towering and rusted.

It was October and dead leaves blew in whirls across my hood. I used my windshield wipers to swish them away, keeping an eye out for the turnoff to the Number Nine mine. My last hope was that I would make the press conference so at least I'd have some bit of information, anything, to call in to the newsroom by midnight. If I completely failed, Mr. Salvo would suspect that I'd blown off the assignment for a roll in the hay with Stiletto and I'd never get another opportunity like this again.

Mr. Salvo rarely assigned me breaking news stories as it was. Those were reserved for the newsroom stars, the elite Columbia Journalism School graduates or the seasoned veteran reporters. As a full-time hairdresser with a GED and eight years of Two Guys Community College under my belt, what I usually got were the dregs—strawberry festivals and county fairs.

For months I'd been begging Mr. Salvo to throw me a bone, to give me a chance at hard news. And here he had given in and what had I done? Dropped the ball. Why? Because of sex. Sex. Sex. Sex. It has cursed me all my life. Got me knocked up in high school and shotgun wedded to my now ex, Dan the Man. I should Superglue my legs together.

Who was I kidding? Not even Superglue could hold up against a Mel Gibson dead ringer like Stiletto. His long, slow kisses could melt steel. And, oh, the possibilities of what he looked like under those well-worn Levis of his, well. . . .

I was so deep in my naked Stiletto fantasy that I nearly missed the turnoff to the mine's access road, which was unpaved, rocky and rough. A couple of times the Camaro scraped bottom and the engine whined pitifully as my poor, two-toned car crept up the vertical hill. I had to stand on the gas pedal to get to the top.

As it turned out, I needn't have bothered.

Not only was I late for the press conference, I had missed it entirely. The clearing around the mine entrance was deserted. No cops or news vans in sight. I'd have expected yellow police tape marking the murder scene or a patrolman to shoo away curiosity seekers. But there were only black and bare trees.

That's when I really got worried. Perhaps I had misread Mr. Salvo's directions. Maybe the press conference was underway right now, except it was back at the police station or at another location.

I flicked on the map light. It blinked twice. Not a good sign as my battery was on its last legs. My watch indicated it was a little after eleven thirty, so I wasn't that late. I scanned Mr. Salvo's note for clues and found none except the sending fax number. All the *News-Times* exchanges began with 457. This one was 238. And the area code was local to this part of Pennsylvania—570, not Lehigh's 610.

Mr. Salvo hadn't sent this fax at all.

A mournful howl echoed from the hills and I suddenly felt very alone and small.

Moments like these I needed a cell phone. I don't have one because they scare me. Not because of brain cancer or distracted driving. With my pathetic technical skills, I'm afraid I'll accidentally leave one on and be stuck with a thousand dollar bill and yet another collection agency after my overcharged tail.

I opened the glove compartment and pulled out my yellow flashlight from Shop Rite. Then I gathered my purse, including my Reporter's Notebook, and exited the car to do a quick inspection before heading back to the Passion Peak. To cover all my bases, so to speak.

A chilly breeze blew across the mountain and I folded my arms tightly to keep warm. Too bad I hadn't thought to bring a coat since my 98 percent spandex turtleneck provided all the insulation of Kleenex. I ventured a few yards, my heels crunching on the gravelly surface as I surveyed the area. The place smelled of rotting leaves and faint traces of wood smoke while the flashlight revealed no signs of a press conference having been held minutes ago. There was only an empty coal car perched at the mine entrance. A slag heap. A few molding wood beams.

And a late model gold Lexus with the license plate STINKYK4.

STINKYK4! I stopped in my tracks.

Couldn't be. Why, that rat. That fink! There was only one Stinky K in my life and he lived right here in Slagville. His real name was Carl Koolball and he was a consummate, pencil-necked geek. Stinky annoyed everyone with his practical jokes. He was always slipping whoopee cushions onto coworker's seats or unscrewing the salt shaker caps in his company's cafeteria—that is when he wasn't engrossed in his job as a cartographer for a mining company.

Unfortunately, he was also the husband of my absolutely favorite cousin, Roxanne, who, besides introducing me to the exciting world of neighborhood hairdressing, snuck me into my first Journey concert when I was fifteen.

Leave it to Stinky Koolball to play a prank on me. Mama must have let it slip to Roxanne about my stay at the Passion Peak and he took it from there. But how did he get hold of *News-Times* letterhead?

The Lexus was vacant and locked. That could only mean Stinky was somewhere in the woods spying on me, having a laugh at my expense.

"I hope you're happy, Stinky Koolball!" I hollered. "You completely ruined my night."

I cocked an ear. No response. I tried a different approach. "Come on, Stinky, puhleeese. This isn't funny anymore."

Still nothing. Fine. I spun on my heels and headed back to the Camaro. What a waste of time. I got into the car and turned the key in the ignition. Maybe, if I hurried, Stiletto would be still be at the Passion Peak, relaxing on the circular bed, a glass of champagne on the nightstand. Then again, maybe he figured I'd chickened out and split.

Geesh. I wished the car would start. The ignition beeped once, whirred and then died. Click. Click. Nothing more. I turned the key again, although this time I couldn't even conjure a whir or a beep. The car was dead. Not even a spark. What luck.

I slumped in the front seat and let out one sigh short of a sob. The Fates were against me. It was as though some cosmic force—in this case, my cousin's husband—didn't want me to get together with Stiletto, didn't want my life to take a positive upswing with a man who might actually love me forever. A man who sent a tingle of sexual electricity to my lilac fingertips every time he smiled with that generous mouth.

The wind intensified, whipping my car mercilessly. No heat. No light. No radio. No way to communicate to the outside world. I'd just have to wait for Stinky to return to his Lexus so he could give me a jump.

I didn't wait long. For somewhere in the distance, over by the coal car I estimated, echoed the sizzling crack of a gun shot.

My heart stopped. Deer season come early? I thought optimistically. A coal cracker jacker?

But then there was another shot. And this one came straight from the mouth of the mine.

Like a thunderclap, the gravity of the situation hit me. Here I was, a single mother alone in the woods, possibly the victim of cruel mischief, miles from any home or business, with a dead battery and a nutcase shooting guns off in a mine.

I considered my predicament. I could sit here, cowering in my Camaro, or I could find Stinky and get him to stop scaring me and start jumping my battery.

"Stinky!" I shouted again, getting out of the Camaro and marching over to the mine. I leaned against the rotting wood beam and poked my head into the dark abyss. "Stinky Koolball, come out of there. Come out or you'll have to answer to LuLu Yablonsky." Great, evoking my mother's wrath like I was back in grade school.

"Ohhhh. Ugghh. Ohhh."

There was a moaning sound. And it was coming from right behind me.

I froze for a minute, unsure of what to do. Carefully, slowly, I directed the flashlight beam into the coal car and gasped at what it revealed. A man's body, legs at odd positions, a white oxford shirt torn and stained with brown patches. Face bloodied.

It couldn't be. It was.

Stiletto.

PENGUIN GROUP (USA) INC.
Online

Your Internet gateway to a virtual environment with hundreds of entertaining and enlightening books from Penguin Group (USA) Inc.

While you're there, get the latest buzz on the best authors and books around—

Tom Clancy, Patricia Cornwell, W.E.B. Griffin, Nora Roberts, William Gibson, Robin Cook, Brian Jacques, Catherine Coulter, Stephen King, Ken Follett, Terry McMillan, and many more!

Penguin Group (USA) Inc. Online is located at http://www.penguinputnam.com

PENGUIN GROUP (USA) Inc. NEWS

Every month you'll get an inside look at our upcoming books and new features on our site. This is an ongoing effort to provide you with the most up-to-date information about our books and authors.

Subscribe to Penguin Group (USA) Inc. News at
http://www.penguinputnam.com/newsletters